PUFFIN BOOKS

THE WAY OF THE SWORD

Praise for *Young Samurai: The Way of the Warrior*:

'. . . a fantastic adventure that floors the reader on page one and keeps them there until the end. The pace is furious and the martial arts detail authentic' – Eoin Colfer, author of the bestselling Artemis Fowl series

'Bradford comes out swinging in this fast-paced adventure . . . an adventure novel to rank among the genre's best. This book earns the literary equivalent of a black belt' – *Publishers Weekly*

'I promise you will hold your breath until the end . . . this is a super novel' – *First News*

'The story brims with energy, suspense and thrilling, if violent, action' – *Books for Keeps*

'This is a very fast-paced book, with tons of action . . . the book keeps things moving right along with no dull moments' – *School Library Journal*

'A cutting-edge James Bond thriller, Oriental style' – *Japan Times*

Chris Bradford likes to fly through the air. He has thrown himself over Victoria Falls on a bungee cord, out of an airplane in New Zealand and off a French mountain on a paraglider, but he has always managed to land safely – something he learnt from his martial arts . . .

Chris joined a judo club aged seven where his love of throwing people over his shoulder, punching the air and bowing lots started. Since those early years, he has trained in karate, kickboxing, samurai swordmanship and has earned his black belt in *taijutsu*, the secret fighting art of the ninja.

Before writing the Young Samurai series, Chris was a professional musician and songwriter. He's even performed for HRH Queen Elizabeth II (but he suspects she found his band a bit noisy).

Chris lives in a village on the South Downs with his wife, Sarah, and two cats called Tigger and Rhubarb.

To discover more about Chris go to *youngsamurai.com*

Books by Chris Bradford

The Young Samurai series:
THE WAY OF THE WARRIOR
THE WAY OF THE SWORD

YOUNG SAMURAI

THE WAY OF THE SWORD

CHRIS BRADFORD

PUFFIN

PUFFIN BOOKS

Published by the Penguin Group
Penguin Books Ltd, 80 Strand, London WC2R 0RL, England
Penguin Group (USA) Inc., 375 Hudson Street, New York, New York 10014, USA
Penguin Group (Canada), 90 Eglinton Avenue East, Suite 700, Toronto, Ontario, Canada M4P 2Y3
(a division of Pearson Penguin Canada Inc.)
Penguin Ireland, 25 St Stephen's Green, Dublin 2, Ireland (a division of Penguin Books Ltd)
Penguin Group (Australia), 250 Camberwell Road, Camberwell, Victoria 3124, Australia
(a division of Pearson Australia Group Pty Ltd)
Penguin Books India Pvt Ltd, 11 Community Centre, Panchsheel Park, New Delhi – 110 017, India
Penguin Group (NZ), 67 Apollo Drive, Rosedale, North Shore 0632, New Zealand
(a division of Pearson New Zealand Ltd)
Penguin Books (South Africa) (Pty) Ltd, 24 Sturdee Avenue, Rosebank,
Johannesburg 2196, South Africa

Penguin Books Ltd, Registered Offices: 80 Strand, London WC2R 0RL, England

puffinbooks.com

First published 2009
7

Text copyright © Chris Bradford, 2009
Cover illustration copyright © Paul Young, 2009
Map copyright © Robert Nelmes, 2008
All rights reserved

The moral right of the author and illustrator has been asserted

Set in 11.5/15.5pt Bembo Pro
Typeset by Palimpsest Book Production Limited, Grangemouth, Stirlingshire
Made and printed in England by Clays Ltd, St Ives plc

British Library Cataloguing in Publication Data
A CIP catalogue record for this book is available from the British Library

ISBN: 978-0-141-32431-9

Disclaimer: *Young Samurai: The Way of the Sword* is a work of fiction, and while based on
real historical figures, events and locations, the book does not profess to be accurate in this regard.
Young Samurai: The Way of the Sword is more an echo of the times than a re-enactment of history.

Warning: Do not attempt any of the techniques described within this book without the
supervision of a qualified martial arts instructor. These can be highly dangerous moves and
result in fatal injuries. The author and publisher take no responsibility for any
injuries resulting from attempting these techniques.

www.greenpenguin.co.uk

Mixed Sources
Product group from well-managed
forests and other controlled sources
www.fsc.org Cert no. SA-COC-1592
© 1996 Forest Stewardship Council
FSC

Penguin Books is committed to a sustainable future
for our business, our readers and our planet.
The book in your hands is made from paper
certified by the Forest Stewardship Council.

For my mother

CONTENTS

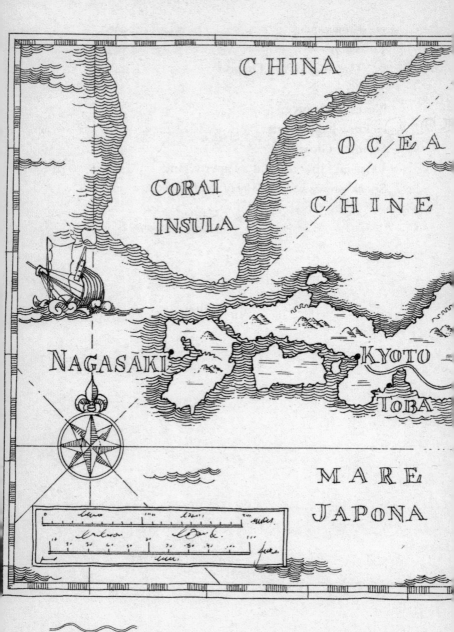

CHINA

OCEA
CHINE

CORAI
INSULA

NAGASAKI

KYOTO
TOBA

MARE
JAPONA

TOKAIDO ROAD

TERRA DE
IESSO

...ANUS
...NUS
...NSIS

...EDO

THE
JAPANS
17 TH
CENTURY

PROLOGUE
DOKUJUTSU

Japan, August 1612

'The Deathstalker is the most poisonous scorpion known to man,' explained the ninja, taking a large black specimen from a wooden box and placing it into his student's trembling hand. 'Armed, silent and deadly, it's the ultimate assassin.'

The student tried in vain to control her shaking as the eight-legged creature crawled over her skin, its stinger glistening in the half-light.

She knelt before the ninja in a small candlelit room crammed full of ceramic jars, wooden boxes and little cages. Inside these containers were an array of poisonous potions, powders, plants and creatures. The ninja had already shown her blood-red berries, bulbous blowfish, brightly coloured frogs, long-legged spiders and coils of black-hooded snakes – each specimen lethal to humans.

'One sting from a Deathstalker and the victim suffers unbearable pain,' the ninja went on, observing the fear flare in his student's eyes. 'Convulsions are followed by paralysis, loss of consciousness and finally death.'

At this, the student became still as stone, her eyes fixed on the scorpion crawling up her arm and towards her neck. Paying no attention to the imminent danger his student was in, the ninja continued with his instruction.

'As part of your *ninjutsu* training, you must learn *doku-jutsu*, the Art of Poison. When you're sent on missions, you'll discover that stabbing your victim with a knife is messy and there's a high chance of failure. But poisoning is silent, hard to detect and, when administered properly, guaranteed to work.'

The scorpion had now reached her neck, having crept into the inviting dark of her long black hair. She turned her head away, trying to distance herself from the creature's approach, her breathing shallow and rapid with panic. The ninja ignored her plight.

'I will teach you how to extract the poison from different plants and animals, and which ones you should apply to your weapons, mix in food and lace your victim's drink with,' the ninja said, running his fingers over a cage and making the snake inside strike at the bars. 'You must also build a tolerance to these poisons, since there's nothing to be gained from dying by your own hand.'

He turned to see his student raising her arm to brush away the scorpion nestled in the crook of her neck. He gently shook his head.

'Many toxins have an antidote. I will show you how to mix these. Others can be overcome by taking small amounts of the poison over time until your body has built a natural defence against it. There are others, though, for which no antidote exists.'

He pointed to a tiny blue-ringed octopus, no bigger than a baby's fist, in a trough of water. 'Beautiful as it is, this animal's venom is so powerful it will kill a man in minutes. I recommend using this one in drinks like *saké* and *sencha*, since it is tasteless.'

The student could no longer bear the scorpion on her. She swiped at the creature, dislodging it from her hair, and screamed as it sank its barb deep into her hand. The flesh round the wound immediately began to swell.

'Help me . . .' she moaned as searing pain exploded up her arm.

The ninja gazed unsympathetically at his convulsing student. 'You'll live,' he replied, picking up the scorpion by its tail and dropping it back into its box. 'He's old and large. It's the small female ones you have to watch out for.'

The student collapsed unconscious to the floor.

1

KNUCKLEBONES

'You're cheating!' said the little girl.

'No, I'm not!' protested Jack, who knelt opposite his little sister in the back garden of their parents' cottage.

'Yes, you are! You're supposed to clap before picking up the bones.'

Jack stopped protesting; his look of mock innocence didn't fool Jess one bit. As much as he loved his sister, a slight girl of seven with light-blue eyes and mousey-blonde hair, he knew she was a stickler for the rules. Most days Jess was as harmless as a buttercup, but when they played Knucklebones, she became as strict and severe as their mother was about the household chores.

Jack picked up the five sheep's knucklebones from the ground and started again. They were the size of small pebbles, their edges rubbed smooth from all the play he and Jess had subjected them to during the summer. Despite the oppressive heat, the white bones felt oddly cold in his hands.

'Bet you can't beat my twosies!' dared Jess.

Taking up the challenge, Jack cast four bones on to the

ground. He then threw the fifth bone high into the air, clapped and seized a knuckle out of the grass before catching the falling bone. He repeated the process with practised ease until he had all five back in his hand.

'Onesies,' said Jack.

Unimpressed, Jess plucked a daisy out of the grass in pretend boredom.

Jack recast the bones, completing the second round in a couple of easy swipes.

'Twosies!' he announced, before tossing the knuckles back on to the grass. Then, throwing one up in the air and clapping, he grabbed three before capturing the falling bone.

'*Threesies!*' exclaimed Jess, unable to contain her astonishment.

Grinning, Jack recast the knucklebones a final time.

In the distance, the sound of thunder rolled heavily across the darkening sky. The air was becoming thick and muggy with an encroaching summer storm, but Jack ignored the change in weather. Instead he concentrated on the challenge of picking up all four bones at once.

Jack tossed the single knuckle high into the air and clapped just as there was an almighty *crack!* A shaft of jagged white lightning scorched the sky, striking a distant hilltop and setting a tree ablaze. It burned blood red against the blackening sky. But Jack was too focused on the game to be distracted. He snatched up the four knucklebones before catching the fifth only a hand's breadth from the earth.

'I did it! I did it! Four in one go!' enthused Jack.

He looked up triumphantly and saw that Jess had disappeared.

So too had the sun. Thunderous clouds as black as pitch now raced across a boiling sky.

Jack stared in bewilderment at the sudden ferocity of the weather. Then he became vaguely aware of something crawling inside his clasped hand. The knucklebones felt like they were *moving*.

Tentatively, he opened his hand.

He gasped. Scurrying across his palm were four tiny black scorpions.

They surrounded the remaining white knuckle, their deadly tails striking at the bone, each of their venomous barbs dripping lethal poison.

One of the scorpions turned and scuttled up his forearm. In a wild panic, Jack shook it off, dropping all the scorpions into the grass, and ran headlong for the house.

'Mother! Mother!' he screamed, then immediately thought of Jess. Where was she?

Large drops of rain began to fall and the garden was cast into shadow. He could just make out the five knucklebones lying discarded in the grass, but there was no sign of the scorpions or of Jess.

'*Jess? Mother?*' he cried at the top of his lungs.

No one answered.

Then he heard the soft singing of his mother coming from the kitchen:

> '*A man of words and not of deeds*
> *Is like a garden full of weeds*
> *And when the weeds begin to grow*
> *It's like a garden full of snow . . .*'

Jack darted along the narrow corridor towards the kitchen.

The cottage was all shadows, as murky and dank as a catacomb. A glimmer of light seeped through a small crack in the kitchen door. From within, his mother's voice faded and rose like the sighing of the wind:

> '*And when the snow begins to fall*
> *It's like a bird upon the wall*
> *And when the bird away does fly*
> *It's like a hawk up in the sky . . .*'

Jack put his eye to the crack and could see his mother sitting in her apron with her back to the door, peeling potatoes with a large curved knife. A single candle lit the room, making the knife's shadow upon the wall appear as monstrous as a samurai sword.

> '*And when the sky begins to roar*
> *It's like a lion at the door . . .*'

Jack pushed at the kitchen door. It grated over the stone-clad flooring, but still his mother did not look round.

'Mother?' he asked. 'Did you hear me . . . ?'

> '*And when the door begins to crack*
> *It's like a stick across your back . . .*'

'Mother! Why won't you answer me?'

The rain was now falling so hard outside it sounded like fish frying in a pan. Jack stepped across the threshold and approached his mother. She kept her back towards him, her fingers working feverishly with the knife, stripping the skin off potato after potato.

> *'And when your back begins to smart*
> *It's like a penknife in your heart . . .'*

Jack tugged on her apron. 'Mother? Are you all right?'

From the other room, Jack heard a stifled scream, and in that moment his mother turned on him, her voice suddenly harsh and grating:

> *'And when your heart begins to bleed*
> *You're dead, and dead, and dead indeed.'*

Jack found himself staring directly into the sunken eye sockets of an old hag, her oily grey hair crawling with lice. The figure, whom he had believed to be his mother, now raised the knife to Jack's throat, a sliver of potato hanging from the blade like freshly peeled skin.

'You're dead indeed, *gaijin*!' rasped the shrivelled witch, her rotten breath making Jack gag.

She gave a callous laugh as Jack ran screaming for the door.

Jack could hear Jess's anguished cries deep within the cottage. He burst into the front room.

The large armchair, where his father always sat, faced the fire in the grate. The flickering flames silhouetted a shrouded figure seated in it.

'Father?' enquired Jack tentatively.

'No, *gaijin*. Your father's dead.'

A gnarly finger protruded from a black-gloved hand and pointed to the prone body of Jack's father, who lay broken and bleeding on the wooden floorboards in the far corner of the room. Jack recoiled at the gruesome fate of his father, and the floor began to heave like the deck of a ship.

With a single leap, the shrouded figure flew from the chair to the latticed casement window. The intruder clutched Jess in his arms.

Jack's heart stopped.

He recognized the single jade-green eye glowering at him through the slit in the hood. The figure, dressed head-to-toe in the black *shinobi shozoku* of a ninja, was Dokugan Ryu.

Dragon Eye. The ninja who had killed his father and hunted Jack ruthlessly and was now kidnapping his little sister.

'No!' screamed Jack as he flung himself across the room to save her.

But other ninja, like black widow spiders, materialized from the walls to stop him. Jack fought them off with all his might, but every faceless ninja he defeated was immediately replaced by the next.

'Another time, *gaijin*!' hissed Dragon Eye as he turned and disappeared into the raging storm. 'The *rutter* is not forgotten.'

2

THE RUTTER

The pale light of dawn filtered through the tiny window and rain continued to drip sluggishly from the lintel to the sill.

A single eye stared through the gloom at Jack.

But it was not Dokugan Ryu's.

It belonged to the Daruma Doll that Sensei Yamada, his Zen teacher, had given him during his first week of samurai training at the *Niten Ichi Ryū*, the 'One School of Two Heavens' in Kyoto.

More than a year had passed since Jack's fateful arrival in Japan when a ninja attack upon the trading ship his father piloted had left him stranded and fighting for his life. The sole survivor, Jack had been rescued by the legendary warrior Masamoto Takeshi, the founder of this particular samurai school.

Injured, unable to speak the language and without friends or family to look after him, Jack had had little choice but to do as he was told. Besides, Masamoto was not the sort of man to have his authority questioned – a fact proven when he adopted Jack, a foreigner, as his son.

Of course, Jack dreamed of going home and being with his sister, Jess, the only family he had left, but these dreams often became nightmares infiltrated by his nemesis, Dragon Eye. The ninja wanted the *rutter*, his father's navigational logbook, at any cost, even if that meant killing a boy Jack's age.

The little wooden Daruma Doll with its round painted face continued to stare at him in the darkness, its lone eye mocking his predicament. Jack recalled the day Sensei Yamada had instructed him to paint in the right eye of the doll and make a wish – the other to be added only when the wish came true. Jack realized to his dismay that *his* wish was no closer to fulfilment than when he had first filled in the eye at the beginning of the year.

He rolled over in despair, burying his head in the *futon*. The other trainee warriors were bound to have heard his cries through the paper-thin walls of his tiny room in the *Shishi-no-ma*, the Hall of Lions.

'Jack, are you all right?' came a whisper in Japanese from the other side of the *shoji* door.

He heard the door slide open and recognized the dim outlines of his best friend Akiko and her cousin Yamato, the second-born son of Masamoto. They slipped inside quietly. Dressed in a cream silk night kimono, her long dark hair tied back, Akiko came and knelt by Jack's bed.

'We heard a shout,' continued Akiko, her half-moon eyes studying his pale face with concern.

'We thought you might be in trouble,' said Yamato, a wiry boy the same age as Jack with chestnut-brown eyes and spiky black hair. 'You look like you've seen a ghost.'

Jack wiped his brow with a trembling hand and tried to calm his nerves. The dream, so vivid and real, had left him shaken and the image of Jess being snatched lingered in his mind.

'I dreamt of Dragon Eye . . . He'd broken into my parents' house . . . He kidnapped my little sister . . .' Jack swallowed hard, trying to calm himself.

Akiko looked like she might reach out to comfort him, but Jack knew Japanese formality prevented any such outward displays of affection. She offered him a sad smile instead.

'Jack, it's just a dream,' said Akiko.

Yamato nodded in agreement, adding, 'It's impossible for Dragon Eye to be in England.'

'I know,' Jack conceded, taking a deep breath, 'but I'm not in England either. If the *Alexandria* hadn't been attacked, I'd be halfway home by now. Instead, I'm stranded on the other side of the world. There's no telling what's happened to Jess. I may be under the protection of your father here, but she has no one.'

Jack's vision blurred with tears.

'But isn't your sister being looked after by a neighbour?' asked Akiko.

'Mrs Winters is old,' said Jack, shaking his head dismissively. 'She can't work and soon she'll have run out of the money my father gave her. Besides, she could have become sick and died . . . just like my mother! Jess will be sent to a workhouse if there's no one to care for her.'

'What's a workhouse?' Yamato asked.

'They're like prisons, but for beggars and orphans. She'll

have to break stones for roads, pick apart old ropes, maybe even crush bones for fertilizer. There's little food, so they end up fighting over the rotting pieces just to eat. How could she ever survive that?'

Jack buried his head in his hands. He was powerless to save what remained of his family. Just as he had been when his father had needed his help fighting the ninja who had boarded their ship. Jack punched his pillow, frustrated at his inability to do anything about it. Akiko and Yamato watched silently as their friend vented his anger.

'Why did the *Alexandria* have to sail into that storm? If her hull had held, we wouldn't have been shipwrecked. We wouldn't have been attacked. And my father would still be alive!'

Even now Jack could see the wire garrotte, slick with his father's blood, Dragon Eye wrenching back on it harder as John Fletcher struggled to get free. Jack remembered how he had simply stood there, his body paralysed with fear, the knife hanging limp in his hand. His father, gasping for breath, the veins in his neck fit to burst, desperately reaching out to him . . .

Angry with himself for his failure to act, Jack threw his pillow across the room.

'Jack. Calm down. You're with us now, it'll be all right,' soothed Akiko. She exchanged a worried glance with Yamato. They had never seen him like this.

'No, it's not all right,' replied Jack, slowly shaking his head and rubbing his eyes in an attempt to clear his mind of the nightmarish vision.

'Jack, it's no wonder you're sleeping so badly. There's a

book under your *futon*!' exclaimed Yamato, picking up the leatherbound tome he'd spotted.

Jack snatched it out of his hands.

It was his father's *rutter*. He'd kept it hidden under his *futon* since there was no other place he could conceal it in his tiny featureless room. The *rutter* was his sole link to his father and Jack cherished every page, every note and every word his father had written. The information it contained was highly valuable and Jack had sworn to his father to keep it secret.

'Easy, Jack. It's only a dictionary,' said Yamato, taken aback at Jack's unexpected aggressiveness.

Jack stared wide-eyed at Yamato, realizing his friend had mistaken the *rutter* for the Portuguese–Japanese dictionary the late Father Lucius had given him the previous year. The one he was supposed to deliver to the priest's superior, Father Bobadillo, in Osaka when he got the chance. But it wasn't the dictionary. Though they both had similar leather bindings, *this* was his father's *rutter*.

Jack had never told Yamato the truth about the *rutter*, even denying its existence to him. And for good reason. Until their victory and reconciliation at the inter-school *Taryu-Jiai* contest that summer, he'd had no reason to trust Yamato.

When Masamoto had first adopted Jack, Yamato had taken an instant dislike to him. His older brother, Tenno, had been killed and he saw Jack as his father's attempt to replace his eldest son. To Yamato, Jack was stealing his father from him. It took a near-drowning experience for Jack to convince Yamato otherwise and to bind them as allies.

Jack knew it was a risk to tell Yamato about something

14

as precious as his father's *rutter*. And Jack had no idea how he would react. But perhaps now was the time to trust his new friend with the secret.

'It's not Father Lucius's dictionary,' confessed Jack.

'What is it then?' asked Yamato, a perplexed look on his face.

'It's my father's *rutter*.'

3

THE DARUMA WISH

'Your father's *rutter*!' exclaimed Yamato, confusion turning to disbelief. 'But when Dragon Eye attacked Akiko's house, you denied all knowledge of it!'

'I lied. I had no choice at the time.'

Jack couldn't bring himself to meet Yamato's eyes. He knew his friend felt betrayed.

Yamato turned to Akiko. 'Did you know about this?'

Akiko nodded, her face flushing with shame.

Yamato fumed. 'I don't believe it. Is this why Dragon Eye keeps coming back? For a stupid book?'

'Yamato, I would have told you,' said Akiko, trying to calm him, 'but I promised Jack I'd keep it secret.'

'How can a *book* be worth Chiro's life?' he said, rising to his feet. 'She may only have been a maid, but she was loyal to our family. Jack's put all of us in danger because of this so-called *rutter*.'

Yamato stared in silent rage at Jack, the old hatred flaring in his eyes. To Jack's horror, Yamato turned to leave.

'I'm going to tell my father about this.'

'Please don't,' Jack pleaded, grabbing Yamato's kimono sleeve. 'It's not just *any* book. It must be kept secret.'

'Why?' Yamato demanded, looking down at Jack's hand in disgust.

Jack let go, but Yamato didn't leave.

Jack wordlessly passed him the book and Yamato flicked through its pages, glancing at but not comprehending the various ocean maps, constellations and their accompanying sea reports.

Jack explained the significance of its contents in hushed tones. 'The *rutter* is a navigational logbook that describes the safe routes across the oceans of the world. The information is so valuable that men have died trying to get their hands on this book. I promised my father I would keep it secret.'

'But why's it so important? Isn't it just a book of directions?'

'No. It's much more than that. It's not only a map of the oceans. My father said it's a powerful political tool. Whoever owns it can control the trade routes between all nations. This means that any country with a *rutter* as accurate as this one rules the seas. That's why England, Spain and Portugal all want it.'

'What does that have to do with Japan?' Yamato said, handing the book back. 'Japan's not like England. I don't think we even have a fleet.'

'I don't know. *I* don't care about politics. I just want to get back to England one day and find Jess. I'm worried about her,' explained Jack, caressing the leather binding of the logbook. 'My father taught me how to use this *rutter* so I could be a pilot like him. That's why, when I do leave

17

Japan, the *rutter* is my ticket home. My future. Without it, I have no trade. Much as I love training in the Way of the Warrior, there's little call for samurai in England.'

'But what's stopping you leaving now?' challenged Yamato, his eyes narrowing.

'Jack can't just go,' interjected Akiko on his behalf. 'Your father's adopted him until he's sixteen and of age. He would need Masamoto-sama's permission. Besides, where would he go to?'

Yamato shrugged.

'Nagasaki,' answered Jack.

They both stared at him.

'That's the port my father was piloting us to before the storm blew us off course. The port might have a ship bound for Europe, or even England.'

'But do you even know where Nagasaki is, Jack?' asked Akiko.

'Sort of . . . there's a rough map in here.'

Jack began to flick through the *rutter*'s pages.

'It's in the far south of Japan in Kyūshū,' said Yamato impatiently.

Akiko rested her hand on the logbook, stopping Jack's search for the map. 'With no food or money, how would you get there? It would take you more than a month to walk from Kyoto.'

'You had better start walking now then, hadn't you?' Yamato said sarcastically.

'Stop it, Yamato! You two are supposed to be friends, remember?' said Akiko. 'Jack can't simply walk to Nagasaki. Dragon Eye's out there. At school, he's under your father's protection and Masamoto-sama seems to be the only person the ninja fears. If Jack left here alone, he could be captured . . . or even killed!'

They all fell silent.

Jack put away the *rutter*, padding the *futon* back over the top. It was such a poor hiding place for something so precious and he realized he needed to find a more secure location for it before Dragon Eye returned.

Yamato slid open the door of the room to leave. Glancing back over his shoulder at Jack, he asked, 'So are *you* going to tell my father about it?'

They held each other's stare, the tension between them growing.

Jack shook his head. 'My father went to great lengths to keep it hidden. On-board ship he had a secret compartment for it. Not even the Captain knew where my father held his logbook. As his son, it's my duty to protect the *rutter*,' explained Jack, knowing he had to get through to Yamato somehow. 'You understand duty. You're samurai. My father made me promise to keep it secret. I'm bound to that promise.'

Yamato nodded ever so slightly and slid the door shut again, before turning back to him.

'I now understand why you haven't told anyone,' Yamato said, unclenching his fists as his anger finally died down. 'I was annoyed that you hadn't told me. That you didn't trust me. You can, you know.'

'Thank you, Yamato,' replied Jack, breathing a sigh of relief.

Yamato sat back down next to Jack. 'I just don't understand why you can't tell my father. He could protect it.'

'No, we mustn't,' insisted Jack. 'When Father Lucius died, he confessed that someone he knew was after the *rutter* and would kill me for it.'

'Dokugan Ryu, of course' said Yamato.

'Yes, Dragon Eye wants the *rutter*,' agreed Jack, 'but you told me ninja were employed for their skills. Somebody's hiring him to steal the *rutter*. It could be someone Masamoto-sama knows. Father Lucius was part of his entourage, so I can't afford to trust anyone. That's why I believe the fewer people who know about it, the better.'

'You mean to say that you don't trust my father? That you think he may want it?' Yamato demanded, offended at the implication.

'No!' replied Jack quickly. 'I'm saying if Masamoto-sama had the *rutter*, he might be murdered for it like my father was. And that's a risk I can't take. I'm trying to *protect* him, Yamato. At least, if Dragon Eye believes I have it, he's only after me. That's why we *must* keep it secret.'

Jack could see his friend weighing the options and for one horrible moment he thought Yamato was still going to tell his father.

'Fine. I promise I won't say anything,' Yamato agreed. 'But what makes you think Dragon Eye will come after it again? We haven't seen him since he tried to assassinate *daimyo* Takatomi during the Gion Festival. Maybe he's dead. Akiko wounded him pretty badly.'

Jack recalled how Akiko had saved his life that night. They'd spotted the ninja entering Nijo Castle, the home of Lord Takatomi, and followed him. However, Dragon Eye overcame Jack and was about to sever his arm when Akiko had flung a *wakizashi* sword to stop him. The short blade pierced Dragon Eye's side, but the ninja had barely flinched. Only the timely arrival of Masamoto and his samurai had prevented the assassin from retaliating. Dragon Eye escaped over the castle walls, but not without promising he'd be back for the *rutter*.

The ninja's threat still haunted him, and Jack didn't doubt that Dragon Eye would return. The ninja was out there, waiting for him.

Akiko was right. While he was at the *Niten Ichi Ryū*, he was under Masamoto's protection. He was safe. But he was dangerously exposed outside the school walls. Travelling alone, he would be lucky to make it beyond the city out-skirts.

Jack had no option but to remain in Kyoto, training at the *Niten Ichi Ryū*. He had to learn the Way of the Sword if he was ever going to survive the journey home.

While the choice wasn't his, the idea of perfecting his skills as a samurai gave Jack a sharp thrill. He was drawn to the discipline and virtues of *bushido* and the thought of wielding a real sword was exhilarating.

'He's out there,' Jack said. 'Dragon Eye will come.'

Reaching across the room, Jack picked up the Daruma Doll. He looked it squarely in the eye and solemnly remade his wish.

'But next time I'll be ready for him.'

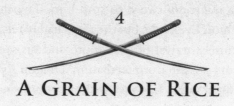

4

A GRAIN OF RICE

'Why have you brought your sword?' barked Sensei Hoso-kawa, a severe-looking samurai with an intimidating stare and a sharp stub of a beard.

Jack looked down at his *katana*. The polished black *saya* gleamed in the morning light, hinting at the razor-sharp blade within. Thrown by his sword teacher's unexpected hostility, he thumbed the golden phoenix *kamon* embossed near the hilt.

'Because . . . this is a *kenjutsu* class, Sensei,' Jack replied, shrugging his shoulders for lack of a better answer.

'Do any other students carry a *katana*?'

Jack glanced at the rest of the class lined down one side of the *Butokuden*, the *dojo* where they trained in the Way of the Sword, *kenjutsu*, and *taijutsu*, unarmed combat. The hall was cavernous, its elevated panel ceiling and immense pillars of dark cypress wood towering over the row of young trainee samurai.

Jack was once again reminded of how utterly different he was from the rest of his class. Not yet fourteen, unlike many of the other students, he was nonetheless the tallest, possessing sky-blue eyes and a mop of hair so blond it stood out like a gold coin among the black-haired uniformity of his class-mates. To the olive-skinned, almond-eyed Japanese, Jack may have been training as a samurai warrior, but he would always be a foreigner – a *gaijin* as his enemies liked to call him.

Looking around, Jack realized that not a single student held a *katana*. They all carried *bokken*, their wooden train-ing swords.

'No, Sensei,' said Jack, abashed.

At the far end of the line, a regal, darkly handsome boy with a shaved head and hooded eyes smirked at Jack's error. Jack ignored Kazuki, knowing his rival would be delight-ing in his loss of face in front of the class.

Despite coming to grips with many of the Japanese cus-toms, like wearing a kimono instead of shirt and breeches, bowing every time he met someone and the etiquette of apologizing for nearly everything, Jack still struggled with the strict ritualized discipline of Japanese life.

He had been late for breakfast that morning, following his nightmare-filled sleep, and had already had to apologize to two of the sensei. It looked like Sensei Hosokawa would be the third.

Jack knew his sensei was a fair but firm teacher who demanded high standards. He expected his students to turn up on time, be dressed smartly and be committed to training hard. Sensei Hosokawa made no allowance for mistakes.

He stood at the centre of the *dojo*'s training area, a broad honey-coloured rectangle of varnished woodblock, glaring at Jack. 'So what makes you think you should bear a *katana* while the others don't?'

Jack knew whatever answer he gave Sensei Hosokawa would be the wrong one. There was a Japanese saying that went 'The stake that sticks out gets hammered down', and Jack was starting to appreciate that living in Japan was a matter of conforming to the rules. No one else in the class carried a sword. Jack, therefore, stuck out and was about to be hammered down.

Yamato, who stood close by, looked as if he was going to speak on his behalf, but Sensei Hosokawa gave him a cautionary glance and he immediately thought better of it.

The silence that had descended upon the *dojo* was almost deafening. Jack could hear the blood rushing through his ears, his mind turning itself over and over for an appropriate response.

The only answer Jack could think of was the truth. Masamoto himself had presented his own *daishō*, the two swords that symbolized the power of the samurai, to Jack in recognition of the school's victory at the *Taryu-Jiai* contest and for his courage in preventing Dragon Eye from assassinating the *daimyo* Takatomi.

'Having won the *Taryu-Jiai*,' ventured Jack, 'I thought I'd earned the right to use them.'

'The right? *Kenjutsu* is not a game, Jack-kun. Winning one little competition doesn't make you a competent *kendoka*.'

Jack fell silent under Sensei Hosokawa's glare.

'I will tell you when you can bring your *katana* to class. Until then, you will only use *bokken*. Understand, Jack-kun?'

'*Hai*, Sensei,' submitted Jack. 'I just hoped I could use a real sword for once.'

'A real one?' snorted the sensei. 'Do you *really* think you're ready?'

Jack shrugged uncertainly. 'I suppose so. Masamoto-sama gave me his swords, so he must think I am.'

'You're not in Masamoto-sama's class yet,' said Sensei Hosokawa, tightening his grip on the hilt of his own sword so that his knuckles turned white. 'Jack-kun, you hold the power of life and death in your hands. Can you handle the consequences of your actions?'

Before Jack could answer, the sensei beckoned him over.

'Come here! You too, Yamato-kun.'

Jack and a startled Yamato stepped out of line and approached Sensei Hosokawa.

'*Seiza*,' he ordered and the two of them knelt down. 'Not you, Jack-kun. I need you to understand what it means to carry a *katana*. Withdraw your sword.'

Jack unsheathed his *katana*. The blade gleamed, its edge so sharp that it appeared to cut the very air itself.

Uncertain as to what Sensei Hosokawa expected of him, he fell into stance. His sword was stretched out in front of him and he gripped the hilt with both hands. His feet were set wide apart, the *kissaki* level with the throat of his imaginary enemy.

Masamoto's sword felt unusually heavy in his hands. Over the course of a year of *kenjutsu* training, his own *bokken* had become an extension of his arm. He knew its weight, its feel and how it cut through the air.

But this sword was different. Weightier and more visceral.

It had killed people. Sliced them in half. And Jack suddenly sensed its bloody history in his hands.

He was starting to regret his rashness in bringing the sword.

The sensei, noting the visible trembling of Jack's *katana* with grim satisfaction, proceeded to remove a single grain of rice from his *inro*, the small wooden carrying case attached to his *obi*. He then placed the grain on top of Yamato's head.

'Cut it in half,' he ordered Jack.

'What?' blurted Yamato, his eyes wide with shock.

'But it's on his head —' protested Jack.

'Do it!' commanded Hosokawa, pointing at the tiny grain of rice.

'But . . . but . . . I can't . . .'

'If you think you're ready for such responsibility, now is your chance to prove it.'

'But I could kill Yamato!' exclaimed Jack.

'This is what it means to carry a sword. People get killed. Now cut the grain.'

'I can't,' said Jack, lowering his *katana*.

'*Can't?*' exclaimed Hosokawa. 'I command you, as your sensei, to strike at his head and slice that grain in half.'

Sensei Hosokawa grabbed Jack's hands and brought the sword into direct line with Yamato's exposed head. The miniscule grain of rice perched there, a white speck among the mass of black hair.

Jack knew that the blade would slice through Yamato's head as if it were little more than a watermelon. Jack's arms quivered uncontrollably and Yamato gave him a despairing look, his face completely drained of blood.

'DO IT NOW!' commanded Hosokawa, lifting Jack's arms to force him to strike.

The rest of the students watched with dread fascination.

Akiko looked on fearfully. Beside her, her best friend Kiku, a petite girl with dark shoulder-length hair and hazelnut-coloured eyes, was almost on the point of tears. Kazuki, though, was apparently relishing the moment. He nudged his ally Nobu, a large boy with the build of a mini-Sumo wrestler, and whispered in his ear, loud enough for Jack to hear.

'I bet you the *gaijin* chops off Yamato's ear!'

'Or maybe his nose!' chortled Nobu, a fat grin spreading across his podgy face.

The sword wavered in the air. Jack felt all control over the weapon drain from his body.

'I . . . I . . . can't,' Jack stammered. 'I'll kill him.'

Defeated, he lowered the *katana* to the floor.

'Then I'll do it for you,' said Sensei Hosokawa.

Yamato, who had let out a sigh of relief, instantly froze.

In the blink of an eye, the sensei withdrew his own sword and cut down on to Yamato's head. Kiku screamed as the blade buried itself in his hair. Her cry reverberated throughout the *Butokuden*.

Yamato fell forward, his head dropping to the ground.

Jack saw the tiny grain of rice peel apart and fall in two separate pieces on to the *dojo* floor.

Yamato remained bowed, trembling like a leaf, trying to regain control of his breathing. Otherwise, he was completely unscathed. The blade had not even grazed his scalp.

Jack stood motionless, overwhelmed at Sensei Hosokawa's skill. What a fool he had been to question his sensei's judgement. *Now* he understood the responsibility that came with a sword. The choice of life over death was truly in his hands. This was no game.

'Until you have complete control,' said Sensei Hosokawa, fixing Jack with a stern look as he resheathed his *katana*, 'you don't have the skill to warrant carrying a real blade. You're not ready for the Way of the Sword.'

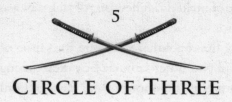

5

CIRCLE OF THREE

'YOUNG SAMURAI!' thundered Masamoto down the length of the *Chō-no-ma*, the ceremonial dining hall that earned its name from the lavishly decorated panelled walls of painted butterflies.

The students, who were kneeling in regimented rows, stiffened and prepared for Masamoto's opening address. Jack, his legs already becoming numb from being in the *seiza* posture, shifted himself in order to get a better view of the proceedings. Masamoto sat in his usual place, raised upon a dais behind a low table of black-lacquered cedar. The table was laid with cups of steaming *sencha*, the bitter green tea the samurai enjoyed.

Masamoto took a measured sip from his cup, letting the silence sink in.

Dressed in a flame-red kimono emblazoned with his golden phoenix *kamon*, Masamoto was a man who commanded total authority and deep respect from both his students and fellow samurai. His strength of presence was such that Jack no longer registered the crimson scarring that disfigured the entire left-hand side of the man's face like a mask of melted candlewax. All Jack saw was an invincible warrior.

Flanking him on either side were the sensei of the *Niten Ichi Ryū* and two other samurai Jack didn't recognize.

'This dinner is in honour of our *daimyo*, Lord of Kyoto Province, Takatomi Hideaki,' announced Masamoto, bowing humbly to the man on his immediate left.

Every student and sensei did likewise.

This was the first time Jack had laid eyes upon the *daimyo* whose life he'd saved. A genial man with large dewy eyes, a brushstroke of a moustache and a generous rounded belly, he wore a flamboyant ceremonial kimono decorated with five *kamon* of a white crane, two on the sleeves, two on the chest and one on the back. He gave a short respectful nod of his head in acknowledgement of Masamoto's respect.

Masamoto sat back up. Then the sensei and students straightened in rank order, the new students being the last to raise their heads.

'Takatomi-sama has graced us with his presence in recognition of our victory at the *Taryu-Jiai* against the *Yagyu Ryū*.'

The school let loose a great cheer.

'And following our prevention of the attempt on his life he has generously extended his sponsorship of the *Niten Ichi Ryū*, securing the future of this school indefinitely.'

The students chanted and clapped in unison three times.

'TAKATOMI!' *CLAP!* 'TAKATOMI!' *CLAP!* 'TAKATOMI!' *CLAP!*

The *daimyo* gave a cordial smile and the briefest of bows in response.

'Furthermore, he has bestowed upon the school a new training hall: the *Taka-no-ma*, the Hall of The Hawk!'

The students erupted into applause and fevered discussion broke out. A new hall meant the possibility of another martial art being taught. Masamoto held his hand up for silence. Immediately, the students checked their enthusiasm and he continued his address.

'Before we commence the meal, allow me to introduce our second guest.'

Masamoto directed his attention to a large barrel of a man whose round head was covered in a fuzz of short black hair and a similarly fuzzy beard.

'Sensei Kano is a *bōjutsu* master visiting us from the *Mugan Ryū*, our sister school in Osaka. Under his tutelage, you will learn how to defend and attack with the *bō* staff. Sensei Kano is a man of great heart and greater skill. You could not ask for a better teacher in the Art of the *Bō*.'

Despite the new teacher's presence dominating the dais, the immense samurai appeared to shrink under Masamoto's praise. He gave a humble bow to the room, his smoky-grey eyes staring blankly down the hall as if he was trying to avoid everyone's gaze.

The students bowed respectfully in return.

'Finally, as some of you are aware, it has been three years since the last Circle of Three . . .'

The atmosphere in the *Chō-no-ma* instantly became tense with excitement, every student kneeling ramrod straight in anticipation. Jack, though, was at a complete loss, having no idea what Masamoto was talking about. He looked over to Akiko for an explanation, but like the rest of the school her eyes remained fixed upon Masamoto.

'For those students who have the courage and the ability, the time has come to prove you are worthy to be called samurai of the *Niten Ichi Ryū*. And those who do will progress on to the Two Heavens without the need for further training.'

Jack had an inkling of what the Two Heavens was. He'd heard it was Masamoto's secret martial art technique and that only the very best students were given the privilege of learning from the great man himself. But beyond that the Two Heavens remained a mystery.

'The Circle of Three, as tradition dictates, will commence when the winds blow the cherry blossom from the branches,' continued Masamoto. 'Those of you who believe you are ready to meet the Circle's three challenges of Mind, Body and Spirit should log their names with Sensei Kyuzo at the end of this evening. A series of four selection trials will then be held at first snowfall to test your strength, skill, intellect and courage. The five students deemed the best in these trials will go through to the Circle.'

Masamoto spread his arms wide so that the sleeves of his flame-red kimono appeared to transform him into the fiery phoenix of his *kamon*.

'Be warned! The Circle of Three is not to be entered into lightly. It demands you understand the seven virtues of *bushido* if you are to have any hope of surviving.' The great warrior paused, his gaze taking in all his students. 'So tell me what is *bushido*?'

'*Rectitude! Courage! Benevolence! Respect! Honesty! Honour! Loyalty!*' boomed the students down the *Chō-no-ma*.

32

Masamoto nodded with satisfaction. 'And it is the virtue of courage that you will need most,' he cautioned. 'So during these coming months of training, remember this: *learn today so that you may live tomorrow!*'

With the declaration of the school's maxim, Masamoto brought the address to an end and the students thundered their response.

'MASAMOTO! MASAMOTO! MASAMOTO!'

The refrain died away and servants entered, carrying several long lacquered tables. These were laid in two rows that stretched the entire length of the *Chō-no-ma*. Jack seated himself between Akiko and Yamato, feeling a small thrill that they weren't positioned right next to the entrance. They were no longer the new students and this meant that they had moved several symbolic places nearer the head table.

Jack always enjoyed ceremonial dinners. The formality of such events demanded that a vast array of dishes be provided in honour of the guest. On this occasion, *sushi* was high on the menu, alongside *tofu*, noodles, *tempura*, bowls of miso soup, pickled yellow *daikon* and purple eggplant. Steaming pots of *sencha* were accompanied by vast quantities of rice piled high in bowls across their table. The centrepiece was an overflowing plate of sliced eel, grilled and smothered in a sticky red sauce.

'*Itadakimasu!*' proclaimed Masamoto.

'*Itadakimasu!*' responded the students, picking up their *hashi* and tucking into the banquet.

Despite the delicious spread, Jack was distracted from the meal by his desperate desire to know more about the

Circle of Three. Everybody else, though, was focused upon devouring the feast before them.

'Jack, you should try the *unagi*,' suggested Saburo, a slightly rotund, plain-looking boy with a chubby face made even chubbier by a mouthful of food.

Jack looked doubtfully across the table at his friend, whose thick black eyebrows bounced up and down in unison with his enthusiastic chewing of a grey stringy lump of eel's liver. It didn't look particularly appetizing, thought Jack, but he could remember the first time he'd been faced with *sushi*. The thought of uncooked fish had almost turned his stomach over, whereas now he relished the soft, succulent flesh of tuna, mackerel and salmon. Eel's liver, though, was another matter.

'It's good for your health,' Akiko reassured him, spooning some rice into her bowl, but avoiding the eel herself.

Jack tentatively picked up a grey lump and lowered it into his mouth. When he bit into the liver, he almost gagged at the intensity of the flavour. It was as if a thousand wriggling eels had exploded on his tongue.

He forced a grimace of a smile for Akiko's benefit and kept chewing. The eel's liver had *better* be good for his health, he thought.

'So who's going to enter for the Circle of Three?' Saburo blurted between mouthfuls, expressing what was clearly on everyone's minds.

'Not me!' replied Kiku. 'I heard a student died last time.'

Beside her, Yori, a small mouse-like boy, gave a wide-eyed look of dread and shook his head vigorously in response to Saburo's question.

34

'That's just a rumour spread by the sensei to scare us,' reassured Akiko, giving Yori an encouraging smile.

'No, it's not. My father's expressly forbidden me from entering,' said Kiku. 'He told me it's needlessly dangerous.'

'But what exactly *is* the Circle?' asked Jack.

'The Circle of Three,' explained Akiko, putting down her *hashi*, 'are the three highest peaks in the Iga mountain range where trainee samurai face the three challenges of Mind, Body and Spirit.'

'So what are the challenges?'

Akiko shook her head apologetically. 'I don't know. They're kept a secret.'

'Whatever they are,' said Yamato, 'my father will be expecting *me* to enter, so I guess I'll find out first hand. What about you, Saburo? Are you going to enter?'

'I'm considering it,' replied Saburo, swallowing down another piece of *unagi*.

'That means no. Obviously, you're too scared! How about you, Jack?'

Jack thought for a moment as Saburo sat open-mouthed, uncertain whether to protest or not. 'I don't know. Is it worth the risk? I know it leads to the Two Heavens, but I'm still not sure what the Two Heavens actually is.'

'Jack, you've seen the Two Heavens,' stated Akiko.

Jack gave her a perplexed look. 'When?'

'On the beach in Toba. Remember how Masamoto-sama fought against the samurai Godai? He used both the *katana* and the *wakizashi*, rather than just his *katana* sword. That is the Two Heavens. The technique is extremely difficult to master, but when you do, you are virtually invincible.'

'My father fought over sixty duels while on his warrior pilgrimage,' announced Yamato proudly. 'Not once was he defeated.'

Jack's mind began to race.

He'd been made aware that he needed to become a better swordsman. By succeeding in the Circle of Three, he would be given the opportunity to be taught by both Sensei Hosokawa *and* Masamoto. Not only that, he would learn how to use *two* swords. The idea filled him with hope. For if he could master the Two Heavens, then he would be invincible like Masamoto. No longer would he need to fear the return of Dragon Eye.

'Are all students who conquer the Circle taught the technique of Two Heavens?' asked Jack.

'Yes, of course,' replied Akiko.

Jack smiled. Surely the Circle of Three was the solution to his predicament.

'Then I will enter.'

THE INVITATION

'REI, SENSEI!' came the cry.

Dinner had drawn to a close and all the students stood to bow as the sensei filed out of the hall. Masamoto, accompanied by *daimyo* Takatomi, led the entourage. As they passed Jack, the *daimyo* paused.

'Jack-kun? I am presuming it's you, considering you are the only blond-haired samurai present,' said Takatomi, broadening his genial smile.

'*Hai*, Sensei,' responded Jack, bowing even lower.

'No, I'm not your sensei,' laughed Takatomi. 'However, I would like you, Akiko-chan and Yamato-kun to join me for *cha-no-yu* in Nijo Castle tomorrow evening.'

A murmur of astonishment spread among the bowing students. Even Masamoto's typically stoic expression registered surprise at this unprecedented invitation. A tea ceremony was regarded as the purest art form, one that took years, if not a lifetime, to perfect. For a student, let alone a foreigner, to be invited to a *cha-no-yu* hosted by the *daimyo* himself was a momentous event.

'I have not had the chance to express my gratitude to

you personally for what you accomplished in stopping Dokugan Ryu,' continued Takatomi. 'My beautiful daughter will be joining us. I believe you're already acquainted with Emi, for she has spoken of you on a number of occasions.'

Jack glanced over to a tall, slender girl with long straight hair and a rose-petal mouth. She smiled sweetly at him, exuding such warmth that Jack had to bow again to hide his reddening face. Not that it went unnoticed by Akiko, who had looked up and spotted the exchange.

'Takatomi-sama, they would be honoured to attend,' answered Masamoto on Jack's behalf, before leading the *daimyo* out of the *Chō-no-ma* and into the night.

There was a great buzz of excitement in the air when the sensei left. Groups of students clustered together, everyone discussing the Circle of Three and watching to see who would enter first.

Sensei Kyuzo, their master in *taijutsu*, a dwarf-sized man whose ability at hand-to-hand combat was legendary, sat at the head table, a roll of parchment before him. He waited impatiently for the first entrant.

As was typical of the sensei, he picked at nuts from a small bowl and crushed them with his bare hands, just as he was inclined to do with Jack's spirit at each and every opportunity. The man despised Jack, and made no effort to disguise the fact that he resented a foreigner being taught the secrets of their martial arts.

After a moment's hesitation, a strong boy with broad shoulders and a bronzed face walked over to the dais. He picked up the ink scribe and wrote his name upon the parchment. Soon afterwards three other students approached, encouraging a steady stream of hopefuls to queue up too.

'Come on,' said Yamato, striding over to the growing line.

Jack looked to Akiko for final reassurance, but she was already in line. Jack should have known. Akiko was no ordinary girl. She was samurai and, being the niece of Masamoto, courage was in her blood.

He joined her in the queue. When they reached the head table, Jack watched Akiko as she wrote her name on the parchment with a series of brushstrokes that formed a beautiful but mysterious pattern of Japanese *kanji* characters. The symbols made little sense to Jack.

Sensei Kyuzo glared over Akiko's shoulder at Jack.

'*You* are entering the Circle?' said Sensei Kyuzo, giving a short incredulous snort at Jack's appearance.

'*Hai*, Sensei,' responded Jack, ignoring his teacher's contempt. He had waited with the others in the queue to sign his name and was not going to be put off by Sensei Kyuzo's antagonism now.

'A *gaijin* has never partaken in the Circle,' stated Kyuzo, with deliberate emphasis placed on his use of the derogatory term for a foreigner.

'Then this will be the first time, Sensei,' said Akiko, pretending not to notice his blatant disrespect towards Jack.

'Sign here,' ordered Sensei Kyuzo. 'In *kanji*.'

Jack paused as he looked at the paper. The names of

the participants were all carefully inked in the Japanese characters.

A cruel smile cut across Sensei Kyuzo's lips. 'Or maybe you can't? Entry must be in *kanji*. It's the rules.'

To Jack's frustration, the sensei was right. He didn't know *kanji*. Jack could write easily enough. His mother had been a fine teacher. But only in Roman characters. While Akiko's guidance, together with the formal lessons provided by Father Lucius, had enabled him to speak in Japanese, he had only limited experience of *kanji*. In Japan, the way of writing, *shodo*, was as much an art form as hand-to-hand combat and swordsmanship. The skill took years to perfect.

Sensei Kyuzo savoured Jack's discomfort.

'That's a shame,' he said. 'Maybe you can enter in another three years' time, when you've learnt to write. Next!'

Jack was elbowed out of the way by a student from behind and he could have guessed it would be Kazuki. The boy had been on his back ever since his arrival at samurai school. Now that Jack had gained the respect of the other students by beating their rival school, the *Yagyu Ryū*, in the *Taryu-Jiai* competition, Kazuki was on the lookout for any excuse to bully or belittle him.

'I wouldn't worry, *gaijin*,' smirked Kazuki, signing his own name in the place where Jack's should have been. 'You won't be around to participate anyway.'

Jack rounded on Kazuki even as he felt Akiko guiding him away. 'What do you mean?'

'Surely even you've heard the news?' said Kazuki with vindictive pleasure. 'The *daimyo* Kamakura Katsuro is expelling Christians from Japan.'

40

Nobu peered over Kazuki's shoulder. He gave Jack a farewell wave of the hand and laughed, 'Sayonara, gaijin!'

'He's going to kill any *gaijin* he finds in Japan,' added Kazuki spitefully, before turning to Nobu with triumph in his eyes at being the first to tell Jack the bad news.

'Ignore them, Jack,' said Akiko, shaking her head in disgust. 'They're making it up.'

But Jack couldn't help thinking that there *might* be a grain of truth in Kazuki's story. Kamakura was the *daimyo* of Edo Province and the head of the *Yagyu Ryū*, the rival school to the *Niten Ichi Ryū*. He was a cruel, vindictive man with too much power. Jack's overriding image of the *daimyo* was his gleeful face as he watched one of his samurai behead an elderly tea merchant, merely because the old man hadn't heard the command to bow. Despite Akiko's assurance, Jack realized Kamakura was more than capable of ordering the exile and death of foreigners.

If it were true, then it wouldn't matter whether he was in the Circle of Three. His life would be in greater danger than ever before, not only from Dragon Eye and his ninja clan, but also from Kamakura and his samurai.

Perhaps he should start planning how to get to Nagasaki before it was too late, thought Jack. But first, he needed to find out whether Kazuki was lying or not.

'Where are you going?' asked Akiko as Jack headed purposefully out of the *Chō-no-ma*.

Glancing over his shoulder at Kazuki and Nobu, who were still sniggering to one another, he replied, 'Somewhere far away from those two!'

RANDORI

Jack lay there, unable to move.

The impact upon the *dojo* floor had knocked the wind clean out of him.

'I'm so sorry,' said Akiko, looking down at him with concern. 'I didn't mean to throw you so hard.'

'Don't . . . apologize,' replied Jack, gasping for air and trying not to throw up his breakfast from earlier that morning. 'It was . . . my fault . . . for not break-falling . . . properly.'

Akiko had tossed Jack over her shoulder like a sack of rice in a move called *seoi nage*. Not that her remarkable fighting abilities were anything unexpected. He'd learnt early on never to underestimate Akiko, having witnessed her single-handedly despatch two ninja with only the knotted *obi* of her kimono.

He was also more than capable of break-falling and should have landed safely. However, Akiko had told him something that completely broke his concentration.

'What did you just say?' asked Jack, sitting up carefully.

'You're in the trials for the Circle of Three.'

'I don't understand. How can that be?'

'Kiku's entered for you,' she explained, a mischievous grin on her face. 'I asked her to write down your name instead of hers.'

Jack stared at Akiko in disbelief. She'd got round the entry rules for him.

He smiled. The Two Heavens was suddenly a possibility again. His training now had real purpose. And with only five places available in the Circle of Three, he knew he would have to work hard to get selected.

'Why have you stopped?' demanded Sensei Kyuzo, standing over Jack, his mean black-pebble eyes boring into him.

'I'm just catching my breath, Sensei,' replied Jack, grinning up at him, unable to hide the glee he felt at Akiko's news.

Sensei Kyuzo eyed Jack with suspicion. 'Get up! Are any of the other students resting? Is Kazuki-kun over there tired?'

The sensei nodded his head towards his favoured student, who was driving Saburo into the ground with a devastating *seoi nage* of his own.

'No, Sensei,' replied Jack through pursed lips.

'Some samurai you'll be!' spat Sensei Kyuzo.

He spun on his heel and crossed to the centre of the *Butokuden*.

'*Yame!*' he ordered.

Every student ceased their training, kneeling down on one knee to listen to their sensei.

'*Taijutsu* is like boiling water: if you do not keep the flame high, it turns tepid!' bellowed Sensei Kyuzo.

'*HAI*, SENSEI!' shouted the students in unison.

'Don't be like Jack-kun and stop merely because you're tired!'

Jack felt all the eyes in the *dojo* turn towards him and he fumed with rage. Why did the sensei always have to make an example of him? There were numerous other students who weren't half as competent as he was and several had stopped training long before Jack.

'If any of you have put your name down for the trials for the Circle of Three, you'll need greater stamina and strength than this. Do you want to give up?' Sensei Kyuzo challenged.

'NO, SENSEI!' responded the exhausted students, their breathing rapid, their *gi* soaked in sweat.

'Good. Then it's time for *randori*!' he announced. 'Line up!'

Hurriedly the students knelt down one side of the *Butokuden* in preparation for free-sparring.

'During this session, I want you to practise your *nage waza* and *katame waza* only,' said Sensei Kyuzo, referring to the various throwing and grappling techniques they had been concentrating on during the past few lessons.

'Kazuki-kun, you're up first. You can show them how it's done.'

Kazuki snapped to his feet and took up position on his teacher's right-hand side.

'Now your opponent will be . . .' considered Sensei Kyuzo, pulling wistfully at the tuft of moustache beneath his pudgy nose, 'Jack-kun.'

Jack knew it. He wasn't going to be given any time to

44

recover. Usually he enjoyed *randori* since it was exciting and challenging. But Kazuki was vindictive. In free-sparring, punches were supposed to be 'pulled', kicks held back, throws executed with due care, and locks released immediately an opponent tapped for submission. But given the slightest chance, Kazuki would apply his techniques with full force and ignore any calls for submission.

With little choice in the matter, Jack got up and stood on Sensei Kyuzo's left-hand side.

'*Rei!*' said Sensei Kyuzo and they both bowed to him.

'*Rei!*' repeated Sensei Kyuzo, and Jack and Kazuki bowed to one another as was required etiquette.

'*Hajime!*' announced the sensei, and the *randori* began.

They each darted in to get their grip, grabbing at the lapels and sleeves of each other's *gi* in an attempt to gain the upper hand.

Like a dazzling but violent dance, they tussled for domination. They pulled and pushed, whirled and zigzagged, trying to unbalance one another, looking for an opportunity for a throw or a leg reap.

The other students watched eagerly, Yamato and Saburo clenching their fists in silent support, Akiko tugging anxiously at the folds of her *gi*.

Jack, spotting his chance, twisted his body in towards Kazuki for *seoi nage*, but Kazuki was quick to counter, shifting his hips out of the way and throwing his leg behind Jack's for a valley drop throw.

The move would have been successful if Jack had been off-balance, but he was still grounded so drove his weight into Kazuki, countering with an inner leg reap.

Kazuki almost fell, but somehow managed to untangle his leg from behind Jack's. Kazuki stumbled backwards and Jack pressed forward with his attack.

Too late . . . Jack realized he'd been tricked.

Kazuki's loss of balance had been a ploy to get Jack to over-commit to his own attack. He was now the target of a sacrifice throw.

Kazuki rolled backwards, pulling Jack on top of him. At the same time, he thrust his foot into Jack's stomach, flipping Jack in a large arc over his head.

Jack had no chance of avoiding Kazuki's *tomoe nage* stomach throw. Landing hard upon his back on the *dojo* floor, he had the wind knocked out of him for the second time that day. Before he could even snatch a breath, Kazuki had rolled on top and locked down on him in a neck hold.

'Very impressive, Kazuki!' commended Sensei Kyuzo from the sidelines. 'See if you can hold him down for a count of ten.'

Kazuki clamped on to Jack, his right forearm wrapping tightly round the back of Jack's neck, while restraining Jack's right arm under his armpit. He spread his legs out to the side and now dropped all his weight on to Jack's ribcage, digging his head in tight beside Jack's.

Jack was pinned to the ground.

'ONE!' called the sensei.

Jack rolled into Kazuki, trying to dislodge him, his free hand scrabbling to find purchase on Kazuki's *gi*.

'Forget it, *gaijin*,' rasped Kazuki into Jack's ear, 'there's no way on earth I'm letting you up!'

'TWO!'

Jack flung himself the other way to turn Kazuki over. He used every ounce of strength he possessed, but Kazuki's legs were spread too wide and his weight prevented Jack rolling him.

'THREE!'

Jack lay helpless, his energy spent.

'Pathetic!' taunted Kazuki.

'FOUR!'

Incensed, Jack renewed his efforts. He shuffled his feet round towards Kazuki's outstretched legs, drawing his body close to his rival. He tried to trap his rear leg and turn him over. Feeling the movement, Kazuki shifted his legs out of the way.

'You'll have to try harder than that!'

'FIVE!'

Jack arched his back, pushing with the balls of his feet to form a bridge with his body. He managed to create a gap between his back and the floor and began to twist into Kazuki, turning his head out of the hold.

Kazuki forced himself back on to Jack's ribcage, driving Jack's body to the floor.

'Squirm all you like. You've lost!'

'SIX!'

Frantic, Jack struggled even harder, but Kazuki's tightened his iron grip.

'While I've got your attention,' whispered Kazuki into Jack's ear. 'I've got fresh news for you. A *gaijin*, just like you, has been burnt alive by the *daimyo* Kamakura.'

SUBMISSION

The words slammed into Jack's brain like a fist and he stopped struggling.

Was this another of Kazuki's false taunts? Jack hadn't yet been able to speak with Masamoto or any of the sensei to discover whether the rumours were true, though he had taken some comfort from the fact that none of the students in the school, aside from Kazuki and his cohorts, appeared to know anything about *daimyo* Kamakura's declaration against Christians.

'SEVEN!'

'They said his flesh fell off in lumps before he died, like a barbecued pig. Imagine that, *gaijin*!'

Kazuki's mocking cruelty was what spurred Jack to retaliate. For a brief moment, he had a flashback of the storm that had shipwrecked the *Alexandria* and the sailor who had been set on fire by lightning. Jack could remember the agony etched on to the dead man's face and the gut-wrenching smell of charred flesh. His anger boiled over at the thought and a surge of adrenalin flooded through him.

'EIGHT!'

In one simultaneous movement, Jack arched his body, flung his legs round Kazuki's back leg and grabbed his opponent's head with his free hand. His fingers found Kazuki's nostrils and he wrenched back hard.

'NINE!'

Kazuki grunted in pain and was spun over.

Jack rolled on top. He trapped Kazuki with a chest hold, lying across Kazuki's shoulders and driving his elbow and knee into either side of Kazuki's head to lock it in place.

Now it was Kazuki's turn to be counted out.

Through the matting of hair that plastered his face, Jack caught a glimpse of Yamato and Saburo willing him on. Despite his exhaustion, he allowed himself the smallest of victory smiles.

'One,' said the sensei half-heartedly.

Kazuki was pinned and going nowhere.

'Two.'

But away from anyone's line of sight, Kazuki managed to free an arm and began to hammer Jack in the kidneys.

'Three.'

Only Sensei Kyuzo could see it, but he turned a blind eye as Kazuki landed another unofficial blow. The sensei deliberately slowed his count.

'Four . . .'

Kazuki struck again. Jack's side flared with pain and he was forced to relinquish his grip. Throwing Jack off, Kazuki countered hard, putting him into a choking hold.

'That's not very nice – going for the face!' spat Kazuki, who now lay on top of Jack, one forearm behind Jack's neck, the other across his throat.

49

Kazuki wrenched his forearms together, closing them like a vice.

Jack spluttered in shock.

His windpipe was instantly cut off and he couldn't breathe.

'Excellent, Kazuki,' praised Sensei Kyuzo, pleased to see his protégé back in control.

Blatantly ignoring the escalating violence of the *randori*, Sensei Kyuzo turned to instruct the class.

'Notice the switch from the pin to the choke. This is an extremely effective manoeuvre and will guarantee submission from any enemy.'

Encouraged, Kazuki bore down even harder with his stranglehold, a sadistic glint in his eyes.

Jack felt his throat being crushed. His head pounded under the pressure. His lungs starved of oxygen, darkness seeped into the corners of Jack's vision and he tapped wildly on the floor for submission.

Kazuki merely looked on, savouring Jack's agony.

Jack teetered on the edge of consciousness.

But Kazuki kept the choke on.

Stars exploded in front of Jack's eyes and, for a terrifying moment, Kazuki's grinning face metamorphosed into Dragon Eye's. The mask of a blackened skull with a single green eye flashed before him.

Jack's submissive tapping became weaker, his hand flapping like a dying fish. Then, as if from the depths of a murky pool, he heard Akiko shout, 'Sensei! He's killing him!'

Sensei Kyuzo observed the blue tinge to Jack's lips with

mild interest, saying, 'That's enough, Kazuki. It's clear you've beaten him . . .'

Kazuki released the choke and air flooded back into Jack's lungs.

Jack gulped it down like water. The instant the oxygen hit his brain, Jack's fury exploded with a vengeance. On survival instinct alone, he drove his fist squarely into Kazuki's face. The punch connected and sent his enemy flying backwards.

'*YAME!*' bellowed Sensei Kyuzo, dragging Jack to his feet by the scruff of his *gi*.

His thumb sought out a pressure point in Jack's neck and the sensei pressed down hard. Jack's body was instantly paralysed with pain. He hung there like a rag doll. To the students, Jack merely appeared exhausted from the *randori*. For Jack, it was as if Sensei Kyuzo had inserted a molten iron rod into his spine.

'What did I say?' breathed Sensei Kyuzo into Jack's face with hardened contempt. '*Nage waza* and *katame waza* only. Since when was punching part of grappling technique?'

'Since when . . . was murder . . . encouraged during *randori*?' replied Jack through clenched teeth as he fought against the spasms of pain.

Kazuki lay in the centre of the *dojo*, nursing a split lip, his *gi* stained in bright red patches with his own blood.

'You have much to learn,' said Sensei Kyuzo, 'the first principle being *fudoshin*. You're clearly too unbalanced to be samurai!'

Jack was dumbfounded, not only by the agony Sensei Kyuzo was inflicting upon him, but by the injustice of it all.

'As punishment for your lack of self-control,' announced Sensei Kyuzo so that the whole class could hear, 'you will return here at dinner and polish every single woodblock in this *dojo*. And you will not go to bed until you have finished. Do you understand?'

'But, Sensei, I have to go to tea with *daimyo* Takatomi tonight.'

Sensei Kyuzo fumed at Jack, knowing he couldn't force him to miss such an important appointment. 'Tomorrow night then!'

'*Hai*, Sensei,' replied Jack grimly.

The sensei leant forward, screwing his thumb further into Jack's pressure point and sending another excruciating wave of pain through him. He bent down to whisper in his ear, 'I don't know how you got your name on the submission for the Circle of Three, but, mark my words, I will personally ensure that you're not selected during the trials.'

9

FUDOSHIN

'What's *fudoshin* anyway?' groaned Jack, rubbing his tender neck as he and his small group of friends wound their way through the streets of Kyoto after lunch.

'I'm not sure,' admitted Yamato.

Jack looked to the others for an answer, but Akiko mutely shook her head, appearing to be equally baffled. Saburo stroked his chin in contemplation, but he clearly hadn't a clue either, for he quickly went back to munching on his *yakatori,* the stick of grilled chicken he'd just bought from a passing street vendor.

'It means "immovable spirit",' said Kiku.

Yori, who was trailing beside her, nodded in agreement as if that explained everything.

'But what does it mean to have an "immovable spirit"?' asked Jack.

'My father said *fudoshin* is about taking control of your emotions,' replied Kiku. 'A samurai must remain calm at all times – even in the face of danger.'

'So how do you get *fudoshin*?'

'I don't know . . . My father's good at explaining things, but not at teaching them.'

Kiku gave Jack an apologetic smile, then Yori piped up, 'I think *fudoshin* is a bit like being a willow tree.'

'A willow tree?' Jack repeated, his eyebrows wrinkling in puzzlement.

'Yes, like a willow tree you must grow deep roots into the ground to weather the storm, but also be soft and yielding against the winds that blow through.'

'That's easier said than done!' laughed Jack. 'You try keeping calm when you're being strangled and getting told that foreigners are being burnt alive – and that you're next!'

'You shouldn't listen to Kazuki, Jack,' said Akiko, sighing with concern. 'He's just making up stories to scare you.'

'Sorry,' interrupted Saburo, a sheepish look on his face as he swallowed his last bit of chicken, 'but Kazuki's right.'

All eyes fell upon Saburo.

'I didn't want to tell you, Jack, but the *daimyo* Kamakura supposedly did kill a Christian priest. There was a sign about it in the street . . .'

Saburo trailed off as he saw the blood drain from Jack's face.

Listening to his friend's revelation, Jack felt the warmth of the midday sun disappear, a chill running down his spine like a sliver of ice. So Kazuki *had* been telling the truth. Jack had to know more and was about to ask Saburo when, turning a corner into a large square, he was suddenly confronted by the gleaming blade of a samurai sword.

Held high in the air by a warrior in a dark-blue kimono with the *kamon* of a bamboo shoot, the arc of lethal metal

54

was poised to strike. All thoughts of Kamakura and the dead priest were wiped from Jack's mind.

But the blade wasn't directed at Jack — rather at a battle-hardened warrior, dressed in a plain brown kimono with the *kamon* of a crescent moon and star, standing motionless three sword lengths from his opponent.

'A duel!' exclaimed Saburo with a yelp of delight, dragging Jack out of the way. 'Quick, over here!'

A crowd had gathered in the duelling ground. Some of them eyed Jack's arrival with suspicion, whispering to one another behind their hands. Even the warrior in blue glanced over, distracted from the impending duel by the strange spectacle of a blond-haired foreigner dressed in a kimono.

Jack ignored them. He was used to the curiosity he generated wherever he went.

'Hello, Jack. I didn't expect to see you here.'

Jack turned to see Emi, dressed in an elegant sea-green kimono, accompanied by her two friends, Cho and Kai, along with an elderly samurai chaperone. The two groups of students bowed to one another.

'Why are they fighting?' Jack asked Emi as she took up position by his side.

'The samurai in blue is on his *musha shugyo*,' replied Emi.

The warrior who had been distracted by Jack's appearance was several years younger than his opponent, who looked about thirty. His kimono was dusty and faded in patches and his face weathered by the elements.

'What's a *musha shugyo*?' asked Jack.

'It's a warrior pilgrimage. When samurai finish their

training, they go on a quest throughout Japan to test their strength and refine their fighting skills. Warriors challenge one another to prove who is the best.'

'The loser can be knocked out or disabled, and sometimes even killed!' interrupted Saburo, a little too enthusiastically for Jack's liking.

'Killed? That seems a rather idiotic way to test yourself.'

'Well, how else are they going to know if they're any good or not?' replied Emi matter-of-factly.

Jack turned his attention to the two contesting samurai. They stared at one another. Neither seemed willing to make the first move. In the heat of the midday sun, a bead of sweat ran down the side of the blue-clothed warrior's face, but he disregarded it.

'Why isn't he attacking?' asked Jack.

'They're trying to hide any weaknesses they may have,' Yamato answered. 'My father told me that even the smallest movement can reveal a flaw in your fighting technique, which your opponent can then take advantage of.'

The crowd, sensing the growing tension, was now motionless too. Even the children gathered round the edges were quiet. The only sound that could be heard was the chime of temple bells marking the beginning of midday prayers.

The samurai in blue shifted uneasily and dust swirled in little eddies across the ground. His opponent, however, remained perfectly calm, his sword still sheathed inside its *saya*.

Then as the last ring of temple bells died away, the older samurai withdrew his *katana* in one fluid movement.

The crowd shuffled backwards.

The duel had begun.

The two samurai circled one another warily.

Suddenly the warrior in blue screamed, '*KIAI!*'

Brandishing his sword, he advanced on the older samurai. Ignoring this display of bravado, the older man merely dropped back into a wide stance, side-on to his enemy. At the same time, he raised his own sword over his head then dropped it down behind his body, so that his opponent could no longer see his blade.

The older samurai waited.

'*KIAAAIIIIIII!*'

The samurai in blue screamed again, summoning all his fighting spirit, and launched an attack. He cut down with his sword on to the exposed neck of the warrior, victory assured.

Still the older samurai didn't move and Jack was sure he was as good as dead.

Then at the last second, the older samurai shifted off-line, avoiding the lethal arc of the blade, and with a short cry of '*Kiai!*' cut his own sword across the unguarded side of his attacker.

For what seemed an eternity, the two samurai froze, face-to-face.

Neither broke eye contact.

One sword dripped blood.

There was a disturbing absence of sound, as if death itself had muffled the ears of the world. Not even a temple bell chimed.

Then, with a low groan, the younger samurai leant to

one side and crumpled to the ground, dead. His body threw up clouds of dust that billowed away as if they were the warrior's fleeing spirit.

The older samurai maintained his focus a moment longer, ensuring the duel was over. Then he straightened up and flicked the blood from his blade in a move Jack recognized as *chiburi*. Resheathing his sword, the samurai walked away without looking back.

'I suppose that's what Sensei Kyuzo means by *fudoshin*,' breathed Saburo in awe. 'That samurai didn't even blink when the sword was going for his head.'

But Jack wasn't listening. He was transfixed by the blood seeping into the dusty ground. The duel had reminded him of how brutal and unforgiving Japan could be. The news that the priest's death was true meant that *daimyo* Kamakura's plan to wipe out Christians *had* to be too. The question was how long did Jack have left in this violent land?

10

THE NIGHTINGALE FLOOR

'Run!' whispered Akiko urgently later that night. 'They're coming!'

Jack bolted from their hiding place underneath the staircase. He hurried down the corridor and into a room with a large silk-screen painting of two ferocious tigers. He heard a cry from behind and realized the guards had already caught Akiko. They would be after him now.

Opening the *shoji* door on the other side of the Tiger Room, he glanced down the hallway, saw it was deserted and ran. He switched left at the end, then took the first right. He had no idea where he was going, since the *daimyo*'s castle was a complete labyrinth of rooms, corridors and passageways.

Running on tiptoe so that he made as little sound as possible upon the wooden floorboards, he followed the corridor round past two closed *shoji* doors and then bore left. But it was a dead end.

He heard a guard's voice and spun round. But the corridor was empty.

Jack retraced his steps, stopping where the corridor

switched right. He then listened for the sound of approaching feet.

Dead silence.

Warily, he peeked round the corner.

The corridor was windowless and only one of the paper lanterns that hung from the beams had been lit. In the flickering gloom, he could see a single *shoji* at the far end of the passageway.

With no sight or sound of anyone, he stepped out.

And his foot disappeared through the floor.

He cried out as he plummeted downwards. In sheer desperation, he flung himself to one side, grabbing at the wall. His fingers found purchase on a wooden crosspiece and Jack clung on for all his life was worth.

To his alarm, he hung over a gaping hole in the woodblock floor. A sliding trapdoor had been opened to catch unsuspecting intruders.

Jack peered into the depths. A small set of steps led down into unfathomable darkness. Jack cursed himself for his hastiness. He could easily have broken his leg, or even his neck. Here was all the proof he needed that escape was futile.

Regaining his composure, he edged backwards until his feet found solid ground again.

'Come on! This way!'

A guard had heard his cry and they were now in pursuit.

Skirting the hole, Jack made his way down the corridor, but he could hear footsteps rapidly approaching.

'He's not in here.'

Jack quickened his pace, keeping one eye on the floor

and one eye on where he was headed. His pursuers would soon turn the corner and discover him.

He reached the end of the corridor, slid the *shoji* open and stepped through, swiftly closing the door behind him.

The rectangular room he had entered was large enough for twenty *tatami* straw mats. Jack guessed it was a reception room of some kind. At the rear was a polished cedar dais, adorned with a single *zabuton* cushion, behind which was a large silk wall hanging of a white crane in flight. Otherwise, the fawn-coloured walls were completely bare.

No windows. No other doors. No escape.

Jack could hear his pursuers running down the corridor.

He was trapped.

Then Jack noticed the crane shifting slightly as if caught in a breeze. But with no windows or doors, something had to be causing it to move.

Jack hurried over to inspect the hanging more closely. There, concealed behind the silk screen, was a secret bolt-hole. Without a second thought, Jack scrambled through, pulling the wall hanging back to hide the entrance just as the *shoji* was jerked open.

'So where is he?' demanded a voice.

'He can't have vanished,' replied another, this one female.

Jack held his breath. He could hear the two of them pacing the room.

'Well, he's not here,' said the first voice. 'Maybe he doubled back?'

'I told you we should have checked that first room. Come on!'

The *shoji* slid shut with a soft *whoosh* and the voices receded down the hallway. Jack let out a relieved sigh. That had been *too* close. If he'd got caught, it would have been all over for him.

In the gloom of the bolt-hole, Jack noticed a narrow passage leading off to his left. With no other choice open to him, he turned and slipped along the walkway. He had no idea where he was headed, but after a couple of turns the passage lightened, a dim glow filtering through the translucent walls.

'Where can he have gone?' said a voice, close by his ear.

Jack froze, then realized his hidden walkway ran parallel to one of the main corridors. He could see his pursuers' silhouettes through the paper-thin wall. Yet, as he was in shadow, they were completely oblivious to his presence, barely a knife thrust away.

'Let's try down here. He can't have got far.'

Jack heard their bare feet pad away down the corridor before continuing along the passageway until, to his surprise, he hit another dead end.

Convinced the passage must lead somewhere, Jack felt around for a door. He tried to slide the wall panels back, but nothing shifted. He gave one a firm push to see if it opened that way. All of a sudden, the lower section gave way and he was catapulted into the main corridor.

'There he is!' came a shout.

Jack jumped to his feet as the false wall sprang back into place. He ran as fast as he could, dodging left and right down the warren of corridors. Spotting a narrow staircase, he was up the stairs in three quick bounds. As he landed on the top step, the entire staircase retracted upwards, Jack's weight triggering the hidden fulcrum. From the corridor below, the staircase had completely disappeared into the ceiling.

Astounded as he was by the remarkable staircase, Jack had the wits to remain silent and still. Oblivious to his presence above their heads, his pursuers shot by beneath.

Walking carefully back along the steps, the staircase descended to its original position and Jack backtracked down the now deserted corridor until he found a door he hadn't yet tried. On the other side was a long corridor with a highly polished wooden floor. It ended in a wooden gateway that *had* to be the way out.

With barely the length of a ship's quarterdeck to cross, he knew he could escape the *daimyo*'s castle. Jack started for the exit, but as his foot went down, the floorboard warbled like a bird. He tried to lighten his movements, but however softly he trod the floor sang out with every step he took, mocking his attempted flight.

He could hear the pounding of feet coming his way.

Jack ran as the floor sang even louder.

'Got you!' said the guard, grabbing hold of Jack. 'The game's up.'

11

THE GOLDEN TEA ROOM

Jack let himself be led back down the corridor and towards the reception room with the wall hanging of the white crane. Upon entering, Jack immediately knelt down and bowed low until his head touched the *tatami* in deference to the *daimyo*.

'So you were caught out by my Nightingale Floor?'

Daimyo Takatomi sat cross-legged upon the cedar dais, guarded by six samurai who lined the walls like stone statues.

'Yes,' Jack admitted.

'Excellent!' he cried, a satisfied grin on his face. 'The Nightingale Floor is the new security feature in my palace that I'm most proud of. The bird sound is produced by metal hinges under the floorboards that are triggered with the pressure of a single foot. This makes it impossible to cross without being detected. I think our little game of "Escape" has proved its effectiveness.'

'What I would like to know, Father,' asked Emi, who knelt between Yamato and Akiko, 'is how Jack got out of *this* room.'

Jack smiled to himself. While he hadn't managed to avoid all the traps during the *daimyo*'s challenge to each of them to escape his castle undetected, he had evaded the guards longer than anyone else.

'Emi-chan,' said her father reproachfully, 'I cannot believe my own daughter didn't spot the other door.'

Jack glanced over to see the *daimyo* indicating the blank wall to their right. They all studied it, bemused. Takatomi, with a wave of his hand, prompted one of his samurai guards to push at the central wall panel. It gave a soft *click*, then pivoted on a central axis.

The samurai disappeared in the blink of an eye.

A moment later, the wall revolved again and the guard was back in the room. Jack, Akiko, Yamato and Emi looked at one another, dumbfounded by the hidden door. For even now, though they knew it was there, the wall appeared solid and unbroken.

'As I said before, children, Nijo Castle is now ninja-proof, but you can never be too careful. I have a guard behind that door every time I receive guests in this room.'

'So that's how you escaped,' said Emi, shaking her head in disbelief. 'I can't believe you spotted it and we didn't.'

Jack was going to correct her, but decided against it. Clearly, the *daimyo* thought no one had discovered his bolt-hole behind the wall hanging of the crane.

It was *daimyo* Takatomi's secret.

Now it was Jack's too.

'But enough of the games for this evening,' announced the *daimyo*. 'It is time for *cha-no-yu*.'

★ ★ ★

'The host will sometimes spend days going over every detail to ensure that the ceremony is perfect,' explained Emi in hushed tones.

They were entering the *roji*, a tiny cultivated garden, devoid of flowers but sprinkled with water so that all the mossy rocks, ferns and stepping-stones glistened like morning dew. Emi led the way and seated herself on a bench, indicating for Jack, Akiko and Yamato to join her.

'Here we wait,' informed Emi softly, 'in order that we may rid ourselves of the dust of the world.'

Jack's anticipation grew. He didn't particularly like green tea, but he knew the tea ceremony was of the greatest significance. Emi had tried to explain the ritual, but there was so much symbolism attached to every action, movement and moment that Jack understood very little of what she said.

'There are four guiding principles to the tea ceremony,' she had explained. 'Harmony, respect, purity and tranquillity. At its deepest level, you should experience the same qualities in your own heart and mind.'

As they sat there, silently absorbing the peace of the *roji*, Jack began to understand some of Emi's meaning. The soft trickle of flowing water sounded like distant bells and the simplicity of the garden somehow eased his mind. The setting was almost magical and he felt his spirits begin to lift.

'Now remember, Jack,' whispered Emi after a moment of silence, 'when we go in, do not step on the joins between mats. Do not walk on or touch the central *tatami* where the hearth is. You must remain in the kneeling *seiza* position throughout the ceremony, and don't forget to admire the hanging scroll, study the kettle and hearth and comment favourably on the scoop and tea container when they're offered to you for inspection.'

'Is that all?' exclaimed Jack, his brain bursting with so much etiquette.

'Don't worry. Simply follow what I do,' said Akiko softly, seeing Jack's growing alarm.

She gave him a tender look and Jack felt reassured. With Akiko by his side, he should be able to avoid the most embarrassing of mistakes.

'You have to be quiet now,' ordered Emi under her breath, straightening out her kimono as her father appeared.

Daimyo Takatomi, dressed in a stark-white kimono, approached along a black-pebbled path. He paused by a large stone basin set among rocks and filled it with fresh water from the stream. Jack watched as the *daimyo* took a small wooden ladle from beside the basin, scooped up some of the water and washed both his hands and mouth. Once he had completed the purification ritual, he made his way through the *chumon* gate, and silently welcomed his guests with a courteous bow. They responded like-wise before following the *daimyo* back through the *chumon*, which Emi had informed Jack was a symbolic doorway between the physical world and the spiritual world of the *cha-no-yu*.

They each took up the wooden ladle in turn and puri-fied their hands and mouth, before continuing along the path to the tea house. Here, the entrance was only a few feet high, so they had to crouch to enter. Emi had explained that the doorway was constructed like this so that everyone had to bow their heads, stressing that all were equal in *cha-no-yu*, irrespective of status or social position. It also meant a samurai could not carry a sword inside.

Jack was the last to enter. He slipped off his sandals and ducked through the entrance. As he stood up, he gasped in astonishment. The small square room was decorated entirely in gold leaf. To Jack, it was like standing inside a bar of solid gold. Even the ceiling was gilded. The only adornment in the room was a single scroll hanging in the alcove. The *tatami*, while not gold, were lined with rich red gossamer, so that the tea room's magnificence totally overwhelmed the senses.

Jack had been under the impression from Akiko that tea rooms were modest, simple buildings made of wood and decorated in subdued colours, but this tea house was grand beyond imagination.

Akiko and Yamato looked equally dumbstruck and the *daimyo* Takatomi was clearly pleased with their reactions. He gestured for them to kneel and join him.

Emi stepped towards the alcove, taking her time to admire the scroll painting before seating herself in front of the hearth and examining the kettle appreciatively. Akiko and Yamato performed the same ritual, then Jack tried to copy their actions.

He approached the alcove and studied the scroll, a simple yet exquisite painting of a kingfisher upon a bare branch, with *kanji* scripture traced in ink down its right-hand side.

'The *kanji* says *Ichi-go, Ichi-e*: one time, one meeting,' explained Takatomi. 'The scroll reminds me that each tea ceremony is unique and must be savoured for what it gives.'

The others nodded appreciatively at Takatomi's wisdom.

'The script may also be interpreted as "One chance in a lifetime". This reminds me that in any conflict of life and death, there is no chance to try again. You must seize life with both hands.'

Ichi-go, Ichi-e, repeated Jack quietly. The *daimyo*'s words rang true. Having lost so much, Jack understood the fragility of life.

Takatomi indicated for Jack to join the others, then the *daimyo* lit a small charcoal fire in the hearth and fed the flames with incense. The heady aroma of sandalwood soon filled the air.

Retiring to a preparation room through a discreet door to his right, Takatomi collected a black tea bowl containing a bamboo whisk, a white linen cloth and a slender ivory scoop. On his return, he meticulously arranged these by a large oval water jar placed on the central *tatami*.

Next Takatomi brought in a second water bowl, a bamboo water ladle and a green bamboo rest for the kettle lid. Closing the *shoji* door behind him, he then arranged himself in *seiza*.

With due ceremony, he removed a fine silk cloth of bright purple from his *obi* and began a ritual cleansing of the scoop and tea container. The level of concentration the *daimyo* applied to the process was quite remarkable. Every movement was painstakingly precise and heavy with a symbolism that remained a mystery to Jack.

As the *daimyo* ladled hot water from the kettle into the

tea bowl, he spoke once again. 'When tea is made with water drawn from the depths of the mind, whose bottom is beyond measure, we really have what is called *cha-no-yu*.'

And so the Way of Tea began.

12

TAMASHIWARI

'Four hours for a cup of tea!' exclaimed Jack as they made their way back to the *Shishi-no-ma* under a star-filled night.

'Yes, how wonderful!' enthused Akiko, misinterpreting Jack's incredulity for awe. 'The ceremony was perfect. The *daimyo* certainly has a flair for *cha-no-yu*, a rare master of *sado*. You should feel greatly honoured.'

'I feel greatly sore!' mumbled Jack in English, still suffering from his knees having locked up after the first hour. 'God forbid tea ever arrives on our shores!'

'Sorry, what was that?' asked Akiko.

'I said, we have yet to have tea in England,' Jack mistranslated in Japanese.

'Your countrymen can sail so far, but you don't have tea! How sad to miss out on such perfection.'

'We have other drinks,' countered Jack, though he had to admit the drink on-board ship was an acquired taste too.

'Oh, I'm sure they're nice . . . but what about the Golden Tea Room?' she continued. 'To think that the *daimyo* once moved the entire tea room to the Imperial

Palace to entertain the Emperor himself! We are *truly* honoured guests.'

Jack let Akiko talk uninterrupted. The Japanese were usually very reserved in expressing their emotions and he was happy to see her so buoyant. While Akiko continued discussing the ceremony with Yamato, Jack thought about Nijo Castle and its inner palace. He was astounded at the lengths the *daimyo* had gone to protect himself. Takatomi was clearly proud of the new security features he had installed since Dragon Eye's assassination attempt. Hence the escape challenge the *daimyo* had arranged to demonstrate its effectiveness.

'Ninja-proof,' the *daimyo* had said.

If that were so, reasoned Jack, then the bolt-hole behind the hanging of the crane was the most secure location to hide the *rutter* from Dragon Eye. Certainly far better than under a flimsy *futon* or in the grounds of the *Niten Ichi Ryū*. Besides, the school was the first place the ninja would look. Jack realized he had no choice but to somehow arrange a return visit to the castle and hide the logbook.

'KIAI!' screamed Akiko.

Her fist slammed into the solid block of wood.

And rebounded . . .

The strike looked exceedingly painful and Jack winced for her. Akiko cradled her hand, tears welling up in her eyes, her joy of the previous night completely extinguished by their first class of the day, *taijutsu*.

'Next!' shouted Sensei Kyuzo, without a hint of sympathy.

Akiko knelt back in line to allow Jack to take up position

in front of the short rectangular plank. The cedar was as thick as his thumb and appeared indestructible with bare hands. Still Sensei Kyuzo had placed it upon two stable blocks in the middle of the *Butokuden* and instructed every student to break the board with their fists.

So far no one had even dented it.

Jack clenched his right hand in preparation to strike. With all his might, he drove his arm down on to the cedar plank. His fist collided with the block, sending a shuddering jolt up his arm. The wood didn't even splinter, but Jack felt as if every bone in his hand had shattered.

'Pathetic,' snarled Sensei Kyuzo, waving him dismissively back into line.

Jack rejoined the rest of class, who were all nursing bruised hands and aching arms.

'Iron is full of impurities that weaken it,' lectured Sensei Kyuzo, ignoring the suffering of his students. 'Through forging, it becomes steel and is transformed into a razor-sharp sword. Samurai develop in the same fashion. Those wishing to prove they're strong enough to be chosen for the Circle of Three will be required to break through three such blocks, at the same time.'

Sensei Kyuzo suddenly attacked the cedar block, dropping his tiny body downwards and driving his fist through the wood with a shout of 'KIAI!'

CRACK! The cedar split in two as if it were no more than a chopstick.

'You're all merely iron waiting to be forged into mighty warriors,' continued Sensei Kyuzo without skipping a beat, 'and your forge is *tamashiwari*, Trial by Wood.'

73

He looked pointedly in Jack's direction.

'It's just that some of you have more impurities than others,' he added as he strode over to one of the *Butokuden*'s mighty wooden pillars.

Jack bit down on his lip, determined not to rise to the sensei's bait.

'Like iron, you must beat out these weaknesses,' Sensei Kyuzo explained, indicating a pad of rice straw bound by cord at chest height to the pillar.

He punched it with his fist. The wooden column boomed deeply under the force of the blow.

'This is a *makiwara*. I've set up these striking posts on each pillar of the training hall. You're to hit these repeatedly to strengthen the bones in your hands. It's good conditioning for all samurai. Twenty punches each. Begin!'

Jack lined himself up behind Saburo, who was already preparing to make his first strike.

'One!' shouted Saburo, working himself up for the punch.

Saburo's fist collided with the straw pad. There was a crunch followed by a feeble groan as his hand crumpled against the rigid pillar. Saburo, his eyes screwed up in pain, stepped aside for Jack.

'Your turn,' he moaned through gritted teeth.

'Three blocks!' exclaimed Saburo, who was having trouble holding his *hashi* during dinner that evening. He wiggled his fingers trying to get movement back into his bruised hand. 'I'm glad it's you and not me going for the Circle of

Three. One's hard enough. How on earth are you supposed to break three blocks?'

'You think Trial by Wood's hard? This is only the beginning. We're being judged on three other trials too,' said Yamato, putting down his rice bowl.

He nodded towards the head table, where their *kyujutsu* teacher sat. Sensei Yosa, the only female samurai among the teachers and their instructor in the Art of the Bow, was looking as radiant as ever, the ruby-red scar that cut across her right cheek discreetly hidden behind her beautiful mane of black hair. 'I've heard Sensei Yosa's Trial by Fire is to snuff out a candle.'

'That doesn't sound so bad,' said Jack, his hand also stiff as he struggled to pick up a piece of *sashimi* from the centre plate.

'No, but in order to prove your skill for the Circle you have to do it with an arrow, fired at long distance.'

Jack dropped his *sashimi* in disbelief.

'At this rate, none of you will be entering the Circle,' observed Kiku.

Jack glumly retrieved his piece of fish from the table. Kiku was probably right. His own archery skills were passable, but he knew he had little hope of achieving such a feat as Trial by Fire.

'Do you know what the other two trials are? Are they any easier?' asked Jack hopefully.

'Sensei Yamada is setting a Trial by *Koan*,' revealed Akiko. 'Our answer to the question will be used to assess our intellect.'

'Yori, you'd better be careful,' said Saburo, arching his eyebrows into a look of serious concern. 'As the king of solving *koans*, you might be entered for the Circle whether you like it or not!'

Yori looked up from his bowl of miso soup, a startled expression on his face.

'Stop teasing him!' scolded Kiku.

Saburo shrugged an apology before slurping appreciatively on his noodles.

'So what's the final trial?' asked Jack.

'That's Sensei Hosokawa's Trial by Sword,' answered Akiko. 'To test our courage.'

'I've heard the older students call it the Gauntlet,' added Saburo.

'Why's that?' asked Jack.

'I don't know, but I'm sure you'll find out.'

13

ORIGAMI

'Can anyone tell me what this is?' asked Sensei Yamada, indicating a bright white square of paper at his feet.

The ancient monk sat, cross-legged, in his usual position on the raised dais at the rear of the Buddha Hall, his hands gently folded in his lap. Trails of incense weaved a curtain of smoke around him and mingled with his grey spiderweb of a beard, making him appear ghost-like, as if the slightest breeze could blow him away.

The students, also sitting in the half-lotus position, studied the squares of paper laid out before them like large snowflakes.

'Paper, Sensei,' scoffed Nobu from the back of the class, grinning at Kazuki for approval. But Kazuki just shook his head in disbelief at his friend's idiocy.

'Never assume the obvious is true, Nobu-kun,' said Sensei Yamada. 'That's what it is, but it's much more than that. What else is it?'

Nobu fell silent under Sensei Yamada's glare. The sensei may have been an old man, but Jack knew he'd been *sohei*, one of the notoriously fearsome warrior monks of

Enryakuji, once the most powerful Buddhist monastery in Japan. It was rumoured the fighting spirit of these monks had been so strong, they could kill a man without even touching him.

Sensei Yamada clapped his hands and called, '*Mokuso!*' signalling the start of the class's meditation. The *koan* had been set: 'It is paper, but what else is it?'

Jack settled himself on his *zabuton* cushion in preparation for his *zazen* meditation. Half closing his eyes, he slowed his breathing and let his mind empty.

As a Christian, Jack had never encountered meditation, or even Buddhism, prior to his arrival in Japan. At first he had found the process and concepts difficult to grasp. He questioned whether, as a Christian, he should be accepting them so readily, but three things had helped him change his mind.

First, when he had raised the conflict of faith with Sensei Yamada, the monk had explained to him that Buddhism was a philosophy open to all religions. This was why the Japanese had no issues with following Shintoism – their native religion – practising Buddhism, and even converting to Christianity, at the same time.

'They're all strands of the same rug,' Sensei Yamada had said, 'only different colours.'

Second, Jack had discovered that meditation was quite similar to the act of praying. Both required focus, peaceful surroundings and, usually, reflections upon life and how it should be led. So Jack decided he would think of meditation as simply another form of praying to God.

Third, during a particularly deep meditation, he had

experienced the vision of a butterfly overcoming a demon and this vision had helped him win his *taijutsu* fight in the *Taryu-Jiai* contest.

This had been the proof that encouraged Jack to open his mind to the possibilities and benefits of Buddhism, even if he remained a Christian at heart.

Through daily practice he had become adept at meditation, and in no time at all his mind was focused on the piece of paper before him, trying to unravel the mystery of the *koan*. Even though no answer was immediately forthcoming, he wasn't worried. He knew enlightenment, *satori* as Sensei Yamada called it, took patience and intense concentration.

Yet, whichever way he looked at the paper, it was still merely a sheet of paper.

A whole stick of incense had burnt through by the time Sensei Yamada called a halt to the meditation, and Jack was no closer to experiencing *satori*.

'*Mokuso yame!*' said the sensei, clapping his hands once more. 'So, do you have an answer for me, Nobu-kun?'

'No, Sensei,' mumbled Nobu, bowing his head in shame.

'Anyone else?' invited the sensei.

Kiku raised her hand tentatively. 'Is it *kozo*, Sensei?'

'What makes you say that?'

'The paper is made from the fibres of the *kozo* tree,' explained Kiku.

'A fair suggestion, but you are still thinking too literally. How about if I do this?'

Sensei Yamada picked up his paper and folded it several

times. Initially shaping it into a smaller square, he then bent the sheet in increasingly intricate folds. Within moments, the flat piece of paper had been transformed into a small bird.

He placed the paper model on the floor for all to see.

'So what is it?'

'A crane!' said Emi excitedly. 'Our symbol of peace.'

'Excellent, Emi. And folding a paper crane is like making peace – some of the steps are awkward. At first, it may even seem impossible. But, with patience, the result is always a thing of beauty. This is the art of *origami*.'

Sensei Yamada took a fresh piece of paper from a small pile behind him.

'So let me rephrase my opening question for you to meditate on. The *koan* is now: what is it that *origami* teaches us? But first watch me closely, so that you can all make your own cranes.'

Sensei Yamada repeated the complex combination of folds that would create the little bird. There were more than twenty individual steps. When the sensei made his last move, pulling at the corners of the model to form the wings, he was left with a perfect miniature crane in his palm.

In Jack's hand, though, was a crumpled piece of paper.

Jack realized that *origami* was far more difficult than it appeared. He looked around at the others. The attempts by Yamato and Saburo were equally flawed, and even Akiko's model appeared rather lopsided with one wing vastly larger than the other. The only student to have folded a crane perfectly was Yori, who was pulling at its tail and making the little bird's wings flap.

'It seems some of you need more practice,' observed Sensei Yamada, who selected a second piece of paper and laid it in front of him. 'So who can tell me what this is?'

'A crane!' chimed the class in unison.

'Certainly not!' admonished Sensei Yamada, much to the confusion of his students. 'Use the eyes of your mind, not the eyes in your head.'

Picking up the paper, he folded and bent the sheet, his fingers dexterously manipulating it into ever more complex shapes. The students gasped in astonishment at the finished model.

'This is quite clearly a butterfly,' said the sensei with a wry smile, and in his hand was a lifelike replica of a butterfly, complete with antennae. 'Tonight, I want you all to practise making a paper crane like I showed you. And while you do this, meditate on what *origami* is teaching you.'

The class collected up their pieces of paper and filed out of the Buddha Hall.

'Remember the answer is in the paper!' Sensei Yamada called after his departing students.

Jack, however, remained behind. He waited until everyone had gone, then approached his sensei.

'You appear troubled, Jack-kun. What's on your mind?' asked Sensei Yamada, arranging his butterfly and crane models on the altar at the foot of the shrine's great Buddha statue.

Jack summoned up the courage to speak about his personal fears. 'I've been told that a Christian priest has been killed by *daimyo* Kamakura. Is this true?'

Sensei Yamada nodded sadly. 'I've heard this news too. It's an unfortunate case.'

'So the *daimyo does* intend to kill all Christians in Japan?' exclaimed Jack, alarmed to hear that the rumours were right.

'Who told you that?' said Sensei Yamada, raising his eyebrows in surprise. 'As I understand, the death was not religiously motivated. The priest bribed a court official and so was punished for his crime. Granted, such a thing has never happened before and *daimyo* Kamakura does seem to be taking a hard line with foreigners, but this doesn't automatically mean all Christians are under threat.'

'But I'd heard that the *daimyo* was going to expel all foreigners by force,' Jack insisted. 'And that would include me!'

'You needn't worry,' replied Sensei Yamada, smiling warmly at Jack. 'If Masamoto-sama thought you were in danger, he would make moves to ensure your safety.'

Jack realized that Sensei Yamada was right and his idea of escaping to Nagasaki on his own had been idiotic, as well as completely unnecessary with Masamoto as his protector. But he was also aware of the strict hierarchy of Japanese rule. Kamakura, as the *daimyo* of Edo, was an influential man, and Jack wondered whether Masamoto wielded enough power to guard him from the higher authority of a lord.

'But isn't a *daimyo* more powerful than a samurai?' he asked. 'Can Masamoto-sama really protect me from him?'

'We're talking about Masamoto-sama here. Possibly the greatest swordsman to have lived,' said Sensei Yamada, chuckling at the idea. 'Besides, even if *daimyo* Kamakura was contemplating such a foolish notion, he would have little support for such ideas. Foreigners are needed in Japan since they bring in good trade.'

Sensei Yamada got up and walked Jack to the Buddha Hall's entrance. From the top of the stone steps, he pointed across the rooftops to Nijo Castle.

'As you're well aware, the ruling lord here in Kyoto is *daimyo* Takatomi. But *daimyo* Takatomi is not just responsible for this province. He governs Japan as one of the appointed regents and he's popular among the samurai lords. He likes Christians and foreigners. In fact, he likes them so much, I've heard that he's converting to Christianity himself. So he wouldn't allow anything like that to happen here.'

Sensei Yamada smiled and placed a reassuring hand on Jack's shoulder.

'Jack, you are perfectly safe.'

INTRUDER

Following Sensei Yamada's reassurance that his fears were unfounded, Jack would have been in good spirits that evening had Yamato not reminded him of Sensei Kyuzo's punishment. So, while everyone folded cranes and sought a solution to Sensei Yamada's *koan*, Jack was hard at work polishing block after block of the *Butokuden*'s training area.

The wooden floor seemed as vast as an ocean to Jack as he rocked back and forth with the polishing oil, his shadow ebbing and flowing like a tiny wave across its surface.

'Put your back into it!' snarled Sensei Kyuzo, who was eating his dinner in the ceremonial alcove of the large hall.

The tantalizing aroma of grilled mackerel wafted past and Jack's stomach rumbled with hunger.

'I'll return in the morning,' the sensei suddenly announced, having finished his meal, 'and I expect the *Butokuden* to be gleaming. Or else you will miss breakfast too.'

'*Hai*, Sensei,' Jack mumbled, bowing his head all the way to the floor.

However much he despised this samurai, he had to show the appropriate respect.

When Sensei Kyuzo had left, Jack resumed his punishment. He had no intention of being here in the morning and intended to work until his fingers were raw and his knees felt like granite, if need be.

Despite the injustice of the punishment, Jack found solace in the chore. He was reminded of all the times he'd had to holystone the decks of the *Alexandria*. Though it had meant toiling under the blistering heat of a Pacific sun with the rest of the crew, the task had been necessary work to maintain the ship, not a punishment. Scouring the decks became a time of songs and merry tales, when friendships were made and worries forgotten.

He was reminded of Ginsel, his shark-toothed friend, who now lay dead at the bottom of the ocean. He missed their camaraderie. In fact, he missed all the crew, even the Bosun, who had kept the men in check with the threat of the cat-o'-nine-tails!

But most of all, he missed his father. His murder had left a gaping hole in Jack's life. His father had been the one he'd always turned to, the one who had guided and protected him, the one who had believed in him.

Jack wiped an unexpected tear from his eye and turned back to the task in hand.

The moon had nearly completed its arc across the heavens by the time Jack had polished every block of the wooden floor. The inky black sky was showing the first signs of dawn on the horizon as he emerged from the *Butokuden*, exhausted and light-headed with hunger.

At least breakfast would soon be served, thought Jack. Not that he was particularly looking forward to it. Miso soup, cold fish and rice were hard to stomach early in the morning. How he longed for a normal English breakfast of crusty buttered bread, fried eggs and ham.

Out of the corner of his eye, he caught sight of a movement on the opposite side of the courtyard. At first he thought his eyes were deceiving him, for who else would be up at this time?

He looked harder.

A shadow flitted along the edge of the Hall of Lions.

Whoever it was, they didn't want to be seen. Dressed all in black, the figure kept close to the wall and barely made a sound as it crept towards the entrance of the Hall of Lions, where the students slept.

Jack's senses went on alert. The intruder looked like a ninja.

Retreating behind the *Butokuden*'s doorway, Jack watched the ninja's progress.

So Dragon Eye had finally returned.

'*Another time,* gaijin*! The* rutter *is not forgotten.*' The ninja's words resounded in Jack's head. He cursed himself for not having spoken with Emi yet to arrange going back to Nijo Castle to hide the logbook. But Jack had foolishly begun to think that Yamato had been right and that Dragon Eye had died from his wounds, for there had been no sight or sound of his sworn enemy for months.

But it appeared that Dragon Eye *wasn't* dead.

Akiko had suggested that the ninja, as an assassin for hire, had simply been employed by someone else on another mission. Clearly that assignment was over and he'd returned to finish his original job.

The figure in black reached the doorway and, as it turned to enter the *Shishi-no-ma*, the moonlight caught the intruder's face.

Jack drew back in surprise. It was a fleeting glimpse, but he could have sworn it was Akiko.

15

SENSEI KANO

Jack sprinted across the courtyard.

Reaching the doorway, he slid back the *shoji* and peered in. All of the lamps had burnt out so it was hard to see anything, but the corridor seemed empty.

He silently made his way down the girls' corridor towards Akiko's room. When he got there, he found that her door was slightly ajar. He peeked in through the gap.

Akiko was fast asleep under the covers of her *futon* – and looked like she had been there for some time.

Seeing her asleep, Jack became aware of just how exhausted he was. Suffering from hunger and lack of sleep, could he have imagined the intruder?

He decided he would speak with Akiko in the morning, but now the pull of his own bed was too much to resist and he stumbled back to his room. Collapsing on to his *futon*, Jack's mind whirled. He stared at his Daruma Doll, willing himself to sleep, and after a while he felt his eyelids grow heavy.

He could have sworn he'd closed his eyes for only a moment before Yamato was at his door, the bright morning sunshine flooding his room.

'Come on, Jack!' said Yamato, rousing him out of bed. 'You've missed breakfast and Sensei Kano's said we're to meet at the *Butokuden* right now. We've got our first lesson in the Art of the *Bō*.'

Leaving the bustle of Kyoto city behind, the students crossed the wide wooden bridge that spanned the Kamogawa River and headed north-east in the direction of Mount Hiei. Despite being the tail end of summer, the weather was warm and dry, the sky cloudless, and in the sharp light of morning the burnt-out temples, that could be seen scattered over the mountain's forested slopes, glinted like broken teeth.

The enormous bulk of Sensei Kano, a mountain in himself, strode out in front, his great white *bō* staff striking the ground with each step. Like sheep following their shepherd, his students trailed behind in two regimented rows, their pace dictated by the rhythmic *thunk-thunk* of the sensei's staff.

As instructed, the class had gathered outside the *Butokuden* to await their new teacher. Jack and the others had been watching the early morning workers digging the foundations for the new Hall of the Hawk when Sensei Kano appeared. He acknowledged his students with a brief bow before instructing them to collect a wooden *bō* staff from a pile stacked against the weapons wall inside the *Butokuden*. They had then left the school at a brisk march.

Their teacher hadn't spoken a word since.

By the time they reached the foot of the mountain, the

morning sun had risen high in the sky. The forced march, combined with the dust of the road, soon left the students hot and thirsty, so the cool shade of the cedar trees was a welcome relief when they entered the forest and began their ascent of Mount Hiei.

As they weaved their way up its slope, the students spread out a little and Jack finally spotted an opportunity to speak with Akiko.

'So where do you think Sensei Kano's taking us?' he asked nonchalantly.

'Enryakuji, I presume.'

'Why there? Didn't you tell me a samurai general destroyed it?'

'Yes, General Nobunaga.'

'So what's there left to see?' asked Jack.

'Nothing. Apart from the remains of several hundred deserted temples. Enryakuji has been a tomb for over forty years.'

'It seems a rather odd place to take us to train.' Jack drew closer, checking no one was listening before he whispered, 'By the way, what were you doing last night?'

Akiko momentarily faltered at the question. Then, keeping her gaze fixed on the path, replied, 'I was folding cranes.'

'No, I mean just before dawn,' pressed Jack. 'I'm sure I saw you outside the *Shishi-no-ma*. You were dressed all in black like a ninja!'

Akiko's face was an odd mixture of disbelief and alarm.

'You must be mistaken, Jack. I was asleep. Like everyone else.'

'Well, I saw *someone* – and I swear it looked like you. But when I got inside, there was no one around.'

'Are you sure you didn't imagine it?' She studied his face with concern. 'You look dead on your feet. Did you get any sleep last night?'

Jack shook his head wearily and was about to question her further, when the students behind caught them up.

Out of the corner of his eye, Jack continued to study Akiko, but her face gave nothing away. Perhaps he *had* been mistaken. Akiko had no reason to lie to him. But if it wasn't Akiko, then who else could it have been?

THUNK!

Jack's thoughts were interrupted by the final beat of Sensei Kano's *bō* staff upon the ground. The students all came to an abrupt halt.

'We cross here,' announced Sensei Kano. His voice was deep and booming, as if a temple gong had been rung inside his chest.

The students gathered round. Jack edged his way forward with Yamato and Akiko by his side. In front of them was a ravine splitting the forest in two, with a fast-flowing river far below. Shimmering in the watery mist, the remains of a footbridge jutted out over the abyss.

'Where shall we cross, Sensei?' asked Yamato.

'Is there not a bridge?' enquired Sensei Kano.

'*Hai* Sensei,' Yamato replied, bemused at the question, 'but it's been destroyed.'

Sensei Kano raised his eyes to heaven, as if listening to some distant sound, then said, 'What about the log?'

A little way down from the bridge, spanning the gorge,

was a small felled cedar tree, its branches pruned, the trunk stripped bare of its bark.

'But, Sensei,' objected Yamato, a tremor in his voice, 'the log is barely wide enough for one foot . . . it's covered in moss . . . and it's wet . . . someone could easily slip and fall.'

'Nonsense. You'll all cross here. Indeed you, Yamato-kun, will go first. You are Masamoto's son, aren't you?'

Yamato's mouth fell open, his face going a touch pale. '*Hai*, Sensei,' he replied weakly.

'Good, then lead the way!'

The sensei gave Yamato an encouraging prod with his staff and Yamato shuffled to the edge of the ravine. He stopped at its lip.

'Why haven't you crossed yet?' asked Sensei Kano.

'S-s-sorry . . . Sensei,' stammered Yamato, 'I . . . can't do it.'

Jack knew his friend was scared of heights. He had discovered Yamato's phobia when they had climbed the Sound of Feathers waterfall at the culmination of the *Taryu-Jiai* contest. The same vertigo was defeating him again.

'Nonsense. If it's the height that scaring you, simply don't look,' instructed Sensei Kano.

'What? Close my eyes!' exclaimed Yamato, backing away from the chasm.

'Yes. Become blind to your fear.'

Everyone stared at the sensei, aghast. The thought of crossing the log was unnerving enough, but to cross it with one's eyes closed. That was sheer lunacy!

'It's perfectly safe. I'll even go first,' said Sensei Kano, slipping off his sandals and threading them on his staff. 'It would be helpful, though, if someone could show me where the log is.'

The students exchanged bewildered looks. The log was in plain sight. After a brief pause, several of the students pointed to the makeshift crossing.

'No use pointing,' said Sensei Kano. 'I'm blind.'

Jack, along with the rest of the class, was stunned. Sensei Kano had led them all the way to the gorge without a guide or even a single request for directions. How could he be blind?

Jack studied his new sensei properly for the first time. Sensei Kano's sheer size dominated his appearance, being a head taller than most Japanese. Upon closer inspection, though, Jack realized that Sensei Kano's eyes were not grey by nature, but clouded as if a sea mist had seeped into them.

'Excuse me, Sensei,' said Akiko, recovering first. 'The log's almost in front of you, no more than eight *shaku* ahead and twelve *shaku* to your left.'

'Thank you,' replied Sensei Kano, striding confidently up to the lip of the ravine.

His *bō* found the edge and he followed it to his left until it struck the fallen tree. Without a moment's hesitation, he stepped on to the narrow log. Holding his staff out in front of him for balance, he crossed in several easy strides.

'You have just witnessed your first lesson,' announced Sensei Kano from the opposite side. 'If one sees with the eyes of the heart, rather than the eyes of the head, there is nothing to fear.'

As if in response to his words of wisdom, a shaft of sunlight broke through the forest canopy, suspending a tiny rainbow within the veil of mist that swirled above the void.

'Now it's your turn.'

16

MUGAN RYŪ

The roar of the river filled Jack's ears as he stepped out over the abyss and a sliver of fear took hold.

He couldn't see the gorge he knew gaped beneath him like the open mouth of a shark. Yet with each step into the unknown, his confidence grew. Having been a rigging monkey on-board the *Alexandria*, the soles of his feet gripped the slippery surface of the log as if he were back upon the yardarm.

He was also aware that without his sight he would have to rely upon his other senses, and tried to judge his progress across the log by the changing echoes of the river below.

Eventually, his feet found the grassy bank on the opposite side and he opened his eyes, amazed he had crossed without looking once.

Akiko now approached the log. She closed her eyes and nimbly negotiated the gorge in several quick steps, her balance as perfect as a dancer's, making everyone else's attempts so far appear awkward and ungainly.

They waited for Yamato. But he put off his crossing by

politely inviting Emi to go first. She was across in no time, so he stepped aside for others in the class. Saburo shuffled along in fits and bursts, then Yori scampered over, followed by Kiku. Nobu ended up groping his way along astride the trunk, while Kazuki strolled across not even bothering to close his eyes.

Eventually there were no more left for Yamato to invite.

'Don't worry,' called Jack. 'Just keep your eyes closed, walk straight and you'll be fine.'

'I know!' said Yamato irritably, but he remained at the end of the log all the same, his staff trembling in his hands.

'Use the eyes of your heart and believe in yourself, then you have nothing to fear,' advised Sensei Kano, who waited for him at the opposite end.

Yamato screwed his eyes tight shut, took a deep breath and stepped out on to the log. In painstakingly tiny steps, he edged himself along. Halfway across, he wobbled wildly. The class drew in breath expecting him to fall. But Yamato regained his balance and resumed his snail-like progress.

'You're nearly there,' encouraged Saburo when Yamato was little more than four steps from the end.

Unfortunately that was the wrong thing to say. Yamato opened his eyes, looked down and saw the dizzying drop beneath him. Panic seized his senses. Rushing the last few steps, his feet slipped from under him.

Yamato screamed and plunged head first into the chasm.

But, just as Yamato lost his footing, Sensei Kano shot out his *bō* staff, catching him across the chest and flinging him up and over to safety. Yamato landed in a quivering heap upon the grass.

'You opened your eyes and let fear in, didn't you?' said Sensei Kano. 'You'll learn soon enough not to be so swayed by what you see.'

Without waiting for a response, the sensei turned and led the students deeper into the forest.

Jack, Akiko and Saburo ran to help Yamato back to his feet, but he shrugged them off moodily, furious with himself for having lost face in front of the class.

'How on earth did Sensei Kano do that?' exclaimed Jack to the others, astounded at the *bō* master's lightning reactions. 'He's blind!'

'All will become clear when we reach the monastery, Jack-kun,' shouted Sensei Kano from afar.

They stared at one another in amazement. Sensei Kano was already out of sight, yet he had still heard them.

'This temple is where Sensei Sorimachi, the founder of the *Mugan Ryū*, the School of No Eyes, began his training,' explained Sensei Kano. 'The school is based upon the insight that "To see with eyes alone is not to see at all".'

The class listened obediently, standing in two rows, their staffs held tightly by their sides. Sensei Kano had brought them to a large open courtyard that faced the ruined remains of the Kompon Chu-do, the largest temple of the once great and powerful Enryakuji monastery.

The temple's long curved roof had collapsed in several places, and red and green tiles lay scattered on the floor like discarded dragon scales. The broken bones of wooden pillars rested at odd angles and battered gap-toothed walls revealed ransacked shrines and cracked stone idols. To all intents and purposes, the monastery was dead.

Yet deep inside, a single light glimmered. This, Sensei Kano explained, was the 'Eternal Light'. A lantern lit by the temple's founding priest, Saicho, over eight hundred years ago, it was still burning, tended by a solitary monk. 'Belief never burns out,' observed Sensei Kano before starting the lesson.

'As a samurai warrior, you must not become blinded by what you see. You must use all your senses to conquer your enemy – sight, hearing, touch, taste and smell. You must be at one with your body at all times, maintaining perfect balance and complete awareness of where each limb is in relation to the others.'

The sensei turned to face Jack, his misty grey eyes staring directly at him. The effect was unsettling, as if the sensei was somehow looking into Jack's very soul.

'You asked me, Jack-kun, how I managed to save your friend without being able to see. Simple. I sensed his panic. My staff was moving before he fell. I heard his foot slip on the log and then his scream, so I knew exactly where he was. The hard part was ensuring he didn't land on any of you!'

A ripple of laughter spread among the students.

'But how can such skills be used to fight an enemy you can't see?' asked Kazuki with scepticism.

'I will demonstrate,' replied Sensei Kano, turning his clouded gaze towards Kazuki. 'Your name?'

'Oda Kazuki, Sensei.'

'Well, Kazuki-kun, try to steal my *inro* without me knowing and it's yours to keep.'

Kazuki grinned at the challenge. The little carrying box hung freely from the *obi* of the sensei's kimono, easy pickings for even the most inept thief.

Kazuki crept out of line and advanced silently towards the sensei. As he passed Nobu, he indicated to him and another lad, a thin, wiry stick insect of a boy called Hiroto, to follow him. Kazuki then resumed his approach, with Nobu moving off to his right and Hiroto to the left. Each converged on Sensei Kano from a different direction.

They were four paces away when Sensei Kano whipped his *bō* staff round, catching Hiroto by the ankle and sweeping him off his feet. Spinning round, the sensei thrust his staff in between Nobu's legs, knocking them apart. A single jab to the stomach sent the startled Nobu toppling to the floor. Finally, without pausing, he attacked Kazuki, driving his *bō* directly at the boy's throat.

Kazuki froze, an audible swallow of panic coming from him as the end of the staff stopped a hair's breadth from his Adam's apple.

'Very clever, Kazuki-kun, employing decoys, but your friend over there smells of three-day-old sushi,' he explained, nodding towards the fallen figure of Hiroto. 'You breathe as loud as a baby dragon, and that boy treads like an elephant!' he said, indicating Nobu, who lay on the floor rubbing his bruised belly.

The class broke into uncontrollable sniggering.

'Enough!' interrupted Sensei Kano, bringing an abrupt end to the laughter. 'It's time to start your training or you'll never learn how to fight blind. Space yourselves out so that you have enough room to swing your *bō*.'

The class obediently spread out across the stone court-yard.

'First you need be at one with the weight and feel of the *bō*. I want you all to spin your staffs as I do.'

Sensei Kano held out his staff in his right hand, gripping it halfway along the shaft. He began to spin the *bō*, swapping hands in the process. He started slowly, then built up speed until the staff was a blur either side of his body.

'Once you're confident enough spinning the *bō* between your hands, close your eyes. Learn to sense its movement, rather than relying on your sight to follow it.'

The class began to twirl their staffs. Several students immediately fumbled their weapons and dropped them.

'Start off slowly. Get the hand movements right first,' advised Sensei Kano.

To begin with, Jack found it difficult to swap the staff over. Shattered from lack of sleep, his reactions were sluggish and his movements clumsy.

Yamato, on the other hand, took to the weapon like he had been born with it in his hands. His friend already had his eyes closed.

'Good work, Yamato-kun,' Sensei Kano commended as he listened to Yamato's *bō* whistle through the air. Yamato smiled, his loss of face at crossing the gorge regained as he became the first student to master the technique.

Yet it was not long before Jack had his own staff spinning, albeit at a more sedate pace. With continued practice, his confidence grew until he braved closing his eyes. He tried to feel the weapon, hear it, sense it, rather than having to see it.

He increased his speed.

The *bō* was flying, each spin sending a blast of air past his ears.

He had mastered it!

'Owwww!' Jack cried out as pain leapt up his leg.

The *bō* had struck his shin and shot out of his hands, clattering across the stone courtyard. Jack hobbled after the fallen weapon.

The *bō* rolled to a stop . . . at Kazuki's feet.

Jack stooped to retrieve it, but before he could get to it, he was struck across the back of the head. Jack glared up at Kazuki.

'Careful, *gaijin*,' said Kazuki, giving him a look of mock innocence.

The hatred between them flared and Jack tensed himself in readiness for a fight.

'Don't even think about it,' whispered Kazuki, checking to see Sensei Kano was nowhere nearby. 'You wouldn't even get close.'

Kazuki stopped his *bō* directly in line with Jack's nose, forcing Jack's head back. Jack stepped away, then feigned to his left before ducking and snatching up his staff with the other hand. But Kazuki was ready for it and brought the tip of his own staff down on to Jack's fingers, knocking the *bō* back to the floor with a clatter.

'The student who keeps dropping their *bō* would be best advised to keep their eyes open until they're more competent,' said Sensei Kano from the other side of the courtyard.

Jack and Kazuki silently opposed one another, each waiting for the other to make the next move.

'Eyes open or closed, you're a worthless excuse for a samurai,' goaded Kazuki under his breath. 'Even you must realize that no one at the school likes you. Your so-called friends are only *polite* to you, because Masamoto-sama commands it.'

Jack was riled by the accusation and fought to control his anger.

'And the student who keeps talking would be advised to channel his energies into more positive practice,' added Sensei Kano pointedly.

But the damage had been done. Kazuki had hit a raw nerve. Jack couldn't deny that there was a grain of truth in his taunt. When he had first arrived in Japan, Yamato had only tolerated his presence due to a direct order from his father. It had taken their victory in the *Taryu-Jiai* to bring them together as friends. Then there was Akiko. Despite being his closest friend, she hid her feelings so well that Jack wouldn't be able to tell if she was faking their friendship or not.

Maybe Kazuki was right.

Despite her denial of last night's mysterious appearance, Jack had the feeling she was hiding something from him.

Seeing the internal battle played out on Jack's face, Kazuki grinned.

'Go home, *gaijin*,' he mouthed silently.

17

PLANTING SEEDS

'Go home, gaijin! Go home, gaijin! Go home, gaijin!'

Jack sat immobilized by fear in his father's high-backed arm-chair as he watched Dragon Eye slash with his sword, scoring the phrase over and over again on to every wall of his parents' cottage. Like open wounds, the red letters seeped in crimson streaks, and Jack realized Dragon Eye was using his father's blood as ink.

Hearing a scuttling sound approach, Jack clasped the rutter closer to his chest. Glancing down, he was confronted by four black scorpions, each the size of a fist, crawling their way over the floorboards and up his bare legs, their poisoned barbs crack-ling in the darkness . . .

'Are you coming?'

Jack was jolted awake by Akiko's voice.

He sat up and rubbed his eyes against the bright morn-ing light that poured in through the tiny window of his room.

'I'm not . . . quite ready . . . you go ahead,' replied Jack, his voice shaky as he pulled back the covers of his *futon*.

'Are you all right?' she asked from the other side of his *shoji* door.

'I'm fine . . . just sleepy.'

But Jack was far from fine. Akiko had woken him from another nightmare.

'I'll meet you in the *Chō-no-ma* for breakfast,' he added hurriedly.

'Try not to be late this time,' Akiko cautioned, and Jack heard her soft footsteps pad along the passageway.

He got up, groggy from his dream of Dragon Eye and the four scorpions. He wondered whether it could be a premonition like the butterfly and demon vision. But that vision had been induced by meditation. This was a nightmare, something darker, more primitive. If it happened again, he promised himself he would consult Sensei Yamada.

Jack packed away his *futon*, tucking the *rutter* carefully inside the folds of the mattress. It was too obvious a hiding place. He urgently needed to speak with Emi to arrange a return visit to the castle. The problem was that he could never get her alone. Her two friends, Cho and Kai, followed her around like handmaidens. Besides, Jack hadn't yet thought of how to broach the subject with her without revealing his true purpose.

Hurriedly he put on his training *gi*, wrapping the upper section round his body, ensuring the lapel went left over right. He didn't want to dress like a corpse by having them the other way. He then tied the jacket off with a white *obi* round his waist.

Before leaving for breakfast and his first lesson of the day, Jack tended to his *bonsai* perched on the narrow window sill. He treasured the tiny cherry-blossom tree, a parting gift from Uekiya, the gardener in Toba. It was a constant reminder of the kindness the old man had shown him that first summer. He watered it religiously, pruned its branches and removed any dead leaves. The ritual always calmed him, and soon the cruel taunts of his nightmare faded until they were little more than a whisper in his head.

That morning, several of the *bonsai*'s miniature green leaves showed tints of golden brown and fiery red, announcing the arrival of autumn. With only a season left to go before snow heralded the selection trials for the Circle of Three, the sensei had intensified their training, increasing the complexity of the techniques and pushing the students to their limits. Jack was really starting to struggle with the regime.

Securing his *bokken* in his *obi*, he summoned up the energy he would need to get through the day.

'Again, *kata* four!' ordered Sensei Hosokawa.

The students sliced the air with their *bokken*, repeating the prescribed series of moves. They had performed hundreds of cuts already that morning, but Sensei Hosokawa's lesson was relentless.

Jack's arms were burning with the exertion, sweat poured down him and his *bokken* felt as heavy as lead.

'No, Jack-kun!' corrected Sensei Hosokawa. 'The *kissaki* stops at *chudan*. You are slicing through the belly of your enemy – not trying to chop off their feet.'

Jack, who usually excelled during the sword class, was having great difficulty keeping up. His aching limbs just wouldn't respond and the *bokken* kept dropping way past its target.

'Concentrate!' commanded Sensei Hosokawa, rounding on Jack. 'Don't make me remind you again.'

He grabbed Jack's sword arm, sternly lifting the *bokken* to the appropriate height. Jack's arms trembled with the effort.

'These *kata* are the basics of *kenjutsu*,' reinforced Sensei Hosokawa, addressing the entire class now. 'You cannot run before you've learnt to walk. It is imperative you assimilate these moves so that they become instinctive, so that the *bokken* becomes part of you. When the sword becomes "no sword" in your hands, then you are ready. Only then will you truly comprehend the Way of the Sword!'

'*HAI*, SENSEI!' yelled the class.

Sensei Hosokawa fixed Jack with a stern gaze, 'Don't forget your training, Jack-kun. You should have mastered the basics by now.'

The arrow soared clear of the target, disappearing among the branches of the ancient pine tree. A pair of doves, nestling in the foliage, cooed indignantly and fluttered off towards the safety of the *Butsuden*'s temple roof.

'This is impossible!' complained Jack, his frustration getting the better of him.

Unlike Akiko, who struck the furthest target with apparent ease, archery didn't come so naturally to Jack. And now that Sensei Yosa had doubled the length of the range, setting the targets at the far end of the *Nanzen-niwa*, not one of Jack's shots had even come close. If he couldn't hit a target at this distance, how on earth was he supposed to snuff out a candle?

To make matters worse, Kazuki and his friends had been trying to put him off, commenting loudly on each of his failed attempts.

Noticing that Jack was struggling, his *kyujutsu* teacher approached, her hawk-like eyes studying his form and noting his problem.

'Relax, Jack-kun,' Sensei Yosa instructed as Jack returned his bow to the rack and knelt back into line. 'Hitting the target is unimportant.'

'But it is to me,' Jack insisted. 'I want to be able to pass your trial.'

'You misunderstand,' said Sensei Yosa, smiling warmly at his keenness. 'You must abandon the idea of *having* to hit the target. When the archer does not think about the target, then they may unfold the Way of the Bow.'

Jack's brow creased in confusion. 'But won't I be more likely to miss if I don't think about it?' he asked.

'There are no mysteries in *kyujutsu*, Jack-kun,' continued Sensei Yosa, shaking her head in response. 'Like any art, the secret is revealed through dedication, hard work and constant practice.'

But I am practising hard, Jack wanted to say, *and I don't seem to be getting any better.*

Later that day, Jack's fifth attempt at *origami* lay in a crumpled heap on the floor.

The rest of the students were deep in studied concentration, cross-legged on their *zabuton* cushions within the

Buddha Hall. Today their meditation model was a frog, and all that could be heard was the delicate crimping of countless pieces of paper.

Sensei Yamada had once again set his class a *zazen* mediation on *origami*, repeating the *koan*, 'What does *origami* teach us?' No one as yet had provided him with a satisfactory answer.

'Watch how I do it, Jack,' Yori offered, turning so that Jack could see his moves.

Jack tried again, but only succeeded in tearing a hole in the fragile paper. He cursed out loud in English and Yori gave him a puzzled look. Jack smiled apologetically.

'How am I going to be able to answer Sensei Yamada's *Koan* trial if I can't even fold a paper frog?' said Jack, taking another sheet from the pile.

'I don't think it matters if you can or can't,' replied Yori kindly. 'The frog is not the focus. Remember what Sensei Yamada said? The answer is in the paper.'

Yori admired his own perfect frog before setting it on the floor next to the perfect *origami* crane, butterfly and goldfish he had already made.

'But surely the process must help,' maintained Jack, waving his flat square of paper despondently in the air. 'Otherwise why would he be getting us all to do *origami*? I seem to be making such slow progress.'

Jack was now very concerned about his chances in the forthcoming trials. There were only five places and if he didn't pass any of the trials, he wouldn't earn his place in the Circle of Three, let alone be taught the Two Heavens technique.

'Don't judge each day by the harvest you reap,' said a calm voice in his ear.

Sensei Yamada had appeared at Jack's shoulder and leant over to take the paper from his hands. He scored, folded and bent the sheet in front of Jack's eyes, transforming it into a beautiful flowering rose.

'Judge it by the seeds you plant.'

'You're having a bad week, that's all,' said Akiko, trying to console Jack during dinner that evening.

'But I haven't hit the archery targets for nearly a month now,' Jack replied, half-heartedly spearing a piece of *sushi* with his *hashi* before reminding himself that it was bad etiquette.

'It's just a matter of getting used to the distance,' encouraged Yamato. 'Don't you remember how you scored in *kyujutsu* during the *Taryu-Jiai*? It's not as if you can't do it.'

'I suppose you're right,' conceded Jack, putting down his *hashi*. 'But it feels like I've hit a brick wall with my training. Even in *kenjutsu* Sensei Hosokawa's constantly on my back, correcting every little mistake. However hard I try, I don't seem to be getting any better.'

'But you heard what Sensei Yamada said,' reminded Yori. '*Don't judge each day by the harvest you reap . . .*'

'Yes, but what seeds am I actually planting?' sighed Jack, burying his head in his hands. 'Perhaps Kazuki's right. I'm not meant to be samurai.'

'You're not listening to Kazuki again, are you?' exclaimed Akiko in exasperation. 'He's poisoning your mind! Of course you're worthy to be samurai. Masamoto-sama would not have adopted you, or invited you to his school if he thought you were anything less. Becoming a true samurai takes time.'

Jack gazed despondently out of the tiny window of his room in the *Shishi-no-ma*. The night sky was a blanket of stars. A waning moon shone its ghostly light and washed out all colour from the buildings of the *Niten Ichi Ryū*.

On the horizon, Jack could see storm clouds brewing. They were blotting out the stars one by one. The prayer flags at the entrance to the *Butsuden* started to flutter like a ship's sails as a chill wind cut through the open courtyard.

Jack began to imagine he was back on-board the *Alexandria* with his father, learning to navigate by the heavens. That was something he *was* good at. Being a pilot came naturally. He could name the stars and planets and use them to calculate the ship's position and course, even in rough seas.

He had been destined to be a ship's pilot by blood and birth. Not a samurai.

Suddenly Jack felt the pressure of life in Japan like a coiled spring in the pit of his stomach, getting wound tighter and tighter until he thought he was going to explode. The headache of speaking Japanese every day. The rigid etiquette of Japanese life as if he was walking on eggshells all the time. The painstaking progress he was making with his training. The constant threat of Dragon Eye and whether he would be ready to face him in time. The gaping absence of his parents. The thought of Jess alone, with the threat of a workhouse hanging over her . . .

Lost in his despair, Jack almost missed the movement of several shrouded figures crossing the school's courtyard. Hugging the shadows, they skirted under the lee of the *Butokuden* before disappearing inside.

Determined to discover who the intruders were this time, Jack grabbed his *katana* and sprinted out of the room.

18

IREZUMI

'Akiko? Are you there?' whispered Jack through the paper-thin door of her room.

There was no reply. He drew back the *shoji* and peeked inside. Akiko was nowhere to be seen. Her *futon* was untouched even though she should have been in bed by now.

Perhaps she had gone to the bathhouse, thought Jack, or else . . .

He shut the door and hurried on. A lantern was still burning within Yori's room.

'Yori?' he called.

The little boy slid open his *shoji*.

'Have you seen Akiko?'

'Not since supper,' replied Yori, shaking his head. 'Isn't she in her room?'

'No, I think she's . . .' Jack trailed off, distracted by the sight of countless paper cranes littering Yori's floor. 'What *are* you doing?'

'I'm folding cranes.'

'I can see that, but *origami* in bed! You take Sensei

Yamada's lessons far too seriously,' accused Jack. 'Listen, if you hear Akiko come back, can you let her know that I've gone over to the *Butokuden*.'

'The training hall? And you accuse me of studying too hard!' Yori glanced dubiously at Jack's *katana*. 'Isn't it rather late to be practising your sword *kata*?'

'I don't have time to explain. Just tell Akiko.'

Jack sped off, not bothering to wait for Yori's response.

As he reached the main door, he briefly considered alerting Yamato and Saburo, but they would be asleep and he had wasted too much time already. The intruders might have gone by the time they all reached the *Butokuden*.

Jack rushed across the courtyard. The storm was approaching fast and icy blasts of wind stabbed through his thin night kimono like a *tantō* blade. Pressing himself flat against the *Butokuden*'s wall, he edged towards its main entrance. Poking his head round the wooden door frame, he searched for the intruders.

In the gloom of the great hall, he could distinguish a number of hunched figures sitting in a tight circle within the ceremonial alcove. But from this distance, he was unable to make out their faces or hear what they were saying.

Jack hurried to the back of the *Butokuden*, where the slatted windows behind the dais were within easy reach. As quietly as he could, he eased open a wooden shutter. Peering through, he discovered he had a direct line of sight to the alcove.

Jack counted four intruders in total. They each wore a

heavy cowl so their faces remained cast in shadow. Pressing his ear close to the slatted opening, he listened.

'. . . the *daimyo* Kamakura Katsura is going to wage war against the Christians,' whispered a youthful yet commanding male voice in the darkness.

A husky female voice took over. 'The *gaijin* are a threat to our traditions and the orderly society of Japan.'

'But there are so few. How can they be a threat?' queried a third voice, high and thin like a bamboo flute.

'Their priests are spreading an evil belief, converting honourable Japanese *daimyo* and their samurai with their lies,' explained the male voice. 'They're trying to overthrow our society from within. They want to destroy our culture, control Japan and its people.'

'They *must* be stopped!' interjected the female voice.

'The *daimyo* is drawing loyal samurai to his cause in preparation for an all-out assault on every Christian,' explained the first voice. 'My father, Oda Satoshi, has joined his ranks and sworn allegiance to this righteous cause.'

'*Gaijin* are the germ of a great disaster and must be crushed,' hissed the female voice with venom.

'But what can *we* do about it?' asked the fourth shadow.

'We can prepare for war!' stated the male and female voice in unison.

Jack could hardly believe his ears. He had been right all along. Sensei Yamada was mistaken. The killing of the Christian priest was not an isolated case. It had been just the beginning. The *daimyo* Kamakura was intent on slaughtering every Christian in Japan.

Yet what chilled Jack's blood most was the fact that he

knew who the ringleader of this mysterious group was. He recognized his voice. It was Kazuki, following in his father's footsteps and calling for war.

Outside, the first drops of rain began to fall. The shower quickly became a torrent and within moments Jack was soaked to the skin and numb with cold. But he was determined to stay and learn all he could. Ignoring his discomfort, he strained to hear the ongoing conversation above the rain, which was now beating an insistent rhythm upon the *Butokuden*'s roof.

'. . . all Christians will be forced to leave on pain of death,' continued Kazuki. 'Some may try to hide, but it will be our duty to hunt them down.'

'What about Jack?' asked the thin reedy voice. 'Surely he's protected by Masamoto-sama.'

'The great Masamoto-sama's got more important things to worry about than some *gaijin*. I mean, have you seen Masamoto-sama at school recently? No. His duty is to *daimyo* Takatomi. He couldn't care less about Jack.'

'And without his samurai guardian around,' mocked the female voice, 'there'll be no rock the *gaijin* can crawl under where we won't find him!'

All of sudden, Jack felt very vulnerable. He'd been so busy with training for the trials, he hadn't noticed the continued absence of Masamoto. It only now occurred to him that his guardian's seat at the head table during dinner had been empty for almost a month. The last time Jack had seen Masamoto was when the samurai had overseen the start of the construction of the Hall of the Hawk. Where had he gone? If the situation suddenly turned serious, Jack had no one in authority at the school with a personal interest in protecting him.

'We must be ready for the call to arms from our *daimyo*,' continued Kazuki. 'That is the purpose of the *Sasori* Gang. We must now all swear our allegiance to this righteous cause.'

'I'll need some light for the initiation ritual,' demanded the husky female voice.

Jack heard the sound of a flint being struck and a couple of sparks flared in the gloom. A moment later, a small oil lamp burned like a solitary firefly in the cavernous hall.

Jack gasped in astonishment. The flickering flame illuminated a girl's bleached-white face. Her oval eyes were like coals in a fire and a pair of blood-red lips parted to reveal teeth painted black as tar. Jack instantly recognized her as Moriko, the female samurai who had competed against Akiko in the *Taryu-Jiai*. A cruel, vicious fighter, she trained at the rival *Yagyu* School in Kyoto. Jack couldn't believe *she* was inside the walls of the *Niten Ichi Ryū*.

'That's better,' she rasped, taking an inkpot and several bamboo needles from her *inro* and laying them beside the lamp. She then uncorked a small bottle of *saké* and poured a measure of the clear liquid into a cup. This was placed in the centre of the group. 'So who will be first for *irezumi*?'

'I will,' said Kazuki, opening his overcoat and kimono to expose his chest.

Moriko inspected one of the needles, turning it slowly over the flame. Satisfied, she then dipped its sharpened point into the pot of black ink. With her other hand, she held Kazuki's skin taut above his heart.

'This will hurt,' she said, puncturing Kazuki's skin with the tip and inserting a drop of ink beneath.

Kazuki grimaced, but made no sound. Moriko recharged her needle before piercing his chest again. She continued slowly and methodically, adding more dots of ink to the design.

Jack had seen such work performed before, on the sailors of the *Alexandria* when they had had their arms tattooed. To Jack it had always seemed like a great deal of pain for what amounted to a poor image of an anchor or the name of some sweetheart the sailor soon forgot once they docked at another port.

'Done,' said Moriko, a black slit of a smile spreading across her face.

'This is your mark,' announced Kazuki with pride, turning so that the others could see. 'The *sasori*!'

Jack was too stunned to breathe. Tattooed above Kazuki's heart was a small black scorpion – the creature of Jack's nightmares.

However hard his Christian beliefs tried to deny it, the coincidence of this tattoo and his dream was too great to ignore.

Kazuki raised the cup of *saké*.

'Once you have your *sasori* and have shared *saké* from this cup, you're forever a brother of the Scorpion Gang. Death to all *gaijin*!' toasted Kazuki, drinking from the cup.

'Death to all *gaijin*!' echoed the others, pledging their allegiance and eagerly opening up their kimonos for Moriko to begin the *irezumi*.

Outside the *Butokuden*, the storm thundered its approval.

Jack shook uncontrollably. He hugged himself for warmth, pressing his body against the wall in an attempt to shelter from the relentless downpour.

His mind, like the elements, was a whirlwind of confusion. What should he do? He'd heard all the testimony he needed. Japan was being turned against foreigners. If someone didn't stop Kamakura, Jack would become an outcast. The enemy. He needed to tell Masamoto, but how could his guardian protect him against such forces?

Crack!

A blast of wind caught the wooden shutter, slamming it against the window frame. Startled, Jack dropped his *katana* and it went clattering across the stone-clad courtyard, disappearing into the darkness.

'Someone's there!' cried Moriko from within.

Panic rose up in Jack's chest. He quickly searched for his weapon, but he could hear the Scorpion Gang fast approaching.

Leaving his *katana* behind, he ran for his life.

19

FIGHTING BLIND

Jack sprinted round the corner of the *Butokuden*, but he knew he wouldn't make it across the courtyard without being spotted by Kazuki and his Scorpion Gang.

Glancing around, the only cover within reach was the building works of the Hall of the Hawk. Jack ran and dived into a waterlogged hole in the newly dug foundations just as several figures burst out of the *Butokuden*.

Peering over the muddy lip, he watched as they hunted for him. The first two went round the far side of the training hall, while the other two headed in Jack's direction. Jack slipped further into the murky depths of the hole. As they drew closer, he could hear the squelch of their feet in the mud. They stopped at the edge of the flooded foundations.

'There's no way I'm going in there,' protested a voice.

'Go on!' ordered Kazuki. 'You need an excuse for a bath.'

Jack heard three more squelching footsteps and looked up. Above him towered the bulk of Nobu.

'I can't go any further. I'm sinking!' complained Nobu, oblivious to Jack's presence right at his feet.

'You're useless! Come back then.'

Turning round, Nobu slipped and wobbled on the edge. For a moment it looked like he might fall into the hole, but to Jack's relief the oaf regained his balance.

'Do you think it was one of the sensei?' asked Nobu as he slowly made his way back to Kazuki.

'No,' replied Kazuki. 'A sensei wouldn't run away! But whoever it was, we need to convince them to join the gang. Or else silence them. Come on. Let's go find the others.'

Jack, shivering with a combination of cold, fear and anger, waited until he was sure Kazuki and Nobu were gone, then crawled out of the hole. As much as he wanted to go back to his room, he first had to find his sword. Masamoto had instructed him that 'it must never fall into the hands of your enemy'. He couldn't risk Kazuki finding it.

Jack hurried to the back of the *Butokuden*, but in the darkness and downpour it was impossible to see anything. He scrabbled around on his hands and knees, praying his fingers would come across it.

Suddenly he was aware of footsteps running up behind him.

Loath to leave his sword, he realized he had no choice but to escape while he could.

Jack sensed the blow a fraction before he was caught hard across the gut. He reeled, gasping for breath. Struggling to keep his feet, he heard movement to his left and turned to face his enemy.

The problem was that Jack couldn't see. The darkness completely enveloped him. But he could hear Kazuki snorting with laughter in the background and the sound of shuffling feet. Apart from that, he had no other way of knowing where the next attack might come from.

Out of nowhere the *swoosh* of a weapon came rocketing towards his head. More by luck than skill, Jack lurched sideways and avoided the blow. In blind retaliation, he swung wildly at his assailant. Missing his target, he flailed through empty air.

Before Jack could follow through, he was struck across the shins. His legs went from under him and he fell to the ground face first. He tried to roll out of the fall, but was too disorientated. Jack grunted in pain as his shoulder ploughed into the stony earth.

'*Yame!*' boomed the voice of Sensei Kano, bringing the fight to a halt.

Jack pulled off his blindfold, squinting into the bright light of the midday sun. Kazuki was kneeling in line with the other students, delighting in Jack's defeat.

'Sorry, Jack,' apologized Yamato, taking off his own blindfold and offering his hand to help him up. 'I didn't mean to hit you so hard. It's just I couldn't see where you were . . .'

'Don't worry, I'm fine,' grimaced Jack, pulling himself to his feet.

'Good work, both of you,' commended Sensei Kano, who sat upon the worn steps of the Kompon Chu-do Temple.

Once again, Sensei Kano had led his students at dawn up Mount Hiei for their lesson in the Art of the *Bō*. He considered the long walk good conditioning for them and the mountain air beneficial to training.

'I heard three attacks avoided. And you, Yamato-kun, were highly aware of your surroundings. Two strikes on target are praiseworthy for a first attempt at blind *kumite*, but please control your strength next time. It sounds like Jack-kun took quite a tumble. Let's have the next two students.'

Relieved the free-fighting session was over, Jack handed over his blindfold to another student and knelt back in line between Yori and Akiko. He massaged his aching shoulder, groaning as his fingers found the bruise.

'Are you hurt badly?' asked Akiko, noting Jack's pained expression.

'No, I'm fine . . . but I'm still not sure why we're learning to fight blindfolded,' replied Jack under his breath, 'when all of us can see.'

'As I explained before, Jack-kun,' interrupted Sensei Kano, whose acute sense of hearing had picked up the comment from the opposite side of the courtyard, 'to see with eyes alone is not to see at all. In my lessons, you're learning *not* to rely upon your eyes to defend yourself. As soon as you open your eyes, you begin to make mistakes.'

'But wouldn't I make fewer mistakes if I could see what my enemy was doing?' asked Jack.

'No, young samurai. You must remember the eyes are the windows to your mind,' explained Sensei Kano. 'Come stand on this step before me and I will show what I mean.'

Sensei Kano beckoned him over. Jack got to his feet and joined him on the steps.

'Look at my feet,' instructed the sensei.

Jack studied his teacher's open-toed sandals and was instantly struck on top of the head by the sensei's *bō* staff.

'My apologies, I'm blind and sometimes clumsy,' said Sensei Kano. 'Please keep an eye on my staff for me.'

Jack followed the tip of the white staff, ensuring he was not caught out again.

Sensei Kano kicked him sharply in the shin.

'Oww!' Jack exclaimed, hobbling backwards.

The students all sniggered behind their hands.

'Lesson over,' stated Sensei Kano. 'Now do you understand?'

'Not really, Sensei . . .' said Jack, rubbing his sore shin.

'Think about it! If you look at an opponent's feet your attention will be directed to his feet, and if you look to his weapon your attention will be drawn to his weapon. So it follows, when you look to the left you forget the right, and when you look to the right you forget the left.'

Sensei Kano let the message sink in. He pointed to his own sightless eyes.

'Whatever is being contemplated within never fails to be revealed through the eyes. Your enemy will take advantage of this. In order to fight without giving yourself away, you must learn to fight without relying on your eyes.'

Jack put down his writing brush. After his humiliation in front of Sensei Kyuzo over not being able to write *kanji*, Akiko had offered to teach him the basics of calligraphy. Whenever they had free time before dinner, they would meet in her room and she would show him a new *kanji* character and the correct order of brushstrokes needed to form it.

Akiko looked up at Jack, wondering why he had

stopped halfway through her explanation of the character for 'temple'.

Jack took a breath. Since his discovery of the Scorpion Gang and losing his sword, this was the first opportunity he'd had to speak with Akiko alone and he was uncertain how to tackle the mystery of her absence the previous evening.

'Where were you last night?' Jack eventually asked. 'You weren't in your room.'

She blinked once, her mouth visibly tightening at Jack's inappropriate directness.

'I don't know what it's like in England, but that's not the sort of question you ask a lady in Japan,' she replied coolly and started to pack away her writing tools. 'Perhaps the question that should be asked is, where were *you*?'

'Me? I was at the *Butokuden* . . .'

'That will explain why I found this,' she snapped, sliding open the door of her wall closet and taking out Jack's *katana*.

Jack was completely thrown, both by Akiko's harshness and his sword's unexpected appearance.

The previous night when he'd heard footsteps approaching, he'd run back to the Hall of Lions empty-handed, afraid it was Kazuki and his gang. On returning to the training hall at first light, his sword was nowhere to be seen. He assumed Kazuki had taken it and had been worrying ever since, for to confront him about it would mean revealing he knew about the Scorpion Gang.

Miraculously, though, Akiko had it. He stared at her in curious amazement.

'Thank you, Akiko. I've been looking for it everywhere,' he eventually said, bowing to receive his sword.

'Jack, this sword is your soul,' she continued gravely, ignoring Jack's outstretched hands. 'It's unforgivable to lose such a possession. The shame is even greater considering this was a gift from Masamoto-sama and his first sword. Why didn't you tell anyone you'd lost it?'

'I only lost it last night. I was hoping I'd be able to find it. Akiko, *please* don't tell Masamoto-sama,' pleaded Jack, mortified at his mistake.

Akiko stared impassively at him and Jack couldn't tell whether she was disappointed or pitying him for his care-lessness. Then the hardness in her expression softened and she handed over the weapon. 'I won't. But what was it doing at the back of the *Butokuden*?'

This was not how Jack had envisaged the conversation going. He had wanted to find out where Akiko had been and whether she knew about Kazuki's plans. He hadn't expected to have to account for his own actions.

'I spotted intruders in the courtyard again. I thought they could be ninja breaking into the school,' confided Jack, hoping that if he was straight with her, she would be with him. 'But it wasn't.'

'Who was it?'

'It was Kazuki, Nobu, someone else and, you won't believe this, Moriko from the *Yagyu Ryū*.'

'Moriko? In our school?' she replied, alarmed at the idea. 'Have you told Masamoto-sama?'

'Not yet. He's still not returned, but we must tell him. Not just about Moriko, but about Kazuki's Scorpion Gang.'

Akiko listened intently while Jack described what he had overheard about *daimyo* Kamakura and the Scorpion Gang.

After some thought, Akiko replied, 'Jack, there are always rumours of war. Of *daimyo* threatening *daimyo*. We're in a time of peace now and there's no reason why this won't continue. You've met *daimyo* Kamakura. He's hot-headed and power hungry. Masamoto-sama often complains about how he's always stirring up trouble. But it never comes to anything. He never has the support.'

'That's what Sensei Yamada said. But what if he *is* getting the support?' insisted Jack. 'What if —?'

'Jack! There you are!'

Jack looked up as Yamato burst into the room with Saburo.

'You two look like you've been busy,' he said, picking up a piece of paper with one of Jack's attempts at *kanji*. 'It'll be dinner soon and we all need to get a bath. What's keeping you?'

'Jack saw Kazuki in the *Butokuden* last night,' explained Akiko in hushed tones, indicating for Saburo to close the *shoji* behind him. 'He and some others were getting a tattoo from that Moriko girl from the *Yagyu* School.'

'Moriko?' said Yamato, alarmed. 'What was she doing here?'

'Supposedly, Kazuki's formed an anti-*gaijin* gang.'

'But tattoos? They're the mark of a prisoner!' exclaimed Saburo.

'They used to be,' corrected Akiko. 'But now merchants, and even some samurai, are getting them as marks of bravery or declarations of love.'

Saburo laughed and gave Jack a reassuring grin. 'Jack, whatever it is you're worried about, you certainly don't need to be afraid of a gang of convicts and lovers.'

'It's no laughing matter, Saburo,' retorted Jack. 'Kazuki's serious. He has it in for me.'

Yamato nodded thoughtfully. 'It sounds like Kazuki thinks he's a warlord or something. I know what we should do – me and Saburo will become your official body-guards.'

'And we'll arrange to see Masamoto-sama as soon as he returns,' added Akiko.

'Anyway, Jack, you should be less concerned about Kazuki and more worried about how much you smell!' Yamato teased, throwing Jack a towel. 'Come on, let's get to the bathhouse before they serve dinner. I'm hungry.'

Sighing with bliss, Jack eased himself into the steaming hot water of the *ofuro*.

There had been a time when he would have run scared of a bath. In England, it was considered dangerous for your health, a surefire way to catch the flux. But his time in Japan had soon changed that opinion and now the *ofuro* was one of the highlights of his day.

Having first scrubbed and sluiced himself down in cold water, he then slipped into a large square wooden tub of hot water. Jack began to relax. Sensei Yamada and Akiko had both dismissed his fears about *daimyo* Kamakura. Perhaps the combination of the night and the raging storm had distorted his perception of the whole situation. Maybe Kazuki's war amounted to little more than a figment of his rival's imagination. Anyway, with Yamato and Saburo looking out for him, he should be safe.

Jack allowed the steaming water to loosen his muscles, easing the tension in his bruised shoulder. His worries began to disappear too, seeming to dissolve in the heat of the bath. After a while, he got out and towelled himself down before joining the others for dinner.

'How's your shoulder, Jack?' asked Yamato as they headed over to the *Chō-no-ma* with Saburo.

'It's much better thanks to the bath, but don't worry about it. I'll get you back in *kenjutsu* tomorrow!' promised Jack, punching Yamato on the arm.

Yamato gave an expression of mock pain and they all laughed.

'That's a devastating right hook,' commented a voice from behind. 'I'd better watch out.'

Their amusement ceased as Kazuki, flanked by Nobu and Hiroto, strode towards them.

Jack clenched his fists, preparing for a fight.

Perhaps the Scorpion Gang *was* more than just a game. Perhaps Kazuki *really* believed he was a warlord.

20

THE SCORPION GANG

'What do you want?' demanded Yamato, stepping between Jack and the approaching gang.

The two groups of boys confronted one another.

It was getting dark in the school courtyard, the only light coming from the entrance to the Hall of Butterflies. Other students passed by, oblivious to the impending conflict, and there were no sensei in sight to witness a fight.

The tension grew as Yamato waited for an answer, his eyes daring Kazuki to make a move.

'Dinner,' said Kazuki cheerfully in response, before walking on past with his friends, laughing.

For the next month, Yamato and Saburo stuck close by, but there appeared little need. Kazuki and his gang ignored Jack as if he no longer existed. Kazuki in particular seemed more intent on training for the Circle of Three selection. Jack had spotted him several times in the *Butokuden* receiving extra tuition from Sensei Kyuzo.

Although neither of his friends said anything, Jack sensed they were beginning to doubt his story.

Even though Masamoto had returned to the school, Jack hadn't managed to meet with him before he was called away on yet another assignment for *daimyo* Takatomi. But with the apparent threat coming to nothing, and Moriko not having been seen in the grounds since, there seemed little point in meeting with him anyway.

'I'm going for a walk,' said Jack, passing by Yamato's room on the way out of the Hall of Lions. 'I need some air before bed.'

'At this time of night?' observed Yamato, frowning. 'Do you need me to come with you?'

Despite the offer, Yamato looked far from willing. He had already settled down on his *futon*, it was cold outside and the *Shishi-no-ma* was warm.

'No, don't worry. I'll be fine.'

Besides, Jack needed time alone to think.

Stepping outside, he wandered round the courtyard before perching upon one of the beams that would eventually support the floor of the Hall of the Hawk.

The new building was rapidly taking shape. The foundations had been completed and the main wooden pillars were now in place. When finished, the hall, although half the size of the *Butokuden*, would nonetheless be an impressive addition to the school.

Like all the other students, Jack wondered what martial art he would learn within it. That was if he was still around.

Although his fears of an anti-*gaijin* campaign were supposedly unfounded, he couldn't help noticing that certain students seemed less friendly towards him. He had always been isolated by the fact that he was different. During his first year at the school, Akiko had been his only true ally, but after his victory at the *Taryu-Jiai* most of the students accepted him. Now, many had started to ignore him again, looking through him like glass.

Of course, he could be imagining it. He was struggling with his training and had lost confidence in making it into the top five in the forthcoming Circle of Three selection trials. It had been getting him down and this could be distorting his perception. But did he really have any hope of entering the Circle and going on to learn the Two Heavens?

Jack looked up at the night sky for an answer, but this time the familiar constellations his father had taught him offered cold comfort. The nights were drawing in and autumn would soon give way to winter, signalling the start of the trials.

'Eh, *gaijin!* Where are your bodyguards?' demanded a voice that made Jack's heart sink.

He turned to face Kazuki. This was the last thing he needed.

'Leave me alone, Kazuki,' replied Jack, slipping off the cross-beam and walking away.

But other students emerged from the darkness to surround him. Jack looked towards the *Shishi-no-ma* for help, but there was no one around. Akiko, Yamato and Saburo would be in bed, if not asleep, by now.

'Leave you alone?' ridiculed Kazuki. 'Why can't your kind leave *us* alone? I mean, what do you think you're doing in *our* land, pretending to be samurai? You should give up and go home.'

'Yeah, go home, *gaijin!*' echoed Nobu and Hiroto.

The circle of boys took up the chant.

'Go home, *gaijin*! Go home, *gaijin*! Go home, *gaijin*!'

Despite himself, Jack felt his face flush with humiliation at the taunts. He desperately *wanted* to go home, to be with his sister, Jess, but he was stranded in a foreign land that now didn't want him.

'Just leave . . . me . . . alone!'

Jack tried to escape the circle, but Nobu stepped forward and pushed him back. Jack collided with one of the other boys who shoved him the opposite way. He stumbled into the cross-beam and, as he fell to the ground, Jack caught hold of a boy's kimono, ripping it open.

'Now look what you've done!' exclaimed the boy, kicking Jack in the leg.

Jack was curled up with pain. Still he couldn't help staring at the boy's exposed chest.

'What? You want another?' asked the boy, drawing back his leg for another kick.

'Goro, I think he's admiring your tattoo,' said Hiroto in the same thin, reedy voice Jack now recognized as belonging to the fourth person at the *irezumi* ceremony.

'Look great, don't they? We've all got one, you know.' Hiroto pulled back his own kimono, revealing a small black scorpion. Then he gave Jack a cruel kick in the ribs.

He kicked him again for good measure and the Scorpion Gang laughed as each of the boys revealed their tattoos and lined up to kick Jack too.

'Leave him!' Kazuki ordered. 'A sensei's coming.'

The boys scattered.

As Jack lay there, shaking with a combination of pain,

rage and shame, he heard the familiar click of a walking stick upon the stone courtyard and Sensei Yamada shuffled up.

Leaning upon his bamboo stick, he looked down at Jack just as he had done almost a year previously when Kazuki had first threatened him.

'You shouldn't play on building sites. They can be dangerous.'

'Thanks for the warning, Sensei,' said Jack bitterly, trying to hide his humiliation.

'Someone giving you trouble again?'

Jack nodded and sat up, inspecting his bruised ribs. 'Some of my class want me to give up and go home. The thing is I just wish I *could* go home . . .'

'Anyone can give up, Jack-kun, it's the easiest thing in the world to do,' Sensei Yamada cautioned as he helped Jack back to his feet. 'But to keep it together when everyone else would expect you to fall apart, now that's true strength.'

Jack glanced uncertainly at his teacher, but met only a look of complete belief in him.

'I would ask you who it was,' continued Sensei Yamada, 'but it would be of little consequence. You must fight your own battles, if you're to stand on your own feet. And I know you can.'

Sensei Yamada accompanied Jack back to the *Shishi-no-ma*. Before departing for his own quarters, he offered Jack one final piece of counsel: 'Remember, there is no failure except in no longer trying.'

Once he had gone, Jack considered the sensei's advice.

Maybe the old monk was right. He had to keep trying. The alternative was giving up, but that would be exactly what Kazuki wanted him to do and he had no intention of letting his rival beat him like that.

Gazing at the cold crescent moon that hung low in the sky, Jack vowed to renew his training efforts. He would get up early in the morning and practise his sword work. He would also ask Akiko for help with his archery. He had to do whatever it took to be among the top five in the trials.

He had to learn the Two Heavens — if not to protect himself from Dragon Eye, then to defend himself from the Scorpion Gang.

As he turned to enter the Hall of Lions and go to bed, Jack spotted Akiko, dressed all in black, rounding the far corner of the *Butokuden*. She was hurrying towards the side gate of the school.

Stunned, Jack now *knew* he hadn't been mistaken about the identity of that first intruder. He *had* seen Akiko that night.

Jack ran across the courtyard in an effort to catch up with her, but she'd disappeared by the time he reached the gate.

Luckily, the streets were deserted at this time of night and, glancing left, he spotted a lone figure turn down an alleyway at the far end of the road. This had to be her, but where was she going and why the secrecy of night?

This time Jack wanted answers and hurried after her.

21

TEMPLE OF THE PEACEFUL DRAGON

The alleyway swung left, then right, and Jack emerged into a small courtyard. But Akiko was nowhere to be seen.

He heard footsteps receding down a passageway off to his right. He followed the sound until the passage opened out into a large tree-lined courtyard. Before him was a temple with an arched roof of compact green tiles overlapping like the scales of a snake. A set of stone steps led up to a pair of solid wooden doors.

Jack cautiously approached the entrance. Above the door was a wooden sign upon which the name of the temple had been carved.

龍安寺

He immediately recognized the last symbol as 'temple' and tried to remember the other *kanji* characters Akiko had taught him. He thought the first might be 'dragon', the second 'peace'.

The sign spelt *Ryōanji*.

The Temple of the Peaceful Dragon.

He tried the door, but it was locked.

Jack sat down on the steps to consider what to do next. It was then that he noticed a tiny gap in the outer wall of the temple, on one side of the doorway.

The wall was constructed of an alternating pattern of dark cedar panelling and white-washed stone. One of the wooden panels was not quite flush to the wall. Jack put an eye to the gap and was rewarded with a glimpse of an inner garden. A series of small stepping stones led across a mossy manicured lawn to a wooden veranda on the opposite side.

Jack pushed his fingers into the gap and the panel slid smoothly aside. Through the concealed entrance, Jack slipped into the temple garden. Perhaps this was where Akiko had disappeared to.

He crossed over to the veranda and followed it round to where it bordered a long rectangular Zen garden of raked grey pebbles, in which fifteen large black stones had been placed in a pattern of five irregular groups. Under the pale moonlight, the garden looked like a ridge of mountain tops thrusting through a sea of clouds.

The garden was deserted.

Through an archway on the far side, Jack spied a smaller plot of raked pebbles, decorated with one or two shrubs but little else. At the end of a stone pathway that bisected the garden was a simple wooden shrine. Its *shoji* doors were drawn shut, but the warm halo of a candle could be seen through the *washi* paper and Jack thought he heard voices coming from within.

He stepped off the wooden walkway towards the shrine, the pebbles crunching underfoot.

The voices stopped suddenly and the candle was extinguished.

Jack jumped back on to the walkway, silently cursing his haste to cross the stone garden. He hurried round the edge, keeping close to the shadows. He hid in an alcove near the entrance to the shrine and waited.

No one emerged.

After what seemed an age, Jack decided to risk a peek inside. Ever so slowly, he approached the *shoji* and slid it back a touch. There was a waft of freshly burnt incense. A statue of a Buddha sat upon a small stone pedestal surrounded by offerings of fruit, rice and *saké*, but otherwise the shrine was empty.

'Can I help you?' asked an authoritative voice.

Jack spun round, his heart in his mouth.

A monk in black and grey robes stood over him. The middle-aged man was muscular and compact, with a shaved head and dark glinting eyes. Jack thought about running, but there was something in this man's demeanour that suggested it wouldn't be a good idea. The monk exuded a lethal stillness. The tips of his fingers were held together as if in prayer, but his hands looked as deadly as two *tantō* blades.

'I . . . was looking for a friend,' stammered Jack.

'In the middle of the night?'

'Yes . . . I was worried for her.'

'Is she in trouble?'

'No, but I didn't know where she was going —'

'So you were following her?'

'Yes,' replied Jack, the guilt striking him like a slap across the face.

'You should respect people's privacy, boy. If your friend needed you, she would have asked for your company. She is clearly not here, so I think it's time you left.'

'Yes. I'm sorry. It was a mistake . . .' said Jack, bowing low.

'It is only a mistake if you do it twice,' interrupted the monk, though his expression remained unforgiving. 'Mistakes are lessons of wisdom. I trust you will learn from this one.'

Without another word, the monk escorted Jack back to the main gate and indicated for him to leave.

'I do not expect to see you here again.'

He then closed the double doors and Jack was left alone on the stone steps.

Jack walked slowly back to school, contemplating his actions. The monk was right. What business did he have spying on Akiko? She had only ever shown him trust. When he'd asked her to keep his father's *rutter* secret, she had. He, on the other hand, had not respected her privacy and was breaking her trust by following her around. Jack hated himself for it.

Still, doubt plagued his mind. Akiko had denied going out at night, so what was she doing that was so secret she had to lie about it?

When he returned to the Hall of Lions, he passed Akiko's room and couldn't help peeking inside. He realized then that he must have followed someone else to the Temple of the Peaceful Dragon.

For there Akiko was, fast asleep in her bed.

22

MAPLE LEAF VIEWING

'And I thought the cherry blossom in spring was beautiful,' said Jack, looking around in awe at the maple trees as they wandered through the gardens of the Eikan-Do Temple.

Akiko had taken Jack and the others to the temple to view *momiji gari*, an event similar to the spring *hanami* party, but held in autumn when the leaves of the maple trees turned into a magical kaleidoscope of colour. Jack was astounded by the display. The hillside was ablaze with red, gold, yellow and orange leaves as far as the eye could see.

'Let's go up to the *Tahoto*,' proposed Akiko, pointing to the three-tiered pagoda that poked through the flaming canopy like a spear. 'There's a wonderful view from there.'

With Akiko leading the way, Jack, Yamato, Saburo, Yori and Kiku climbed to the top tier, where they could look down on to the trees below. Each leaf was as beautiful and delicate as a golden snowflake.

'Glorious, isn't it?' commented a deep barrelled voice from behind.

They all turned to see Sensei Kano, their *bōjutsu* master. Despite being blind, it seemed he was admiring the view as well.

'Yes . . . but surely you can't see it. Can you?' asked Jack, not wishing to offend.

'No, Jack-kun, but life isn't bound by what you can or can't see,' replied Sensei Kano. 'I may not be able to see the trees, but I can still appreciate *momiji gari*. I can taste the colours, smell the maple's life and feel the canopy's decay. I can hear the individual leaves fall like a million fluttering butterflies. Close your eyes and you'll hear what I mean.'

They all did so. At first, Jack heard only an indistinct wash of sound, but it soon separated out into a rain-like pitter-patter of dry leaves. Then, just as he was starting to enjoy the experience, he heard giggling.

'Stop it!' cried Kiku.

Jack opened his eyes to see Saburo tickling Kiku's ear with a twig. She grabbed a handful of dead leaves and threw them in his face, but also got Yamato. In a matter of moments, they were all involved in a riotous battle of leaves.

'I suppose time spent laughing is time spent with the gods,' observed Sensei Kano ruefully, and walked off, leaving the young samurai convulsed with laughter as they played among the leaves.

They spent the rest of the afternoon exploring the expansive temple gardens. They crossed over wooden bridges and circled a large pond on which people rowed in little boats, playing *koto* harps and admiring the autumnal views.

Jack spotted Kazuki and his friends in one of the boats on the far shore. They hadn't seen him but seemed to be having too much fun splashing one another to care about Jack. Then Jack saw Emi walking across one of the bridges. At last this was his chance to speak with her alone.

'I'll catch up with you,' said Jack to the rest of the group, who were heading towards a small shrine on the other side of the pond. 'I just need to ask Emi something.'

Yamato and Akiko both stopped. Akiko raised her eyebrows in curiosity but said nothing.

'Come on, you three,' Saburo called impatiently. 'Once we've seen this last shrine, we can hire a boat and go paddling.'

Yamato hesitated a moment longer. Jack knew his friend still felt guilty for not being there when Kazuki and his gang had jumped him at the Hall of the Hawk. He hadn't left his side since.

'Let's go,' said Akiko, walking off. 'We'll see him on the way back.'

'We'll be just over there if you need us,' Yamato said, following Akiko with reluctance.

Jack watched as the two of them headed off to join the others. In her honey-coloured kimono, Akiko appeared to float away like a leaf on a stream. Jack hurried over to Emi. She was standing on the bridge, admiring a maple tree that hung over the water like a tongue of flame. Emi bowed as he approached.

'Enjoying *momiji gari*?' she asked, smiling.

'Yes. And you?' replied Jack, returning the bow.

'Very much. It's my favourite time of year.'

Jack glanced over at the nearby maple tree, trying to think of what to say next.

'Is it ever like this in your country?' Emi asked.

'Sometimes,' replied Jack, watching a leaf fall through the air and land on the surface of the pond. 'But most of the time it rains . . .'

An awkward silence fell between them as he summoned up the courage to speak. 'May I ask you a favour?'

'Of course.'

'Can I visit your father's palace again?'

She looked at him, her eyes registering surprise. 'Any particular reason?'

'Yes . . . When we were there for the tea ceremony, I noticed some screen paintings of tigers. I'd like to see them again.'

Jack had thought carefully about this answer, but when he said it now the excuse sounded weak, and he cringed.

'I didn't know you were interested in art,' she said, the corners of her mouth crinkling into a mischievous smile.

Jack nodded.

'I'm sure it can be arranged. I would have to speak with my father, of course, when he gets back.'

'Of course,' Jack agreed. Then he heard laughter and turned to see that Cho and Kai had caught up with Emi and were giggling behind their hands.

'I have to go,' Emi said, bowing before joining her friends and their elderly chaperone.

Jack watched them leave, whispering to one another and glancing over their shoulders at him before bursting into fits of giggles again. Had they overheard him speaking with Emi? Or were they laughing simply because they had discovered him and Emi alone together? He needed to keep the visit to the castle private so the *rutter* would remain safe, and it wouldn't help if those two started spreading rumours about them.

The sun was now beginning to set; its golden rays glinted upon the water and shone through the leaves of the maple trees like a patchwork of paper lanterns. Jack absently opened up his *inro*, the wooden carrying case that had been a gift from *daimyo* Takatomo, and took out the picture Jess had drawn and given to their father some three years ago, when they had set sail from Limehouse Docks for the Japans. He now kept the picture with him as a constant reminder of his little sister.

He opened the parchment, ragged and worn from repeated handling. In the dappled sunlight, he traced the outlines of his family. His little sister's summer smock, his father's black scribble of a ponytail, his own head drawn three times too big on a stick-thin body, and lastly the angel wings of his mother.

One day he *would* return home, he promised himself.

Jack closed his eyes. Listening to the breeze in the trees and the ripples on the water, he could almost imagine he was on a boat heading back to England. He was so entranced by the idea that he hardly noticed the group returning.

They quietly surrounded him.

'Enjoying your last days of *momiji gari*, are you?'

Startled, Jack spun round to find himself confronted, not by Akiko or his friends, but by Kazuki and his Scorpion Gang.

'Have you heard another foreign priest has died?' revealed Kazuki, as if he was merely discussing the weather. 'He was preaching to his followers to obey the Church over their *daimyo*. Loyal samurai punished him for his treachery by setting fire to his house, with him inside. It won't be long before we get rid of all your kind.'

'*Gaijin* Jack should go back!' said Nobu, his belly bobbing up and down with laughter, clearly delighted with his taunt.

Jack backed away, but was stopped by the handrail of the bridge.

'All on your own?' smirked Hiroto. 'No bodyguards? I thought you would have learnt from last time – or do you need another kick in the ribs to remind you?'

Jack said nothing, knowing Hiroto was looking for any excuse to strike him.

'Cat got your tongue?' asked Moriko, hissing in delight. 'Or are you just too brainless to understand?'

Jack tried to keep calm. He was outnumbered, but determined not to be intimidated this time.

'No one likes *gaijin*,' rasped Moriko, baring her black teeth at him. 'They're filthy, stupid and ugly.'

Jack stared back at her. He was above this.

Moriko, frustrated at his lack of reaction, spat at Jack's feet.

'What have we got here?' Kazuki demanded, snatching Jess's picture out of Jack's hand before he could react.

Jack flew at Kazuki. 'Give it back!'

Nobu and Hiroto caught hold of his arms and put him in a lock.

'Look at this, gang. Hasn't Jack been a clever boy? He's

learnt to draw,' teased Kazuki, holding the piece of paper in the air for all of them to see.

'Give it back NOW, Kazuki!' Jack demanded, struggling to escape.

'Why could you possibly want to keep this? It's terrible. It's like a little girl's drawn it!'

Jack shook with rage as Kazuki dangled the picture in front of his nose.

'Say goodbye to your masterpiece, *gaijin*.' Kazuki threw the picture into the air.

Jack watched in anguish as the drawing fluttered away on the breeze.

'Look! The *gaijin* is about to cry like a baby,' squealed Moriko and the Scorpion Gang laughed.

Jack hardly heard the taunts. His entire focus was on the fragile piece of paper flying away. He thrashed wildly in Nobu and Hiroto's grip as his only bond with Jess disappeared into the sky. It lifted high above the pond before getting caught in the upper branches of a maple tree.

'Leave him alone!' ordered Yamato, running on to the bridge with Akiko and his friends.

Jack felt a small wave of relief. At least he was not alone in this fight.

'Let Jack go,' demanded Akiko, pulling at Hiroto's arms.

'Look who it is; the *gaijin* lover!' announced Kazuki, looking her up and down scornfully. 'Do as she says. It's only fair to give them a fighting chance. Scorpions!'

At Kazuki's command, the Scorpion Gang dropped into

fighting guard, facing off against each of Jack's friends. Yamato and Saburo stood their ground, but Yori trembled as a boy twice his size loomed over him. Ignoring Kiku with a sneer, Moriko squared up to Akiko and hissed into her face like a wildcat.

'Come on! Make the first move,' Moriko dared, baring her blackened teeth and fingernails that had been sharpened into claws. 'Give me the excuse I need to scar you!'

23

BREAKING BOARDS

Akiko slipped into stance, preparing to defend herself. She knew from experience that Moriko fought viciously. But just as the fight was about to kick off, a *bō* struck the wooden bridge with tremendous force and everyone froze.

'Do we have a problem?' enquired Sensei Kano. 'In a setting such as this, there should be no need for raised voices.'

Nobu and Hiroto immediately released Jack.

'No, Sensei,' replied Kazuki in a friendly voice. 'Jack's lost his picture and is a bit upset. There was a misunderstanding, but it's all sorted now. Isn't it, Jack?'

Jack glared at Kazuki, but there was little else he could do. He had no proof of what had happened. Sensei Kano would never be able to see the truth.

'Yes,' he replied flatly, not taking his eyes off his enemy.

'I understand the situation perfectly,' stated Sensei Kano. 'I think it is time that you all went back to the school.'

Kazuki signed to his Scorpion Gang to follow him and they left without another word.

Jack looked up in despair at his sister's drawing caught

high in the topmost branches of the maple tree. Even with his skills as a rigging monkey, there was no way he could get to it. The upper branches would snap under his weight.

'Don't worry, Jack,' said Akiko, seeing the sorrow well up in Jack's eyes, 'I'll get it for you.'

With astounding grace, Akiko launched herself from the bridge, kicking off from the handrail and catching hold of the nearest branch of the maple tree. She swung herself up to the next level, then flew up the tree swift as a sparrow. Fearlessly walking out on to an upper branch, she caught hold of the fluttering paper.

With the same unparalleled skill, Akiko dropped down the tree and back on to the bridge. She handed Jack his sister's drawing and bowed.

Jack was speechless, only managing a nod of the head to show his appreciation. The others appeared equally impressed.

'I've always enjoyed climbing trees,' she said by way of an excuse, heading towards the school without a backward glance.

Where had Akiko's remarkable ability come from? None of them had been taught those skills at the *Niten Ichi Ryū*. Her agility reminded Jack of the ninja who had flown like bats through the rigging of the *Alexandria*, and of the one person he'd seen scale a castle wall as if he was a spider – Dragon Eye.

Is this what Akiko had been up to on her nightly outings? Learning ninja skills?

But that was absurd. The samurai hated the ninja and all they stood for, and surely ninja felt the same way about samurai. What sort of ninja would want to teach a samurai their tricks? The whole idea was ludicrous. Besides, only men became ninja. Jack immediately dismissed the idea.

CRACK!

Kazuki's fist drove through the cedar board, smashing it into two pieces.

The class applauded loudly as Kazuki became the first student to break wood in the run-up to the trials.

But he was not the only one to succeed at *tamashiwari* that morning. The constant training inflicted by Sensei Kyuzo on the *makiwara* over the past month was paying off as Hiroto, Goro, Yamato and then Emi and Akiko all snapped their single pieces of board. With more time, the students realized that one board would become two, and eventually the three required in the Trial by Wood.

Jack was preparing for his attempt when Sensei Kyuzo suddenly shouted, '*REI!*'

The whole class bowed as Masamoto strode into the *Butokuden*. Jack was taken aback at his guardian's unexpected appearance.

'Please, Sensei Kyuzo,' said Masamoto, with a wave of his hand, 'continue as if I wasn't here. I just wish to check on progress for the trials.'

Sensei Kyuzo bowed and returned to his class.

'Jack-kun, step up!' he ordered.

Jack hurried to the centre of the *Butokuden* and waited as Sensei Kyuzo positioned a single cedar board between the two stable blocks. He then placed a second board on top of the first.

'But —' Jack protested.

Sensei Kyuzo cut him off with a withering look.

Jack groaned inwardly. Sensei Kyuzo had promised he would do everything in his power to ruin Jack's chances of entering the Circle of Three. Now the sensei was setting him up to fail in front of Masamoto.

Jack could see that Yamato and Akiko were equally appalled by the unfairness, but they were in no position to say anything.

Jack's only choice was to prove Sensei Kyuzo wrong.

During their training, Jack had come to understand that the *tamashiwari* technique required more than brute strength. It demanded total commitment, concentration and focus.

He had to strike *through* the wood, not at it.

The power came from his body, not the arm itself.

He needed to condense his *ki*, his spiritual energy, and transfer it through his fist into the object he was striking. And most crucial of all, he had to truly believe that he was capable of breaking the block.

Jack took all the anger, frustration and hate he had suffered at the hands of Sensei Kyuzo, Kazuki and his Scorpion Gang and channelled it into the wooden blocks. With an explosive force that even surprised Jack, he slammed his fist through the wood, screaming '*KIAIIIII!*'

With the sound of a gunshot, the two blocks shattered apart, the splinters flying through the air.

There was a moment of awed silence then the class erupted into applause.

Jack was euphoric. A rush of adrenaline pulsed through him as he experienced a sudden release of all his frustrations. For that brief moment, he was all-powerful.

As the clapping died down, one pair of hands kept applauding.

'Very impressive,' commended Masamoto, stepping forward. 'You have been training your students well, Sensei Kyuzo. May I borrow Jack-kun for a moment?'

Sensei Kyuzo bowed in acknowledgement, but Jack noticed the burning frustration in the samurai's eyes.

Masamoto beckoned Jack over and led him outside.

'I haven't had an opportunity to speak with you for a while,' he began as they walked past the construction works of the Hall of the Hawk, where several carpenters were busy hammering down floorboards and putting up roof beams. Masamoto and Jack entered the sanctuary of the Southern Zen Garden to escape the noise.

'How are you coping as a young samurai?' enquired Masamoto.

Jack, still buzzing from the *tamashiwari*, replied, 'Great, but the training's been harder than I expected.'

Masamoto laughed. 'The training is easy. It's your expectations that are making it hard,' he observed. 'I must apologize for not being around much this year to guide you, but affairs of state have taken priority. I'm sure you understand.'

Jack nodded. He assumed Masamoto was referring to Kamakura's anti-Christian campaign. There had been more reports of persecution in Edo, Kazuki ensuring Jack was made fully aware of each one. Jack now wondered how widespread the problem had become to require so much of his guardian's time in serving *daimyo* Takatomi.

'The good news is that we have dealt with the situation and you'll be seeing far more of me for the rest of the year,' Masamoto said, a smile spreading across the unscarred side of his face.

'Has *daimyo* Kamakura been stopped?' Jack blurted, unable to hide the relief in his voice.

'Kamakura?' queried Masamoto, the smile disappearing. 'So you are aware of the issue?'

He looked hard at Jack, his stare as penetrating as steel blade. For a moment Jack wondered if he had spoken out of turn.

'There's no reason to concern yourself with such matters,' continued his guardian, indicating for Jack to sit down next to him on the veranda that overlooked the Zen garden and a small stone water feature. 'Still, to allay your fears I can tell you in strictest confidence that *daimyo* Takatomi has required my services to deal with . . . how should I say, "disagreements" over the running of our country and who should be welcome upon our shores. I've been carrying out assignments to establish the positions of other provincial lords on this matter. The vast majority are on our side. You have nothing to worry about.'

'But what about all the priests who've died, and *daimyo* Kamakura's order to kill all Christians and foreigners who don't leave?'

'I can assure you that's purely the prejudice of one *daimyo*.'

'But might it not spread among the other lords?' insisted Jack. 'I mean, if it did, surely I'd be in danger and could get killed before I return home.'

'Return home?' said Masamoto, raising his eyebrows in surprise. 'But *this* is your home.'

Jack didn't know what to say in reply. Though he couldn't deny that Japan was now in his blood, England was where his heart truly lay and always would.

'You're my son,' affirmed Masamoto proudly. 'No one would dare harm you. Besides, you're samurai now, and with a few years' more training you won't need me to protect you.'

Masamoto clapped Jack firmly on the back and laughed.

Jack forced a smile. Masamoto had never asked for anything in return for his kindness and Jack knew that contradicting his guardian now would be the most disrespectful thing he could do. He would be throwing all that generosity back into the samurai's face. However much he wanted to go home and find Jess, Jack owed Masamoto his life and, as a samurai, his service too.

Jack decided he would bide his time and dedicate himself to mastering the Two Heavens. Then, once he'd proved he could look after himself, he would ask for Masamoto's permission to leave.

'I understand, Masamoto-sama,' said Jack, bowing his head in deference. 'I was just worried that the situation was getting out of control. But I'm determined to enter the Circle of Three and learn the Two Heavens.'

'*That's* the samurai spirit I'm looking for. I can appreciate how you must yearn for your homeland,' conceded Masamoto. 'But I made a promise to the memory of your father, and the honour of my dear departed son, Tenno, that I would take care of you. You are *my* responsibility. And you are perfectly safe.'

Despite Jack's fears that Kamakura's campaign would become bigger than even the great Masamoto could handle, he knew deep down that his guardian would fight to his last breath protecting him.

Masamoto turned to Jack, concern now etched in his brow. 'I've been made aware that you're experiencing some difficulties with other students in the school. Is this right?'

Jack nodded once. 'But it's nothing that I can't handle,' he added quickly.

'I'm sure it isn't,' replied Masamoto, noting Jack's bravado with pride. 'Nonetheless, now that I am back, I will be making it very clear that I won't tolerate bullying or prejudice in my school. At the same time, I wish to give you some advice that stood me well in my youth.'

Jack had never witnessed Masamoto like this before. Severe, austere and commanding, yes. But paternal – this was something very different. Jack felt a pang of grief for his true father.

'I realize it's hard being different. The truth is that they're envious of your skills as a swordsman and samurai, but, if you ignore their taunts, they will ignore you.'

'How can I?' said Jack. 'It's not as if I blend in.'

'Do I?' Masamoto asked, turning so that the reddened mass of scars down the left-hand side of his face was fully visible to Jack.

Jack said nothing.

'Apply *fudoshin*,' instructed Masamoto, reaching forward and dipping his finger into the large stone bowl in the water feature. He traced a circular pattern upon its surface and watched the ripples ebb away.

'Instead of allowing yourself to be led and trapped by your feelings, let them disappear as they form like letters drawn upon water with a finger. They cannot hurt you, unless you let them.'

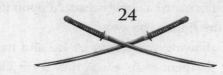

24

TRIAL BY WOOD AND FIRE

A wintery smudge of sun rose in the sky to reveal a world bleached white with snow. The curved eaves of the *Butsuden* hung heavy with powder drifts and the school was oddly peaceful, all sound muffled by the abrupt change in season from autumn to winter.

Jack's breath billowed out in front of him like smoke as he sliced through the frozen air with his *katana*.

Every morning since Kazuki and his Scorpion Gang had attacked him in the Hall of the Hawk, Jack had risen early to practise his *kenjutsu* in the Southern Zen Garden, performing a ritual of one hundred cuts of every *kata* before breakfast – just as he had vowed he would. Sensei Hosokawa may have forbidden him to use his sword in class, but that wasn't going to stop Jack practising with it in his own time. He was determined to succeed in the Gauntlet, whatever the Trial by Sword entailed.

Jack would then head over to *Butokuden* and strike the *makiwara* fifty times with each fist, conditioning his bones for the Trial by Wood. He would hit the padded post so hard that his hands would still be trembling during breakfast and he'd struggle to hold his *hashi*.

In the afternoons following classes, he joined Akiko in the garden as she perfected her *kyujutsu* skills in preparation for the Trial by Fire. Between arrows, she would correct his stance, guide his aim and help him 'forget' the target. Occasionally Jack would even hit it. Afterwards, when they had time, she would test him on his *kanji* and teach him a new character.

Once during these unofficial lessons, Jack had brought up the matter of her extraordinary tree-climbing skill, but she just dismissed it as natural ability, laughing at his suggestion of ninja training and ending the discussion by exclaiming, 'I'm no more a ninja than you are Japanese.'

Jack even joined Yori in his nightly ritual of folding cranes, hoping to increase his chances in Sensei Yamada's Trial by *Koan*. He had now mastered the various folds and was finding the process of *origami* to be somewhat soothing, though why Yori needed so many of the paper models was beyond Jack's comprehension. His friend's tiny room was overflowing with hundreds of the little white birds.

Through this daily routine, Jack's life in Japan acquired a steady rhythm and day by day, brick by brick, the invisible wall that stood in the way of his samurai training was crumbling. He knew he'd improved, but would it be enough to secure him a place in the Circle?

If it had not been for Kazuki and his Scorpion Gang, he would have been almost content with his life at the school. Following Masamoto's decree, Jack was no longer physically threatened by any of the gang members, but it didn't stop them from taunting him, spitting insults or whispering 'Go home, *gaijin*!' whenever the opportunity presented itself. These were the attacks Masamoto couldn't protect him from. The ones he needed to apply *fudoshin* against.

Initially Jack was able to let the empty threats wash over him, but it became harder as more students began to sympathize with Kazuki's point of view. It was as if a split was forming in the school between those who accepted foreigners and those who didn't.

He was beginning to wonder if Masamoto had been entirely truthful with him regarding Kamakura's influence over Japan. Despite his promise, the samurai had been summoned away twice in the past three weeks by *daimyo* Takatomi, and Jack would occasionally bump into students discussing the news of another Christian who had been persecuted or banished by *daimyo* Kamakura and his samurai. Any time this happened, the students would appear embarrassed by Jack's presence, the conversation grinding to a halt, before they made their excuses and walked away. Jack got a real sense that, though some of them still liked him, they could no longer afford to be associated with him. He was quickly learning who his true friends were.

Jack, raising his sword to make the final cut of his practice session, heard the crisp crunch of snow behind him. He spun round, half expecting to see Kazuki or one of his cohorts.

'I thought I'd find you out here,' said Akiko. She was wrapped in several layers of kimono against the cold, but her warm smile thawed the winter chill in the air.

Jack dropped his guard and sheathed his sword.

Akiko glanced around at the thick blanket of snow that had fallen overnight. 'You do know what this means, don't you?'

Jack nodded.

'The trials for the Circle of Three.'

Later that morning, stepping up to the three wooden blocks carefully stacked in the centre of the *Butokuden*, Jack prayed all his efforts would carry him through the trials. He needed to be among the top five, but it was just his luck the selection began with the toughest of these trials – *tamashiwari*.

No one so far had broken through three blocks and Jack knew he had only one chance to get this trial right.

The entire school lined the length of the *Butokuden* to watch. They fell silent as Jack positioned himself to strike.

Jack rubbed his hands for warmth, even though the morning sunlight was filtering through the slatted windows. Making his final preparations, he tried to summon the explosive energy he'd tapped into when he had demolished the two blocks in front of Masamoto.

Sensei Kyuzo, who was the official adjudicator of this trial, stood to one side, his arms crossed. 'When you are ready,' he said, staring irritably at Jack. 'Not that you'll ever be,' he added under his breath as Jack raised his fist.

Jack tried to ignore the comment, but his concentration had been thrown by the sensei's deliberate distraction. Implanted in the back of his mind was now the thought that he wasn't ready, that the combination of three blocks was too thick.

THUNK!

Jack's fist collided with the wood. The first two boards broke, but the third layer of cedar held and Jack's hand was brought to an abrupt halt, sending a sickening wave of pain up his arm.

A murmur of disappointment washed through the *dojo*.

Jack massaged his throbbing hand, infuriated at himself for allowing Sensei Kyuzo's comment to break his concentration. It had been that sliver of doubt that had prevented the break.

He hastily bowed his respects to Masamoto, who was watching the proceedings from the ceremonial alcove with the other sensei. His guardian had returned to the school that morning for the selection trials and the journey appeared to have left him tired and irritable. His scarring was inflamed and he slowly shook his head, clearly as disappointed with Jack's performance as Jack was with himself.

As he knelt back into line with the thirty students who'd entered the trials, Jack caught Sensei Kyuzo grinning smugly.

'Don't worry, Jack,' said Akiko, who had also been defeated by *tamashiwari*. 'We still have three more trials to prove ourselves.'

Jack was reassured by her words until Kazuki stepped up to the challenge accompanied by shouts of encouragement.

Sensei Kyuzo replaced the cracked blocks with new ones, while whispering in his protégé's ear.

Kazuki nodded once, then focused his attention on the blocks of wood. With an unwavering look of determination, he smashed his fist through all three blocks, splintered pieces of wood flying through the air.

The school erupted in a huge cheer while Masamoto and his sensei applauded respectfully. Even Jack had to admit that the feat was impressive. Kazuki bowed smartly to Masamoto, his reputation affirmed as the first student to pass a trial.

The *dojo* was cleared and reset for Sensei Yosa's Trial by Fire. An archery target was positioned at the far end, a tall wooden candleholder placed before it and a slim white candle fitted on top so that the wick was in line with the bullseye.

The trial participants prepared themselves at the other end of the *Butokuden*, choosing bows from the weapons rack and checking that their arrows were in good order.

Jack went to select his, but Kazuki, Hiroto and Goro pushed in front to seize the best ones. The only bow left was well-used and past its prime. Jack tested the draw strength and knew straight away that it had lost much of its power.

'The first trial by Sensei Kyuzo tested strength,' proclaimed Masamoto to the assembled students. 'Strength of body and strength of mind. The next trial will be led by Sensei Yosa and will assess your skill and technical ability.'

Sensei Yosa stood and made her way to the target, her long black hair shimmering in waves down the back of her blood-red kimono. She held a burning taper in her hand, which she used to light the wick. The candle flickered into life, its flame a tiny petal of light before the bullseye.

'Your challenge is to snuff out the candle,' explained Sensei Yosa. 'You will be allowed two attempts.'

'Good luck,' Yamato whispered to Jack.

'I think I'll need more than luck,' replied Jack, glancing down at his bow.

The firing distance was equal to the length of the Southern Zen Garden, making it a difficult shot even without the additional factor of the flame.

The first to step up was Goro. Jack's earlier annoyance over the selection of the bows was tempered by the boy's appalling performance. A ripple of laughter broke out as one of his arrows missed the target completely and glanced off one of the pillars, narrowly missing Sensei Yosa.

Then it was Akiko's turn.

She finished tending to the bamboo bow and hawk feather arrows that Sensei Yosa had presented to her earlier that summer. Being the only student to have her own weapon, she hadn't needed to fight over the school's. She lined herself up with the target, nocked an arrow on to her bowstring, then raised the weapon above her head. She did all this with an ease and elegance that was reminiscent of Sensei Yosa herself.

Akiko's first arrow pierced the bullseye with a resounding thump like a heartbeat.

There was a moment of awed silence.

Akiko didn't need to fire a second. Her arrow had flown so true that it had actually sliced the flame in half as the feathered flights snuffed out the candle.

The *Butokuden* was drowned in ecstatic applause.

Akiko's performance put everyone else to shame. Each

162

entrant filed through, firing to the best of their ability, but no one could match Akiko's skill. Yamato struck the target both times, but missed the candle. Kazuki's performance was more impressive, his second arrow slicing the edge of the candle and almost cutting it in half. To Jack's relief, though, the flame stayed lit. Even Emi, who was usually on a par with Akiko, didn't extinguish the flame, though she did get two bullseyes. Hiroto was the only one to prove the exception. His second arrow clipped the wick of the candle, snuffing the flame out.

Then it was Jack's turn.

With Kazuki, Akiko and Hiroto having succeeded in a trial and therefore standing a good chance of being chosen to enter the Circle of Three, he was starting to feel the pressure.

He had to be chosen. He had to prove himself.

He had to learn the Two Heavens.

Drawing upon all his reserves of concentration, Jack took up position at the mark. He focused on the tiny flame at the far end of the hall, no larger than a rosebud. He drew back on his bow, moving fluidly between each movement as Akiko had instructed, and let loose his first arrow.

Jack grimaced in disappointment. It was a good hand's width below the bullseye. The bow's limited draw strength had thrown his aim off. He adjusted his stance to compensate. Focusing hard on the flickering light, he was about to fire his second arrow when he remembered Sensei Yosa's words: '*When the archer does not think about the target, then they may unfold the Way of the Bow.*'

Jack finally understood what she meant. He was so

focused on the flickering candle that he hadn't noticed his body tensing up.

He stopped thinking about the target, let his mind go and relaxed with the bow. Starting again, he gave each moment of the draw his full attention. As he breathed out, he released the arrow. It whistled down the length of the *dojo*, straight towards the centre of the flame.

It struck the bullseye.

The whole *dojo* stared at the candle, the arrow quivering slightly above it. The flame guttered briefly and some of the students began to clap, but their premature applause died as soon as the candle flared back into life.

The next moment, the arrow's feathered flights burst into flames like a terrible omen.

Jack had failed the second trial.

MORE THAN A PIECE OF PAPER

Perched upon a *zabuton* at the front of the *Butokuden*'s ceremonial alcove, Sensei Yamada leant forward to listen to a petite girl with a short sweep of dark-brown hair. The girl whispering in his ear was Harumi, who, despite her size and to everyone's astonishment, had demolished the three blocks during the Trial by Wood. Having given her answer to the Trial by *Koan*, she bowed and waited for Sensei Yamada's verdict, her pale round face delicate as a porcelain doll's.

After a few moments contemplation, Sensei Yamada gave a resigned shake of the head and dismissed Harumi back into line.

'Can no one provide Sensei Yamada with a satisfactory answer?' demanded Masamoto, glowering at the trial participants who knelt before him. His indignation at everyone's failure to solve this third trial was marked, a fact conveyed by the reddening of his scars. 'Are you telling me that there is not one student in my *dojo* who can demonstrate intellect and insight worthy of a samurai?'

He was greeted by shamed silence, the entrants' disgrace growing with each empty second.

Jack joined the others in bowing his head. Despite the fact that, thanks to Yori, he could fold a paper crane, frog or goldfish with practised ease, the solution to the riddle remained elusive. When his turn had come, Jack's suggestion was that *origami* taught patience, but Sensei Yamada had reluctantly shaken his head in response.

'Very well. I now open this trial to all trainee samurai of the *Niten Ichi Ryū*,' Masamoto announced, 'not just those vying for entry into the Circle of Three. So, what does *origami* teach us?'

The rest of the school suddenly stiffened to attention as his eyes raked the students for a solution. No one dared move in case the irate Masamoto thought they had the answer. The tension grew unbearable, dishonour now tainting everyone who failed to respond.

Just as Masamoto appeared ready to explode, a small hand raised itself among the sea of shamefaced samurai.

'Yes, Yori-kun? You have an answer?'

Yori meekly nodded his head.

'Then step forward and take part in the trial.'

Yori approached in quick hesitant steps like a dormouse seeking a bolt-hole.

'Please, Yori-kun,' invited Sensei Yamada, his wrinkly face warm and welcoming in contrast to the fearsome expression of Masamoto, 'reveal your answer to me.'

The hall fell silent as the entire school strained to hear Yori's words.

Yori finished his explanation, every word a secret in his sensei's ear, then stepped back and bowed. Sensei Yamada studied him a moment, twisting his grey beard through his fingers. Ever so slowly, he turned his head towards Masamoto and nodded once, allowing a wide, gap-toothed smile to spread across his face.

'Excellent,' said Masamoto, his thunderous mood dissipating at once. 'At least one trainee warrior here has the aptitude to think like a true samurai. Yori-kun, enlighten your peers with an answer worthy of the *Niten Ichi Ryū*.'

Yori looked startled. Quiet at the best of times, he quaked under the pressure of addressing the whole school.

'Have courage, young samurai. Speak!'

Yori's voice came out in a petrified squeak, 'Nothing . . . is as it appears.'

He swallowed hard to regain control of his voice.

'Just like a piece of paper can be more than a piece of paper in *origami*, becoming a crane, a fish or a flower; so . . . so . . .'

'A samurai should never underestimate their own potential to bend and fold to life,' continued Sensei Yamada, taking over before Yori completely stuttered to a halt. 'To strive to become more than they first appear, to go beyond their obvious limits.'

Yori nodded gratefully, finishing in a small voice, 'This is what *origami* teaches us.'

'The Gauntlet is your last trial,' announced Sensei Hosokawa, pacing the *dojo* floor in front of the entrants who knelt respectfully in a line. 'It is a test of courage, your final chance to prove yourselves worthy for the Circle of Three. Judging by the previous trial, you all have a great deal to prove.'

The *Butokuden*'s training area was empty, giving no clue as to what was involved in the Gauntlet.

'Your goal is to walk from one end of the *Butokuden* to the other,' he continued, indicating a route that ran straight down the centre of the *dojo*.

That didn't seem too hard, thought Jack, glancing at Yamato who appeared to be thinking the exact same thing. But Akiko gave them both a dubious shake of the head, indicating that there was definitely more to this challenge than a mere walk.

'The Gauntlet is your Trial by Sword, so you should carry your *bokken*. If you can run the Gauntlet and reach the other end, you will pass the test. I now ask all participants to leave the *dojo*.'

Jack and the others hesitated. What was so different about this trial that they were required to leave?

'NOW!' commanded Sensei Hosokawa.

A moment later, they were on their feet and marching from the *Butokuden*.

'Wait in the courtyard until you are called for,' ordered Sensei Hosokawa before re-entering the *dojo* and closing the large wooden doors behind him.

'What do you think he's got planned?' asked Yamato as they stood shivering, ankle deep in the snow.

They could hear the sound of movement and the shuffling of a multitude of feet.

'Perhaps he's setting up an obstacle course,' Jack suggested.

'Or releasing a *gaijin*-eating tiger!' snarled Hiroto, laughing with Kazuki.

Jack turned to confront them, his nerves already on edge with the forthcoming trial. The Trial by Sword was Jack's last opportunity to prove himself. His only chance.

'Save your energy for the Gauntlet,' advised Akiko, ensuring her *bokken* was secure on her hip. 'Sensei Hosokawa hasn't been drilling us hard without good reason.'

Jack backed down and tended to his own *bokken*.

'HIROTO-KUN!' summoned Sensei Hosokawa from within the *Butokuden*.

Hiroto's laughter died at the mention of his name, his narrow lips suddenly drawing tight with tension. He strode valiantly across the courtyard, but couldn't disguise a shudder of nerves as he approached the entrance. As soon as Hiroto was inside, the *Butokuden*'s doors slammed shut with an ominous thud. Outside, the rest of the participants waited and listened.

For a while, they heard nothing but the light patter of snow falling around them from the cold grey sky. Then a thundering '*KIAI!*' broke from the *dojo*, followed by the sound of fighting and a loud scream.

A moment later there was deathly silence.

The entrants looked at one another in shock.

They waited, expecting to hear more, but no further sound came from Hiroto.

'YAMATO-KUN!' Sensei Hosokawa beckoned, opening the doors and breaking the silence.

Yamato took three deep breaths, then made his way across the courtyard to the hall. Jack gave him an encouraging look, but he barely acknowledged it. Yamato was already in the moment, utterly focused on the unknown trial that awaited him.

Once again, the doors closed.

The hush from within the *dojo* was unsettling and Jack was reminded of the calm that preceded the most violent of storms.

All of a sudden the air was punctuated with screams of *kiai*, shouts of combat and the soft dull thud of *bokken* against flesh.

This time, the battle seemed to stretch on and on before a great guttural cheer exploded from the hall.

Then Sensei Hosokawa's voice issued forth.

'EMI-CHAN!'

'Good luck,' said Jack.

Emi smiled warmly at him, but her eyes belied the fear she really felt.

'Remember what the painting in the Tiger Room said,' Jack added, hoping to reassure her. '*If you don't enter the tiger's cave, you won't catch its cub.*'

Emi disappeared inside the *Butokuden*.

'When were you in the Tiger Room at Nijo Castle?' enquired Akiko, her voice slightly strained. 'We didn't visit it during the tea ceremony.'

'No. I went back.'

'What? Just the two of you?'

'Well . . . yes,' mumbled Jack. 'I wanted to see more of the castle.'

Pursing her lips, Akiko nodded curtly and glanced up into the sky, concentrating on the snowflakes as they fell and settled upon the ground.

A single *kiai* from Emi was heard within the hall and it was not long before the next participant was summoned. Several more entered before Sensei Hosokawa cried, 'AKIKO-CHAN!'

Jack offered her a reassuring smile, but she was staring straight ahead as she strode over to the entrance. He hoped she wasn't upset that he hadn't told her about his second visit with Emi. But why should she be? He knew there were things that Akiko didn't tell him.

In the courtyard, the snow continued to fall, settling upon everyone's heads and shoulders. Jack heard Akiko *kiai* several times above the cries of battle, but just as he was wondering how far she had got, an ominous silence descended upon the *Butokuden*.

The dwindling group of entrants tensed to hear whose name would be called out next.

Eventually only Jack and Kazuki remained. They ignored one another, the tension of the Gauntlet getting to both of them.

'KAZUKI-KUN!'

Kazuki straightened his *gi* and headed confidently towards the entrance.

'Good luck,' said Jack on the spur of the moment.

Kazuki glanced back over his shoulder, a grim smile on his face. 'You too,' he replied with uncharacteristic cama-raderie. 'We'll need it.'

Then he stepped inside and closed the doors behind him.

From the shouts that ensued, Kazuki seemed to be doing well, but Jack's body was too stiff with cold for him to care whether Kazuki succeeded or not.

'JACK-KUN!'

Summoned at last, he tried to rub some warmth back into his bones. He didn't know if he was shaking more from cold or trepidation. He gripped the hilt of his *bokken* in an attempt to steady himself.

Stepping through the doors of the *dojo*, he entered the Gauntlet.

26

THE GAUNTLET

Jack dared not move.

Down either side of the *dojo* were lined the students of the *Niten Ichi Ryū*, appearing at first glance to be a ceremonial welcoming party. They formed a narrow corridor of samurai, stretching from the entrance to Hosokawa himself at the opposite end.

At various points behind these two rows, Jack noticed the other Circle of Three entrants. All of them looked thoroughly beaten, some nursing bruised limbs, others bloody faces. Jack spotted Akiko halfway down the hall. She didn't look too injured, though she clutched her side, wincing in pain as she shifted to get a better view of Jack.

'Welcome to the Gauntlet,' greeted Sensei Hosokawa from the far end of the hall. 'Please join me so we can begin.'

Jack took a wary step forward.

Nothing happened.

He glanced to one side, eyeing a burly student from the year above. The boy ignored him.

Jack made another move, but the two rows remained stock-still. Perhaps they *were* just a welcoming party, with the Gauntlet starting only once he reached Sensei Hoso-kawa. Jack began to walk towards the sensei, but the moment he did, a shout of '*KIAI!*' erupted from behind him.

Jack heard the *swoosh* of a *bokken*.

Instinctively he ducked, the wooden sword barely miss-ing his shoulder. Jack spun round, unsheathing his own *bokken* to protect himself against any follow-up attack. The student from the year above had been the culprit and was now bringing his sword back down on to Jack's head.

Jack countered, blocking the strike and swinging his own sword across his attacker's gut. The blow winded the boy, bending him double. Jack kicked him hard in the side and the boy fell to the ground.

But no sooner had Jack dispatched his first assailant than a girl broke from the ranks and thrust a wooden *tantō* at his stomach. Jack leapt to the side, parrying the girl's assault with his hand and knocking the knife from her grip. Slip-ping to her off-guard side, he brought his own weapon round in a low arc. The girl jumped to avoid it, but Jack raised the blade at the last second and caught her ankle. The girl was swept off her feet and landed in a crumpled heap upon the floor.

A faint rustle alerted Jack to an attack from behind. Two students were bearing down on him. They struck simulta-neously, one sword at his head, the other at his stomach.

With no time to think, Jack dived beneath the two *bokken*, rolling between his assailants. As he passed through, he struck the knee of the boy to his left, hobbling him. Flipping back to his feet, Jack followed through with a back kick that caught the other in the kidneys, dropping the boy like a stone.

As more assailants stepped from the ranks, Jack continued to fight his way down the centre of the Gauntlet, fending off attack after attack. All his extra training was now paying off. Each sword movement flowed into the next, the *bokken* gliding through the air in a series of controlled arcs and executing strikes with devastating accuracy.

But with each new wave of attack, Jack became a little slower, a touch weaker. A sense of dread consumed him as he realized that he wasn't *meant* to complete the Gauntlet unscathed. The Gauntlet wasn't about testing his skill with a sword. It was about his courage and spirit to survive against all the odds.

Jack was now three-quarters of the way down the hall and had levelled with Kazuki, who bore a nasty gash on his left cheek. His rival watched Jack's progress through hooded eyes, one of which was swollen half-shut. The only other entrant who had got as far as him was Yamato, but it seemed no one had reached Sensei Hosokawa.

With the end in sight, Jack rushed forwards, but was confronted by a girl wielding a *bō*. The girl twirled her staff like a whirling dervish and prevented him from passing. By the way she moved, Jack could tell she was as quick as a cobra, and the reach of her weapon gave her a distinct advantage over Jack's *bokken*. Jack couldn't even get close. He dodged and weaved, but was unable to land a single strike.

She thrust her *bō* at Jack with lightning speed, catching him directly in the stomach. Jack felt his insides turn over. She whipped her staff up, knocking him under the chin.

He saw stars and almost blacked out. But Jack instinctively swung his *bokken* up, somehow managing to deflect what would have been her finishing blow to his neck.

He staggered backwards, continuing to fend off her attacks, but then her staff hit his sword hand, breaking his grip, and the *bokken* went skittering across the *dojo* floor.

Defenceless, Jack could only jump from side to side as she drove her staff at him. He went to slip past her, but was pinioned from behind by another student in line.

The *bō* girl grinned and drove forward to deliver her conquering strike.

At the last second, Jack stamped on the foot of his captor, twisting sideways so that the *bō* connected with the boy's stomach instead. The boy yelled in surprise, relinquishing Jack from his grip.

In one fluid movement, Jack seized the boy's *bokken* and brought it down hard on to the girl's lead hand. Her *bō* clattered to the ground.

Jack shoulder-barged her out of the way and charged for the end of the Gauntlet.

He had made it!

He had run the Gauntlet.

He had managed to complete a trial.

Bruised and battered as he was, he proudly faced Sensei Hosokawa, who returned his gaze with a satisfied nod of the head. Jack could only hope that he had done enough to be selected for the Circle of Three. He bowed his respects to Sensei Hosokawa.

Strangely, there was no applause from the students. The anti-*gaijin* sentiment surely hadn't gone so far in the school that they wouldn't recognize his achievement. Jack was about to look up, when out of the corner of his eye, he glimpsed the sensei shift his body weight. Something whistled through the air.

The next thing Jack heard was, 'How many times have I told you . . .'

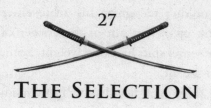

27

THE SELECTION

'. . . never let your guard down!'

The words rang in Jack's head as painfully as the *bokken* that struck him across the back of his neck, knocking him senseless to the floor.

The Gauntlet didn't finish at Sensei Hosokawa.

Sensei Hosokawa *was* the final trial.

Nursing a stiff neck, Jack now stood with the Circle of Three entrants in three lines at the centre of the *Butokuden*. They all looked like they'd been through a war, not one of them having escaped without injury.

While the rest of the school waited patiently in *seiza* around the edges of the *dojo*, Masamoto and Sensei Hosokawa, Yosa, Kyuzo and Yamada sat in a circle within the ceremonial alcove, quietly discussing the fate of the students.

Sensei Kano knelt to one side, his white *bō* leaning against a nearby pillar. As a visiting teacher to the *Niten Ichi Ryū*, he was not involved in the selection process, but Jack could tell the man was listening intently to the ongoing debate.

The selection process appeared to progress smoothly, until all of a sudden the discussion became heated and voices were raised.

'I object!' protested Sensei Kyuzo, slamming a rock-like fist on to the wooden floor. 'He didn't complete the trial.'

Every eye and ear in the *dojo* focused upon the quarrelling sensei and, despite Masamoto's attempts to subdue the dispute, snatches of the argument were still clearly audible.

'. . . your opinion is somewhat biased,' accused Sensei Kyuzo of Masamoto, his annoyance getting the better of his discretion.

'Can you honestly say you're impartial?' interjected Sensei Yosa.

'That's beside the point. The boy failed the trial. You cannot bend the rules for one individual!'

Masamoto held his hand up for calm. 'Enough. If my vote is contentious, I withdraw it . . .'

The row nonetheless rumbled on, but in tense whispered exchanges so that the students were no longer able to overhear. Jack's heart sank. Sensei Kyuzo had promised he would do everything in his power to stop him entering the Circle.

'What is your opinion, Sensei Kano?' Masamoto asked of the *bō* master a moment later. 'We are in a stalemate situation and require your vote.'

The great man leant forward to give his opinion. A few moments later, the issue was apparently resolved as the teachers returned to a more amicable discussion, though Sensei Kyuzo still looked sour as vinegar.

★　★　★

Like a cannon shot, a single handclap resounded in the *Butokuden* and Masamoto announced, 'The time has come!'

The entire school stiffened to attention as the selection panel turned to face the students, their expressions stony. Behind them, the school's carved gilded phoenix *kamon* hung proudly above the sensei's heads.

'Young samurai! To all those who participated in the trials, we bow to you.'

With a single sweeping glance, Masamoto took in the three lines of students, the power of his gaze making it appear as if he had looked at each of them in turn.

'We've carefully considered your performances today. The five students selected for entry to the Circle of Three are those who completed at least one trial and acted like a samurai in all by showing true *bushido* spirit,' explained Masamoto. 'When your name is called, step forward to receive our judgement.'

Jack let go of any remaining hope, biting back on the bitter disappointment he now felt. Having not completed a trial, he realized the Circle of Three would remain a distant dream, the Two Heavens technique a mystery to him for many more years to come.

'Emi-chan,' summoned Masamoto.

Emi limped out of line to take her place in front of the judging panel, the Gauntlet clearly having taken its toll upon her.

'You performed well. You're a fine *kyudoka* and although you were frightened by the Gauntlet we were most impressed with the way you regained your composure in the face of such danger. That took courage. However, your overall result was not quite good enough to warrant you entering the Circle. I'm sure your father would agree in this instance. Three to two against.'

Emi-chan bowed to the panel. As Jack watched her hobble over to the sidelines, it dawned on him just how challenging the Circle of Three must be, if even the daughter of the school's benefactor was rejected.

A sense of disappointment descended over the school as the next six entrants also failed to make the grade. Jack, however, felt a little better knowing that the bar had been set so high.

'Tadashi-kun,' summoned Masamoto.

A strong boy with broad shoulders and dark half-moon eyebrows stepped forward. Jack recognized him as the boy who had first entered his name for the Circle.

Masamoto nodded once. 'Formidable spirit throughout, especially in the *tamashiwari*. It was a shame you were knocked down towards the end of the Gauntlet, but no matter. Four to one in agreement. You are through to the Circle.'

The school gave a great cheer. At last one of the entrants was deemed good enough. Tadashi, a broad grin on his face, bowed his respects before taking up position in the middle of the *dojo*. The celebrations were short-lived, though, as the following seven contenders were all dismissed in quick succession.

Then Masamoto summoned Akiko.

She approached the panel and Jack crossed his fingers behind his back, silently wishing her luck.

'What can I say? The only one to kill the candle with their first arrow,' Masamoto said. Jack could see Sensei Yosa beaming at her protégé. 'But you only made it halfway down the Gauntlet. You appeared somewhat distracted during the fight. We had really expected more from you.'

Akiko bit her lower lip, and Jack felt his own mouth go dry. Had his offhand comment about his visit to the castle with Emi put her concentration off?

'Still, you have shown such *bushido* spirit and inner strength in all your other trials,' continued Masamoto, 'that it would be unjust for us to deny you this opportunity. Three to two in favour. Please join Tadashi.'

The *Butokuden* filled with applause again. Akiko remained where she was, astonished by the decision, and it took a few moments before she regained her composure, bowed and joined Tadashi.

The next ten competitors, including to Jack's satisfaction Goro, added to the growing number of failed students gathering on the sidelines. Only one of them was passed: Harumi, the petite girl with the doll-like face who had amazingly succeeded in the Trial by Wood. Two places now remained.

Kazuki was summoned.

Jack watched as his rival stepped up, the gash on his cheek now even more swollen and his eye completely closed.

'An outstanding performance in every aspect. All in favour. You are through to the Circle.'

Kazuki was the first entrant to be awarded a unanimous decision. He had triumphed in the eyes of all the sensei and, by the cheers that erupted from the hall, it was apparent that the school saw him as the favourite to conquer the

Circle. Despite the hostility between them, Jack was forced to admit Kazuki had performed brilliantly and deserved his place.

This left only one place and three entrants: Yamato, Hiroto and himself. Jack, assured of his own failure, silently prayed Yamato would triumph over Hiroto.

'Yamato-kun,' called Masamoto.

Yamato stepped forward, clutching his side and breathing between his teeth in short pained gasps. He glanced apprehensively at his father.

'I'm proud to say you fought like a true Masamoto in the Gauntlet, so this was a tough decision to make. However, without a clear victory in any of the trials, the committee voted three to two against. I'm sorry, but you are not one of the five.'

Yamato's eyes widened in dismay. He looked as if he wanted the *dojo* floor to swallow him up. Jack couldn't believe it. It must have been Yamato the sensei had been arguing over, not Jack. That was why Masamoto had deferred his vote to Sensei Kano. The decision must have been a great disappointment for the samurai.

Yamato hung his head and crossed the *dojo* to the sidelines, his frustration at his performance apparent in every weary step.

Masamoto then called out Jack's name.

Jack readied himself for the inevitable.

'Jack-kun, yours was a very controversial decision. I was of the mind that you had shown true *bushido* spirit throughout the trials and therefore proved your worth to enter the Circle of Three. Still, I had to be impartial in all decisions, especially as you are my adopted son, and you did not actually complete a single trial.'

Jack now knew for certain that Hiroto had beaten him. Now he just wanted to get the formality over with so he could join Yamato on the sidelines, but his guardian continued, 'You didn't finish the Gauntlet. Then again, no one has ever reached the end of the Gauntlet as you did. Sensei Hosokawa was most impressed with your performance. He passed you, despite your error at the last stage. But there were opposing opinions. We therefore agreed to defer the final decision to Sensei Kano.'

So it *hadn't* been Yamato the sensei had argued over. It had been him all along. Jack felt the great grey eyes of the *bō* master upon him, and although he knew the man could not see, Jack knew the sensei was observing him with all his other senses.

'I need not remind you that the Circle of Three is not only difficult but dangerous. It can even be fatal. Therefore we do not make such decisions lightly. On balance, while Sensei Kano feels you are worthy, this is only on his proviso that you undertake extra training sessions with him, in addition to any Circle preparation required.'

For a moment Jack was unsure that he had heard correctly. Did this mean he had gained entry to the Circle or not?

Then the students began clapping, though not with the enthusiasm afforded Kazuki and the other successful entrants. But Jack didn't care. He was in the Circle and Hiroto wasn't! Karma for the kick in the ribs, thought Jack as Hiroto slunk off to the sidelines, glaring at Jack all the way.

'Now I want to remind all the entrants who didn't succeed that simply by participating you've proved you have the courage to become a samurai warrior,' reaffirmed Masamoto, and he personally acknowledged the group on the sidelines by bowing his head to indicate the sincerity of his respect.

Then he faced the five successful students in the centre of the hall: Tadashi, Akiko, Harumi, Kazuki and Jack.

'For the five who journey onwards, I have this advice. In a fight between a strong body and a strong technique, technique will prevail. In a fight between a strong technique and a strong mind, mind will prevail because it will find the weak point in your opponent. While many of you are approaching this understanding, only one student has embraced the knowledge necessary to achieve this.'

Kazuki allowed himself a self-satisfied smile at the forthcoming praise which he believed was his due. But the smile twisted into a grimace of disbelief as Masamoto announced, 'Yori, step forward. You will join them in the Circle.'

A gasp of astonishment arose from the school and everyone looked around for the little boy. A reluctant Yori was pushed forward by the students closest to him and he shuffled into the centre, as startled and helpless as a newborn lamb.

28

BREAK-IN

'I still can't believe he hit you while you were bowing, Jack,' said Saburo the following day as they relaxed in the Southern Zen Garden between lessons. They had gathered on the wooden veranda overlooking the water feature and standing stones. The garden was now cloaked in so much snow that it looked like a miniature landscape of white clouds and snow-capped mountain peaks.

Jack gave Saburo a pained smile and massaged his neck where the *bokken* had struck.

'Sensei Hosokawa *was* the final part of the Gauntlet,' Akiko reminded them as she played *ohajiki* with Kiku, flicking one coin-shaped pebble across the ground at another, then claiming it as it was struck out of play. 'Would you bow in the middle of a fight?'

'No, but you have to admit it was rather sneaky of him.'

'Well, I still don't see why Jack got in and I didn't,' muttered Yamato, moodily poking at the snow with his *bokken*. 'It's favouritism if you ask me, just because he's *gai—*'

'Yamato!' exclaimed Akiko, glaring at her cousin. 'Jack

got further than any student in the history of the Gauntlet. He deserves to be entered.'

'Sorry,' said Yamato, offering Jack an apologetic smile. 'I'm still a little sore about it all.'

Yamato pulled aside the jacket of his training *gi* to inspect the purple mass of bruises spread across his right side. Jack realized he must have been hit extremely hard during the Gauntlet. He also recognized his friend was hurting badly from the shame of failing in the trials. Jack let the insult go and hoped that their friendship wouldn't be ruined by the turn of events.

'I bet that hurts,' Saburo said, giving Yamato's side an explorative prod with his finger.

'Oww!' exclaimed Yamato, shoving Saburo's hand away.

'You big baby,' teased Saburo.

'Well, see how you like it!'

Yamato began to pummel Saburo with his fists. The others laughed as Saburo cartwheeled backwards off the veranda and into the snow.

'You forget, Saburo, I went through all that pain and training for *nothing*!' yelled Yamato, jumping down and grabbing a handful of snow before shoving it in Saburo's face.

'Leave him alone, Yamato,' chided Akiko, worried that Yamato's anger at himself was turning nasty.

'That's easy for *you* to say. You and Jack are in the Circle. I'm not!'

'Don't forget . . . Yori,' spluttered Saburo under the continuing barrage of blows and snow.

'That's a point. Where is Yori?' asked Kiku quickly, trying to divert Yamato from the escalating fight.

Yamato stopped his assault. 'The ungrateful little genius is over there.' He indicated the gnarled pine tree at the far end of the garden, its trunk propped up by the wooden crutch.

Yori was squatting under one of its snow-shrouded branches, listlessly pulling at the tail of an *origami* crane, making its wings flap. Despite their best efforts to console him, Yori hadn't uttered a single word since the shock announcement in the *Butokuden* the day before.

'Don't be such a sore loser,' said Akiko to Yamato. 'Yori hadn't entered and didn't want to.'

'So why should he get to go? The sensei had said only five students would be entered in the Circle. There are plenty of other students who would give their sword arms for that extra place. And *I'm* one of them,' said Yamato, releasing Saburo and dusting the snow from his kimono in angry swipes.

'But he did pass a trial, Yamato. And I'm sorry, but you didn't.'

'I know,' admitted Yamato, slumping back down on the veranda. 'But Yori wasn't even tested in the physical trials. How do they know he's ready?'

'Are any of us?' said Jack.

'Well, you aren't. You were only *just* accepted,' Yamato was quick to point out.

'Yes. That's why I have to take extra tuition from Sensei Kano,' added Jack by way of an excuse.

'You'll need it.'

'You're right. I will. And I'll need your help too, if you're up for it.'

'What do you mean?' demanded Yamato, turning to face Jack.

'Sensei Kano said I needed a training partner. I was hoping it would be you.'

Yamato deliberated before answering and Jack thought he would refuse as a matter of pride.

'Come on. It would be like our old sparring days in Toba,' urged Jack.

Recognizing the gesture for what it was, his friend managed to muster up a half-hearted smile. 'Thanks, Jack. Of course I will. You know I'd never miss an opportunity to beat you up!'

Later that evening, Jack heard Yori sobbing in his room. Deciding that his friend needed company, he knocked on his door.

'Come in,' sniffled Yori.

Jack slid back the *shoji* and stepped inside. There was barely enough space for him to stand, let alone sit down, not just because the bedroom was so small, but due to the fact that Yori's room was littered with *origami* cranes. Despite this, Yori was still making more, and there was a feverish anxiety to his labours.

Jack cleared a space and sat down beside his friend. Yori barely acknowledged him, so Jack decided to help him in his task. After folding his fifth crane, though, he could no longer contain his curiosity.

'Yori, why are you folding so many paper cranes? You've solved the *koan*.'

'*Senbazuru Orikata*,' replied Yori sullenly.

'What's that?' Jack asked, his brow wrinkling in puzzlement.

'According to legend,' Yori continued, tetchy at being distracted from his task, 'anyone who folds a thousand *origami* cranes will be granted their wish by a crane.'

'Really? So what's your wish going to be?'

'Can't you guess . . . ?'

Jack thought he could, but, since Yori was in no mood to talk, he let the matter rest. As all conversation died, Jack stood to stretch his legs and stepped over to the little window. He stared out over the courtyard and gazed at the snowflakes floating through the night. If he had the patience to fold one thousand cranes, Jack knew what he would wish for. It would be the same wish he had asked of the Daruma Doll.

His thoughts wandered to Jess. What would his little sister be doing now? He hoped she was getting up to have breakfast with Mrs Winters. He didn't want to think of the alternative.

Not wanting to worsen the mood in the room with his own melancholic thoughts, Jack returned to the task at hand. He picked up a sheet of paper to fold yet another crane.

The pile of *origami* paper was soon used up, and Yori quietly thanked him for his help and said he would get more the next day. While he couldn't quite muster a smile, he did seem less despondent about his situation and he had stopped crying, so Jack left and headed to bed. Sliding open the *shoji* to his own room, he stopped dead in his tracks.

His bedroom had been ransacked.

The *futon* was unrolled and ripped open; his ceremonial

kimono, training *gi* and *bokken* lay discarded upon the floor; and the Daruma Doll and *bonsai* had been knocked off the window sill, the little tree now lying on its side, its roots exposed and earth spilt everywhere.

Jack's first thought was *Kazuki*. It was exactly the sort of thing he or one of his Scorpion Gang would do. He scanned the room to see if anything had been taken. To his relief, he found Masamoto's swords under the ceremonial kimono and spotted his sister's drawing crumpled but intact beneath the *bonsai*'s pot, his *inro* carrying case discarded to one side. He then looked under the *futon* and realized what was missing.

Jack stormed up the now deserted corridor to Kazuki's room and flung open his *shoji*.

'Where is it?' accused Jack.

'Where's what?' replied an indignant Kazuki, who was in the process of polishing a gleaming samurai sword of black and gold that his father had presented to him upon the news of his acceptance into the Circle.

'You know exactly what I mean. Now give it back!'

Kazuki glared at Jack, his left eye still swollen and discoloured by the bruising he had sustained during the Gauntlet. 'Get out of my room!' he demanded. 'What sort of samurai do you think I am to steal from you? That might be something a *gaijin* would do, but never a Japanese.'

Then a malicious smile spread across his face as he saw Jack's distress. 'But if you do find out who did it, remind me to thank them.'

Jack cursed. Despite Kazuki's arrogance, he seemingly had nothing to do with the break-in. Perhaps it had been

Hiroto, getting his own back for Jack beating him in the trials. Jack glanced down the empty corridor and froze.

Creeping out of his room was a figure dressed head-to-toe in white. It held the leatherbound book in its grasp.

'Stop!' cried Jack.

The dark pebble eyes of the ghostly figure locked with his. It fled down the corridor as silent as the falling snow and out of the *Shishi-no-ma*.

Jack flew after it. He raced past startled students, who had emerged to see what the disturbance was, and out into the cold night air.

He spotted the figure sprinting across the courtyard and followed.

'Give it back!' Jack shouted, gaining on the intruder.

The figure reached the edge of the courtyard and launched itself at the school walls. Jack clambered up after the thief, his hands grabbing hold of the bottom of a white jacket. He wrenched back as hard as he could, but was kicked in the chest for his efforts and sent sprawling into the snow. Momentarily stunned, Jack could only watch as the intruder continued to scale the wall with cat-like grace.

Then, without looking back, the white-clad figure disappeared into the snowy night.

29

THE DECOY

'Do you really think it was Dragon Eye?' asked Yamato as he helped Jack tidy his room. 'It's been a long time since he showed himself.'

Jack was smoothing out his sister's picture and wiping off the earth that had fallen on to it from the *bonsai*. Since Jack usually kept the drawing hidden in his *inro*, the intruder had clearly been carrying out a thorough search of his room.

'It had to be, but he sent someone else this time. Unless he's managed to grow another eye!' replied Jack sarcastically, remembering the two dark eyes that had peered at him through the slit of the ninja's hood.

'But who's ever heard of a white ninja? It must have been a disguise. Are you sure it wasn't one of Kazuki's Scorpion Gang playing a trick on you? I mean, ninja always wear black.'

'At night, yes,' interrupted Akiko, who suddenly appeared at the doorway, dressed in a pink petal sleeping kimono. 'But with the snow, they would stand out as if it was the middle of the day. Their *shinobi shozoku* is for camouflage and concealment, so they wear black at night, white in the winter and green in the forests.'

'Where have you been all this time?' demanded Jack, irritable she'd not been around to help.

It was now very late and, apart from Yamato and Akiko, the other students had got bored and gone to bed. No one else but Jack had seen the white ninja. That was fine with Jack. He didn't want people asking questions. He had even told Saburo that Hiroto had wrecked his room, so that he didn't have to reveal the existence of the *rutter* to another of his friends.

'I was having a bath,' replied Akiko, looking round the overturned room in shock. 'What happened here? Has anything been stolen?'

'Dragon Eye returned,' replied Jack, gathering up his swords, 'and yes, something was taken.'

'Not the *rutter*!' she exclaimed.

Jack shook his head.

'No. Father Lucius's Japanese dictionary. The one he gave me in Toba. The one that I was supposed to deliver to Father Bobadilla in Osaka when I got the chance. Looks like I'll have to break that promise.'

'Why would anyone want to take a dictionary?' asked Yamato, his brow wrinkling in puzzlement.

'I don't think they were looking for the dictionary, do you?' Jack replied, picking up the Daruma Doll and putting it back on the window sill next to the *bonsai*. 'At a glance, Father Lucius's book could be mistaken for the *rutter*. I left the dictionary under my *futon* as a decoy. Whoever took it wouldn't have known the difference unless they looked inside. I must have disturbed them in the middle of their search.'

'What? The ninja was in here with you?' asked an incredulous Yamato. 'Why didn't you see him?'

'He must have been hanging over my head,' explained Jack, shuddering. 'See those damp patches on the wall above the door. That's where snow's melted. The ninja must have wedged himself between the cross-beam and the ceiling.'

'It's possible,' agreed Akiko. 'Ninja learn from an early age how to climb and perform acrobatics. Supposedly, they're taught how to hang on to tree branches with just one finger.'

'How do you know all this?' asked Yamato, amazed.

'So where's the *rutter* now if Dragon Eye hasn't got it?' Akiko continued, ignoring her cousin.

Jack hesitated. He couldn't afford to take any more risks with his father's logbook and was reluctant to tell them. When he had visited Nijo Castle with Emi, he'd managed to excuse himself from her company under pretext of needing to relieve himself. He'd been on his own long enough to hide it behind the wall hanging of the white crane. The *rutter* was safe for the time being. It was the perfect hiding place, but only as long as no one else knew about it.

'Jack, you can trust us,' insisted Akiko. 'Besides we can help protect it, if we know where it is. Dragon Eye will realize soon enough that he has stolen a decoy and will come seeking the real *rutter*.'

Jack considered them both a moment longer. They were his friends. His closest friends. He had to trust them and

Akiko was right. They might be able to help him. But he wouldn't tell them everything – not yet.

'You know I mentioned that I'd returned to Nijo Castle with Emi . . . ?'

'Yes,' said Akiko rather coolly.

'I'm sorry I didn't tell you at the time, but I'm sure there are things you don't tell me too,' added Jack tetchily, allowing the accusation to hang in the air for the briefest of moments. 'Anyway, I went alone with Emi for a reason. I've hidden the *rutter* inside the castle.'

'In the castle? But why there?' Yamato asked.

'*Daimyo* Takatomi has made the castle ninja-proof. Where better to hide the *rutter* from a ninja as devious as Dragon Eye?'

'Jack, I can't believe you've done this,' Akiko snapped, glaring at him as if he'd just committed a terrible crime.

'What do you mean?' said Jack. 'It's the safest place for it. Why are you acting as if I've killed someone?'

'You haven't yet, but you *have* put the *daimyo* Takatomi's life in danger!' she said, shaking her head in disbelief at Jack's stupidity. 'Dragon Eye will now break into the castle to get it.'

'How can that possibly happen? Even if Dragon Eye did try, he'd be caught out by the Nightingale Floor and captured by the guards before he got anywhere near the *daimyo*,' argued Jack. 'Besides, how can the *daimyo* be in danger when only the three of us know the *rutter*'s location? Dragon Eye would never think of looking there, and we're certainly not going to tell him.'

30

STICKY HANDS

'Shall I let you into a secret? I'm not really blind . . .'

Jack knew it. The *bō* master had been faking all the time. That would explain why he could guide his students into the mountains, trick Kazuki and wield the *bō* so skilfully. He simply fooled people into believing he was blind.

'I just can't see,' finished Sensei Kano in his deep sonorous voice.

'I don't understand,' said Jack and Yamato in unison, the icy winter air making their breath puff out in large clouds of mist.

They had returned to the gardens of the Eikan-Do Temple. The glorious reds and oranges of autumn were all gone now, replaced with bare skeletons of trees frosted in winter snow. The three of them sat on a stone bench next to a slender wooden footbridge. The wide stream passing beneath it was iced over, though further up the slope a small waterfall still trickled and ran beneath the surface to the frozen pond in the middle of the gardens.

'People think that seeing is the perception of the world

through the eyes. But is it?' questioned Sensei Kano, waving the tip of his staff at the scene before them.

He picked up some pebbles from the path and passed one to each of his two trainees.

'When you see a stone, you are also feeling it with your mind's hand. Seeing is as much touching as it is sight, but because the sense of vision is so overwhelming, you are unaware of the importance of touch.'

'But without being able to see, how did you ever learn to fight in the first place?' Yamato asked.

'Disability doesn't mean inability,' the sensei replied, throwing his own pebble into the air and striking it with his staff. The pebble landed on the pond and skittered across the ice. 'It just means adaptability. I've had to use my other senses. I've learnt to feel my way through life. I've become adept at sniffing out danger and tasting fear in the air. And I've taught myself to listen to the world around me.'

Sensei Kano stood up and walked towards the stream.

'Close your eyes and I will show you what I mean.' He continued to talk to them while moving around, emphasizing each step with the thud of his *bō* striking the ground. 'In these sessions, I'm going to train you in sensitivity techniques. You're going to learn to use everything but your sight. Can you both point to where I am standing?'

Jack and Yamato raised their hands to indicate his position.

'Open your eyes. Were you correct in your assumption?'

'*Hai*, Sensei,' they replied in unison, pointing to their teacher on the bridge.

198

'I would hope so. If you can hear me, then you know where I am. Close your eyes again. Aside from the sounds that your opponent may make, don't forget the background noise that will also indicate where they are. The human body creates a sound shadow, just like a light shadow cast by the sun. If you listen out for the hole in the background noise, you can determine the position of your attacker even if they remain silent. So listen to the sounds around you, then tell me where I've moved to.'

Jack tried to follow the *bō* master's movements with his ears, but, with Sensei Kano now maintaining silence, it was impossible to judge his progress. Instead Jack had to focus on the noises he could hear.

Yamato's breathing.

The trickle of the waterfall.

The distant bustle of the city.

A lone bird calling among the treetops.

Then . . . he swore he heard the waterfall fade ever so slightly.

'You're in front of the waterfall,' deduced Jack.

'Excellent. Very perceptive, Jack-kun,' praised Sensei Kano as Yamato and Jack reopened their eyes. 'We will begin with that exercise every day until you can recognize a sound shadow in most environments. Now let's progress on to the touch techniques of *chi sao*.'

'*Chi sao*?' queried Yamato. 'What does that mean? It's not Japanese.'

'No, it's Chinese. *Chi sao* means "sticky hands",' explained Sensei Kano. 'It's a technique I learnt from a blind Chinese warrior in Beijing.'

Jack nudged Yamato and whispered, 'The blind leading the blind, eh?'

They both laughed. Yamato, apparently over his disappointment at not being selected for the Circle of Three, had apologized for his behaviour the day before and their friendship was back on solid ground.

'You could say that, Jack-kun,' Sensei Kano continued, giving them both a sharp rap on the head with his staff for their impudence, 'but *chi sao* is your gateway to understanding the internal aspects of martial arts – sensitivity, reflex, timing, coordination and positioning. It will teach you to undo your body's natural instinct to resist force with force and you will learn to yield to an attack and redirect it. Most importantly, you will learn to *see* with your hands. Come here, Jack-kun, and stand opposite me in fighting stance.'

When Jack was in position, Sensei Kano knelt on one knee so they were more or less of equal height. He then rested each of his hands on the outside of Jack's guard, so that he mirrored his stance.

'I want you to attack me. Any kick or punch will do. You're at zero range so you should be able to land something on an old blind man.'

Jack wasn't so sure, but he gave it a go anyway. He went for a basic jab to the face, direct and quick.

Instantly he found himself off-balance, his lead hand trapped and Sensei Kano's own fist in his face, the knuckles pressing against the tip of his nose.

'Try again.'

This time Jack kicked, a roundhouse to the ribs, but before he had even moved Sensei Kano had pushed against his shoulder. Jack had to step backwards to regain his balance. At the same time, Sensei Kano had thrust a spearhand strike directly at a pressure point in his throat, stopping just short.

Jack swallowed in astonishment.

He had lost before he had even started. It was as though Sensei Kano could read his mind.

'How do you do that?' asked Jack, amazed.

'I'm hearing you with my hands. I use my fingers to feel where your power is and as soon as you start to move, I counter by redirecting your energies then striking in retaliation,' he explained. 'You will learn this technique too. With time, you'll be able to intercept an attack before your opponent has completed a single move.'

Sensei Kano stood up and indicated for Yamato to take his place.

'To begin with, I want you to simply maintain contact with one another. Push and roll your forearms in a circle,' tutored Sensei Kano, guiding them in their initial circular movements. 'Stay relaxed. You're trying to feel the movements of your opponent and find gaps in their defence. The main principle in *chi sao* is to greet what arrives, escort what leaves and rush in upon any loss of contact.'

Jack and Yamato were clumsy at first and had to restart several times before they managed to achieve any kind of fluidity.

'No, don't lean into it, Jack-kun,' Sensei Kano instructed, his hands resting upon their shoulders so that he could judge their progress. 'The key to *chi sao* is to keep your centre and stay relaxed. Think of yourselves as bamboo shoots in the wind. Be rooted yet remain flexible. Then you will grow to be strong.'

The winter sun was low in the sky by the time Sensei Kano called an end to their training. Jack and Yamato had continued with the same drill all afternoon until Jack thought his arms were about to drop off, but gradually the two of them had found their rhythm and the circular motions had become faster and more fluid.

'Excellent work, boys,' commended the *bō* master as they wended their way through the snow-laden gardens and icy waterways in the direction of the *Niten Ichi Ryū*. 'In a few more sessions, I'll teach you how to trap one another's arms and spot the gaps you can attack into. It won't be long before you're doing *chi sao* blindfolded.'

'We'll never be able to do that,' snorted Yamato. 'It's hard enough now and we can see what we're doing.'

Without breaking his stride, Sensei Kano turned and walked straight across the frozen pond.

'Watch out!' cried Jack.

There was a splintering crack at the edges as the surface took Sensei Kano's weight, but incredibly the ice held.

'You would be amazed what things you can accomplish,' shouted Sensei Kano over his shoulder to his two astonished students, 'if only you have the courage to believe in yourself and trust your senses.'

31

YUKI GASSEN

'How's your training going?' enquired Tadashi.

He sat down next to Jack and the others on the stone steps of the *Butsuden*. Tadashi had been the first student to be chosen for the Circle of Three and, following the selection, had politely introduced himself to the other entrants. Tadashi and Jack then found themselves paired together in sword training, striking up an easy friendship.

'Good, I think,' replied Jack. 'Sensei Kano's tough, though. I just hope I'll be ready in time.'

Spring was now only two moons away and with it the flowering of the cherry-blossom trees that would herald the Circle of Three. Consequently, the sensei had begun to push their charges harder and harder. Jack and the five other entrants had been preparing for the Circle of Three for over a month and, like Jack, each of the participants had acquired a mentor. Yori's was Sensei Yamada. Akiko and Harumi had been taken on by Sensei Yosa, while Kazuki was on an intense training schedule set by Sensei Kyuzo. In addition to his own lessons with Sensei Kano, Jack was being coached along with Tadashi under the watchful eye of Sensei Hosokawa.

'And how about you, little warrior?' Tadashi asked, turning to Yori.

Yori didn't respond, but continued to gaze out at the thick blanket of snow covering the school's courtyard. Tadashi gave Jack a nudge and mouthed to ask if Yori was all right. Jack nodded, pointing to the side of his head to indicate Yori was a deep thinker.

'Sensei Yamada told me not to eat an elephant for lunch,' Yori eventually replied.

Everyone stared at Yori, bewildered by his statement. Jack began to wonder exactly what sort of lessons Sensei Yamada was teaching his little friend.

'How's that going to help you in the Circle of Three?' asked Saburo, looking baffled. 'It's impossible to eat an *entire* elephant.'

'Precisely,' said Kiku, shaking her head in exasperation. 'Don't you understand anything Sensei Yamada teaches us?'

'I would if he didn't always speak in riddles.'

'He's telling Yori not to get worried about the entire Circle of Three. Instead he should concentrate on one challenge at a time,' Kiku explained. Then, seeing Saburo's blank face, she continued, 'In other words, if you broke a large meal down into smaller pieces, you'd be able to eat it all without choking like a pig!'

'Got it!' exclaimed Saburo. 'Why didn't you just say that before?'

'That's good advice,' agreed Tadashi, 'but has anyone discovered what the three Circle challenges actually are?'

They all shook their heads. Beyond knowing that the

Circle referred to the three highest peaks in the Iga mountain range, the actual three challenges of Mind, Body and Spirit remained a mystery.

'It seems bizarre to me that you're training for something you know nothing about,' commented Yamato, kicking the snow off the step below. Despite his best efforts to remain cheerful, he was clearly still upset at not being selected for the Circle of Three.

'Sensei Yamada told me that's the point. Only the unknown terrifies man,' Yori revealed, his tiny hands trembling at the thought. 'We're preparing for the unknown.'

A snowball slammed into the side of Jack's face.

Jack cried out in shock, his cheek smarting with the cold.

'Bullseye!' shouted a familiar voice.

Jack wiped the icy remains away and glared at Kazuki, who had entered the courtyard with his friends. They all carried snowballs and were playfully tossing them them at one another.

Kazuki ducked as Moriko, the black-toothed wildcat from the rival *Yagyu Ryū*, threw one back at him. She squealed as Kazuki plastered her with two in quick succession. Jack now wasn't certain if Kazuki had purposely aimed at him or had simply missed Moriko. Kazuki and his friends continued to bombard one another.

To Jack's surprise, he noticed Kazuki's two hulking cousins among the group. Raiden and Toru were the twin brothers who had attacked Jack at the *hanami* party the previous year. Not only did it appear that Kazuki was recruiting Scorpion Gang members from the rival school, but he was bold enough to invite such students into the grounds of the *Niten Ichi Ryū* in broad daylight.

'Kazuki, you've dropped your *inro*,' said Tadashi casually, while reaching behind to scrape off a layer of snow from a higher step and compacting it into a ball behind his back.

Without thinking, Kazuki glanced down to look for his wooden carrying case. On looking up, he realized too late that he'd been tricked. Tadashi's snowball struck him square in the face. He yowled in surprise as half of it disappeared into his mouth.

Tadashi gave Jack a sly grin and they both burst into laughter. Everyone else joined in, even Kazuki's friends.

'Attack! Attack!' spluttered Kazuki, spitting out snow.

Spurred into action, the Scorpion Gang hurled their snowballs as hard as they could. Jack and Tadashi attempted to evade the barrage, but it was useless. They were completely exposed and several hit home.

Other students from the *Niten Ichi Ryū*, seeing the snowball fight start, began to congregate in the courtyard.

'Look, we've got spectators!' said Kazuki, a genuine smile spreading across his face. 'Let's have a game of *Yuki Gassen*?'

'You're on!' shouted Tadashi, gathering more snow.

There was a murmur of excitement from the gathering crowd, whose numbers swelled as word of a snowball contest spread. Even the men working on the Hall of the Hawk downed tools to watch.

'How do you play *Yuki Gassen*?' Jack asked, seeing several groups of students start to build waist-high walls of snow across the courtyard.

'The aim is to capture the other team's *bokken*,' explained Yamato as Tadashi began to kick snow into a large pile a couple of paces in front of the *Butsuden*'s steps. 'Each team is allowed ninety balls. You can hide behind the snow walls, but if you get hit by a snowball, you're out.'

Tadashi removed his *bokken* and thrust it vertically into their mound like a flagless standard at the start of a battle. At the other end of the courtyard Kazuki did the same, then selected five of his friends to form his team. They huddled under the snow-laden eaves of the Hall of the Hawk's nearly completed roof.

'So who's going to be in our team?' asked Tadashi.

'You can count me out,' said Kiku immediately, hurrying over to the sidelines.

'Well, that leaves six,' he said, looking at Akiko, Yori, Saburo, Jack and Yamato. 'We have our team.'

They all began to build up their arsenal of snowballs. Soon they had six equal stacks around their *bokken*.

'Ready?' shouted Tadashi to Kazuki.

'Hang on,' replied Kazuki, poking his head up from his team huddle. 'We're discussing team tactics.'

'What are *our* tactics?' asked Yori, in a timorous voice.

Tadashi studied the layout of the battle area. At the centre of the rectangular courtyard was a waist-high wall of snow. Set back on either side were two shorter snow-wall shelters, then a couple of sloping mounds and finally a waist-high semi-circular wall around each team's *bokken*.

Tadashi frowned. 'Kazuki's clever, he's pitched his *bokken* right next to the Hall of the Hawk and the building work stops us approaching from behind.'

The team glanced at their own *bokken*, which was dangerously exposed to attack from the rear.

'OK, here's the plan. Yori and Yamato, you stay back to defend the *bokken*.' Yamato was about to protest, but Tadashi continued. 'We need strength at the back and Yamato, you look to be the best thrower among us. Saburo and Akiko, you take the middle ground to cover Jack and me, while we launch the attack.'

They all nodded in agreement and took up their positions to start.

Kazuki and his team gave a great shout, then split apart and positioned themselves strategically across the courtyard. Nobu and Raiden stayed at the back, while Goro and Moriko took midfield, leaving Kazuki and Hiroto up front.

'Who's going to referee?' shouted Tadashi.

'I will,' offered Emi, emerging from the crowd.

She beckoned the team leaders over.

Kazuki and Tadashi faced off.

'Remember, this is a friendly game and my decisions are final,' said Emi, making eye contact with both of them to ensure their understanding.

Jack immediately recognized her father's natural authority in her.

'What are your team names?' she asked.

'The Scorpions,' stated Kazuki with pride, raising his arms skyward.

A loyal cheer erupted from the sidelines.

'And your team, Tadashi?'

Tadashi looked back over his shoulder at Yamato.

'The Phoenix Team,' he replied, a round of applause immediately breaking from the crowd.

Jack saw Yamato nod at Tadashi and grin. It was a good choice, the phoenix being Yamato's family *kamon*.

'Take up your positions,' announced Emi, and the excited spectators roared their approval. '*Yuki Gassen* will begin in five . . . four . . . three . . . two . . . one!'

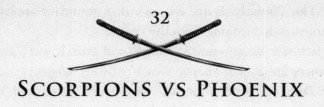

32

SCORPIONS VS PHOENIX

A volley of snowballs flew through the air and Jack dived behind the nearest snow wall.

'OUT!' cried Emi.

There was a great cheer from the crowd and for a moment Jack thought he'd already been caught. Then he saw Saburo wiping the remains of two snowballs from the front of his kimono. His friend gave a half-hearted bow before slouching off to the sidelines.

'Jack! To your right!' warned Akiko.

Taking advantage of Saburo's departure, Hiroto was sneaking forward and now had Jack directly in his line of fire.

Jack ducked as a snowball whizzed past his head. He threw two balls back in retaliation but they missed, striking the spectators instead. A mixture of catcalls and boos broke from the crowd. Jack retreated to behind a snow mound on his left, randomly throwing balls as he ran.

'They're going to overrun us if we don't attack!' shouted Tadashi over the growing chants of the Scorpion Team's supporters.

With that he launched several snowballs at Moriko, who was advancing down the right.

'OUT!' cried Emi.

Pretending she hadn't heard, Moriko kept lobbing snowballs.

'OUT! Or forfeit the game!'

Moriko kicked the nearest snow wall in frustration and hissed at Emi. The Phoenix supporters booed Moriko's dishonourable behaviour.

'Cover me!' shouted Jack as he sprinted forward to join Tadashi behind the central wall.

Akiko and Yori let loose a round of snowballs. Three of them struck the lumbering figure of Raiden as he stepped out from behind his defence to target Jack.

'OUT!' announced Emi.

The Scorpion Team retaliated with a barrage of snowballs. A moment later, there was a squeal of pain from behind.

'OUT!'

'They're using ice balls!' cried Yori, a large bump already swelling on his forehead as he staggered to the sidelines.

Tadashi gave Jack an uneasy look. 'And I thought this was supposed to be a friendly game.'

Tadashi stood up and quickly blasted Kazuki's team with several balls. The rest of the Phoenix Team joined in, but despite a courageous offensive, a long shot from Kazuki took out Akiko. Fortunately the ice ball struck her arm and not her face.

Only Jack, Tadashi and Yamato were now left against four Scorpions.

Tadashi spotted Nobu trying to ferry ice balls to Kazuki.

Launching a lightning attack, he managed to smack Nobu twice in the rear.

'OUT!'

'Shame we're not using ice balls,' commented Tadashi, giving Jack a mischievous grin.

'Or snowballs for that matter,' replied Jack. 'I've run out.'

With the fight now three on three, their main problem was the dwindling supply of ammunition. Tadashi indicated he only had five left, but he nonetheless passed three to Jack.

Tadashi then spotted Saburo's original stockpile by the *bokken* and signed his intention to get them. Jack threw a covering shot at Kazuki while Tadashi zigzagged towards them. Tadashi dived the last few paces but was plastered by two ice balls from Hiroto and Goro.

'OUT!'

Tadashi thumped the snow in annoyance, then got up and and walked off the court. As he did so, he secretly signed to Jack where one of the Scorpion Team was hiding. Jack nodded his understanding.

'*Scorpions! Scorpions! Scorpions!*' chanted the supporters of Kazuki's team.

Jack and Yamato now stood alone in defence of the Phoenix *bokken* and the small group keeping up a chorus of 'Phoenix!' were in danger of being drowned out.

Yamato indicated to Jack he was out of snowballs. Jack pointed to Saburo's pile. Yamato took a deep breath and darted over to them, sliding behind the semi-circular snow wall as an ice ball skimmed overhead.

As Yamato attempted to pass Jack some snowballs, Goro had a clear view of him. He emerged from behind his defence but Jack, having been tipped off by Tadashi, was ready for him and flung a snowball at the Scorpion. It struck him cleanly, but too late. Goro had already launched his ice ball at Yamato.

'OUT! OUT!' declared Emi in quick succession, dismissing both Goro and Yamato.

Now it was two against one.

Jack peered from behind the protection of his shelter, trying to locate Kazuki and Hiroto. They had retreated to their *bokken* and were huddled safely behind the semi-circular rear wall plotting their strategy to get the Phoenix's *bokken* without being hit by Jack.

Jack had one snowball left. How on earth was he going to defeat them both? Jack ran for Saburo's remaining stockpile, but a barrage of ice balls sent him diving for cover behind the nearest mound. It was then that Jack's eyes fell upon the shattered remains of one of the ice balls. Hidden inside was a shard of rock. Not only had the Scorpions compacted their snowballs into ice, they had now made them doubly dangerous.

Jack didn't know what to do. He had a single snowball. He could attempt to reach the remaining stockpile, but he would surely get hit and seriously injured. He could surrender, but he was certain Kazuki would throw his lethal iceballs anyway. Or . . .

Carefully peering round the edge of his snow mound, he spotted the perfect target. Ducking back down as an ice ball sailed past, he grabbed a couple of handfuls of extra snow and squeezed them together with his remaining snowball until he'd compacted it into a large ice ball of his own. Then, with all his strength, he lobbed it high and hard over the heads of Kazuki and Hiroto.

The Scorpions' supporters heckled loudly at Jack's wild pitch.

Jack ignored them. Instead he watched the ice ball sail up on to the peak of the Hall of the Hawk's roof. He smiled in satisfaction as it slowly began to roll down the steep angled roof.

'Pathetic!' cried Kazuki with glee.

But, unbeknown to Kazuki, the ice ball had picked up speed gathering powder snow as it went. As it reached the heavily laden eaves, its momentum caused the amassed snow to cascade like an avalanche. Kazuki and Hiroto glanced up just in time to see a wave of powder snow come crashing down on them. Within seconds, they were buried up to their necks. As more and more snow slid off the roof, they rapidly disappeared from view, much to the amusement of the crowd.

Jack emerged from behind his shelter, strolled over to the Scorpion Team's *bokken* and lifted it high above his head in a victory salute.

'I pronounce the Phoenix Team the winners!' Emi announced, smiling broadly at Jack.

The rest of the Phoenix Team rushed over, lifting Jack high into the air to cheers from all the spectators.

'Brilliant!' shouted Yamato.

'Inspired!' agreed Tadashi, slapping Jack hard on the back.

However, their celebrations were cut short by the jeering from the Scorpion Team.

'The *gaijin* cheated!'

'He played without honour!'

'Nothing in the rules require snowballs to be aimed directly at an opponent,' declared Tadashi above the shouting. 'No question about it, we won.'

Jack couldn't help but smile as he watched Kazuki and Hiroto being dug out of the snow. He had beaten the Scorpion Team.

But his smile faded as an irate and shamed Kazuki shouted for all to hear, '*Gaijin*, you're going to pay for that with your life!'

33

MUSHIN

'I'm going to kill you!' roared the samurai.

Jack didn't know what to do. The sudden attack had taken him off-guard.

Sensei Hosokawa had gone crazy, his dark eyes merciless and intent on murder. He was charging directly at him with a razor-sharp *katana* and Jack realized that in the blink of an eye he'd be sliced open like a pig, his guts spilled out across the *dojo* floor.

Only a few moments before Jack had been training with Tadashi in the *Butokuden* in preparation for the Circle, barely a month away. Suddenly, out of nowhere, Jack had caught a gleam of steel and had spun round to see Sensei Hosokawa bearing down on him, his sword drawn.

Sensei Hosokawa struck with lightning speed, the *katana* emitting a high whistling sound as it carved across Jack's chest and down past his stomach.

Jack shakily looked down, afraid of what he might see. But his entrails weren't spread all over the floor. His belly remained intact. He was completely unharmed. The only thing cleaved apart had been his *obi*. The belt, sliced in two, fell to the floor in a defeated heap.

'You're dead,' stated Sensei Hosokawa.

Jack swallowed back his shock, unable to respond. Gradually it dawned on him that this attack had been a ruthless lesson in martial arts.

'You were thinking too much,' Sensei Hosokawa continued, resheathing his sword. 'You allowed yourself to be scared and it caused you to hesitate. If you hesitate in battle, you die.'

Sensei Hosokawa looked at both his students, ensuring they understood the warning.

'B–but I thought you'd gone crazy,' stammered Jack, suddenly regaining his voice. He trembled with a combination of shock and shame at being the victim of a sword stunt in front of his new friend Tadashi. He felt belittled. 'I really thought you were going to kill me!'

'No, but next time the attack could be for real,' replied Sensei Hosokawa gravely. 'The three evils for a samurai are fear, doubt and confusion. You just displayed all of them.'

'So I'm not good enough? Is that what you're telling me?' snapped Jack, his frustration at his progress boiling to the surface. 'Am I ever going to be? It seems there's always something wrong with my technique. Why aren't I getting any better?'

'Mastering the Way of the Sword is a long road,' explained Sensei Hosokawa kindly. 'Rushing it only hastens your death. *Ichi-go, Ichi-e*. Have you heard that phrase before?'

Jack nodded, remembering the calligraphy on the scroll in *daimyo* Takatomi's golden tea room.

'One chance in a lifetime. That is all you ever get in a

sword fight.' Sensei Hosokawa looked Jack in the eye. 'I want to give you that chance.'

Jack studied his feet, embarrassed by his outburst when his teacher was only trying to help.

'The Gauntlet was all about *fudoshin*,' Sensei Hosokawa continued. 'You were being tested on whether you were able to control your body *and* mind under the pressure of an impossible battle. You proved yourself capable of *fudoshin* then, but fear and confusion during my attack now made you hesitate. You must learn to stare death in the face and react without hesitation. No fear. No confusion. No hesitation. No doubt.'

'But how could I have known that you would attack me? I was concentrating on sparring with Tadashi.'

'*Mushin*,' stated Sensei Hosokawa.

'*Mushin*?'

'*Mushin* means possessing a state of "no mind".'

Sensei Hosokawa began to pace the floor as he always did when he lectured a class. 'When a samurai is faced by an opponent, he must not mind the opponent; he must not mind himself; he must not mind the movement of his enemy's sword. A samurai possessing *mushin* doesn't rely on what move they think should be next. They act intuitively. *Mushin* is a spontaneous knowledge of every situation as it occurs.'

'But how should I know what's going to happen in a fight? Do you mean samurai have to see into the future?'

Sensei Hosokawa chuckled, amused at Jack's suggestion.

'No, Jack-kun, though it may appear that they do. You have to train your mind to be like water, openly flowing

218

towards any possibility. This is the ideal mental state of a warrior in combat, one where you expect nothing, but are ready for anything.'

'So how do I get *mushin*?'

'First you must practise your cuts many thousands of times, until you can perform them instinctively, without conscious thought or hesitation. Until your sword becomes "no sword".'

Jack glanced at Tadashi, who quietly stood by absorbing everything that was said. He wondered if Tadashi under-stood this concept of 'no sword'.

'I don't understand,' Jack admitted, hoping he wouldn't appear stupid. 'How can my *katana* become "no sword"? How can it no longer exist?'

'Your aim is to achieve unity between yourself and the sword.'

Sensei Hosokawa swiftly unsheathed his *katana* and held it aloft.

'Once the sword exists only in your heart and mind,' said Sensei Hosokawa, pressing the tip of his blade against Jack's chest exactly where his heart lay, 'then it becomes "no sword". For when you strike, it isn't you but the sword in the hand of your mind that strikes.'

Jack understood only a little of what his sensei was say-ing. He realized the sword master was teaching him great things, vital skills that he needed, but at the same time the sensei seemed to be tying one arm behind his back. If he was worthy of the Circle of Three and this concept of 'no sword' was so important, why wouldn't Sensei Hosokawa allow him to train with a real blade?

'But, with all respect, if you won't let me use my *katana*, how can I make my sword become "no sword"?'

Sensei Hosokawa's face suddenly became hard as stone. 'When you begin to grasp *mushin*, then I will permit you to train with a sword.'

Jack grasped at this new glimmer of hope. Eager to pursue 'no mind' training, he asked, 'How long will it take me to master *mushin*?'

'Five years,' replied Sensei Hosokawa.

'That long! I can't wait five years,' despaired Jack. 'What if I work really hard at it?'

'Then you will need ten years.'

Mystified by this illogical answer, Jack asked, 'Well, how about if I devote all my time to *mushin*?'

'Then you will need twenty years.'

34

GANJITSU

The immense temple bell, the size of a mountain boulder, rang out for the one hundred and eighth time, its deep sonorous *dong* resonating into the night. Spirals of incense smoke swirled through the air and candles fluttered in all corners of the Buddha Hall like a heavenly constellation of stars.

Jack stood in silence with the entire school as they waited for the slow swing of the long wooden pendulum hammer to come to a rest.

'GOOD FORTUNE FOR THE NEW YEAR!' announced Masamoto.

Dressed in his ceremonial flame-red phoenix robes, he stood before a large bronze statue of the Buddha.

The *Niten Ichi Ryū* was celebrating *Ganjitsu*, a festival that marked the beginning of the New Year. Jack had discovered that the Japanese celebrated New Year, not on the first of January like most Western countries, but according to the Chinese calendar several weeks later in anticipation of the arrival of spring.

It had been Sensei Yamada's honour to strike the temple

bell for the final time to mark midnight, and he now knelt before the Buddha shrine in order to bestow blessings upon the school.

Robed in their finest kimono, the students formed a line that coiled round the hall like a bejewelled dragon. Jack wore the burgundy silk kimono that Akiko's mother, Hiroko, had given him on leaving Toba. It bore Masamoto's phoenix *kamon*, picked out in fine golden thread so that it caught the light every time he moved. That though was nothing compared to Akiko's attire. She had a purple orchid in her hair and was dressed in a glorious yellow, green and blue sparkling kimono that appeared to be woven out of hundreds of butterfly wings.

'So why was the bell tolled exactly one hundred and eight times?' Jack asked as they waited in line to receive their first blessing of the year. The rituals of Buddhism were still bizarre to his Christian way of thinking.

Akiko didn't respond. When Jack looked, her attention was elsewhere, her eyes far away, and her face appeared paler than usual.

'Are you all right?' he asked.

Akiko blinked and her eyes came back into focus. 'Yes, I'm fine.'

Jack studied her a moment longer. She smiled back in response to his concern, but her eyes looked rheumy.

Beside her, Yori was fumbling with the sleeves of his kimono, which hung too long for his tiny frame. He answered Jack's question instead. 'Buddhists believe that man suffers from one hundred and eight desires or sins.

With each ring of the bell, one of these sins is driven out and the evils of the previous year forgiven.'

What a curious way to be pardoned, thought Jack, having been brought up believing only God and Christ alone had the power to forgive sins. Despite his scepticism, Jack thought he could still hear the bell ringing inside his head.

Then he realized Sensei Yamada was gently striking a large brass bowl while hammering out a hypnotic rhythm upon a wooden block and chanting softly to each student in turn. The bowl sounded as if it was singing, the note going round and round in an undying circle.

When it became their turn to be blessed, Akiko whispered, 'Follow what I do.'

Jack had considered not participating in the Buddhist ceremony, but he realized that with the growing animosity towards Christians and foreigners he needed to blend in as much as possible. Showing his willingness to accept Japanese beliefs might help him to win favour. Besides, as Sensei Yamada had once said, their religions were 'all strands of the same rug, only different colours'.

Jack carefully watched Akiko step up to a large urn full of sand, take a stick of incense from a nearby box and light it with a candle. She stuck the incense among the forest of burning sticks, the urn now resembling a huge smoking pincushion. Akiko then bowed twice in the direction of the bronze Buddha, following this with two hand claps and a final bow. Sensei Yamada beckoned Akiko over. She knelt down before him, bowed once more, then offered the monk her orchid as a gift.

Jack suddenly realized he hadn't brought a gift to offer

the Buddha. But before he could do anything about it, it was his turn. Without any other alternative, Jack stepped up to the urn, a large waft of woody incense filling his nostrils, and repeated the ritual that he had seen Akiko perform. He then knelt and bowed awkwardly before Sensei Yamada.

'I'm sorry, Sensei,' began Jack, bowing again by way of an apology, 'but I don't have anything to give.'

'Don't worry, Jack-kun. You're not yet familiar with all our customs,' said the old monk, smiling serenely back at him. 'The most perfect gift to offer is an honest and sincere heart. It is clear to me that is exactly what you've just brought to the altar and in return I will bestow my blessings upon you for the year.'

Sensei Yamada began a Buddhist chant that rolled from his lips and flowed warm and hypnotic into Jack's ears . . .

> *'Just as the soft rains fill the streams,*
> *pour into the rivers and join together in the oceans . . .'*

. . . the silken words weaved in and out of the chimes of the singing bowl and Jack felt his eyes begin to close . . .

> *'So may the power of every moment of your goodness*
> *flow forth to awaken and heal all beings . . .'*

. . . Jack's ears thrummed with each beat of the wooden block and he began to drift, his whole being gently vibrating . . .

> *'Those here now, those gone before, those yet to come.'*

He opened his eyes, his mind calmed and his heart filled with an expansive joy.

His Zen master bowed to indicate the blessing was over. Jack thanked him and got up to depart, when on an impulse he said, 'Sensei, may I ask you something?'

The old monk nodded. Recalling Sensei Hosokawa's riddle of the years, Jack continued, 'I have to master *mushin* quickly, but I don't understand how the harder I work at it, the longer it will take.'

'The answer is to slow down,' replied Sensei Yamada.

Jack stared at his teacher, mystified by yet another contradiction. 'But won't that take even longer?'

Sensei Yamada shook his head. 'Impatience is a hindrance. As with all things, if you attempt to take short cuts, the final destination will rarely be as good and may even be unattainable.'

Jack thought he understood and Sensei Yamada smiled, recognizing the glimmer of enlightenment in Jack's eyes.

'More haste, less speed, young samurai.'

Outside, the courtyard was empty of snow and the early signs of spring could be seen in the budding flowers of the surrounding cherry-blossom trees. Jack, Akiko and the others made their way over to the Hall of Butterflies where the *Ganjitsu* celebrations were to continue until dawn.

Inside the *Chō-no-ma*, tables had been laid with bowls of *ozoni* soup and plates piled high with sticky white rice cakes called *mochi*. Several groups of students were already tucking into the feast. A small crowd was gathered around two girls in the middle of the hall who were giggling loudly

225

as they batted a feathered shuttlecock between them with wooden paddles. Jack noticed that the face of one of the girls was covered in large black spots.

'What's going on?' asked Jack, sitting down at a free table.

'*Hanetsuki*,' Akiko replied, pouring each of them a cup of steaming *sencha*. 'If you fail to hit the shuttlecock, your face is marked with ink.'

A cheer and more laughter erupted as the girl missed the shuttlecock again and had to suffer another blotch of ink.

'May I join you?' asked Tadashi, bearing a plate of rice cakes.

Yamato and Saburo shuffled along to make room for him beside Jack.

'Here, try this,' suggested Tadashi, offering Jack a *mochi*.

Jack bit into the rice cake. While it was tasty, it was also very glutinous and he found it difficult to swallow. Tadashi laughed and slapped him on the back to stop him choking. Jack took several swigs of *sencha* to wash the rice cake down.

Tadashi offered the rice cakes to the rest of the table. Everyone tucked in, though Jack noticed Akiko didn't touch her food. Then he spotted Kazuki and his Scorpion Gang sit down at the table opposite.

Kazuki glanced over at Jack but ignored him. His friends began to clear the table of plates, while Kazuki dealt out a deck of cards across its surface. They huddled close as he selected a card from another pile and read its contents to the group. Immediately, there began a frenzy of card-snatching and boisterous shouting at one another.

'What's that they're playing?' asked Jack.

'*Obake Karuta*,' replied Tadashi, putting down his soup. 'One person reads out clues and the others have to match it to a legendary character or monster featured on one of the upturned cards. The player who accumulates the most cards by the end of the game wins.'

'Jack, I'll show you a game you should try,' Yamato announced, finishing his *sencha*. '*Fukuwarai*.'

'*Fuku*–what?' repeated Jack.

But Yamato merely beckoned him over to where a group of students was huddled round a picture of a face hung upon the wall. They were all laughing at a blind-folded girl who was trying to pin a mouth on to the face. Judging by the fact that the eyes and nose were located on its chin, she wasn't doing very well.

'Go on, Jack,' encouraged Yamato after the girl had pinned the mouth to the face's forehead, 'you have a go.'

Yamato grabbed Jack, blindfolded him and handed him the mouth. He then positioned him three paces in front of the blank face before spinning him round several times.

Completely disorientated and unable to see, Jack wondered how on earth he would even find the face, let alone pin the mouth in the correct place.

'He's got no chance,' he heard Tadashi say. 'He's not even looking the right way!'

It was then that Jack recalled Sensei Kano's words: '*To see with eyes alone is not to see at all.*' Using the sensitivity skills he'd been taught during the past couple of months, Jack listened to the crowd's whispers, judging where the paper face was in relation to the changes in background noise. Turning until he found the blank spot among the chatter, he figured he was now facing the wall. He then visualized the face in his mind's eye, took three confident paces forward and stuck the mouth on.

'Good work, Jack. Now the eyes and nose.'

Yamato spun him again, then handed him the other features. Once more Jack 'listened' for the face, using all his other senses to judge where to go. Once he finished, a stunned silence filled the air. Then everyone applauded.

'How did he do that?' exclaimed Tadashi to Yamato. 'He must have cheated. Jack, you couldn't see, could you?'

Shaking his head, Jack lifted the blindfold. In front of him was the picture of a perfectly proportioned face. Sensei Kano's *chi sao* training was clearly working.

'Beginner's luck,' explained Yamato, giving Jack a conspiratorial nudge with his elbow. They went back to the table to rejoin the others. Akiko was no longer among them.

'Where's Akiko?' Jack asked.

'She said she wasn't feeling very well and went to bed,' replied Kiku. 'She thinks it's something she drank.'

'Has anyone gone and checked on her?' said Jack, recalling how pale she had looked during the ceremony and her lack of appetite.

They all shook their heads. Worried, Jack excused himself and made his way over to the Hall of Lions.

Akiko wasn't in her room. He checked the bathhouse and toilets. She wasn't there either. He wondered if she had gone back to the party. Jack was about to return to the Hall of Butterflies, when he spotted a lone figure leaving the school via the side gate.

Jack ran out of the school gate and into the midst of a carnival.

35

HATSUHINODE

Kyoto's streets were full of revellers and each temple brimmed with worshippers. The entrances to every house were decorated with pine boughs, bamboo stalks and plum-tree sprigs as an invitation to the protecting spirit *toshigami* to bless the home; while the doors had been hung with plaited ropes festooned with strips of white paper to keep away evil spirits.

Jack spotted Akiko stumbling down the street. Although conscious of the monk's warning to respect his friend's privacy, he was more concerned at this moment about where she was going in such a sickly state. Pushing through the crowds, Jack tried to catch up with Akiko, following her down a side alley, across a market square and into a large tree-lined courtyard thronged with people. A group of drunken samurai bumped into Jack and he lost sight of Akiko among the mass of worshippers.

'Get out my way!' slurred one of the samurai, grabbing Jack by the lapel of his kimono.

The samurai lent close, his breath reeking sharply of *saké*.

'A *gaijin*,' he spat into Jack's face. 'What you doing here? This isn't your country.'

'You'd best leave him be,' advised another in the group, who pointed an unsteady finger at the phoenix *kamon* on Jack's kimono. 'He's Masamoto's. You know, the young *gaijin* samurai.'

The drunken man let go as if Jack's clothing were on fire.

'I'll be glad when *daimyo* Kamakura cleanses Kyoto, like he's doing in Edo,' snarled the samurai before staggering off into the crowd with his friends.

Jack was shaken by the encounter. Until now, he hadn't truly realized the danger he'd put himself in, wandering alone through Kyoto's backstreets. He was comparatively safe within the school grounds. Outside it was only Masamoto's reputation that protected him and he couldn't rely on everyone recognizing his guardian's family crest. He needed to find Akiko before he got himself into even more trouble.

Jack looked around nervously, but the majority of revellers were too wrapped up in their celebrations to give him more than a cursory glance. Then he recognized where he was. In front of him were the stone steps and arched green roof of the Temple of the Peaceful Dragon.

'Why are you following me?'

Jack spun round.

Akiko's ashen face stared at him out of the crowd.

'Kiku said you were sick . . .' replied Jack.

'Jack, I can look after myself. I've just drunk something that didn't agree with me, that's all.' She studied him severely. 'Anyway, you've followed me here before, haven't you?'

Jack nodded, feeling like a criminal caught red-handed.

'I appreciate your concern,' continued Akiko, though there was no warmth in her voice, 'but if I had wanted you to know where I was going, I would have told you.'

Jack realized that he'd lost Akiko's trust in him. 'I'm . . . so sorry, Akiko,' he stammered. 'I didn't mean to. It's just . . .'

Words failed him and he found himself staring at his own feet to avoid her gaze.

'It's just what?' she persisted.

'I . . . care for you and was worried.' The words blurted out of him without warning, then his feelings for her spilled over. 'Ever since I've been stranded here, all you've ever done is look after me. You've been my only true friend. But what have I ever done for you in return? I'm sorry for following you, but you were sick and I thought you might need my help. Can't I watch out for you too sometimes?'

The coldness in Akiko's eyes thawed and the icy distance that had come between them melted.

'Do you really want to know where I was going?' asked Akiko softly.

'Not if you don't want to tell me,' replied Jack, and he turned to leave.

'But I should tell you. You need to know,' insisted Akiko, laying a hand upon his arm to stop him going. 'It's my baby brother's birthday today.'

'You mean Jiro?' said Jack, surprised, remembering the cheerful little boy he had befriended in Toba over a year ago.

'No, I have another brother. His name is Kiyoshi.' Her

eyes misted at the mention of his name. 'Sadly he's no longer with us, so I was going to the shrine to pray for him. He would be eight today.'

The same age as Jess, thought Jack, and he felt a pang of anguish in his heart for his sister.

'I've missed him greatly this past year,' Akiko went on, 'so I've been seeking spiritual comfort from a priest, one of the monks at the Temple of the Peaceful Dragon.'

Jack now felt doubly guilty. This was the real reason behind her mysterious disappearances. She was mourning her baby brother.

'I'm sorry . . . I didn't know –'

'Don't be, Jack,' she interrupted, motioning with a nod of her head for him to follow her up the entrance steps of the temple. 'Why not come with me now to the shrine and make a blessing for my brother? Then we can climb Mount Hiei together in time for *hatsuhinode*.'

Akiko huddled closer to Jack for warmth.

They sat alone, in the shelter of a ruined temple wall at the edge of Enryakuji, overlooking Kyoto, which was hidden by early morning mist in the valley below. The frigid mountain air made them both shiver, but inside Jack was feeling a warm glow.

They had visited the little shrine within the Temple of the Peaceful Dragon. Akiko had briefly spoken with the monk in private and then together they had made their peace offerings and prayers to Kiyoshi. This shared experience was the first time Jack had felt included in Akiko's personal life. It was as if a screen had been pulled back to reveal a delicate tapestry that once seen would never be forgotten.

With Akiko's night excursions now explained, Jack felt at ease with her again. The monk with the knife-like hands seemed an unusual choice for a comforting priest, but who was he to question her choice. Jack still wondered at Akiko's inexplicable tree-scaling skills, but perhaps she had been telling the truth and had always been good at climbing. Whatever the explanation, Jack was just content to be feeling close to Akiko again.

Having wound their way up the steep mountain slopes of Mount Hiei, they now waited for *hatsuhinode*, the first sunrise of the year.

'New Year's Day is the key to unlocking the year,' Akiko explained dreamily, her breath fogging in the chilly air. 'It's a time of new beginnings. We think about the past year, bury the bad and remember the good, then make our resolutions for the New Year. We always pay special attention to the first time something is done, whether it's the first visit to a temple, the first sunrise or the first dream.'

'What's so important about your first dream?' Jack asked.

'It foretells your luck for the forthcoming year.'

Akiko looked up at Jack, her eyes sleepy, and yawned, the tiredness from staying up all night finally taking hold. Her face, though still pale, had lost its deathly pallor since visiting the monk, and her health appeared to be returning with the onset of a brand-new day.

'Dream well tonight,' she whispered.

Akiko drew closer to him and soon fell asleep on his shoulder.

Jack sat in silence, listening to the dawn chorus, as the first rays of the New Year sun began to warm them both.

36

THE NET WIDENS

Akiko lay motionless at the foot of the mountain.

But it was not a mountain Jack recognized. A great black volcanic cone thrusting out of the ground, its peak capped in ice and snow, the mountain dominated the landscape.

Jack stood upon a stony path that wound its way tortuously across broken ground towards the prone body of Akiko, who held a large lobed leaf in her left hand. Between the two of them scurried four black scorpions, their barbed tails twitching, their black beady eyes shiny with malice. A lone hawk soared across an empty sky, emitting a mournful rasping screech. Then suddenly one of the scorpions scuttled over to Akiko and arched its back to strike its stinger into her chest.

'AKIKO!' he screamed . . .

'Jack, I'm here,' came her reply, soft and gentle by his ear.

Jack's eyes snapped open.

Branches hung over him in a bower so thick with pink-white cherry blossom that they blotted out the bright blue sky and shaded him from the hot spring sunshine.

Jack sat up.

Akiko was beside him. Yamato and Kiku were there

too, leaning against the trunk of the tree and observing him with concern. Now he remembered where he was. It was the middle of spring and they had gone to one of Kyoto's many gardens for *hanami*, a flower-viewing party.

A southerly wind blew through and the blossom fell like teardrops on to the ground, some of the petals catching in Akiko's hair.

'It's all right. You were dreaming,' she soothed, brushing the blossom away. 'Was it the same one?'

Jack nodded, his mouth dry with dread. Yes, it was the same dream as his first of the year. He had told Akiko about it the day after New Year, though he still couldn't bring himself to reveal her part in the vision. At the time, he had sought Sensei Yamada's advice and the Zen master had divined, 'The mountain you see is Mount Fuji. Being our highest mountain and the home of many great spirits, its appearance in your dream signifies good luck. The hawk represents strength and quick-wittedness; while the leaf you describe sounds like that of an eggplant. Its name, *nasu*, can mean the achievement of something great. This bodes well for the future.'

Not a believer of dream divination until his experiences in Japan, Jack had breathed a sigh of relief at the sensei's positive reading. But then the old monk had continued, 'On the other hand, the presence of scorpions often symbolizes an act of treachery preventing such greatness. Moreover, the number *shi* is considered very bad luck. The word for "four" can also mean death.'

'You have to see this!' Saburo shouted, disrupting Jack's thoughts.

Saburo hurried breathlessly over to the cherry-blossom tree with Yori in tow. He was pointing to a large wooden sign being erected in the street. They all got up and left the garden to get a closer look.

'It's a declaration,' Yamato explained for Jack's benefit. 'It says, "Whoever wants to challenge me shall be accepted. Leave your name and place of abode upon this sign. Sasaki Bishamon."'

'Nice,' said Kiku in a sarcastic tone. 'A samurai on his warrior pilgrimage and he's named after the God of War!'

'Do you think we'll get to see a duel?' enthused Saburo, acting out a fight against an imaginary opponent.

'We won't be here,' Akiko reminded them as another gust of wind blew blossom from the trees, carpeting the ground in white. The fall of the blossom meant that the time for the Circle of Three had finally arrived.

Jack could not wait to go. He was desperate to discover what the three challenges were. Having trained so hard since his selection, he felt like a rope stretched taut and ready to snap.

'But the sign's just gone up,' persisted Saburo. 'We'll only be in the Iga mountains for a few days. Surely we'll get back in time to see at least one of the fights.'

Kiku gave Saburo a grave look. 'That's if he survives the first one.'

Jack sensed the lunge punch without seeing it. He deflected it neatly past his ear, while countering with a back fist to the head.

Yamato gauged the move, pulling back out of reach and

sweeping his hand across in a combined block and knife-hand strike. Jack caught it, trapped the arm and drove his fist forward. Yamato disengaged, slipping the punch and retaliating with a hammer fist to the bridge of the nose.

All the time they maintained contact with one another.

All the time they sought gaps in each other's defence.

Throughout they were blindfolded.

'Excellent, boys,' praised Sensei Kano, who leant non-chalantly on his white staff in a side garden of the Eikan-Do Temple where the *chi sao* lesson was taking place. 'But I sense you're playing with one another. Go for the kill!'

Sensei Kano had been training them rigorously in the run-up to the Circle of Three and both boys had become adept at the Sticky Hands technique as well as the use of their other senses. Jack could now pick out sound shadows whether in a forest or a Kyoto side street, though he still found the task impossible in a silent room.

This was Jack's final session to prove to Sensei Kano he was ready for the Circle of Three. He concentrated hard on following Yamato's movements with his hands. He and Yamato were evenly matched so their attacks got faster and faster, becoming a blur as they tried to outdo one another.

Strike. Block. Punch. Evade.

Jack sensed Yamato shift his body weight, but was a second too late in retracting his foot. Yamato swept his front leg from under him and Jack lost his balance. The moment's distraction was all Yamato needed. He open-palmed Jack in the head and Jack toppled sideways. With nothing to grab on to, Jack fell and plunged into the water below.

Sensei Kano had instructed them to fight on a narrow

footbridge that straddled the stream running into the pond of the temple. This had been their last training session and this, their final test.

Yamato had won.

Jack had lost.

He came up gasping. The stream was icy cold in contrast to the heat of the day and he climbed out on to the bank, shivering like a leaf.

'Your balance is still off, Jack-kun, but you're ready nonetheless,' said Sensei Kano. 'We'll have to focus on that when you get back from the Circle of Three. I'll get you fighting with *bō* blindfolded on a log. That should sharpen your senses, or else you'll grow gills from being in the water all the time!'

Sensei Kano chuckled deeply at his little joke before wandering off into the gardens. Yamato grinned too and Jack knew why. Not only had Yamato outperformed him in *chi sao*, but he was the best student in their class with the *bō*. He could beat Jack in sparring every time, even if he was blindfolded and Jack wasn't.

With the final test over, Jack hurried back to the *Niten Ichi Ryū*, Yamato in tow, to pack for the next day's arduous trek into the Iga mountain range.

As they entered the school gates, Jack noticed Hiroto and Goro hovering over a small boy from the year below. He was looking up at them and shaking his head vigorously. Goro pushed the boy hard in the chest and the boy stumbled backwards, striking his head against the wall. He began to cry.

Jack and Yamato rushed over.

'Leave him alone,' Jack ordered, grabbing Goro's arm.

'Stay out of it, *gaijin*!' warned Hiroto, advancing on Jack.

'No, we won't,' answered Yamato, stepping between Hiroto and Jack, 'and don't call Jack *gaijin*, unless you want to deal with me too.'

A stalemate occurred and the little boy glanced nervously between them, waiting to see who would make the next move.

'You'll be sorry for sticking your big nose into our business,' threatened Hiroto, stabbing a stick-thin finger into Jack's chest. Hiroto gestured to Goro and they left.

'Are you all right?' asked Jack, once the two Scorpion Gang members had gone.

The boy snuffled, choking back his sobs and rubbing his bruised head. He looked up at Jack, his eyes red with tears, then blurted, 'They said I was a traitor, that I was no longer Japanese, that I was unworthy to be called a samurai and that I would be punished if I didn't renounce my faith.'

'But why should they object to you being a Buddhist?' asked Jack.

'I'm not just a Buddhist. Last year, my family converted to Christianity.'

Jack was taken aback by the boy's revelation. Although he'd been hearing increasing rumours of Christian persecution and the expulsion of *gaijin* around the country, he'd always assumed that the prejudice was directed at foreign Christians. He didn't realize it extended to Japanese Christians as well. If such harassment was happening within the *Niten Ichi Ryū*, Jack could only imagine how bad things were in the rest of the country. The idea of travelling on foot to the Iga mountains for the Circle of Three was no longer an inviting prospect – it was a risk to his life.

37

BODY CHALLENGE

The rain fell as hard as nails.

The single-track road, churned up by the horses' hooves and pedestrian traffic, had become a quagmire of mud slowing their progress to that of a snail's. The tall trees on either side rose up into a sky pregnant with black clouds and blocked out much of the evening's fading light. There was a growing unease among the travellers as they wound their way through the wooded mountain pass to the town of Iga Ueno, for the dark recesses of the forest concealed any number of dangers, from wild boars to pillaging bandits.

The column of students trudged on wearily, headed by Masamoto and Sensei Hosokawa on horseback. Although only six entrants had been accepted into the Circle of Three, there had been an open invitation for supporters to attend. Around half the school had decided to join the expedition. Many were now regretting that decision.

Suddenly something broke from the undergrowth and flew at Sensei Hosokawa.

The sensei's sword flashed in the twilight.

But it stopped short as a black-feathered grouse flew

overhead. The bird would never know how close it had just come to death.

Masamoto laughed. 'Scared of an old bird, my friend? Or were you thinking of killing it for your supper?'

Jack noticed that Sensei Yosa had also gone for her weapon and was cautiously releasing the tension on her bow and returning the arrow to her quiver. In fact, out of all the sensei, only Sensei Kano had remained at ease, seemingly aware from the very start that the threat was harmless.

'Why are the sensei so jumpy?' asked Jack, quickening his pace to walk beside Akiko. Not that he was any less nervous. Despite being under the direct protection of Masamoto, Jack was concerned that some unwitting samurai loyal to *daimyo* Kamakura might try to expel him from Japan, either respectfully or by the sword.

'We're passing through ninja territory,' whispered Akiko.

In Jack's mind, every shadow in the forest suddenly grew eyes. He caught a movement on the edge of his vision, but it turned out to be nothing more than the swaying of a branch. Behind him, Yamato, Saburo, Yori and Kiku, who had overheard their conversation, glanced around nervously, little Yori turning white as a sheet.

'This region is the stronghold of the Iga clans,' continued Akiko under her breath. 'In fact, these mountains provided refuge against General Nobunaga's attempted destruction of the ninja thirty years ago. He brought in over forty thousand troops against some four thousand ninja. The ninja still survived and somewhere in those mountains is Dokugan Ryu's hiding place.'

'But how do you know all this?' asked Jack.

244

'From stories, hearsay, the sensei . . .' She trailed off and pointed up ahead. 'Look, we're nearly there. Hakuhojo, the Castle of the White Phoenix.'

Through the rain and mist, Jack saw that the track had opened out into a small valley basin ringed by mountains. In the distance a three-tiered castle of white wood and grey tiled roofs materialized. However, the mist quickly descended and the castle disappeared as if it were a ghost in a storm.

Night had fallen by the time they reached the outskirts of Iga Ueno and the castle was now only discernible by the lanterns that burned within.

Jack was relieved to enter the safety of the town. The journey from Kyoto had been tough and, like everyone else, he was soaked through, cold and tired. His back was stiff from carrying his pack and his muscles were aching and sore from dragging his feet through the mud. He would be glad to reach their temple lodgings, get a warm bath, food and a good night's sleep.

'Get up!' ordered Sensei Kyuzo, kicking the sleeping form of Jack with his foot. 'The Circle of Three begins now.'

Jack struggled to his feet, bleary-eyed. He'd not been asleep more than an hour when the sensei had begun rounding up the entrants. Jack followed his *taijutsu* master along the corridor and entered the main temple, a dark wood-panelled room lit by softly glowing lanterns. The room was dominated by a large wooden Buddha, which emanated such spiritual energy it seemed to have a life all of its own.

As Jack lined up with the others facing the shrine, he

was greeted by several rows of shaven-headed monks in brilliant white robes chanting a mantra that sounded as if it had been sung since the beginning of time.

'. . . om amogha vairocana mahamudra
manipadma jvala pravarttaya hum . . .'

'It's the Mantra of Light,' whispered Yori reverentially. He stood next to Jack, nervously tugging at a paper crane concealed in his hand. 'The phrase contains the Buddha's wisdom which helps guide these monks to *satori*.'

Jack nodded and gave his friend what he hoped was a confident smile. In reality, he was a bundle of nerves and excitement. After four trials and several months of training, the Circle of Three and its three challenges of Mind, Body and Spirit would be revealed to them.

A sudden stab of doubt struck his heart. Had his impatience to learn the Two Heavens clouded his judgement? Was he ready for such a test? He was so tired from the journey and he now realized their sleep had been disrupted as a trick to unsettle the entrants at the first stage. The challenge of the Circle of Three had already begun.

He glanced down the line in Akiko's direction. Despite the determined look in her eyes, the dark shadows that ringed them showed she too was exhausted from the long journey. Next to her was Harumi, the other girl contender, who appeared equally tired. At the end stood Tadashi. He nodded to Jack and held up a clenched fist as a sign of encouragement. Kazuki then filed in and stood next to Jack, but ignored him completely.

Led by Masamoto, the teachers entered and seated themselves to one side. Then the student supporters filed in and knelt behind them in four neat rows. The monks' chant rolled to an end, receding like the sound of a wave, and the High Priest stood to greet the congregation. The priest's face was old and wrinkled, but his body appeared as resilient as stone and, like the Buddha statue, radiated a powerful inner energy.

'Welcome, Masamoto-sama, to the Tendai Temple,' he said in the serene voice of a man at peace with himself.

'Thank you for allowing us to stay as your humble guests,' Masamoto replied, bowing low to the priest. 'May I present to you our entrants for the Circle of Three? May they prove worthy in Mind, Body and Spirit.'

He gestured towards Jack and the others with a wide sweep of his hand. The priest surveyed the six young samurai, his eyes falling upon Jack last. Jack was hypnotized by the intensity of the old monk's gaze. As deep as a well and as infinite as the sky, it was as if the monk was aware of everything. Jack felt he was staring into the eyes of a living god.

'We shall begin with the Body challenge,' announced the priest.

Stepping forward, he blessed each of the entrants with words that Jack didn't understand, but sensed had great power. Once the priest had finished, six novice monks stepped forward with a cup of water, a bowl of thin miso soup and a small ball of rice. They handed each in turn to the entrants. Realizing how hungry he was, Jack drained his soup and water and devoured the rice ball in a matter of moments.

Next they were presented with three pairs of straw sandals, a white vestment, a sheathed knife, a rope, a book, a paper lantern and a long straw hat shaped like the upturned hull of a boat. The monks helped the entrants into the white robe, tied the hat to their heads and slipped a pair of the sandals on to their bare feet.

Throughout all this, no explanation was given.

'What's all this for?' whispered Jack to the monk who was helping him to dress in the strange assortment of clothing and equipment.

The monk, busy with wrapping the rope round Jack's waist, looked up.

'You're wearing a robe of white, the Buddhist colour of death, to remind you of how close you will come to the limits of life itself,' he whispered. 'The rope is known as "the cord of death". This, together with the knife, serves to remind all novice monks of their duty to take their life if they do not complete their pilgrimage, either by hanging or self-disembowelment.'

Not being a monk, Jack was glad this rule didn't apply to him.

The preparations complete, their lanterns were lit and the six entrants were led outside into the darkened temple courtyard. The rain had eased, but there was a chill wind blowing and Jack gave an involuntary shudder.

The priest, sheltering beneath an umbrella held by one of his monks, beckoned them into the centre of the courtyard. The six of them gathered round, each shivering in their own pool of lantern light, their faces drawn and anxious.

'You are to complete just one day of the Thousand Day

Pilgrimage my Tendai monks have to accomplish as part of their spiritual training,' he announced. 'Our temple believes challenge is a mountain with enlightenment at its peak. Climb the mountain and *satori* is yours.'

The priest pointed into the darkness. Against the thunderous sky, Jack could just make out the shadowy outline of a mountain backlit by sheet lightning.

'You will go to the top of the first Circle of Three and back, praying at each of the twenty shrines marked in your books,' explained the priest. 'You will undertake this challenge alone. You cannot stop to sleep. You are not allowed to eat. And you must return to this temple before the first light of dawn strikes the eyes of the wooden Buddha.'

The priest looked at each of them in turn, his gaze seeming to penetrate their very souls.

'If you hear my monks complete the Mantra of Light, then you are too late.'

38

RUNNING ON EMPTY

Jack had hit his limit.

He couldn't go on. His body was rebelling and a lonesome desperation descended upon him as he listened to the sound of his straw sandals squelching in the mud.

The rain, which had slackened at the start of the challenge, was now cascading in a torrential downpour and Jack was soaked to the skin. His feet were aching blocks of ice, his second pair of straw sandals were already disintegrating, and his muscles burned with a sickening pain.

But he couldn't stop.

He wasn't allowed to.

'To reach the top, you have to climb a mountain step by step,' the High Priest had told the six Circle entrants prior to commencing the Body challenge. 'You will experience pain on this journey, but remember the pain is only a symptom of the effort you're putting into the task. You must break through this barrier.'

But Jack was finding the pain too great to overcome. He'd been running for over half the night. He was hungry and weak from exhaustion; the energy from the pitiful last meal was already burnt up and he had visited only fourteen of the twenty shrines he had to reach before dawn.

Jack stumbled on.

But the fifteenth shrine was still nowhere in sight. Surely he must have passed it by now. He began to question whether the Two Heavens could be worth such physical punishment and all the momentum from his body ebbed away as his mind took hold, coaxing him to stop.

'Climb the mountain and *satori* is yours,' the priest had told them.

Jack no longer cared for enlightenment. All he wanted was a bed and to be warm and dry. He felt his pace almost grinding to a halt.

This challenge was impossible. How was he supposed to find his way along mountain trails, made treacherous by the rain, in complete darkness? Somehow he was meant to cover a distance equivalent to crossing the Channel from England to France, with only a paper lantern to light the way and a tiny book of directions to guide him to each of the twenty shrines.

There was no chance of taking a short cut, since the shrines had to be visited in a set order and his book stamped with an ink woodblock to prove he'd been there. Jack wished he had someone else to follow and encourage him on, but each entrant had been separated by a short period of time measured by the burning of a stick of incense. He was alone in his suffering.

Without food or sleep, he wondered whether *anyone* would get to the temple's main shrine before the first light of dawn struck the eyes of the wooden Buddha.

Despair had Jack in its grip and it weakened the last threads of his determination. His foot struck something solid and he went tumbling forward.

Jack fell to his knees, defeated.

His lantern, miraculously still burning in the downpour, illuminated an old moss-covered gravestone. The whole trail, Jack had discovered, was littered with such burial sites, each one marking the mortal fate of a monk who had failed in his pilgrimage.

He looked down at the rope round his waist and the knife in his belt. That would not be his fate, however desperate things became.

Jack attempted to stand, but the effort was too great and he slumped to his hands and knees in the mud. His body had given up.

The Circle of Three had broken him at the first hurdle.

Jack had no idea how long he stayed there on all fours in the pouring rain, but deep in the recesses of his mind he heard Sensei Yamada's voice, '*Anyone can give up, it's the easiest thing in the world to do. But to hold it together when everyone else would expect you to fall apart, now that's true strength.*'

Jack hung on to these words like a lifeline. His sensei was right. He must continue. This was his path to becoming a true samurai warrior. His fast track to learning the unbeatable Two Heavens technique.

Jack crawled through the mud.

He willed himself to rise above the pain in his legs and knees.

He had to complete the Body challenge.

He reminded himself that this single night's task represented only one day of the Thousand Day Pilgrimage the Tendai monks had to complete as part of their spiritual training. The High Priest had told them that over a period of seven years, his disciples would run the equivalent of the circumference of the world. Only forty-six monks had ever completed this extraordinary ritual in the past four centuries, but the old priest was living proof that it could be done. He was the forty-sixth. If that old man could complete one thousand days, then surely Jack could manage one.

He lifted his head, letting the cool rain wash the grime from his face. In the darkness, a glint of light from his lantern reflected off the fifteenth shrine only a little farther up the path.

Don't try to eat an elephant for lunch.

The phrase popped out of nowhere and Jack laughed at the absurd saying Sensei Yamada had given Yori. But now he understood.

By breaking down the course into smaller sections and tackling it piece by piece, perhaps he could finish the challenge. Jack focused on the fifteenth shrine as his first achievable goal. A trickle of energy seeped into his body and he got back to his feet. He took one unsteady step forward, then another, each step bringing him closer to his goal of the fifteenth shrine.

Reaching the shrine, Jack rejoiced and said a little prayer. The words filled him with optimism. With a renewed determination that masked his aches and pains, he stamped his book and set off down the path to his next goal, the sixteenth shrine.

He was running. He had broken through the pain barrier the High Priest had spoken of. But Jack hadn't gone twenty paces when he spotted two red eyes glaring at him out of the darkness.

A strangled scream erupted from this devilish apparition and it charged straight at him.

39

YORI

Jack barely had time to avoid the bloody tusks as he dived for cover.

The wild boar thundered towards him, its head down to attack. The tusks slashed upwards, missing Jack's left leg by a hair's breadth. The animal careered past before disappearing into the undergrowth.

Jack lay there in the bushes, panting for breath. He listened to the hellish squeal recede until eventually it was drowned out by the storm. In his desperation to evade the wild boar, Jack had dropped his lantern and it now lay crushed and useless in the mud, its flame extinguished.

What was he to do now? It was the middle of the night and the dense forest meant he could barely see more than a few feet in front of him. He would surely get lost on the mountainside if he tried to find his way down in the darkness. And, he reminded himself, he was deep in ninja territory. His chances of finishing the challenge, let alone getting off the mountain alive, were minimal.

Having been the last to start, there was also little point

in waiting to be discovered. If he stayed put, there was a danger of dying from the extreme cold.

His predicament couldn't be much worse. Too tired to cry, he got angry instead. Getting to his feet, Jack stumbled onwards down the path.

He would *not* be defeated by this mountain.

He would survive.

He walked straight into a tree.

Jack cursed, but kept going. He remembered the lesson the Daruma Doll had taught him the previous year in *Taryu-Jiai*. Seven times down, eight times up.

Taking a moment to calm himself, Jack realized he should be using the techniques Sensei Kano had taught him in sensitivity training. With hands outstretched, he cautiously felt and listened his way through the forest.

For the first time ever, Jack began to appreciate what Sensei Kano faced on a daily basis, and his admiration for the blind teacher grew ten thousandfold. For the *bō* master, life was a constant struggle through a pitch-black forest, yet he took it all in his stride.

Having got his own troubles into perspective, Jack battled on.

Rounding a corner and heading down the trail, he noticed a flickering light in the darkness. As he got closer, Jack could hear a low moaning. He quickened his pace. He saw a figure lying in the mud and recognized Yori.

'What happened? Are you all right?' asked Jack, stumbling up to him.

'A boar attacked me,' Yori groaned, his face pale with shock in the glow of his paper lantern.

Jack redirected the light and inspected his friend for injuries. He discovered Yori had a large gash on his right thigh. It was bleeding badly and Jack knew he would have to get his friend off the mountain as soon as possible, if he was to have any chance of surviving. Jack ripped off the sleeve of his robe and tied it tightly round Yori's leg to stem the bleeding.

'Do you think you can stand?'

'I've tried . . . It's no use,' gasped Yori, his eyes screwed up in agony. 'Go and get help.'

'I can't leave you here. You're already shivering. We have to get you off the mountain now.'

'But I can't walk . . .'

'Yes, you can,' said Jack, slipping an arm round Yori's waist. 'Put your arm over my shoulder.'

With great effort, Jack got Yori back to his feet.

'But I'll slow you down,' protested Yori, 'and you won't complete the challenge.'

'I can't see where I'm going anyway. I lost my lantern to that stupid boar. So we need each other. Don't you see, together we have a chance of finishing,' persuaded Jack, smiling his encouragement. 'Look, I'll support you, if you hold the lantern to light our way.'

They took a few faltering steps and stumbled. Yori cried out in pain as they fell against a tree.

'This is stupid,' wheezed Yori. 'We'll never make it at this rate.'

'We'll make it. We just need to find our rhythm.'

Jack looked away before Yori could see the doubt in his eyes.

The lame leading the blind, thought Jack. What hope did they honestly have?

Jack and Yori were lost.

Having agreed that the safest and quickest way down was to follow the route that had been given to them, they'd been making good progress and had been encouraged by the fact that they'd found the next four shrines with little problem. But the twentieth shrine was proving elusive.

'The book definitely says turn right at the stone lantern to reach the stream,' said Jack.

Exhausted and frustrated, he was tempted to throw the guide away. They had reached a junction of four paths in the forest. Yet there was no mention of a crossroads in the directions they had been given.

'So where's the stone lantern?'

'Perhaps we missed it?' offered Yori weakly.

'Wait here,' instructed Jack, lowering Yori on to a nearby rock. 'I'll have another look. There were some smaller paths further back.'

Jack retraced their steps and eventually found the stone lantern concealed behind a pile of foliage. The branches were freshly broken so Jack knew it wasn't an accident of nature that had hidden the marker.

'Kazuki!' he spat in disgust. Just the sort of dishonest tactic his rival would play to ensure his own success and Jack's failure.

Fuelled by anger, Jack ran back to collect Yori.

★ ★ ★

By the time they reached the stream where the twentieth shrine stood, Jack's last pair of straw sandals were mush around his feet. With every step he now suffered from a sharp pain in his left foot, but tried to hide the discomfort from Yori.

'Take mine,' said Yori, slipping off his own sandals.

'What about you?'

'I can't go on any more, Jack.'

Yori's face was now a pallid sheen of sweat and Jack could see his friend had lost a lot of blood.

'Yes, you can,' replied Jack, shouldering more of Yori's weight despite his own overwhelming exhaustion. 'Sensei Yamada once told me "there's no failure except in no longer trying". We must keep trying.'

'But it's nearly dawn.'

Jack looked at the sky. The rain had petered out and the horizon was beginning to lighten. In the valley below, the grey-white silhouette of the Castle of the White Phoenix was now visible.

'But I can see the castle. We've visited all the shrines and just need to get to the temple. We can make it. It's not that far.'

Jack felt Yori collapse in his arms, limp as a rag doll.

'There's no point in us both failing,' wheezed Yori, his breathing rapid and shallow. 'You go on. Complete the Circle.'

In his exhaustion, Jack was almost persuaded by his friend's fevered logic. The Circle was his path to the Two Heavens. The Circle was the key. He had strived for it the whole year, worked too hard to let it slip through his fingers now. On his own, he could still make it.

Jack studied the pale face of his friend and smiled sadly. With the last of his remaining strength, he lifted Yori on to his shoulders.

'The Circle can wait.'

40

THE EYES OF BUDDHA

Jack collapsed into Akiko's arms.

A crowd of students rapidly gathered round the temple's main entrance trying to get a glimpse of Jack, covered in mud and carrying his injured friend upon his back. Two monks hurried over and rushed the unconscious Yori away.

By now, the early morning sun was clipping the temple's rooftops, but it hadn't yet entered the courtyard. Jack shivered uncontrollably from the cold.

'What happened? Where have you been?' Akiko demanded, worry etched in her face as Jack fell to his knees, too tired to stand on his bruised and bloodied feet. 'We were back hours ago.'

Jack didn't answer. Instead he stared at Kazuki, who had come up behind Akiko. His rival had washed and was dressed in a clean robe. He looked fresh and almost unaffected by the night's exertions. Arms crossed, Kazuki observed Jack's shattered form with amused curiosity.

Jack's whole body shook, no longer with cold, but with fury.

'Your cheating almost killed Yori!' he managed to gasp.

'You're delirious, *gaijin*. I didn't cheat. I finished first because I was the best,' Kazuki replied, giving him a contemptuous sneer. 'It's you who's failed. Don't blame me, you pathetic *gaijin*.'

'He hasn't failed yet!' snapped Akiko, glaring up at Kazuki. 'The sun's rays haven't reached Buddha's eyes. He still has time. Come on, Jack.'

Akiko, not caring about the mud getting on her fresh robe, began to half carry, half drag Jack towards the steps of the main temple.

'NO! LEAVE HIM!' came a cry.

Akiko stopped in her tracks. Jack lifted his head to the see the white-robed High Priest standing at the top of the steps, his hand outstretched, ordering them to stop. Behind him through the open *shoji* doors of the shrine, hidden in shadow, Jack glimpsed the wooden Buddha.

'You cannot help him. If he wants to continue in the Circle, then he must complete the journey by himself.'

'But he'll never make it,' pleaded Akiko.

'That's for him to decide, not you. Put the boy down,' instructed the priest.

Akiko gently lowered Jack to the ground and stepped away, her eyes brimming with tears.

Jack knelt where he was. A numbing exhaustion pinned him down as if the weight of the entire sky had dropped upon his shoulders. The Buddha statue was no more than fifty paces away, but it could have been the other side of the world for all he cared. He had expended his last ounce of energy in his desperate marathon to save Yori's life.

Inside, the monks began to chant the Mantra of Light and Jack could see the rest of the school, the sensei and Masamoto waiting to see what he would do. The High Priest beckoned Jack on with a single wave of his hand, then turned and entered the shrine as if expecting him to follow.

Jack didn't.

He couldn't.

He simply had nothing left. This time Jack knew it was not a pain barrier he could break through. This felt like a canyon, a vast vacuum of energy, a void impossible to leap across.

Kazuki knelt down next to him, an arrogant smile upon his face, and whispered gleefully in Jack's ear, 'You'll never make it.'

The sun was halfway down the temple roof and Jack could see it inching its way over each tile. Kazuki was right. It would require a superhuman effort to reach the Buddha in time.

Jack stared dejectedly at the ground in front of him. In his exhausted daze, he watched an ant crossing his path, dragging a leaf five times its size. The little creature struggled, pulled, pushed and prodded, but despite the enormity of the task it didn't give up.

There's no failure except in no longer trying.

Sensei Yamada's words resounded in his head. Jack glanced up and saw the old Zen master staring at him from the doorway of the temple, his eyes radiating belief in him.

'Come on, Jack! You can do it!' cried Yamato, running down the steps towards him, Saburo at his side.

'Come on, Jack!' echoed Saburo.

'It's not that far,' Akiko encouraged, her hands out-stretched, desperately willing him on.

With a Herculean effort and the supporting cheers of his friends, Jack managed to get to his feet. He staggered forward, repeating the mantra with each step, 'There's no failure except in no longer trying. There's no failure except in no longer trying. There's no failure . . .'

Jack dragged one foot in front of the other, his legs as heavy as if a ball and chain had been attached to them. He was falling forward more than walking, but each step carried him closer and closer.

He was at the temple steps now, crawling up them. His friends continued to shout their encouragement, but their words were a distant wash in his ears. The only sound that he was conscious of was the ever-cycling chant of the white-robed monks. The nearer he got, the stronger their mantra became, seeping into his muscles like an elixir.

Now he was inside the shrine.

But so too was the sun.

It had risen above the line of the mountains and now shone brightly on the back wall of the temple, its beam catching motes of dust in the air as it descended towards the Buddha's eyes.

The school, in awe of Jack's supreme effort, were utterly silent as they watched him lurch towards the shrine.

Jack reached out as the sun illuminated the Buddha's eyes. At the same time, the monks ceased their chant. Jack felt the cool sensation of the wood and the smoothness of

264

the Buddha's belly. He smiled briefly before collapsing at the statue's feet.

'You can never conquer the mountain. You can only conquer yourself,' began the High Priest, once the congregation had settled back into the temple following lunch. 'The first challenge of the Circle of Three tested the physical body, taking it to its very limit. Five of you succeeded in reaching the temple before the first light of dawn struck the eyes of Buddha, thus demonstrating your dominion over the body.'

Jack swayed on his feet, dizzy with exhaustion. He'd been given food and water and allowed to rest, but it hadn't been long before they'd woken him again and brought him back to the main temple with the other Circle entrants.

'The Body challenge should have proved to each of you that the mind rules the body. The body can keep going as long as the mind is strong.'

The priest studied each of them with his fathomless eyes, checking they had comprehended this life lesson.

'Once you realize this, there are no limits to what you can achieve. The impossible becomes possible, if only your mind believes it. This truth forms the basis of the second Circle challenge. But first Masamoto-sama wishes to speak.'

Masamoto stood and approached his students, his stance proud and mighty as he appraised Jack and the others.

'I'm honoured to have such strong samurai in my school. The *Niten Ichi Ryū* spirit burns bright in all of you.' He clasped Jack's shoulder with his sword hand and Jack felt the immense strength of the great warrior. 'But today that spirit burnt brightest in Jack-kun.'

Everyone's eyes fell upon Jack.

Jack didn't know where to look, except directly into the scarred face of Masamoto, who returned his gaze with paternal pride.

'Jack-kun demonstrated true *bushido*. When he sacrificed his chances for a fellow samurai in need, he displayed the virtue of loyalty. In bringing that same samurai down off the mountain, he showed courage. He not only conquered himself, but I am of the mind that he conquered the mountain by denying it Yori-kun's life.'

The school bowed as one, honouring Jack's achievement.

Jack glanced around, uncomfortable at being the centre of such attention. Akiko smiled warmly at him, while Tadashi, clearly exhausted from the first challenge, only managed a brief nod of the head in acknowledgement of Jack's achievement. Yori wasn't in the line. He was still recovering from his injury, being tended to by a monk whose medical knowledge was renowned. Jack had been told that Yori would need time to recuperate, but the signs were good and he was responding well to the monk's herbal remedies.

'No allowance, though, can be made for the boy's fatigue,' interjected the High Priest, bowing respectfully to Masamoto. 'The path of a Tendai monk is never-ending, so the challenge of the Mind must begin forthwith.'

41

MIND OVER MATTER

The waterfall thundered down from the second highest peak in the Iga mountain range, cascading in one long roaring curtain of white. Over the centuries, it had gouged a narrow high-sided ravine into the mountain, as if some god had driven a mighty axe into the rock and cleaved it apart.

The monks, students and sensei stood in a large semi-circle round the churning rock pool at the base of the fall. They held their hands together, praying in honour of the mountain spirits and the ancient *kami* of the waterfall, while the High Priest recited a Buddhist blessing and scattered salt as part of the purification ritual.

Jack, dressed in a fresh white robe, looked on with the other entrants, each of them petrified at the prospect of this second challenge. They were to stand upon a large flat rock under the waterfall for the time it took a stick of incense to burn through, using only the power of the mind to defeat the physical. In doing so, they risked the very real danger of death due to freezing in the icy waters.

With the rites over, the priest beckoned the five

remaining young samurai to line up along the ledge that ran behind the fall.

First to enter, Jack kept his back close to the rock face, being careful not to slip on the slimy stone. The spray billowed everywhere and his thin monk's robe was soon plastered to his body. The cold damp air revived him, but he wasn't looking forward to stepping under the freezing falls. On the other side he could just make out the semicircle of spectators, their forms and faces distorted and twisted by the turbulent veil of water. It was as if he was peering into an asylum of Hell.

The others followed close behind, each of them staring in terrified awe at the torrent. Then, with a wave of his arm, the High Priest signalled for the challenge to commence. Bowing as one, the five entrants stepped from the ledge and entered the waterfall's thunderous power.

Jack almost blacked out, instantly overwhelmed by the numbing cold.

He had to fight the urge to escape the furious cascade as the water smashed on to his head as hard as hailstones. He tried to resist the flow, but his muscles were being pummelled into heavy knots of tension.

There was no way on earth he could last a stick of time.

Frantically, he mumbled the mantra he'd been taught to ward off the cold, but it was no use. He was simply too weakened from the Body challenge. His mind had gone blank, he was hyperventilating and his whole being was racked with convulsing shivers. He was vaguely aware that Harumi had exited the waterfall, its power too great for her to bear. Jack felt himself caving in too.

He desperately clung on to the challenge, determined to outlast Kazuki at the very least. But it was no use. His body couldn't take much more of this punishment. He would have to leave.

His feet, though, refused to move.

Something deep within him defied the waterfall. Defied his own will.

The impossible becomes possible if only your mind believes it.

Jack gave one final mental push, trying to detach his mind from the bone-chilling pain. He summoned up the mantra again, but was doubtful whether a Buddhist chant would help a Christian heart. Nevertheless, he repeated the mantra faster and faster until it became a continuous circle of words:

> *My mind is limitless,*
> *a horizon never ending,*
> *a sun never setting,*
> *a sky forever stretching . . .*

Amazingly, by focusing his mind on the mantra, he felt his body transform. With each turn of the phrase, his muscles became softer and more supple so that the waterfall no longer hurt. For a brief moment, the pounding water felt as gentle as a mountain spring.

Then he lost all feeling.

The strange thing about this numbness was that he also lost all care. He didn't mind any more. He realized that the mantra had transported him into one of the curious Buddhist states of meditation. Regardless of his own beliefs, he was experiencing the strangest sensation of his consciousness opening up to the universe around him.

He lost all sense of time.

Had a stick of incense burnt down yet?

A moment later he lost his concentration as Tadashi, escaping the waterfall, bumped into him. The collision disrupted his trance and his body turned instantly ice cold. Despite his best efforts to regain his previous meditative state, Jack was forced to give up.

'Di-di-did I make it?' stammered Jack, stepping out of the falls.

'Of course you did, you frozen idiot!' replied Yamato, laughing incredulously and handing him a dry robe. 'You've been under for ages. The monk has already lit a second incense stick.'

'A-A-Akiko?' shuddered Jack.

'She's still in there, along with Kazuki.'

Akiko and Kazuki shimmered within the cascade of water like ghosts. Jack resigned himself to the fact that Kazuki had defeated him once again, but that didn't mean his rival had to win.

Come on, Akiko, willed Jack. *Outdo Kazuki!*

Akiko was struggling to keep her footing on the slimy rocks and Jack's heart leapt for her as she slipped. Miraculously, despite the pounding of the water, she regained her balance.

Then, without warning, Kazuki crumpled and fell.

Two monks rushed to retrieve him, carrying him out of the falls and rubbing him vigorously with a thick robe. As

Kazuki came round and shakily got to his feet, the school applauded his valiant effort. Jack joined in the clapping, but more in support of Akiko. She still stood under the torrent, at one with the waterfall, her hands clasped in front of her, her lips constantly moving with the mantra.

How much longer could she keep going? wondered Jack.

By all rights, the waterfall should have claimed Akiko's life by now. The incense stick had burnt through a second time and a third one was now lit. Akiko had survived twice the required duration.

'Take her out now!' ordered the High Priest, looking alarmed as the third stick reached its end.

Akiko emerged to triumphant cheering. She walked across to Kiku, who quickly wrapped her in a robe. Jack hurried over and, ignoring Japanese formality, began to rub her hands for warmth. The strange thing was, although Akiko shivered slightly, her body was hot to the touch as if she'd stepped out of a volcanic hot spring instead of a freezing waterfall.

Jack raised his eyebrows in surprise, but she just smiled serenely back at him.

Leaving Kiku to assist Akiko with getting into dry clothes, Jack and Yamato rejoined the rest of the students on the far side of the pool. Passing the High Priest and Masamoto on their way, Jack couldn't help overhearing their conversation.

'Truly remarkable,' said the priest. 'That girl stayed beneath the waterfall longer than any person I've witnessed in my lifetime. She's clearly been taught mind control by a great master.'

'I would agree with you,' said Masamoto. 'Sensei Yamada, you have done a remarkable job in training our students.'

Sensei Yamada shook his head gently, his shrewd eyes glancing over at Akiko in curiosity. 'This is not a skill I've taught my class.'

'In that case, she is a samurai of rare talent,' commended the High Priest.

The priest turned to address the school, casting a considered eye over the remaining Circle entrants. Harumi was now standing to one side with her friends, who were trying to console her.

'In life sometimes you must do the things you think you cannot do,' said the High Priest. 'But always remember, the only limits are those of the mind. By pushing the limits of what you believe, you can accomplish the impossible.'

The High Priest beckoned to Akiko, and Jack felt his heart swell with pride at her achievement.

'This girl is proof that you can expand your mind beyond anything you think it's capable of. And the mind, once expanded, never returns to its former dimensions. Learn from this challenge to be the master of your mind, rather than being mastered by your mind. This knowledge will aid you greatly in tomorrow's Spirit challenge.'

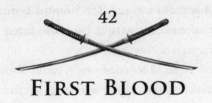

42

FIRST BLOOD

'I got your message,' stated Jack, tossing the paper note at Kazuki's feet. 'So what do you want?'

Kazuki merely smiled, looking like a cat whose prey had just dropped into its lap. He was leaning nonchalantly against the town well. Built of stone, with an aged wooden bucket attached to a rope, it was the only feature of the Iga Ueno's town square, a place enclosed on all sides by shops and two-storey wooden houses.

The shops were now closed for the day, their windows shuttered and doors barred, offering little incentive for people to hang around. Apart from a single villager hurrying home down a side street ahead of the encroaching storm, the place was deserted.

'I don't believe you're here alone,' said Jack, glancing around the darkened alleyways. 'Where's your Scorpion Gang?'

The note Jack had found slipped under the door of his bedroom after dinner that evening had demanded a one-to-one meeting between himself and Kazuki. Akiko had tried to dissuade him from going, but Jack, despite having no idea what Kazuki wanted, felt honour bound to attend. If he didn't appear, he would be considered gutless. He would be branded a coward.

Besides, he wanted to confront Kazuki about Yori.

Kazuki took a step closer to Jack so that they were eyeball-to-eyeball with one another.

'I dislike you, *gaijin*,' Kazuki hissed, his hooded eyes shadowy in the twilight, 'and I don't like accusations of being a cheat. I can easily beat you in the Circle without having to resort to cheating.'

'You barefaced liar! We both know for a fact that you cheated,' exclaimed Jack, his blood boiling at the thought of Yori lying fevered in bed, his leg swollen to twice its usual size.

'I don't lie,' retorted Kazuki, his voice taut with indignation, 'I don't cheat and, for the record, I don't steal things either! Don't judge me by your *gaijin* standards. I come from an honourable family. I am samurai born and bred. Unlike *you*.'

He spat the last two words into Jack's face.

'Your accusation in front of the school caused me to lose face. I summoned you here to defend my honour. I challenge you to a fight. Submission or first blood wins.'

Jack didn't reply immediately. As large drops of rain began to fall out of the thundering sky, he continued to stare at Kazuki, considering his options.

Jack was confident of his ability to fight hand-to-hand, especially since Sensei Kano's *chi sao* training. In fact, the onset of dusk could only increase his chances of victory. On the other hand, Jack knew Kazuki had worked just as hard during his own private training sessions with Sensei Kyuzo and his strength and advanced skill in *taijutsu* meant he might still have the upper hand. Accepting Kazuki's challenge could prove fatal, particularly in Jack's current exhausted condition. To back down, however, would be seen as shameful and he was under no illusion that Kazuki wouldn't hesitate to revel in spreading the word of such a spineless surrender.

When it came down to it, did he actually have a choice?

One look into Kazuki's eyes told Jack his enemy intended to fight him regardless of his answer.

Lightning flared across the sky. The Castle of the White Phoenix was momentarily illuminated, a ghostly apparition against the horizon. As the storm rumbled angrily overhead, the rain became a downpour that drummed loudly on the nearby roofs and a chill wind blasted the cloth signs that hung from the shop awnings.

Seemingly oblivious to the storm, Kazuki waited for Jack's answer.

Jack nodded his head once in assent.

Kazuki grinned.

'Stop!' cried Akiko, running through the rain towards them.

Close behind her were Yamato and Saburo. Although Jack had insisted he should go alone, he was relieved to see his loyal friends.

'Didn't trust me, did you, *gaijin*?' spat Kazuki. 'No matter, it'll be good to have an audience for this. Scorpions!'

He signed to a darkened alleyway and the Scorpion Gang materialized out of the shadows. With a sinking heart, Jack realized this was going to be a fight, not to first blood but his last.

They closed in upon Jack and his friends. There was a tense stand-off, then Kazuki laughed and indicated for his gang to back off and join him.

'This is a matter of honour, between me and the *gaijin*. No need for anyone else to get involved,' he said, passing Nobu his *bokken*. 'On my family's name, I'll follow the samurai code. No weapons. We stop at first blood.'

Akiko turned urgently to Jack and whispered, 'Don't do this, Jack. You know he breaks the rules during *randori*. You think he'll be satisfied with first blood? Kazuki will want to finish you off, once and for all.'

'He just swore on the honour of his family,' Jack countered as he gave Saburo his raincoat. 'He considers himself pure samurai. He won't break *bushido*.'

'Jack, you don't get it, do you? Don't you remember the rocks in the snowballs? The rules don't apply to you. You're *gaijin*.'

Jack was stung by Akiko's use of the insult. Although he realized she hadn't said it out of cruelty, it still cut deeply to hear her call him *gaijin*. He was reminded yet again that however accomplished he became at their language, however well he knew Japan and its customs, however perfectly he followed their etiquette and mastered their martial arts, for the simple reason that he was not born Japanese, he would always be perceived as an outsider – even by Akiko.

Unwittingly, Akiko's comment spurred Jack on and strengthened his determination to fight. He would prove that he was more samurai than any of them.

Jack gave Yamato his *bokken* and stepped forward.

'Destroy him, Kazuki!' yelled Hiroto as Kazuki and Jack faced off in the pouring rain.

Keeping within the tradition of a formal fight, Kazuki bowed to Jack.

Jack returned the bow. But Kazuki had tricked him. He didn't wait for Jack to finish, kicking straight for his face. Jack barely had time to react. He blocked the kick, but the force of the blow sent him staggering backwards.

Kazuki drove into him, trying to blast his way through Jack's desperate guard. Jack ducked, evading Kazuki's hook punch, and countered with two body blows to his stomach. Jack got kneed in the thigh for his efforts and immediately backed off.

'Come on, Jack! You can take him!' urged Saburo in response.

Jack faked a front kick as Kazuki advanced on him. The ruse worked and Kazuki dropped his guard to block it. Jack went on the offensive with a blistering combination of a front jab, reverse punch and spinning back fist. The back fist caught Kazuki hard across the jaw.

Stunned, Kazuki staggered backwards, slipping on the muddy ground and falling unceremoniously on his backside.

Yamato and Saburo let out a cheer.

'I win,' declared Jack in between ragged drawing of breaths.

'It isn't over yet . . .'

'You're bleeding.'

Kazuki wiped his hand across his mouth, a thin stream of

blood running over it before quickly dispersing in the rain.

'I bit my own tongue,' spat Kazuki. 'That doesn't qualify as first blood.'

He then flung a handful of mud into Jack's eyes, blinding him. In that moment of distraction, Kazuki scrambled to his feet and punched Jack in the face. Jack's head rang and he tasted blood as his own lip split open.

'*That* qualifies as first blood,' announced Kazuki with vindictive glee.

But Kazuki didn't halt his assault there. He began to pummel Jack as hard as he could. Instinctively, Jack's *chi sao* training kicked in and he threw up his guard, locking himself against his opponent's arms.

Jack sensed Kazuki's attacks as each technique was thrown. He successfully slipped a series of jabs and attempted a counter. He heard Kazuki cursing in frustration at Jack's unexpected ability to fight without sight.

Jack's skill even amazed himself for a while, but then he was struck on the jaw by an unforeseen roundhouse punch.

His flow broken, Jack began to panic. The pressure of a real blind fight overwhelmed him as another strike from Kazuki caught him in the gut. This was not the same as sparring with Yamato. Kazuki fought differently and Jack was now finding it harder to predict his moves.

Jack lost all contact with Kazuki's guard. An instant later, he found himself flying through the air and splashing down into a large puddle.

Kazuki dropped on top of him.

Before Jack could catch his breath, Kazuki had him in a neck choke and was thrusting him under the water. Jack gagged as his mouth filled with slimy mud. Struggling wildly, he managed to lift his head out of the puddle to snatch a lungful of air. The murky water had washed the remnants of mud from his eyes and he caught a glimpse of Akiko and his friends being restrained by the Scorpion Gang.

'You're going to drown him!' Akiko was screaming as she clawed at Hiroto to free herself.

'Excellent suggestion,' agreed Kazuki, shoving Jack's head back under.

Jack could no longer hear anything but the swirl of muddy water in his ears. He remembered the last time he'd been strangled by Kazuki. If Sensei Kyuzo hadn't stopped the *randori* then, Kazuki would have continued the choke until Jack passed out.

This time, however, there was no teacher in charge.

Kazuki might actually kill him.

Fudoshin.

The word flashed in his mind like lightning as he surfaced again.

Kazuki was laughing in delight at his victory and, clamping down harder, he thrust Jack back under for one final time.

A samurai must remain calm at all times – even in the face of danger.

Sensei Hosokawa's teachings swam through Jack's head.

You must learn to stare death in the face . . .

Wrestling with his fear, Jack regained control of himself and, against all natural instinct, he let his body go limp.

He heard Akiko crying, 'You've killed him! You've killed him!'

Kazuki immediately let go, suddenly aware he'd taken the fight too far.

Jack lay still a second longer.

Then he exploded out of the puddle.

Taking Kazuki completely by surprise, Jack elbowed his rival in the face and rolled on top. Back in control, he locked Kazuki in a head-hold, then drove Kazuki's own face under the surface of the muddy pool.

'SUBMIT!' demanded Jack. 'SUBMIT, YOU CHEAT!'

Jack lifted Kazuki's head up to allow him a mouthful of air before thrusting him back under.

'Admit you cheated, Kazuki. Admit that you hid the lantern!'

Jack held him up for longer this time but didn't release the choking hold.

'Did what?' gasped Kazuki, struggling to control his growing panic.

'Don't play me for an idiot, Kazuki. Tell everyone here how you put branches in front of the stone lantern. Expose yourself to be the dishonourable samurai that you are!' demanded Jack, bobbing Kazuki's head beneath surface in between sentences.

'I didn't . . .' spluttered Kazuki, his voice harsh and grating under the pressure of the choke. 'I didn't cheat . . . I got ahead of Tadashi and Akiko during that challenge. There's no way it could've been me!'

'Liar!' said Jack, dunking him once again.

'JACK, STOP IT!' cried Akiko, breaking free of Hiroto and rushing over to pull Jack off. 'He's telling the truth.'

Jack faltered in his attack.

'I could see the stone lantern when I passed it,' she explained.

Jack looked at her and knew she was telling the truth. All of a sudden, his entire assumption had been undermined. He let go and allowed himself to be dragged off Kazuki by Akiko. He sat staring dumbfounded at the shuddering form of his rival.

Kazuki rolled on to one side, coughing up muddy water.

'Tadashi was in front of you, not Kazuki,' Akiko continued. 'It must have been *him* that cheated. That would explain why, during the Mind challenge, Tadashi fell against me in the waterfall. At the time, I assumed it wasn't intentional, but now I'm not so sure.'

'Tadashi . . . knocked into me too,' confessed Jack, a twisted truth emerging in his head, 'but I thought it was an accident as well.'

'Clearly not,' spat Kazuki, giving Jack a venomous look.

Jack felt ashamed and betrayed. He'd accused Kazuki of cheating with no real proof. He'd jumped to conclusions based solely on his low opinion of his rival, while all along it had been Tadashi, whom he'd thought of as a friend. His own behaviour was no better than Kazuki's, discriminating against him for being a *gaijin*.

'I'm . . . sorry,' admitted Jack, the apology sticking in his throat, each word as heavy and bitter as lead. 'You didn't cheat. It was my mistake.'

Kazuki got unsteadily to his feet with the help of Nobu and Hiroto. He looked down at Jack, pure loathing in his eyes. 'That's right, *gaijin*. You were mistaken. But make no mistake – I will get my own back.'

Jack felt an ice-cold shiver creep down his spine, but oddly it was not in response to Kazuki's threat. It came from the distinct feeling that he was being watched.

'Did you see that?' Nobu whispered, pointing over Kazuki's shoulder to a nearby rooftop.

Everyone turned and peered into the rainsoaked night.

Nothing was visible in the darkness, not even the Castle of the White Phoenix.

A second later, lightning blazed across the heavens and for one terrifying moment a figure in black could be seen silhouetted against the boiling sky.

The thunder roared as Nobu, his chubby face stretched taut with fear, screamed, 'NINJA!'

43

ESCAPE

They fled in different directions.

Jack, Akiko, Yamato and Saburo sprinted across the mud-slicked square towards a side alley that would lead back to the temple. Kazuki and his Scorpion Gang went the opposite way, heading for the castle. As they ran, Jack glanced up and spotted several shadows flitting across the rooftops towards them.

'Hurry!' Jack urged. 'There's a whole gang of them.'

They put on another burst of speed and had almost reached the cover of the alley when Saburo lost his footing, flying face first into the mud.

'Keep going!' Yamato shouted to the rest of them, running back to help their fallen friend.

Jack and Akiko rushed on, entering the alley just as a ninja dropped from the eaves. Glancing over his shoulder, Jack expected to see the assassin bearing down on them. Instead, the ninja let them run away and turned to bar Yamato and Saburo from making their escape.

'We'll meet you at the temple!' cried Yamato, dragging Saburo towards a different alley.

Akiko drove Jack onwards. 'Come on! We'll lose the ninja in the backstreets.'

They switched left, then right, then right again, before entering an enclosed courtyard with only a single unlit passage leading off from it.

'I think we're in the clear,' whispered Akiko, checking over her shoulder for signs of pursuit.

Jack's eyes hunted the dark recesses of the yard, but there was only a large wooden water butt and a small shrub in a clay pot in one corner. He peered into the black hole of the passage where the rain ran in rivulets off the eaves and disappeared, but no enemy threatened to emerge. They were out of danger and he breathed a quiet sigh of relief.

'Do you think it's Dragon Eye?' he whispered to Akiko.

Akiko put a finger to her lips, her eyes scanning the courtyard.

All of a sudden, two ninja materialized out of the night sky, cartwheeling in mid-air to land right between them.

'RUN!' screamed Akiko, snap-kicking her foot into the closest ninja.

She caught him right between the legs and he crumpled to the floor with a feeble groan. Spinning round at lightning speed, she then sent a hook kick directly at the other ninja's head.

But this ninja, quicker than his companion, caught Akiko's foot in mid-air. He raised his other arm to break her leg with a crushing forearm strike.

Akiko didn't falter. She jumped, cartwheeling backwards, and brought her other foot up to connect with her attacker's jaw.

The ninja's head was jerked backwards by the blow and he released her leg. Akiko continued to fly through the air before landing deftly on the eaves above.

Jack stood rooted to the spot, astounded at her agility.

'I said RUN!' ordered Akiko above the storm.

Two more ninja suddenly appeared on the rooftops and began to battle with Akiko.

Jack's first instinct was to clamber up the water butt and help her, but the ninja who'd been kicked first was back on his feet and rushing bow-leggedly in his direction.

Without hesitating, Jack grabbed the clay pot and flung it towards him. The pot smashed into his head and the ninja crumpled to the floor, where he lay unconscious among the shards of pottery.

Jack made for the water butt, but this time found his way blocked by the other assassin. His only option was to escape down the passage.

He plunged into its enveloping darkness, faltering only for a moment to look back at Akiko. She had knocked one ninja off the roof, but now another forced her to leap from building to building in an effort to escape. Jack prayed she would survive.

Then he fled.

Jack held his breath, trying to remain absolutely still.

The ninja raced past, oblivious to his quarry hidden in the darkness of a blind alley, barely noticeable as a narrow gap between two houses. Jack waited a few moments longer. Then, when the ninja did not come back, he allowed himself to relax. He'd managed to escape from his pursuer for the time being, but what should he do now?

He was safe concealed by the darkness, but at the same time he was trapped in a dead end. If a ninja appeared, he would have nowhere to run.

Jack shivered with both cold and fear. Above him, the night sky was just a narrow strip of thundering cloud caught between two rickety buildings. The rain cascaded down the roofs and into the narrow alley, the sound echoing off the walls as if he'd entered a small subterranean cave.

He shivered again, this time with the same uneasy feeling of being watched that he had experienced in the square.

He spun round.

But only the black emptiness of the dead end greeted him.

Still he couldn't shake the sinister sensation.

He checked the main passageway. It was deserted.

Retreating into the security of his blind alley, Jack convinced himself that he was imagining things, his nerves merely on edge.

He hugged himself for warmth, hoping Akiko had also escaped the ninja. It would be remarkable if both of them managed to survive the night. Although he knew Akiko could handle herself, he also knew the ninja were merciless in their pursuit.

The rain softened and Jack glanced up, hopeful that the storm was abating.

The rain hadn't slackened at all.

Only the noise it made. As if there was a sound shadow behind him.

His finely tuned senses blared out a warning. His mouth went dry, his breath caught in his throat. Ever so slowly, he turned his head and stared once more into the dead-end darkness.

There was nothing there.

Then the darkness seemed to rise and Jack found himself face-to-face with the featureless hood of a ninja . . . eye-to-eye with the formidable Dragon Eye.

44

INTERROGATION

A silent scream erupted inside his head, ordering his body to move.

RUN! RUN! RUN! shrieked Jack's mind.

But it was already too late.

As Jack turned to face his foe, Dragon Eye had struck with the swiftness of a scorpion. His fingers, like barbs, had pinpointed nerve centres on Jack's body, paralysing him in five quick successive stabs. Jack was rendered defenceless and completely immobile.

'What . . . have . . . you done to me?' stuttered Jack, hyperventilating as a burning sensation spread through his body and down his arms and legs.

'Be quiet or I'll paralyse your mouth too,' ordered the ninja in a harsh whisper.

Dragon Eye bunched his fingers into the shape of a snakehead and pressed the tips against the skin above Jack's heart.

'One final strike to your heart will kill you.' He dropped the words into Jack's ear with sadistic pleasure while allowing his fingers to linger over their intended target.

'The samurai know and fear this as the Death Touch.'

Jack closed his eyes, half mumbling the Lord's Prayer as Dragon Eye drew back his hand to strike.

'But it can be a far more subtle technique than mere death,' continued Dragon Eye who, instead of killing him, sought out a pressure point beneath Jack's collarbone with his thumb. 'It can also be used to inflict intolerable pain.'

Jack's eyes flew open and he shrieked into the night as the ninja applied pressure with the tip of his thumb. The agony was so intense, Jack felt as if a swarm of wasps had been released inside his chest. He almost passed out, but then Dragon Eye stopped and the pain receded until it was no more than a tingling sensation, like stinging nettles under his skin.

Dragon Eye studied him a moment, watching the pain fade from his victim's eyes. Jack swore that behind that black hood his nemesis was smiling at his suffering.

'Where's the *rutter*?' hissed Dragon Eye.

'It's been stolen,' wheezed Jack, dizzy from the after-shock of the torture.

'That was a decoy! Don't dice with your own death.'

The ninja took hold of Jack's right arm this time and pressed into the middle of his bicep. An unbelievable pressure immediately built up in Jack's right hand, his fingernails became sharp splinters under his skin and he thought his fingers were about to pop. A wave of nausea hit him. But once again Dragon Eye stopped at the threshold of his consciousness.

'I've tortured people before. I can make you suffer beyond anything imaginable – and yet never kill you.'

He took Jack's lolling head in one hand and stared at him with his one eye. Jack couldn't see a single shred of mercy in the ninja's soul.

'It's in Nijo Castle, isn't it?' said Dragon Eye dispassionately.

Jack's eyes flared in alarm. How could he have known that? Had one of his friends betrayed him?

'No need to answer, *gaijin*. Your eyes tell me all I need to know. But where exactly?'

Gripping Jack's head tighter, Dragon Eye placed one finger just below Jack's eye and another on his jawline. The ninja drew closer, his malevolent green eye raking over Jack's face.

'You *are* going to tell me,' he said with ominous finality.

An instant later, Jack thought a molten iron spike had been driven through his eye and out of the back of his skull. The pain was greater than a thousand fires burning, too great for him to even emit a scream. The torture sapped all strength out of him and only a low moan escaped his lips.

Then the pain was gone.

'That is nothing compared to the days of unthinkable agony you will suffer if I let you live. Can you feel that burning sensation in your body?'

Jack nodded weakly, tortured tears rolling down his cheeks.

'That's the pain that I've inflicted upon you so far. It will continue to grow like a furnace until you go mad with suffering. Only I can end it. I ask you one last time. Where is the *rutter*?'

The ninja repositioned his fingers on Jack's face.

'No, please . . .' begged Jack.

Jack felt his resistance break like a tree in a storm. His only remaining hope was that *daimyo* Takatomi's castle was ninja-proof. Even if he died tonight, there was a chance that his tormentor would be caught in the act and ultimately punished for his crimes.

'Behind . . . the wall hanging of the white crane . . . in Takatomi's reception room,' said Jack, gathering what little strength he had left.

'Good. Now tell me what the *rutter* is?'

Jack blinked, unsure if he had heard correctly.

'My father's navigational logbook,' he replied, too stunned to question why Dragon Eye didn't know what he was actually stealing.

'I know that much. My employer insists this *rutter* is more effective than an assassination in gaining power. Tell me why.'

Jack didn't reply.

Dragon Eye gave a sharp stab with his fingers to remind Jack of the pain he could inflict. Jack winced and felt his resistance crumble once more.

'It's the key to the oceans of the known world. The country that possesses this *rutter* can command the trade routes and rule the seas. The fortune of the world is in their hands.'

As Jack explained, he began to understand Dragon Eye's increasing interest in the power of the *rutter*. The ninja may be a hired hand, but he was no fool. Now aware of the importance of such an object, Dragon Eye was perhaps considering the *rutter*'s value for his own purposes.

'You've been more than helpful,' said Dragon Eye. 'But you're now worthless to me. I keep my promises, though, so will release you from your torment. The Death Touch is excruciating but swift. You may not even feel your heart explode.'

Jack's pulse thumped through his body, his heart clamouring to escape, as Dragon Eye formed a snakehead out of his hand and aimed it at Jack's chest.

This was it, Jack realized. This was the face of Death, a featureless black mask with a single green eye. He was staring into it and all he felt was fear. Then, in the last dying moments, a thin smile broke across his bloodless lips.

'What have you got to smile about, *gaijin*?' asked the ninja, astounded at his victim's bravado.

But Jack's smile only broadened as he realized Dragon Eye's efforts were ultimately futile. The key information in the *rutter* was protected by the cipher his father had devised. Only Jack could decode it. Without the key to unlock it, the *rutter* was virtually useless. A jigsaw with a vital piece missing.

Like a lifeline for a drowning sailor, Jack realized the *rutter* could save him.

'Kill me and the *rutter*'s knowledge dies with me,' stated Jack, emboldened by his belief.

'Encrypted, is it?' replied Dragon Eye, unfazed. 'It's of no consequence. I know a Chinese cryptologist who can decode anything.'

With that, Dragon Eye struck and Jack's last hope died in his chest.

45

DIM MAK

Jack's heart thumped against his ribcage as if it was trying to punch its way out through flesh and bone. His lungs became tight and constricted, as if a snake had coiled its way round his chest and was squeezing the breath from him. He collapsed against the alley wall and slid down into the thick mud, where he lay juddering and gasping.

Dragon Eye crouched down to admire his handiwork.

'You have as long as a fish out of water before your heart gives out,' he stated, wiping a strand of Jack's blond hair out of his eyes in a gesture that was almost affectionate. 'You would have made a great samurai, *gaijin*, but I can't risk allowing you to fulfil such a destiny. Maybe in another life, eh?'

Jack was no longer listening. His breath whistled in his ears like wind in a cave and he could feel his blood pulsing through his body, pooling around his dying heart.

Thud . . . thud . . . THUD.

Dragon Eye spun round. A huge figure, large as a mountain bear, confronted him at the mouth of the dead end.

'Move on, blind man,' warned Dragon Eye, spotting the

tall white staff in the man's hand. 'There's nothing here for you to see.' He laughed coldly at his own dark humour.

'I smell blood,' said the figure with distaste.

Despite his disorientation, Jack recognized the deep thrumming voice of Sensei Kano.

'Not just your blood, but the blood of your many victims. Ninja. How I despise your kind.'

'You're too late to save the boy,' hissed Dragon Eye, silently slipping a *shuriken* from his belt as the samurai approached. The ninja threw the deadly silver star at Sensei Kano. 'Or yourself, for that matter!'

The *shuriken* spun through the air with a faint whistle.

The sensei had no time to avoid it. Instead he shifted his staff in front of him and the silver star lodged itself in the wood, striking at a point directly in line with his throat.

'Predictable,' scoffed Sensei Kano.

He then thrust the end of his staff at Dragon Eye, targeting his stomach. Stuck in the narrow passage, the ninja's only choice was to throw himself flat against the wall. He barely avoided the attack. With lightning speed, Sensei Kano struck again. Dragon Eye tried to deflect it, but the tip of the *bō* caught him in the ribs. He grunted with pain and staggered backwards.

Jack's eyes weakly followed Sensei Kano as he stepped over him and drove Dragon Eye further and further back into the dead end.

The ninja was trapped.

The staff was too long and Sensei Kano too swift for Dragon Eye to retaliate. Jack realized that the ninja would soon have nowhere to retreat to and then Sensei Kano could deliver the killing strikes that would finish his enemy's life.

For Jack, though, his life was also fast approaching its end. The crushing pain in his chest was intensifying and his breathing only came in fits and starts. His head felt as though it would crack open like an egg. Blackness crept in at the edges of his consciousness and fingered its way across his vision. He just hoped he would live long enough to see Sensei Kano defeat his father's murderer, the seemingly invincible Dokugan Ryu.

Sensei Kano shot his staff at the ninja's groin. This time Dragon Eye leapt into the air, spreading his legs wide so that he straddled the gap between the two buildings. The *bō* passed harmlessly underneath. Impossibly, Dragon Eye then ran above Sensei Kano using the upper walls as leverage.

Sensei Kano thrust his staff skyward, but missed.

Dragon Eye scuttled overhead like a cockroach and Jack, in his delirious state, felt raindrops falling on him like iron pins. He watched them shower down from the heavens and heard them tinkle on to the ground before realizing that they were real. The area around Jack had been carpeted by the ninja with sharp triangular metal spikes, designed so that one point always faced up.

Dragon Eye reached the end of the alley and dropped back down to the ground.

'Come on, blind man. Let's see how you fight in the open,' he dared.

Sensei Kano charged down the alleyway at Dragon Eye. Jack tried to warn him of the danger, but all he could manage was a feeble croak. At the last second, Sensei Kano planted the end of his staff in the mud and vaulted over Jack. He landed neatly at the entrance to the alleyway, safely clearing all the deadly spikes.

'*Tetsu-bishi*, how uninspired,' commented Sensei Kano. Jack desperately wanted to laugh at Dragon Eye's failure, but the pain proved too great.

Infuriated, the ninja thrust a spear-hand strike at Sensei Kano's throat. The samurai deflected it with his *bō*, then swung the staff round into Dragon Eye's midriff.

Surprisingly, the ninja didn't try to evade it. Instead he absorbed the blow, trapping the staff between his arm and body. Taking Sensei Kano by surprise, he then pulled the huge samurai off-balance before driving him backwards into the alleyway. Sensei Kano remained on his feet, but took one step too many to regain his centre and his rear foot landed on a metal spike. The *tetsu-bishi* went straight through his thin-soled sandal, spearing his flesh.

Sensei Kano dropped to the ground, crying out in shock.

Dragon Eye was on him in an instant. He stamped on the staff, snapping it in two. Then he front-kicked Sensei Kano full force in the face. Jack heard the sensei's nose break and blood gushed out.

'Did you honestly believe you could defeat *me*?' said Dokugan Ryu, grabbing hold of Sensei Kano's head to expose his throat for the killing blow. 'Don't you know that in the land of the blind, the one-eyed man is king?'

With the speed of a cobra, the ninja chopped the knife-edge of his hand at Sensei Kano's windpipe with the intention of snapping it.

Despite his disorientation and pain, Sensei Kano instinctively blocked the attack. Taking hold of Dragon Eye's wrist, he locked the ninja's lead arm and thrust a spear-hand into his face. The ninja barely avoided the counterstrike, but managed to retaliate with a vertical fist punch at the samurai's barrel-sized chest. Sensei Kano's greater strength allowed him to absorb the blow and fight his way back into a standing position.

Through a haze of excruciating pain, Jack watched as the two warriors battled at close range in lethal *chi sao*. The first to make a mistake, Jack knew, would be the one to die.

The speed of their attacks and counters was so fast that Jack only saw their arms as a blur. Their skills were evenly matched and each strike was met with a block, each trap with a counter. Neither gave any ground.

'NINJA!' came a cry.

Dragon Eye glanced up the main passageway and saw a vanguard of castle samurai approaching. Disengaging from Sensei Kano, he vaulted the alley wall with a single mighty leap on to the roof. Taking one last look at Jack, he spat, 'There won't be a next time, *gaijin*. For you, at least!'

A moment later he was gone, a shadow in the night.

Sensei Kano hobbled over to where Jack lay slumped against the wall. 'What's that ninja done to you?'

Jack could hardly breathe now. The world was dim and distant, Sensei Kano's face seemed to be at the opposite end of a long dark tunnel. His heart still thudded hard, but had slowed as the pressure had built. He thought his whole chest was about to explode.

'Death . . . Touch,' Jack somehow managed to gasp.

'*Dim Mak!*' breathed a horrified Sensei Kano.

Immediately, the great sensei ran his hands over Jack's body. Having found what he was feeling for, he pulled Jack forward and, in five rapid strikes with the tips of his fingers, hit Jack at key points on his back and chest.

Like a new spring dawn, Jack's body jerked into life.

He drew in a great breath as his lungs expanded wide. The pressure in his chest vanished as if the gates of a mighty dam had been opened, and his blood flowed through his body in one life-giving flood. His eyesight rushed back and he could now see the bloodstained, bearded face of Sensei Kano, his fingers searching for Jack's pulse in his neck.

'I'm all right, you can stop now,' said Jack wearily as his sensei began to massage his chest.

'I can't. I must ensure your *ki* is flowing freely.'

'But how do you know what to do?'

'I learnt the black art called *Dim Mak* from the same blind Chinese warrior who taught me *chi sao*,' explained Sensei Kano quietly.

He began to work on Jack's limbs.

'*Dim Mak* is the source of the ninja's Death Touch technique. Think of it as the opposite side of the coin to acupuncture. While acupuncture heals using pressure points and nerve centres, *Dim Mak* destroys. You're extremely fortunate to have survived, young samurai.'

He carefully picked up the weakened Jack like a bear cub in his huge arms.

Before heading back to the temple, the great samurai

took a moment to pull out the bloody metal spike that had speared his foot.

'Probably poisoned,' he mumbled, inspecting the *tetsu-bishi*. 'I'll need to keep this for the antidote.'

46

MOUNTAIN MONK

Tadashi ran over to Jack. Pale-faced and sweating, his eyes as wide as saucers, he garbled something incomprehensible then passed out at Jack's feet.

Jack looked down at the comatose traitor. He had little sympathy for his old training partner and false friend who had cheated twice during the Circle of Three. He deserved his fate.

Two monks rushed over and dragged Tadashi to his feet. One threw water over him to try to revive him. The boy spluttered, opened his eyes, screamed at something unseen, then fainted again.

Feverish whispering broke out among the school as they pondered what could have caused such shock and terror in Tadashi during his Spirit challenge.

'What on earth's up there?' asked Kazuki of the High Priest, pointing to the craggy peak of the highest mountain in the Iga range.

This third peak loomed over the small grassy plateau where the final Circle of Three entrants now stood, guarded by a ring of troops from the Castle of the White Phoenix in case of another ninja attack.

'Don't ask yourself what's at the top of the mountain, ask what's on the other side,' the priest replied cryptically. Then he pointed at Jack. 'You're next.'

Jack stepped forward but was held back by Akiko, who had placed her hand on his arm. 'Are you sure you should be doing this?'

'I've come too far to turn back now,' he replied. But Jack's physical and mental fatigue were obvious in the heavy roughness of his voice and the watery glaze to his eyes.

'But you almost died last night,' she pleaded, squeezing his arm gently.

Jack, comforted by Akiko's concern, replied, 'Sensei Kano says I'll be fine. Besides I can rest all I want after this final challenge.'

'That's if you make it. You saw the state of Tadashi. Whatever's up there is not for the faint-hearted. You're not invincible, Jack, however much you may wish you were.'

'I can do this,' Jack asserted, as much for his own reassurance as Akiko's.

She let go of his arm and bowed to hide her fears. 'Be careful, Jack. Don't lose your life in a rush to live.'

Jack had been given nothing but a fresh white robe to climb to the top of the mountain. He had asked if he could take his swords or at least some water for the Spirit challenge, but the High Priest had replied, 'All you need, you already carry with you.'

As Jack set off up the path that wound its way to the peak, he was cheered by his fellow students, all wishing him luck for this final challenge of challenges. He spotted Yamato, Kiku and Saburo shouting their encouragement and, behind them, Emi and her friends waving enthusiastically.

He then passed the line of sensei and bowed his respects to each of them in turn. Sensei Kano was not among the teachers. He was recovering in the temple under the supervision of the medicine monk. The *bō* master had been correct in his assumption that the iron spike was poisoned. Once his wound had been cleaned and bound, he had drunk an evil-smelling antidote concocted by the monk. He had been sick all night as a result. Laughing as he threw up for a fourth time into a nearby bucket, the *bō* master had assured Jack that this was all part of the purging process.

Last in line was Sensei Yamada. The Zen master stepped forward and handed Jack a small *origami* crane.

'From Yori,' he explained with a cheerful smile. 'He wanted you to carry it for luck. He also wanted you to know that he is feeling much better and will be returning to Kyoto with us tomorrow.'

'That's great news,' replied Jack, taking the paper bird. 'Any final words of advice, Sensei?'

'Follow the path and you won't get lost.'

'Is that it?' said Jack, surprised by the plain nature of the Zen master's answer.

'Sometimes that is all that's required.'

★ ★ ★

The path was stony and difficult, wending a steep zigzag up the mountainside. A rock gave way under Jack's foot and a small avalanche of dust and stone clattered down the slope.

He paused to take a much-needed rest and sat down at the edge of the path. The storm of the previous night had passed and a hot spring sun now warmed his aching bones.

Above him, a hawk soared in the clear blue sky and Jack recalled Sensei Yamada's reading of his dream. The bird represented strength and quick-wittedness. Surely, this was a good sign.

Looking over the wide valley basin, Jack could see the school watching him from the grassy plateau below. Up here everything was so calm and peaceful, the air fresh and pure. Life gained a new perspective at this height, he thought. The big became small, his worries disappeared into the distance and the horizon promised new beginnings.

When Sensei Kano had returned with him to the temple after the ninja attack, Jack had been relieved to see that Akiko was already there, safe and sound, along with Yamato, Saburo and everyone else, even Kazuki.

Both Jack and Sensei Kano had been rushed to the temple's medicine monk to be checked out. While Sensei Kano was busy throwing up as a result of the purging potion, Jack was given a sedative to reduce his pain and help him sleep. As he drifted off, Jack overheard Masamoto discussing the raid with the commanding officer of the Castle of the White Phoenix. The Commander believed it to be a raid by a local ninja clan. Jack had groggily mumbled Dragon Eye's name and the Commander had nodded as if he already knew. He confirmed to Masamoto that such attacks by Dokugan Ryu's clan often occurred when there were visiting dignitaries like Masamoto himself.

In the morning Jack had discovered that there had been a unanimous decision to continue with the Circle of Three. Masamoto had announced that no ninja clan would prevent the *Niten Ichi Ryū* completing an ancient samurai tradition. Under armed guard, Jack and the three remaining competitors were led up to the start point of the third and final challenge.

Jack glanced up at the craggy peak that thrust like an arrowhead into the sky. Somewhere up there was the Spirit challenge.

What had terrified Tadashi so badly that he had returned a quivering wreck? Jack couldn't believe that the challenge was any worse than having his heart nearly explode inside his chest with the Death Touch.

Miraculously, he had survived.

Just.

He still had a pounding headache and his body felt as if it had been beaten black and blue with iron rods. His heart throbbed, but he realized he should be thankful that it was still beating at all.

Gazing in the direction of Kyoto, Jack wondered if Dragon Eye was already on his way to Nijo Castle to steal the *rutter*. Jack realized now he must tell Masamoto about it, but then he remembered that the ninja thought he was dead. There would be no urgency for Dragon Eye to retrieve what would always be there. It slowly dawned on Jack that if he could get back to Kyoto before Dragon Eye decided to make his move, he could still save the *rutter*.

Invigorated by this prospect, Jack began scaling the peak anew, fresh hope in his heart.

Jack hesitated outside the entrance to a cave.

A few prayer flags fluttered in the high mountain breeze, but otherwise the peak was desolate and bleak. There was no question that the path led anywhere other than into the dark recesses of the mountain, but Jack was still reluctant to enter. The black hole in the rock face was as inviting as the mouth of a serpent.

Yet he had come this far. There was no point in turning back now.

Jack took a step inside. As soon as he had crossed the line from light to shadow, the warmth of the sun disappeared and was replaced by a damp chill.

He allowed his eyes to adjust to the darkness and saw that the cave was a rough tunnel cut deep into the heart of the mountain. The passageway curved away into pitch-blackness. Taking one last look behind him at the small circle of sunlight that marked his way out, he turned the corner and entered the unknown.

For several moments he saw absolutely nothing. Not even his hand in front of his face. Fighting the urge to flee, he edged deeper into the darkness.

He had no idea how far he had gone when the wall he had been using to guide him suddenly disappeared. Through the large crack in the rock, Jack caught sight of a fiery red glow. With trepidation, he entered a small cavern.

He gave a startled cry at what he saw.

A huge distorted shadow of an ogre towered over him, a massive club in its hand.

'Welcome, young samurai,' spoke a quiet voice.

Jack spun round to where a saffron-robed monk with a bald round head, a skinny neck and a childlike smile was feeding an open fire with a twig.

A pot rested in the flames, happily boiling away.

'I'm just brewing some tea. Would you like some?'

Jack didn't answer. He was still shaken by the appearance of this tiny man whose shadow seemed to have a grotesque life of its own.

'It's the finest *sencha* Japan has to offer,' insisted the monk, indicating with a wave of his hand for Jack to sit.

'Who are you?' asked Jack, warily taking his place on the opposite side of the crackling fire.

'Who am I? A very good question and one that takes a lifetime to answer,' he replied, sprinkling tea leaves into the boiling pot. 'I can tell you what I am. I am Yamabushi.'

Jack looked blankly at the old man.

'Literally, it means "one who hides in the mountains",' he explained, tending the fire, 'but the villagers call me the Mountain Monk. They occasionally come to me for spiritual healing and divination.'

He lifted the pot from the fire and poured a watery green brew into a plain brown teacup. He handed Jack the steaming *sencha*.

'You cannot know who you are, unless you know *how* you are that person.'

Though he didn't like green tea, Jack accepted the drink out of courtesy. He took a sip. It tasted bitter. Certainly not the finest *sencha* Jack had ever tried. Nonetheless, he smiled politely and took another gulp to finish it quickly. Glancing round the cavern, he noticed it was empty apart from a small shrine set into the rock, circled by flickering candles and incense.

'Are you the Spirit challenge?' enquired Jack.

'Me? Of course not,' the monk chuckled, his laughter rebounding off the cavern walls in eerie mocking echoes.

'You are.'

47

SPIRIT COMBAT

The cup in Jack's hand drooped and slowly melted like hot tar to the floor. Jack stared at the gooey mess, then looked up at the Mountain Monk for an explanation.

The skinny monk smiled serenely as if nothing unusual was happening, his saffron robes now an intense orange and his head like a round citrus fruit ripened under the Mediterranean sun. His eyes sparkled as if sprinkled with stardust and his grin was as wide as a crescent moon.

'What's happening?' exclaimed Jack in panic.

'What's happening?' repeated the monk, his words slow and slurred like they were molasses in Jack's ears. 'A very good question and one you must ask when you meet your maker.'

Jack's head swirled. At some point during their conversation, the cavern had expanded to the size of a cathedral and its rock walls now breathed in and out in steady contractions. The circle of candles around the shrine had become a multicoloured rainbow that left tracer lines of light like fireworks exploding inside his eyeballs. The fire between Jack and the monk suddenly roared, flaring into a white-hot furnace too bright to look at.

Jack rubbed his eyes, trying to clear the crazy visions.

When he dared open them again, the fire had died down to glowing embers and the monk had disappeared. Only the teapot remained, lying on its side.

What had just happened? Was his mind playing tricks on him? Was it an after-effect of Dragon Eye's Death Touch?

Jack looked around for the monk, but the cavern was deserted.

Akiko had been right. He had pushed himself too far by taking on this final challenge. He was too drained to cope and now he was seeing things.

Jack picked up the teapot.

It squealed at him and Jack dropped it in shock. The pot suddenly grew hundreds of little black legs like a millipede and scuttled away in a mad panic. Before he could comprehend what he had just seen, he was distracted by a harsh cracking sound behind him.

Jack forced himself to turn his head.

His scream caught in his throat, unable to escape alongside the rush of terror and panic that tried to claw its way out at the same time.

A giant black scorpion, big enough to devour a horse, skittered over the cavern floor towards him. Jack couldn't move for fear. The creature scuttled closer and examined its prey.

'It's not real, it's not real, it's not real . . .' Jack feverishly repeated to himself.

Then the scorpion raised one of its powerful pincers and swiped at Jack. It struck him in the chest and Jack went flying against the cavern wall.

'It's real, it's real, it's real . . .' stammered Jack, struggling to his feet.

The scorpion attacked, its stinger swishing through the air straight at Jack's heart.

Jack dived to the right and the barb ricocheted off the rock face behind. It struck again as he rolled across the floor, just managing to avoid its poisoned tip.

Scrambling to his feet, he ran for the gap in the wall, but the scorpion was too quick and blocked his path. The creature, aware it had him trapped, slowly advanced, its pincers crackling and its stinger flicking like a poisoned spear.

Backed up against the rear wall, Jack had nowhere left to hide. He bent down to pick up a rock to defend himself with and there, lying discarded on the floor, was the little paper crane Yori had made for him.

Origami.

Nothing is as it appears.

All of a sudden, he understood that he was in the midst of the Spirit challenge. The High Priest had instructed them to 'be the master of your mind, rather than being mastered by your mind'.

Whether the scorpion was real or not didn't matter.

His mind believed it was. And . . .

Just like a piece of paper can be more than a piece of paper in origami, *becoming a crane, a fish or a flower; so a samurai should never underestimate their own potential to bend and fold to life.*

Yori's answer to the *origami koan* flashed bright and clear like a beacon in Jack's head. He had to strive to become more than he appeared, to go beyond his natural limits.

Jack roared at the scorpion in defiance.

The creature hesitated a moment.

Then it went for the kill.

Jack roared louder as if he was a lion and struck out with his fist. But it was a fist now armed with the claws of a lion. It batted the scorpion's tail away and Jack pounced cat-like on to the creature's back.

The scorpion bucked and reared, but Jack rode it out, driving his claws deep into the creature's exoskeleton. The scorpion struck wildly with its stinger, Jack dodging from side to side to avoid its poisoned tip.

As it struck yet again, he flung himself on to the creature's head. At the last possible moment he leapt away. It was too late, though, for the creature to pull back its strike. Its barbed tail sunk deep into its own solitary eye, a single green lidless orb that glowed in the dark.

Blinded, the scorpion whirled in frenzied agony, emitting an unholy high-pitched screech that echoed around the cavern. The scream was then drowned out by the sound of a thunderclap and the fire flared again, as bright as the sun.

The scorpion was gone and Jack was sitting opposite the Mountain Monk, who was throwing incense powder on to his fire, each handful turning the flames a bright purple and sending out heady waves of lavender-scented smoke.

'Would you like some?' he asked, handing Jack a cup of lemony liquid.

Jack refused to take it, afraid of what horrors it might unleash.

'I would advise drinking it,' the monk insisted. 'Together with the incense, it counters the effects of the tea.'

Jack did as he was told and within moments he felt his world returning to its normal dimensions.

'Well?' asked Jack as the monk began to prepare another pot of water for a brew.

'Well, what?' replied the Mountain Monk, bemused.

Jack was becoming irritated with the man's obtuse attitude. 'Have I passed?'

'I don't know. Did you?'

'But you set the Spirit challenge, surely you decide.'

'No. You decided your opponent. To know your fears is to know yourself.' He put the teapot down and looked Jack in the eye. 'The key to being a great samurai in peace and war is freedom from fear. If you defeat your nemesis, then you become the master of your fears.'

With a wave of his hand, the monk indicated the way out to Jack. 'Please, I have to prepare for the next guest.'

Jack gave the monk a bewildered bow then headed for the crack in the wall.

'Jack-kun,' called the Mountain Monk just as he reached the hole.

Jack stopped in his tracks, trying to recall when he had told the monk his name.

'Understand that those who successfully complete the Spirit challenge are not free of fear, but are simply no longer afraid to fear.'

★ ★ ★

312

Jack stood in the centre of the grassy plateau alongside Akiko and Kazuki. The sun beat down with a glorious warmth and the three highest peaks of the Iga mountain range towered majestically over them in the bright blue sky.

The students, sensei and temple monks formed three concentric circles around the three of them. On the command of the High Priest, the three circles clapped three times then cheered at the tops of their voices three times, their shouts echoing across the valley.

Jack's heart swelled with pride. He had done it. Against all the odds, he had conquered the Circle. He had survived.

Turning to face Akiko, he saw that she was trying to hold back her own tears, a mixture of relief and delight sparkling in her eyes. When she had come down off the mountain after him, Jack had rejoiced as she recounted how she'd defeated her inner demon, a host of vampire bats, with the aid of her protecting spirit, a pure white falcon. Jack had thought how appropriate that a bird of swift beauty and sharp instinct was her guardian. Akiko had been equally delighted to hear that his spirit had taken the form of a lion.

Then there had been a tense wait, while Kazuki scaled the peak and entered the Spirit cave himself. For a long while, he failed to emerge and Jack, going against the spirit of *bushido*, secretly hoped that Kazuki had failed in his final challenge. But no sooner had this thought occurred than his arch-rival had returned triumphant. Jack didn't discover what Kazuki's protective spirit was, though he assumed it was a snake or something equally venomous.

'Young samurai, the Circle is complete,' announced the

High Priest, stepping up to join them in the centre of the Circle of Three. 'Your mind, body and spirit will forever form a never-ending circle.'

He indicated for the three of them to link hands to form a fourth and final inner circle. Jack and Kazuki reluctantly grasped one another's hand and Akiko couldn't help but laugh at their discomfort.

'But while your body and mind have been strengthened by these challenges,' continued the High Priest, 'always remember that the most important thing for a samurai is not the sword you hold in your hand or the knowledge between your ears; it is what is in your heart. Your spirit is your true shield. If your spirit is strong, you can accomplish anything.'

48

THE CHALLENGE

Akiko stared aghast at Yamato's proposal.

They were back at the *Niten Ichi Ryū*, gathered in Jack's room within the Hall of Lions. The return journey that morning from the Iga mountains had been a relaxed one, made all the more enjoyable by their triumph in the Circle of Three and the splendid spring sunshine that had graced their ride home.

Jack was still tired and all the muscles in his body ached, but following the best nightmare-free sleep he'd had in a long while, he felt rejuvenated. Indeed, in a few days he thought he would be raring to train again. However, the debate they were having at that moment chilled him to the bone.

He had told Yamato and Akiko about his encounter with Dragon Eye and they were now discussing what to do with the *rutter*. With every mention of the ninja's name, his heart burnt as he recalled the assassin's sinister powers.

'I'm serious,' Yamato persisted. 'Dokugan Ryu thinks Jack is dead. We can take him by surprise.'

'No,' countered Akiko. 'You can never surprise a ninja. They're trained in laying traps. Dragon Eye would instinctively sense that something's wrong.'

'Why would he?' said Yamato. 'Besides if we don't get him now, he'll just go after Jack again.'

'We should move the *rutter* first,' Jack suggested, warming to Yamato's plan. 'We have the Circle of Three celebration tonight at *daimyo* Takatomi's castle. We can slip out during the proceedings and hide it elsewhere before Dragon Eye gets his hands on it.'

'That's if he hasn't already got it,' said Akiko, shaking her head in despair. 'This isn't a training game. This is real. The Circle hasn't suddenly made you invincible, Jack. Though Dragon Eye seems to be. He keeps escaping every time and no one's ever defeated him. What makes you think you can now?'

'That's *my* point: until we kill him, he'll always be a threat,' argued Yamato fervently.

'Why are you so fixed on this foolish idea of a trap? It's plain suicide,' said Akiko. 'It's like you've got something to prove.'

'I have!' said Yamato, clenching his fists, his blood boiling as he got more worked up. 'Jack's not the only one who wants revenge. Dokugan Ryu killed my brother, Tenno. Remember? Upholding the Masamoto family honour requires that the ninja dies. This *is* my best chance to prove myself.'

Yamato's thunderous mood, the one Jack knew so well from when he was on the receiving end, appeared to be consuming his friend.

'Calm down, Yamato,' interjected Jack, placing a reassuring hand on his arm.

'Calm down?' exploded Yamato, snatching his arm away. 'Of all the samurai, I thought you'd understand. He murdered your father as he did my brother. Dragon Eye's not all about you and your precious *rutter*, Jack. I feel pain too. Every day. It's just that I don't have anything that ninja still wants. He's already taken the only brother I had from me!'

A tense silence fell between the three of them.

Jack felt ashamed. He hadn't ever considered Yamato's situation that way before. He'd always been concerned with his own predicament, working out ways he could safely get home without the need for Masamoto's protection, worrying about what had become of his little sister, mourning his father's death and wondering how he could defend himself against Dragon Eye. Yamato would be suffering as much as he was. He'd lost his own flesh and blood too.

'I didn't think . . .' began Jack.

'I'm sorry . . .' said Akiko, bowing.

Yamato held up his hand in peace, drawing in a deep breath to calm himself.

'Forget it. I'm sorry I let my temper get the better of me.' He bowed his apologies to both Jack and Akiko. 'We shouldn't be fighting with one another like this. We should be fighting Dragon Eye. He's the cause of it all. Always has been.'

'Don't you think it's time,' suggested Akiko, 'that we told Masamoto about the *rutter*?'

★ ★ ★

Jack knelt before Masamoto, Sensei Hosokawa and Sensei Yamada in the Hall of the Phoenix, the silk-screen painting of the flaming bird rising up behind them like an avenging angel.

'I was delighted with your performance in the Circle of Three, Jack-kun,' said Masamoto, putting down his cup of *sencha* and gazing at Jack with admiration. 'As my adopted son, I am as proud of you as your father would have been.'

Jack had to blink back tears at the mention of his father and the unexpected affection displayed by his guardian. Throughout his time at the samurai school, Jack had missed the encouragement and support his father would have given him. Whether it was a sly wink of approval, or a piece of advice, or just his father enveloping him in arms as strong as the ocean. Those were the precious moments that had been absent in his life over the past two years.

'You completed the Circle challenges with the true *bushido* virtues of loyalty, rectitude and courage,' continued Masamato, 'so I look forward to personally instructing you in the technique of the Two Heavens.'

Jack's heart leapt. Finally, he would get to use Masamoto's swords. At last, he was to be taught this unbeatable skill.

'But now to the heart of this meeting,' said Masamoto, his tone turning serious. 'Is there something you wish to tell me?'

Jack was taken aback by the question. How could he know?

Akiko, Yamato and himself had been discussing whether to raise the issue of the *rutter* with Masamoto, when Jack had received the summons to go to the Hall of the Phoenix to see Masamoto. Before Jack left for this unexpected appointment, the three of them had agreed that they should tell Masamoto about the existence of the *rutter*. Jack realized the consequences of this could be severe and had insisted that Akiko and Yamato remain behind. There was no reason for them to be punished too. He would deny his friends' involvement, maintaining they had no knowledge of the logbook.

Following such praise and assertions of fatherly pride from Masamoto, a wave of guilt now replaced the elation Jack had been feeling. He was ashamed to have to admit to his guardian that he'd lied to him.

'Thank you, Masamoto-sama, for your kind words,' began Jack, bowing low, 'but I don't deserve them.'

Masamoto leant forward, one eyebrow raised in curiosity. 'Why ever not?'

'I know why the ninja attacked us in the Iga mountains. It was Dragon Eye. He was after me. Or, to tell the truth, after my father's *rutter*.'

'What's a *rutter*?' asked Sensei Hosokawa.

Jack told the three of them about the logbook, describing how pilots used it to navigate their ships, and explaining the *rutter*'s importance to trade and politics among the countries of Europe.

'I'm sorry, Masamoto-sama, but I lied to you,' Jack confessed. 'The reason why Dragon Eye attacked Hiroko's house in Toba was because of the *rutter*. I should have told you at the time, but I'd made a promise to my father to keep it secret. I didn't know who to trust and then I was worried if you had the *rutter*, you'd become the target for Dragon Eye, rather than me.'

Masamoto stared at Jack. His stony expression gave little away, but Jack noticed the scars on his face had begun to redden. Sensei Hosokawa's expression was equally severe. Sensei Yamada was the only one who looked kindly upon Jack, his eyes crinkling in sympathy at Jack's predicament.

'We will have to deal with this matter tomorrow,' declared Masamoto tersely. 'Unfortunately there's a more pressing issue to be discussed first.'

Jack wondered what could be worse than breaking the fifth virtue of *bushido* by lying to his guardian.

Masamoto nodded to Sensei Hosokawa. The swordmaster picked up a large scroll of paper and passed it to Jack.

'Explain this!' demanded Masamoto.

Jack stared at the paper. It was the size of a poster with *kanji* scrawled across it. Having been taught the basics of Japanese handwriting by Akiko, Jack recognized his name among the characters.

'What is it?' Jack asked.

The three samurai exchanged confused looks.

'It's a challenge declaration,' replied Masamoto, as if that explained everything.

Jack continued to stare in bewilderment at the scroll.

'You may have succeeded in the Circle of Three, but your confidence in your abilities may be somewhat misguided,' observed Sensei Hosokawa grimly. 'What on earth made you think of entering into a sword duel with an unknown samurai on his *musha shugyo*?'

Jack looked up in shock at the sensei. Surely they were

playing a joke on him. The grave expression on their faces, however, told him otherwise.

'I . . . didn't enter any duel,' stammered Jack.

'Your name's down here, claiming to be the Great Blond Samurai,' replied Sensei Hosokawa, pointing at the *kanji*. 'Sasaki Bishamon, the samurai in question, has accepted your challenge. You are expected in the duelling ground before sunset tonight.'

Jack was stunned into silence. This couldn't be happening. He hadn't written his name down for any challenge. He had no wish to risk his life duelling with a samurai just to prove whose martial arts were the best. And certainly not against a warrior named after the God of War.

His only intention was to retrieve the *rutter*. That was if Masamoto still allowed him to go to Nijo Castle tonight for the Circle of Three celebration. His guardian may have suspended judgement on the issue of the *rutter* until the following day, but the threat of it hung over Jack like a guillotine.

Now Jack had the prospect of a duel to contend with too.

'I didn't write this,' insisted Jack, his eyes pleading. 'I can't fight this samurai.'

Jack's mind whirled in panic. Such a duel could end in him losing a limb, or even in death. Who could have done such a thing?

Kazuki.

The boy had vowed he would get his revenge. This was it. Jack had to admire his rival's genius, though. It was so neat, so Kazuki.

'If not you, then who?' asked Masamoto.

Jack was about to blurt out Kazuki's name, when he remembered how he had falsely accused his rival of cheating in the Circle. How wrong he had been then. He could be as mistaken in his judgement this time, jumping to conclusions based solely on his own prejudices.

Jack looked to the floor and slowly shook his head. 'I don't know.'

'In that case, we are presented with a difficult dilemma,' said Masamoto, taking a thoughtful sip of his *sencha*. 'Your name and the name of this school have been seen on this challenge declaration around Kyoto. If you pull out of the duel now, you will bring shame not only on yourself, but on the Masamoto name and on the *Niten Ichi Ryū*.'

'Can't you explain that it was a mistake?' pleaded Jack.

'It would make no difference. Your challenge has been accepted.'

'But surely I'm too young to fight a duel?'

'How old are you?' asked Sensei Hosokawa.

'Fourteen this month,' replied Jack with hope.

'I fought my first duel at thirteen,' reminisced Masamoto with a hint of pride. 'Against one Arima Kibei, a famous swordsman back then. He too put up a sign appealing for challengers. I was an impetuous boy at the time, so naturally put my name down. In fact, I see a great deal of myself in you, Jack-kun. At least, sometimes. That's why, I must admit, I'm a little disappointed that you didn't actually issue the challenge; and even more disappointed that I find out you've been lying to me.'

Jack felt his cheeks flush with shame and could no longer meet his guardian's eyes.

'But no matter,' continued Masamoto. 'At sundown you will honour this school and prove yourself a mighty young samurai of the *Niten Ichi Ryū*.'

Jack's jaw dropped in disbelief. 'But I haven't sparred with a real sword yet!'

'Neither had I,' retorted Masamoto, with a dismissive wave of the hand. 'I defeated Arima with my *bokken*.'

It was then that Jack realized he was to be given no option. He would have to fight the samurai.

'Looks like you've finally got what you wished for. Your impatience to use your swords in class has caught up with you,' commented Sensei Hosokawa with a wry smile. 'I wouldn't concern yourself too much, though. I've seen you practising with your *katana* in the Southern Zen Garden. Your form's good. You could survive.'

Could? thought Jack, alarmed by his sensei's relaxed attitude.

He hoped his chances were better than that.

49

THE DUELLING GROUND

The young samurai lay twitching in the dust, blood spurting from his severed neck across the duelling ground in miniature rivers of red.

The crowd bayed and whistled, hankering for more bloodshed.

Distraught at the young man's fate, Jack stood at the edge of the makeshift arena of spectators, gripping the hilt of his sword so tightly his knuckles went white and the inlaid metal *menuki* dug painfully into his palm.

Staring down into the samurai's eyes, Jack witnessed the life drain from them like the flame of a guttering candle.

'Next!' bellowed the formidable warrior, who stood victorious in the centre of the duelling ground. The samurai on his *musha shugyo* was dressed in a dark red-and-white *hakama*. He held his *katana* aloft then brought it down sharply, flicking his opponent's blood from the blade – *chiburi*.

Yamato nudged his friend forward. 'He's calling for you, Jack.'

'This is just brilliant, isn't it?' said Saburo, as he stuffed an *obanyaki* into his mouth, the custard filling of the pastry spilling down over his chin.

'How can you say that?' exclaimed Akiko.

'We've got to see a duel! I didn't think we'd get back in time from the Circle of Three.'

'Saburo,' said Jack, mortified at his friend's insensitivity. 'I'm about to die.'

'No, you aren't,' said Saburo, dismissing the idea with a jovial grin. 'Masamoto has agreed with your opponent that your match will be to first blood only. You might get a battle scar, but he won't kill you.'

'But that last duel was supposed to be to first blood too!'

Saburo opened his mouth to reply, but obviously couldn't think of anything to say, so he took another bite of his *obanyaki* instead.

'That challenger was just unlucky, Jack,' said Yamato, trying to calm him. 'He pressed forward at the wrong time and got caught in the neck. An accident, that's all. It won't happen to you.'

Despite his friend's attempt at reassurance, Jack was still doubtful.

'Jack!' came a familiar cry, and the crowd opened up to let a small boy through.

Yori hobbled over, helped by Kiku.

'You should be in bed,' chided Jack. 'Your leg —'

'Don't worry about me,' interrupted Yori, leaning on his crutch. 'You were there for me when I needed you. Besides, I had to bring you this.'

Yori handed him an *origami* crane. It was tiny, smaller than a cherry-blossom petal, but perfectly formed.

'Thanks,' said Jack, 'but I've still got the one you gave me.'

'Yes, but this one's special. I finally finished *Senbazuru Orikata*. This is the thousandth crane. The one that holds the wish.'

For a brief moment, the little bird in Jack's hand seemed to flutter with hope.

'I'm praying my wish can protect you, just as you saved my life,' explained Yori with a hopeful look in his eyes.

Overwhelmed by his friend's compassion, Jack bowed, then tenderly slipped the little bird into the folds of his *obi*.

Masamoto strode over. 'Are you ready?'

Jack gave an unconvincing nod of his head.

'You needn't fear. You have my first swords,' Masamoto reassured him. 'They will serve you well. Just remember to carefully judge the distance between yourself and your adversary. Bring him into your sphere of attack. Draw him out. Whatever you do, don't let him draw you in.'

Jack bowed his appreciation for the advice.

'If you fight with courage,' said Masamoto, speaking low so no one else would overhear, 'you may yet regain your honour and my respect.'

Masamoto returned to his commanding position in the crowd. Jack now felt even more pressure to succeed. He had been given a chance to redeem himself in his guardian's eyes.

Sensei Kano now approached.

'How's your foot?' asked Jack.

Sensei Kano laughed. 'That's what I like about you,

Jack-kun. Always thinking of others before yourself. But what about your predicament? It'll soon be sunset, won't it? So try to attack your enemy at a point where the dying sun shines into his eyes.'

He gripped Jack's shoulders, then let go reluctantly to step aside for Sensei Yosa.

'Maintain your centre and stay balanced. I have faith that you will survive,' she said. Then she tenderly touched Jack's cheek with the back of her hand. 'But if that samurai harms more than a hair on your head, I'll make a pincushion of him with my arrows.'

Everyone seemed to want to offer Jack advice, even Sensei Kyuzo who, on his way to join the other sensei, said abruptly, '*Ichi-go, ichi-e.* You'll only get one chance. Don't make it your last.' The little knot of a man threw Jack a twisted grin, as if it hurt him to smile, then strolled off.

Jack didn't feel any better for the *taijutsu* master's counsel, and his mood plummeted further when he saw Kazuki and his Scorpion Gang swagger over, Moriko close by his side, her black teeth accentuated by her chalk-white face.

Then Kazuki stepped forward and bowed.

'Good luck, Jack,' he said, apparently in earnest.

'Err . . . thank you,' mumbled Jack, caught unawares by Kazuki's sincerity. Perhaps Kazuki wasn't responsible for entering his name after all.

Then, with a straight face, Kazuki asked, 'Can I have your swords after he's finished with you?'

The Scorpion Gang sniggered uncontrollably, revelling in their little joke, then they all strode away, laughing.

Akiko unexpectedly took Jack's hand in hers to comfort him. 'Ignore them, Jack. Don't forget what the High Priest said: *your spirit is your true shield*.'

'*Fudoshin!*' suggested Kiku helpfully. 'You'll need that for the fight too.'

'And remember what Sensei Kano taught us,' Yamato added. 'The eyes are the windows to your mind, so make sure you fight without eyes.'

'Have you eaten?' asked Saburo, offering Jack a skewer of chicken. 'A samurai should never fight on an empty stomach, you know.'

Jack shook his head, thoroughly bewildered by the onslaught of advice.

At that moment, Emi pushed through the crowd and presented Jack with a posy of yellow and red camellia.

'For luck,' she breathed into his ear. 'Don't be late for the celebrations tonight.'

Akiko reached between the two of them, graciously offering to hold the flowers for Jack. Emi gave her a civil smile and handed them over, though her eyes revealed annoyance.

'It's time, Jack-kun,' said Sensei Hosokawa, summoning him over to where the *musha shugyo* samurai waited, sword in hand.

'*Mushin*,' Sensei Hosokawa whispered into Jack's ear, having formally introduced Jack to his opponent, Sasaki Bishamon.

'But you said it would take me years to master *mushin*,' protested Jack as Sensei Hosokawa performed a final check on his sword for him.

'You no longer have the grace of time,' he replied, looking Jack in the eye. 'You have trained hard and you have completed the Circle. As long as you expect nothing and are ready for anything in this fight, *mushin* is within your grasp. Let your sword become no sword.'

With that last piece of counsel, he handed back the *katana* and left Jack alone to face his opponent in the centre of the bloodstained duelling ground.

Up close, Sasaki Bishamon appeared exactly like the God of War his name proclaimed him to be. Scars were visible on both his arms like long, dead snakes and his eyes were as hard and heartless as if they had been chiselled from granite. It was clear even in the way he stood that this samurai was no novice fighter. He had duelled his way across Japan.

What alarmed Jack the most, though, was the *kamon* emblazoned on the jacket of the man's *gi* and his white headband. A circle of four black scorpions.

Jack's first dream of the year flashed before his eyes and he recalled Sensei Yamada's reading. Scorpions symbolized treachery. Four meant death. He had encountered Kazuki's Scorpion Gang, the scorpion in the Spirit challenge and now this warrior's family crest. Was the samurai himself the fourth scorpion?

'I see you've already dressed for your funeral. How appropriate, *gaijin*,' laughed the samurai, pointing at Jack's chest.

Confused, Jack looked down at his own *gi*. In his haste to get ready for the duel, he had folded the right lapel over the left, like a corpse prepared for burial! Why hadn't anyone noticed this before?

'Soon there'll be one less *gaijin* in the world!' shouted someone in the crowd.

'Make his first blood his last!' cried another spectator.

These heckles were followed by a cacophony of cheering and jeering, the spectators seemingly split between *gaijin* supporters and haters.

The shouts grew louder and Jack became disorientated with the noise, heat and confusion of the duelling ground. His head whirled like a storm from all the advice he'd been given. He started to hyperventilate and Sensei Yamada, noticing his panic, shuffled to his side.

'Take a deep breath. You need to focus on the fight.'

'Sensei, I can't. He's going to kill me. Tell me what to do.'

'Nobody can give you wiser counsel than yourself,' replied Sensei Yamada, laying a reassuring hand on Jack's trembling sword arm to steady it. 'Act on the advice you would give to others. Consider what that would be.'

'Come on, you little urchin! No more time-wasting!' shouted the samurai, kicking at the dust.

'Don't be afraid of fear itself,' replied Jack without thinking.

Sensei Yamada nodded. 'Exactly. Remember – this samurai's flesh and blood. He's no Mountain Monk.'

The air was dreadfully dry. Jack's tongue felt like it was caked in dust. He tried to lick his lips, but fear seemed to have drained his mouth of all moisture.

The tips of their opposing *kissaki* glinted golden red in

the dying light of the day. Jack made a final adjustment to his grip on the sword. Masamoto's *katana*, although heavier than his *bokken*, was well balanced, the steel sharp and the blade true. Over the past months of practice, Jack had performed so many cuts with the weapon, he swore he could hear the sword whispering to him.

A calm gradually descended over him.

He was no longer scared but tense. Like the rope of a hangman's noose, he might snap at any moment, but he had already faced down and conquered his fear during the Spirit challenge.

Jack recalled Sensei Hosokawa's words: '*The three evils for a samurai are fear, doubt and confusion.*'

He had defeated his fear.

He had overcome his confusion.

Now there was only doubt.

Jack studied the callous face of his opponent. The man's grey eyes gave nothing away.

Not for the first time, Jack found himself staring into the face of death.

This time, though, he wouldn't hesitate.

Jack noticed the samurai held his *kissaki* slightly too low, exposing a way in straight to the neck.

To every spectator watching, the attack was so quick that it was like the blur of a startled bird. Jack knocked the samurai's sword to one side and struck at his target.

The blade whistled through the air.

And missed.

For the samurai, it had all been part of his plan. Enticing

Jack in with an opportunity and countering with a driving thrust to the stomach that began at Jack's bottom rib and finished its cut at the base of his belly.

A great cry of anguish broke from Akiko, Emi and the others, as Jack was skewered on the samurai's sword.

50

NO SWORD

It was only by the greatest good fortune that Jack had managed to avoid being impaled. The blade had pierced the loose side of his *gi*, slicing straight through his jacket but to one side, almost grazing his flesh. The sword was so close Jack could feel the hard cool steel against his skin.

Stupid! Stupid! Stupid!

Jack cursed himself, driving past his opponent, his *gi* ripping asunder in an effort to escape. He hastily created distance between himself and the samurai.

What had Masamoto said?

'*Whatever you do, don't let him draw you in.*'

That's exactly what he had just done.

The samurai glanced at Jack's exposed midriff, disappointed. 'Don't *gaijin* bleed?'

There was a ripple of laughter from the crowd.

'Of course not!' shouted a spectator. '*Gaijin* are like worms!'

The crowd erupted, some baying for Jack's blood, others defending his honour.

Jack felt his own anger swell at the bigotry of the

spectators. The majority seemed to have no concept of *bushido*. Where was the respect? The honour? The benevolence? The moral integrity of rectitude?

Drawing on his courage, Jack would show them exactly what it meant to be samurai.

Like Masamoto had told him to, Jack tossed his anger on to the water of his mind, letting it disappear in ripples.

He calmed his breathing and considered his strategy.

The first encounter had been too close.

He knew he wouldn't get a second chance.

This time he would wait for the samurai, willing the warrior to enter his sphere of attack. Though Jack was now completely calm inside, he gave an outward impression of being distraught.

He let his sword shake. He appeared to attempt an escape, circling around until his back was to the sun and the samurai had to squint at him. He even began to blubber.

'Please . . . don't kill me . . .' pleaded Jack.

Sasaki Bishamon shook his head, disgusted. There were boos from the crowd and Jack caught Masamoto hanging his head at Jack's shameful surrender.

'You're pathetic. So much for the Great *Gaijin* Samurai,' spat the warrior, flicking his sword at Jack. 'It's time I put you out of your misery.'

The samurai approached in slow deliberate steps, lifting the *katana* high to slice down through Jack, with the clear intent of not only drawing first blood, but making it the last blood Jack ever shed.

Jack willed his mind to flow like water.

Mushin.

No mind.

He let the baying of the crowd fade into the background.

No sound.

He let the samurai's advance become still.

No distraction.

He let the sword in his hand become one with his heart.

No sword.

The samurai struck without mercy.

Time appeared to have slowed as a spontaneous knowledge of the warrior's attack blossomed in Jack's mind. He knew exactly where the samurai was directing his sword. He knew when to step within its arc so he could evade it. He knew where to strike and when.

Jack knew the hand of his mind now wielded the sword.

He acted intuitively.

In three quick swipes, the duel was over.

With the same accuracy that Sensei Hosokawa had cleaved the grain of rice in two, Jack had cut the samurai, slicing through his *obi*, *hakama* trousers and headband.

First the man's *obi* hit the ground.

Then his *hakama* fell in a heap.

Finally the samurai's headband floated down through the air, the scorpion *kamon* cut exactly in half.

The warrior turned on Jack and roared, bringing his sword up to retaliate.

'First blood!" announced Masamoto, quickly stepping between the two of them to halt the fight.

The samurai blinked in disbelief. He had the tiniest trickle of blood running down his forehead from where Jack had nicked him with his *kissaki*.

'My apologies,' said Jack, bowing to stifle a grin. 'I didn't mean to hurt you.'

One of the spectators began to laugh.

Then another joined in. And another. Soon the whole crowd was in fits of laughter, many of the women waving their little fingers at the defeated warrior. Slowly it dawned on the samurai that he was totally naked, his *hakama* around his ankles. The warrior glanced around, mortified at his loss of face. Pulling up the remains of his clothing round him, he fled from the duelling ground.

Jack was swamped by his friends and a whole host of other students from the *Niten Ichi Ryū*, all clamouring to congratulate him.

Jack took in little of what was being said. His mind was lost in the moment of the duel. *Mushin.* He had mastered *mushin.* Or, at the very least, experienced it. More importantly, for a brief moment, his sword had existed in his heart. It had become part of him.

The sword was truly the soul of a samurai.

The crowd opened out to allow Masamoto and Sensei Hosokawa through.

'A masterful ruse, Jack-kun. You had me fooled,' commended Masamoto. 'If you cannot defeat your opponent physically, then you have to trick his mind. You have *earned* my respect.'

'I understand, Masamoto-sama,' replied Jack, bowing, and thanking God that he'd been forgiven for his lie over the *rutter*.

When he looked up again, Sensei Hosokawa stood

before him. His sharp eyes studied Jack as he pulled pensively at the sharp stub of his beard. Then his sword master grinned, broad and proud.

'Jack-kun, you are ready. You've proved to me you truly comprehend the Way of the Sword.'

51

KUNOICHI

The night was unduly warm and the room airless, making Jack sweat uncomfortably as his hand fumbled in the darkness for his father's *rutter*.

The high floating sound of a bamboo flute entwined with the vibrating plucking of a *shamisen* could be heard from the distant Grand Chamber of *daimyo* Takatomo's palace, where everyone was gathered to celebrate the completion of the Circle of Three.

'It's not here!' said Jack, a note of panic entering his voice.

'Are you sure?' queried Yamato.

'Yes. I left it on the upper ledge,' Jack insisted, as he emerged from behind the silk white crane that hung upon the wall of the reception room, 'but it's gone.'

'Let me look,' offered Akiko. She stepped on to the cedar dais and peered into the bolt-hole.

The three of them had slipped out of the celebrations, having left Saburo and Kiku to look after Yori. Their intention had been to retrieve the *rutter* and return before anyone noticed their absence. Masamoto, now aware of the logbook, had asked to see it for himself, requesting that Jack bring it to him the following morning. Jack had agreed, though he hadn't revealed its location in case he further angered the samurai.

But it appeared they were too late. Dragon Eye had already stolen it.

'How could he have got into a ninja-proof castle?' despaired Jack, slumping to the floor.

'Jack!'

Jack was vaguely aware that Akiko was waving something in front of his face.

'Is this what you were looking for?' She smiled, brandishing the oilskin-covered *rutter* in her hand, and placed it in his lap. 'It had just fallen on the floor.'

'You are . . .' began Jack, but he didn't quite know how to express his relief and joy to Akiko.

The music in the Great Chamber came to an end and in the lull a bird could be heard singing.

A nightingale.

The grin on Jack's face faded as he remembered *daimyo* Takatomi's unique alarm system built into the floorboards.

His growing look of horror was mirrored by both Akiko and Yamato.

Someone was coming.

'Quick! Hide the *rutter*,' instructed Akiko.

The Nightingale Floor sang with each approaching footstep.

Jack had no choice. He replaced the logbook on the upper ledge and let the wall hanging fall back into place.

Outside the noise of the floorboards ceased.

The stranger was at the *shoji* door.

They looked at one another. What should they do? If it was a guard, they could they pretend they were lost; but if it wasn't, shouldn't they be getting ready to fight?

The *shoji* slid open.

A figure knelt before them, silhouetted in the corridor, the face veiled in shadow.

No one moved.

Jack noticed the wall hanging was still swinging slightly and desperately willed it to stop.

The figure bowed and stood.

A beautiful woman in a jade-green kimono, her long hair twirled high upon her head and fastened with an ornate hairpin, glided into the room.

'The *daimyo* thought you might like some refreshments for your private party,' the woman said softly, putting a small tray with a teapot and four china cups down on the *tatami*.

She indicated for them to sit.

Bewildered, yet somewhat relieved, the three of them did as they were told. Jack watched the serving woman pour out three cups of *sencha*. She smiled kindly, offering Jack the first drink; her eyes, shiny as black pearls, never leaving his face.

Jack waited for the others to be served before drinking.

The Nightingale Floor sang again and everyone froze.

The woman slipped a fan from her *obi*, flicking open its black metal spine to reveal an exquisite handpainted design of a green dragon entwined in misty mountains.

'It is rather warm,' she commented, fluttering the fan in front of her face. 'You must be thirsty.'

Jack, his mouth dry with dread at the approach of a second visitor, raised the cup to his lips.

The *shoji* slid open a second time and Emi entered.

'My father was wondering where you all were,' she said, her expression rather indignant at not having been invited to their private gathering. 'He wants to . . . Who are *you*?'

Emi stared at the serving woman. 'You don't work here.'

Before anyone could react, the woman flung her tray at Emi, spilling the tea across the floor. The tray went spinning through the air like a large square *shuriken* and struck Emi in the neck. She collapsed to the ground, knocked unconscious.

'*Kunoichi!*' screamed Akiko, rolling away from the imposter.

'Don't drink it, Jack!' Yamato cried as he slapped the cup from his hands. 'Poison!'

Momentarily stunned, Jack could only stare at the *tatami*, which gave off tiny wafts of acrid smoke where the tea had been spilt.

'Ninja?' said Jack in disbelief, looking up at the beautiful woman before him. He'd thought only men were ninja.

The female ninja snapped her dragon fan shut and brought its hardened metal spine down on to Jack's head like a hammer. Yamato threw himself in front of Jack, shoving his friend out of harm's way, but the iron tip of the fan caught Yamato on the temple. He went down and stayed down.

Flipping to her feet, the *kunoichi* leapt over the prone body of Yamato and advanced on Jack. As she raised her hand to strike a second time, Akiko crescent-kicked the iron fan from the woman's grasp.

The ninja immediately retaliated with a devastating sidekick to Akiko's stomach, sending her flying across the room.

In that brief moment of distraction, Jack managed to scramble to his feet. Seeing his friends lying injured around him, his fury fuelled his strength as he went on the attack.

The female ninja retreated before Jack's spinning-hook kick. She ducked while putting a hand to her head. Her hair cascaded down her back in a billowing black cloud and a bolt of lightning flashed out, straight towards Jack's right eye.

Jack staggered backwards to avoid the sharpened hair-pin, its glinting point flying past his eyeball.

She stabbed at his face a second time, but was way off target.

Jack watched as the steel pin passed to his left and suddenly Sensei Kano's lesson 'learn to fight without eyes' came to mind. His eyes had instinctively followed the gleaming weapon, but the wild slash of the ninja had been a distraction tactic.

When he turned back to face her, she held an open palm to her mouth and blew a cloud of glittering black dust into his eyes.

Stung with a combination of sand, sawdust and pepper, tears streamed down Jack's face.

His whole world went dark.

Jack had been blinded.

52

SASORI

'Akiko! I can't see!'

She dived across to protect him, and Jack heard the swish of the hairpin and the dull thud of arms colliding as Akiko blocked another of the *kunoichi*'s attacks. Jack thought he recognized the noise of Akiko retaliating with a front kick, for he heard the woman stumble away, groaning as if winded.

His eyes watered like acrid geysers and he had to screw them up against the pain. Without his sight, he could only follow the sounds of Akiko battling the *kunoichi* in the far corner of the room.

'Watch out!' cried Akiko.

Jack threw up his guard, blindly trying to make contact and use his *chi sao* skills, but the *kunoichi* evaded him. Focusing on the sound of her ragged breathing, Jack pinpointed where she'd moved to, but Akiko jumped between them to intercept an unseen strike from the ninja. Now Jack couldn't attack in case he hit Akiko instead.

Behind him, he thought he caught the sound of a soft rustle from the silk wall hanging and the soft pad of a foot.

Then Jack sensed the cedar dais upon which he stood give ever so slightly under someone else's weight.

Jack spun round, keeping his guard up to protect his face.

His arms collided with a fist that had been aimed directly at the back of his head. Allowing his *chi sao* training to take over, Jack followed the curvature of his attacker's arm and speared his fingers at the throat. His thrust was brushed aside with a countering block and strike. Instantaneously, Jack felt the trajectory of the counter and deflected it with an inner block, rolling his arm over his attacker's and back-fisting his opponent in the face.

He caught his assailant hard on the jaw.

The contact was solid and jarring, but his opponent only laughed, a cold jagged cackle like a rusty broken saw catching in wood.

Jack lost contact, his attacker retreating out of reach.

'Impressive, *gaijin*,' hissed Dokugan Ryu, 'but even more impressive that you're still alive. You should be a ninja, not a samurai!'

Jack's heart gave an aching throb. The proximity of Dragon Eye made his whole body contract, his lungs tighten.

'I'm not scared of you,' said Jack, with as much bravado as he could muster.

'Of course you are,' countered Dragon Eye, circling him slowly. 'I'm the pain that seeps into your bones at night. The scalding fire that burns in your blood. Your worst nightmare. Your father's murderer!'

Dragon Eye struck with such swiftness that Jack was

caught off-guard. The ninja hit a point at the base of his shoulder and a sickening flare of pain rocketed down his right arm. Jack reeled backwards, gasping for breath, feeling as if his arm had been thrust into a white-hot fire.

'But I'm wasting my time here,' spat the ninja, as if bored with torturing his victim. 'I have what I came for.'

Through the agony, Jack was vaguely aware he could see shapes, dark shadows against a grey mist. The pain focused his mind and his vision was clearing.

'Sasori, stop teasing the girl!' ordered Dragon Eye. 'Kill her, then kill the *gaijin*.'

Jack blinked away his tears, catching the vague outline to his left of the hooded ninja against a misty-looking wall.

'Don't disappoint me again, *gaijin*. Stay dead this time.'

Hearing exactly where the ninja was, Jack launched a hook kick at his enemy's head.

His foot passed clean through thin air.

Dragon Eye had disappeared.

A soft exhalation escaped from someone's lips and the next thing Jack heard was a body crumple to the floor.

'Akiko!' exclaimed Jack.

No answer.

'Akiko?' repeated Jack, now afraid for her.

'Your pretty little girlfriend's dead, *gaijin*,' smirked the *kunoichi*. 'I sank my poisoned pin into her pretty little neck.'

A coldness crept into Jack's heart, more agonizing than any torture Dragon Eye could inflict upon him.

Jack flew at Akiko's murderer. He didn't care any more; he

no longer thought about what he was doing. He just struck.

The *kunoichi* struggled against his impassioned onslaught.

Blow after blow rained down upon the ninja.

Jack's forearm slammed into her guard and the *kunoichi* lost her grip on the deadly hairpin, sending it flying across the room.

He drove in harder. The ninja began to buckle under the pressure. Jack then sidekicked her with all his might, catching the *kunoichi* full force in the chest. The ninja fell backwards, landing hard on the dais, and screamed.

'Come on!' Jack roared, his eyes wet with stinging tears, no longer caused by the blinding powder, but by the grief in his heart.

But there was no response.

Jack wiped at his eyes. His vision was blurry, but he could just about see again.

The *kunoichi* lay unmoving in a heap on the dais.

He couldn't have kicked her that hard, thought Jack, not enough to kill her.

He took a cautious step closer and tapped her leg with his foot. There was no reaction. The woman's black eyes were dull and lifeless, their pearl-like shine gone.

Jack rolled her over.

The ninja's ornate steel hairpin protruded out of her back like the barb of a scorpion. Killed by her own poison.

Sasori, thought Jack numbly, Dragon Eye had called her *Sasori*.

Scorpion.

As much as he tried to deny it, his dream had come to be.

Four scorpions.

Kazuki's gang. The Spirit challenge. The warrior. The *kunoichi*.

Four meant death. But it had not been his own that the dream had foretold. It had been Akiko's.

Jack sank to his knees, barely taking in the devastation of the reception room. Yamato was slowly coming to among the broken shards of teacups. Emi still hadn't moved, her neck bruised and swollen, though Jack could see that she was breathing.

The hanging of the white crane had been ripped from the wall and the bolt-hole gaped open, black and empty like the socket of a skull.

Dragon Eye had the *rutter*.

Jack crawled over to Akiko.

She lay utterly still upon the *tatami*, a small prick of blood on her neck where the hairpin had entered. Jack, sobbing in great breaths of anguish, cradled her lifeless body in his arms.

53

THE WAY OF THE DRAGON

'CALL YOURSELF A SAMURAI!'

Masamoto could no longer contain his wrath.

He had kept a cool head when they discovered Jack and the others in the reception room. He had calmly organized a search party for Dokugan Ryu as well as extra protection for the *daimyo*. He had held back while arranging the students' safe return to the *Niten Ichi Ryū*. He had even maintained his composure while Jack had explained the reason for hiding the *rutter* in the *daimyo*'s castle.

But now he bellowed at Jack, who lay prostrate on the floor of the Hall of the Phoenix. Jack quivered with every forceful word Masamoto uttered, each one cutting as sharp as a *katana* blade.

'You sacrificed your friends, violated my trust and above all endangered the *daimyo*'s life, all for the sake of your father's *rutter*!'

Masamoto glared at Jack, fuming with pent-up anger, seemingly unable to express the fury he felt. With each passing moment of raging silence, the scars on Masamoto's face grew redder and redder.

348

'I could forgive you for the lie, but how can I overlook this? You made the *daimyo*'s castle a target for ninja!' he said, almost in a whisper, as if he was scared the violence in his voice would lead to violence in his hands. 'I thought you understood what it meant to be samurai. Your duty is to me and your *daimyo*. You've broken the code of *bushido*! Where was your loyalty? Where was your respect? Had I not proven by my guardianship that you could trust me?'

Masamoto had tears in his eyes. The idea that Jack couldn't trust him, and might not respect him, seemed to disappoint the great samurai the most.

'OUT OF MY SIGHT!'

Jack sat upon the bough of the old pine tree in the corner of the *Nanzen-niwa*. Hidden in darkness, he kicked despondently at the tree's wooden crutch, lashing out harder and harder until the branches shook.

He looked up at the night sky, wishing it would swallow him up, but the stars gave him no comfort either. They just reminded him of how lonely and lost he was. The tide was turning in Japan and foreigners like him were no longer welcome. Not only was he being alienated by the country he lived in, but he had estranged himself from his only protector. He had turned Masamoto against him.

He had nowhere to run and nowhere to hide.

Dragon Eye had finally got his hands on his father's *rutter*.

Jack cursed his stupidity. His failure.

He had failed his father's memory, for the *rutter* was no longer his.

He had failed his little Jess, for he had lost their only

heirloom, the one thing that could help him return home and secure their future.

He had failed his friends, for he'd proved incapable of protecting them.

Jack had lost everything most precious to him.

With his head in his hands, sobs wracking his whole body, Jack wondered whether he should leave the school now, or wait until the morning.

'All is not lost, young samurai. Don't despair.'

Jack glanced up, still weeping. He hadn't even heard the old man approach.

Sensei Yamada leant upon his walking stick, gazing at Jack with concerned affection while pensively twirling the tip of his long wispy beard around one bony finger.

'A storm in the night, that's all,' he said, the gentle kindness in his voice seeking to allay some of Jack's grief. 'In time, his anger will pass and he will see you for the samurai you are. All will be forgiven.'

'How can that be? I've betrayed him,' lamented Jack, the words cutting so deep into his heart he swore they drew blood. 'I've disrespected him. Broken his trust. Gone against the very *bushido* spirit he lives by.'

'Jack-kun, you breathe *bushido*.'

The old Zen master laid a hand upon Jack's arm and patted it lightly. 'Come with me,' he said, guiding Jack out from the darkness of the pine tree and into the pale light of the waxing moon. 'A walk will clear your mind.'

Jack followed blindly by his side as if he were a ghost, not really there, but listening nonetheless to the counsel of his sensei.

'I cannot condone your lying to Masamoto-sama about the *rutter*, but you've proved your honesty by confessing of your own free will,' began the Zen master, flicking a stone from the path with his stick. 'It was unfortunate that you chose the castle in which to hide your precious logbook. You hadn't thought through the consequences of that decision properly.'

Jack solemnly shook his head.

'However, I'm perfectly aware that your decision to put it in the castle was not done out of malice or with the intention of harming the *daimyo*. Your loyalty to your guardian and your respect for his life led you to believe that the lie was safer than the truth, and the castle more secure than the school. However misguided your intentions, you were trying to protect him, to do your duty. This is what Masamoto-sama will undoubtedly come to realize.'

As they reached one of the larger standing stones in the garden, Sensei Yamada rubbed its smooth surface.

'You are headstrong like this rock, Jack-kun. Your boldness in your plans and belief in your ability to deal with problems by yourself is reminiscent of Masamoto-sama's own youth. He too was a fiercely independent spirit.'

Sensei Yamada gave Jack a hard look, which Jack found difficult to meet.

'This is why his emotions are so strong. Masamoto-sama sees himself in you. He's not angry. He's afraid. Afraid that he will lose another son to that demon Dokugan Ryu.'

Sensei Yamada led Jack out of the garden and across the deserted courtyard of the *Niten Ichi Ryū*. Each pebble reflected the moonlight, transforming the square into a great ocean that appeared to ripple as they drifted across its surface towards the Buddha Hall.

'You believe you broke the code of *bushido*?'

Jack nodded his head, too upset to speak.

'Well, you are wrong. What you accomplished tonight, and in every previous encounter with that ninja, proves you are a samurai beyond all doubt. Your courage in the face of such danger can only be applauded. The benevolence you show to others, alongside the compassion you have for your friends, is what binds you together, protects you. It is what keeps you fighting against all the odds. This is a truly honourable principle. The very essence of *bushido*.'

They began to ascend the stone steps of the Buddha Hall, and Jack felt heartened by his sensei's wisdom, each step he took seeming to atone for another of his failings.

'You have always done what you thought was right. This is the first virtue of *bushido*, rectitude. The goodness in your heart is the one thing Dokugan Ryu can never take from you. As long as you possess this, he can never win.'

'But I've made an unforgivable mistake,' protested Jack, 'and I can't take it back.'

'There's no such thing as a mistake, young samurai.'

Sensei Yamada ushered Jack inside the *Butsuden*. The great bronze Buddha sat silent in prayer, surrounded by a ring of flickering candles and the tiny red glowing tips of burning incense sticks. The temple bell hung motionless above the Buddha's head like an ethereal crown, and Jack wondered whether one hundred and eight chimes would ever be enough to absolve him of his sins in the Buddha's eyes. First, though, he had to answer to his own God.

'Mistakes are our teachers,' explained Sensei Yamada, bowing before the Buddha. 'As long as you recognize them for what they are, they can help you learn about life. Each mistake teaches you something new about yourself. There is no failure, remember, except in no longer trying. It is the courage to continue that counts.'

Jack bowed and, in his despair, prayed for both Buddha's and God's blessing.

Sensei Yamada motioned for Jack to enter a side room of the *Butsuden*.

'You may see her now.'

The small room was aglow with candles. Jack bowed his head and entered alone, the richly aromatic smell of white sage and frankincense wafting in the air around him.

Akiko lay upon a thick futon, dressed in a fine silk kimono of cream and gold, delicately embroidered with pale-green bamboo shoots.

Jack approached quietly and knelt by her side.

She looked to be asleep. He took her hand gently in his. It felt cool to the touch.

'So your first dream did foretell our fortunes,' she whispered, her voice hoarse but resilient.

'You're lucky to be alive,' Jack replied, squeezing her hand affectionately.

'Mount Fuji, a hawk and the leaf of a *nasu*,' she laughed weakly. 'Sensei Yamada was right, they brought us all the luck in the world. What more could we have asked for?'

An explanation, thought Jack, but he let it pass. Now wasn't the time to ask about her miraculous survival.

Jack had overheard Sensei Yamada and Sensei Kano, as they laid her in the Buddha Hall to recover in peace, discussing *dokujutsu*, the ninja Art of Poison. The two sensei had both agreed that someone had helped her to build a tolerance against ninja poisons. Jack suspected the monk from the Temple of the Peaceful Dragon was responsible. He recalled how Akiko had appeared ill at New Year. She had told Kiku that it was something she'd drunk and then had gone straight to the monk for help. Had her condition been caused by trying to build up a resistance to such poisons? Akiko had a lot to explain, but for now Jack was just glad she was alive.

'I'm so sorry, Akiko. I should've listened to you. Whatever Sensei Yamada says, I made a stupid mistake in not –'

'Jack, it wasn't your fault,' she interrupted, softly putting a finger to his lips. 'The only mistake was Dragon Eye's – he let you live.'

Akiko beckoned Jack closer, drawing his face towards hers.

Their cheeks touched and Jack felt her warm breath grace his skin. For that brief moment he experienced total peace, safe within her arms.

Whispering in his ear, Akiko said, 'You have to get back the *rutter*. You must follow the Way of the Dragon.'

Notes on Sources

The following quotes and facts are referenced within *Young Samurai: The Way of the Sword* (with the page numbers in square brackets below) and their sources are acknowledged here:

1. [Pages 6 to 8] This old nursery rhyme, 'A man of words and not of deeds', is considered to originate from a play by John Fletcher (playwright, 1579–1625, a contemporary of Shakespeare) called *Lover's Progress* ('Deeds, not words', Sc. 6, Act III).

2. [Page 70] 'When tea is made with water drawn from the depths of mind, whose bottom is beyond measure, we really have what is called *cha-no-yu*' – Toyotomi Hideyoshi (samurai *daimyo*, 1537–98).

3. [Page 71] Tea was first introduced on English shores around 1652 by Dutch traders, who had only begun shipping it back to Europe in 1610. England was a latecomer to the tea scene.

4. [Page 185] 'In a fight between a strong technique and a strong body, technique will prevail. In a fight between

a strong mind and a strong technique, mind will prevail, because it will find the weak point' – Taisen Deshimaru (Japanese Soto Zen Buddhist teacher, 1914–82).

5. [Page 224] 'Those here now, those gone before, those yet to come' – based on a traditional Buddhist blessing and healing chant (anonymous).

ACKNOWLEDGEMENTS

A serious bow of respect and thanks must go to the following people who are all a vital part of the Young Samurai team: Charlie Viney, my agent, for guidance of the Young Samurai project on a worldwide scale and his continuing dedication to my career; Shannon Park, my editor at Puffin, for so ably picking up the editing sword from Sarah Hughes and making just the right cuts and suggestions; Louise Heskett, whose passion, dedication and enthusiasm are worthy of the greatest samurai; Adele Minchin and Penny Webber for launching a great campaign and overcoming the masses; and everyone at wonderful Puffin Books, in particular Francesca Dow; Pippa Le Quesne for early guidance and suggestions; Tessa Girvan at ILA for continuing to discover new countries in which to sell the Young Samurai series; Akemi Solloway Sensei for being such a generous supporter of the Young Samurai books (readers, please visit: *solloway.org*); Trevor Wilson of Authors Abroad for his sterling work in organizing my event bookings; Ian, Nikki and Steffi Chapman for their wonderful backing; David Ansell Sensei of the Shin Ichi Do dojo for his excellent tuition and guidance; my mum for being my number-one fan; my dad, without whom these books would not be so sharp; and my wife, Sarah, for making everything worthwhile. Lastly, all the librarians and teachers who have supported the series (you are my secret ninja force!) and all the Young Samurai readers out there – thank you for buying the book, reading it and sending me emails and letters telling me how much you enjoyed it. It makes all the hard work worthwhile.

JAPANESE GLOSSARY

Bushido

Bushido, meaning the 'Way of the Warrior', is a Japanese code of conduct similar to the concept of chivalry. Samurai warriors were meant to adhere to the seven moral principles in their martial arts training and in their day-to-day lives.

Virtue 1: *Gi* – Rectitude
Gi is the ability to make the right decision with moral confidence and to be fair and equal towards all people no matter what colour, race, gender or age.

Virtue 2: *Yu* – Courage
Yu is the ability to handle any situation with valour and confidence.

仁

Virtue 3: *Jin* – Benevolence

Jin is a combination of compassion and generosity. This virtue works together with *Gi* and discourages samurai from using their skills arrogantly or for domination.

礼

Virtue 4: *Rei* – Respect

Rei is a matter of courtesy and proper behaviour towards others. This virtue means to have respect for all.

真

Virtue 5: *Makoto* – Honesty

Makota is about being honest to oneself as much as to others. It means acting in ways that are morally right and always doing things to the best of your ability.

名誉

Virtue 6: *Meiyo* – Honour

Meiyo is sought with a positive attitude in mind, but will only follow with correct behaviour. Success is an honourable goal to strive for.

忠義

Virtue 7: *Chungi* – Loyalty

Chungi is the foundation of all the virtues; without dedication and loyalty to the task at hand and to one another, one cannot hope to achieve the desired outcome.

A short guide to pronouncing Japanese words

Vowels are pronounced in the following way:
'a' as the 'a' in 'at'
'e' as the 'e' in 'bet'
'i' as the 'i' in 'police
'o' as the 'o' in 'dot'
'u' as the 'u' in 'put'
'ai' as in 'eye'
'ii' as in 'week'
'ō' as in 'go'
'ū' as in 'blue'

Consonants are pronounced in the same way as English:
'g' is hard as in 'get'
'j' is soft as in 'jelly'
'ch' as in 'church'
'z' as in 'zoo'
'ts' as in 'itself'

Each syllable is pronounced separately:
A-ki-ko
Ya-ma-to
Ma-sa-mo-to
Ka-zu-ki

bō	wooden fighting staff
bōjutsu	the Art of the *Bō*
bokken	wooden sword
bushido	the Way of the Warrior

Butokuden	Hall of the Virtues of War
Butsuden	Buddha Hall
cha-no-yu	literally 'tea meeting'
chi sao	sticky hands (or 'sticking hands')
chiburi	to flick blood from the blade
Chō-no-ma	Hall of Butterflies
chudan	middle
daimyo	feudal lord
daishō	the pair of swords, *wakizashi* and *katana*, that are the traditional weapons of the samurai
Dim Mak	Death Touch
dojo	training hall
dokujutsu	the Art of Poison
fudoshin	literally 'immovable heart', a spirit of unshakable calm
fukuwarai	children's game like 'Pin the tail on the donkey'
futon	Japanese bed: flat mattress placed directly on *tatami* flooring, and folded away during the day
gaijin	foreigner, outsider (derogatory term)
Ganjitsu	New Year festival
gi	training uniform
hai	yes
hajime	begin
hakama	traditional Japanese clothing
Hakuhojo	the Castle of the White Phoenix
hanami	cherry-blossom viewing party

hanetsuki	a traditional Japanese game similar to badminton
hashi	chopsticks
hatsuhinode	the 'firsts' of the year: for example, the first visit to a temple in the New Year
inro	a little case for holding small objects
irezumi	a form of tattooing
itadakimasu	let's eat
kami	spirits within objects in the Shinto faith
kamon	family crest
kanji	the Chinese characters used in the Japanese writing system
kata	a prescribed series of moves in martial arts
katame waza	grappling techniques
katana	long sword
kendoka	sword practitioner
kenjutsu	the Art of the Sword
ki	energy flow or life force (Chinese: *chi* or *qi*)
kiai	literally 'concentrated spirit' – used in martial arts as a shout for focusing energy when executing a technique
kissaki	tip of sword
koan	a Buddhist question designed to stimulate intuition

kozo	the paper mulberry tree
kumite	sparring
kunoichi	female ninja
kyudoka	practitioner of archery
kyujutsu	the Art of the Bow
makiwara	padded striking post
menuki	decorative grip ornament
mochi	rice dumpling
mokuso	meditation
momiji gari	maple-leaf viewing
Mugan Ryū	the 'School of "No Eyes"'
musha shugyo	warrior pilgrimage
mushin	a warrior's state of 'no mind'
nage waza	throwing techniques
nasu	eggplant, aubergine
ninjutsu	the Art of Stealth
Niten Ichi Ryū	the 'One School of Two Heavens'
niwa	garden
obake karuta	Japanese card game (monster cards)
obanyaki	sweet bean-filled pastry
obi	belt
ofuro	bath
ohajiki	a game using small coin-shaped playing pieces
origami	the art of folding paper
ozoni	traditional soup served on New Year's Day
randori	free-sparring

rei	call to bow
roji	Japanese garden
Ryōanji	the Temple of the Peaceful Dragon
sado	the Way of Tea
saké	rice wine
sakura	cherry-blossom tree
sashimi	raw fish
sasori	scorpion
satori	enlightenment
saya	scabbard
sayonara	goodbye
seiza	sit/kneel
Senbazuru Orikata	One Thousand Crane origami
sencha	green tea
sensei	teacher
seoi nage	shoulder throw
shaku	unit of length, approximately equal to one foot or thirty centimetres
shamisen	three-stringed musical instrument
shi	the number four, or death
shinobi shozoku	the clothing of a ninja
Shishi-no-ma	Hall of Lions
Shodo	the Way of Writing, Japanese calligraphy
shoji	Japanese sliding door
shuriken	metal throwing stars
sohei	warrior monks

sushi	raw fish on rice
taijutsu	the Art of the Body (hand-to-hand combat)
Taka-no-ma	Hall of the Hawk
tamashiwari	Trial by Wood; woodbreaking
tantō	knife
Taryu-Jiai	inter-school martial arts competition
tatami	floor matting
tempura	deep fried seafood or vegetables
tetsu-bishi	small sharp iron spike
tofu	soya bean curd
tomoe nage	stomach throw
toshigami	spirits of the New Year
wakizashi	side-arm short sword
washi	Japanese paper
yakatori	grilled chicken on a stick
yuki gassen	snow battle
yame	stop!
Yamabushi	mountain monk, literally 'one who hides in the mountains'
zabuton	cushion
zazen	meditation

Japanese names usually consist of a family name (surname) followed by a given name, unlike in the Western world where the given name comes before the surname. In feudal Japan, names reflected a person's social status and spiritual beliefs. Also, when addressing someone, *san* is added to that person's surname (or given names in less formal situations) as a sign of courtesy, in the same way that we use Mr or Mrs in English, and for higher-status people *sama* is used. In Japan, *sensei* is usually added after a person's name if they are a teacher, although in the Young Samurai books a traditional English order has been retained. Boys and girls are usually addressed using *kun* and *chan*, respectively.

Origami: How to Fold a Paper Crane

How to fold a paper crane, by Akemi Solloway (née Tanaka) and Robyn Hondow

Begin with a large square piece of paper – one side coloured and the other plain. In all diagrams, the shaded part represents the coloured side and dotted lines the creases. Make sure all creases are sharp by running your thumbnail along them.

Step 1. Place the paper with the plain side down on the table. Fold it in half diagonally and open. Then fold in half the other way and open.

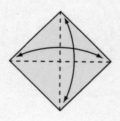

Step 2. Turn the paper over, so it is coloured side down. Fold it in half to make a wide rectangle and open. Then fold it in half to make a tall rectangle and open.

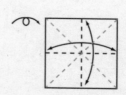

Step 3. With the coloured side down, bring the four corners of the square up and together. Flatten paper so you end up with a small folded square one quarter the size of the original paper.

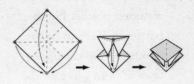

Step 4. Fold the top triangular flaps on the right- and left-hand sides into the centre to make a kite shape. Then unfold.

Step 5. Fold the top corner of the model downwards, crease well and unfold.

Step 6. Take the bottom corner of the upper layer and pull it up, so that it forms a canoe shape. Press down so that the sides of this canoe shape flatten to make a diamond shape. Flatten down, creasing well.

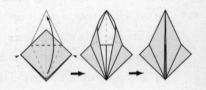

Step 7. Turn the paper over and repeat steps 4, 5 and 6 on the other side. The paper is now a flat diamond shape.

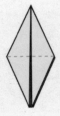

Step 8. The top half of the diamond is solid, but the bottom half seems to have two legs. Fold the upper layer of both legs into the centre line.

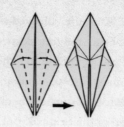

Step 9. Turn over and repeat the fold on the legs on that side, too. The diamond shape is now more like a kite.

Step 10. Fold both legs of the model up, crease very well, then unfold.

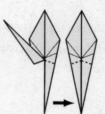

Step 11. Holding the right leg of the kite shape, open it up and reverse fold the leg along the central crease. Raise the leg up and position it inside the top part of the kite then flatten it. Repeat on the other side.

Step 12. There are now two
narrow points sticking out.
These are going to form the
head and tail of the crane.
Take the point on the right
and bend the tip down,
reversing the crease and
pinching it, to form the
beak of the crane.

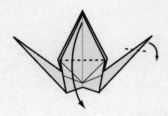

Step 13. Fold down the wings.

Step 14. Finally, pull the wings
and blow into the hole
underneath to open out the
body to complete your *origami* crane

'Congratulations!' says Sensei Yamada. 'A crane isn't easy
to fold, but you have to remember that becoming a true
samurai takes time.'

For other models and additional help, see video at
youngsamurai.com

Credits: lesson by Akemi Solloway Sensei, lecturer of
Japanese culture and eldest daughter of a samurai family,
website *solloway.org*; diagrams courtesy of Robyn Hondow,
website *origami-fun.com*.

CAN'T WAIT FOR THE NEXT JACK FLETCHER BLOCKBUSTER?

THE WAY of the DRAGON

Here's a **sneak preview** . . .

PROLOGUE
THE ASSASSIN

Japan, June 1613

Silent as a shadow, the assassin flitted from roof to roof.

Hidden by the darkness of night, the ninja crossed the moat, scaled the inner bailey wall and infiltrated deep into the castle grounds. His objective, the main tower, was a formidable keep of eight floors that sat at the heart of the supposedly impregnable castle.

Evading the samurai guards on the outer walls had been a simple matter. Lethargic due to the hot, airless night, they were more concerned about their own discomfort than the safety of their *daimyo* within the tower. Besides, their very belief that the castle was impenetrable meant the guards were lax in their duty – who would even attempt to break into such a fortress?

For the assassin, the hardest part would be getting inside the keep. The *daimyo*'s personal bodyguard wouldn't be so negligent and the ninja had come as close as he could by traversing the roofs of the outer buildings. He now had to cross open ground to the solid stone base of the tower.

The ninja dropped from the roof and skirted the edge of a courtyard, using the plum and *sakura* trees for cover. Passing silently through a Zen garden with an oval pond, he made his way to the central well house. The assassin ducked inside as he heard a samurai patrol approach.

When the way was clear, the ninja darted across to the keep and like a black-skinned gecko effortlessly scaled the steep slope of its immense base. Swiftly reaching the third floor, he slipped in through an open window.

Once inside, the assassin knew exactly where he was going. Padding down the darkened corridor, he passed several *shoji* doors then bore right, making for a wooden staircase. He was about to ascend when a guard suddenly appeared at the top of the stairs.

Like smoke, the ninja sank back into the shadows, his all-black *shinobi shozoku* rendering him virtually invisible. Quietly, he drew a *tantō* in readiness to slit the man's throat.

Oblivious to his proximity to death, the guard came down the stairs and walked straight past. The assassin, not wishing to draw attention to his presence within the keep, decided to let the man live. As soon as the guard rounded the corner, the ninja resheathed his blade and climbed the stairs to the upper corridor.

Through the thin paper *shoji* before him, he could see the halos of two candles glowing in the gloom. Sliding open the door a notch, he put a single eye to the crack. A man knelt before an altar deep in prayer. There were no samurai present.

The assassin crept inside.

When he was within striking distance, the ninja reached into a pouch on his belt and removed a rectangular object wrapped in black oilskin. He placed it on the floor beside the worshipping man and gave a brief bow.

'About time,' growled the man.

Without turning round, the man picked up the package and unwrapped it to reveal a worn leatherbound book.

'The *rutter*!' he breathed, caressing its cover, then opening its pages to examine the sea charts, ocean reports and meticulous logging of tides, compass bearings and star constellations. 'Now we possess what is rightfully ours. To think, the fortune of the world is in my hands. The secrets of the oceans laid bare for our nation to command the trade routes. It's our divine right to rule the seas.'

The man placed the logbook on the altar. 'And what of the boy?' he asked, his back to the ninja still. 'Is he dead?'

'No.'

'Why not? My instructions were explicit.'

'As you know, the samurai Masamoto has been training the boy in the Way of the Warrior,' explained the ninja. 'The boy is now highly skilled and has proven somewhat . . . resilient.'

'Resilient? Are you telling me a mere boy has defeated the great Dokugan Ryu?'

Dragon Eye's single emerald-green eye flared in annoyance at the man's mockery. He contemplated snapping the man's neck there and then, but he had yet to receive payment for retrieving the *rutter*. Such pleasures would have to wait.

'I employed you because you were the best. The most

ruthless,' continued the man. 'Am I mistaken in my judgement, Dragon Eye? Why haven't you killed him?'

'Because you may still need him.'

The man turned round, his face cast in shadow.

'What could I possibly want with Jack Fletcher?'

'The *rutter* is encrypted. Only the boy knows the code.'

'How do *you* know that?' demanded the man, a note of alarm registering in his voice. 'Have you been trying to break the cipher yourself?'

'Of course,' revealed the ninja. 'After the mistake of acquiring the Portuguese dictionary, I thought it wise to check the contents before delivery.'

'Did you have any success?' asked the man.

'Not entirely. The unfamiliar combination of Portuguese and English made the task somewhat more complex than anticipated.'

'No matter. It's of little consequence,' said the man, evidently pleased that the knowledge remained secret from the ninja. 'There's a Franciscan monk in the dungeons, fluent in both the languages and a mathematician. The mere promise of freedom should secure his decoding services.'

'And what about the *gaijin* boy?' asked Dragon Eye.

'Once the code's broken, complete your mission,' ordered the man, turning to kneel before the altar once more. 'Kill him.'

THE BATTLE FOR SURVIVAL
HAS ONLY JUST BEGUN

Young SAMURAI

THE WAY OF THE DRAGON

MORE NINJA, MORE ACTION,
MORE JACK.

COMING 2010

MEET CHRIS

HOW OLD WERE YOU WHEN YOU STARTED TRAINING IN MARTIAL ARTS?

I started judo when I was seven years old. I won my first trophy at the age of eight and have since trained in over nine different martial arts.

WHAT'S YOUR FAVOURITE MARTIAL ART AND WHY?

I have enjoyed all my styles – each one has taught me something new – but my favourite must be Zen Kyo Shin *taijutsu*, since it was the first one I earned my black belt in. The style originates from the fighting art of the ninja – my sensei was even taught by a ninja grandmaster!

HAVE YOU EVER MET A REAL SAMURAI WARRIOR?

Yes – I am a student of Akemi Solloway Sensei, who is the eldest daughter of an old samurai family, descended from the *karō* of Iwatsuki Castle (near Tokyo) in the time of Lord Ota Dokan (1432–1486). The name Akemi means 'bright and beautiful' and, because she has no brothers, Akemi has a special responsibility to keep alive the traditions of her samurai ancestors.

WHEN DID YOU START WRITING?

I've been writing all my life, but mostly lyrics for songs. I didn't start writing stories until much later, though I remember making up stories in my head as a child, especially on long car journeys to stop myself getting bored.

HOW LONG DID IT TAKE YOU TO WRITE *THE WAY OF THE WARRIOR*?

I wrote *The Way of the Warrior* very quickly – in two months! The story literally burst out of me and on to the page fully formed.

WHERE DO YOUR IDEAS AND INSPIRATIONS COME FROM?

My heart and my life. The Young Samurai trilogy was inspired by my passion for martial arts. It is the story of a young boy learning about life through martial arts. It could be about me. Equally it could be about you.

WHAT DID YOU USED TO DO BEFORE YOU WERE A WRITER?

I was a songwriter and musician. I sing, play guitar and harmonica. I have performed all over the world, appeared on TV and taught music at the illustrious Academy Of Contemporary Music in Guildford. My musical experience led me to writing my first book on songwriting (*Heart & Soul*) for the British Academy Of Composers & Songwriters.

WHAT'S YOUR FAVOURITE BOOK?

It by Stephen King. The scariest, and his best.

WHAT'S YOUR FAVOURITE PLACE IN THE WORLD AND WHY?

I've travelled to many wonderful places, but my three favourite memories are playing guitar on a beach as the sun set in Fiji, sitting in a tree house in the middle of a jungle in Laos and listening to a temple bell chime at dawn in Kyoto, Japan.

WHAT'S YOUR FAVOURITE TYPE OF FOOD?

Sushi. It's so healthy and very tasty.

WHAT'S YOUR MOST TREASURED POSSESSION?

My samurai sword. The blade gleams like lightning and whistles when it cuts through the air.

WHAT'S YOUR FAVOURITE FILM?

Crouching Tiger, Hidden Dragon. The action scenes are magical and literally defy gravity, the actors are like fighting ballerinas, and it features one of the greatest female movie martial artists, Michelle Yeoh.

JOIN THE DOJO
AND
STEEL YOUR NERVES
FOR

GRIPPING **PODCASTS** AND **VIDEOS**

UNBELIEVABLE **MARTIAL ARTS** MOVES

EXTREME **COMPETITIONS**

SWORD-WIELDING **INTERACTIVE** ACTIVITIES

AND
MUCH MORE
TO GET YOUR
ADRENALIN
RACING!

Let your training commence at
YOUNGSAMURAI.COM

JACK'S BEST MARTIAL ARTS MOVES

KICKS (GERI)

MAE-GERI – This front kick is extremely powerful and can even push an opponent to the ground.

YOKO-GERI – This side-kick is devastating on contact but be careful, it's easier to see it coming than a front kick.

MAWASHI-GERI – Often used to start combat, this roundhouse kick is when you swing your leg up in a circular motion.

USHIRO-GERI – This spinning back kick is one of the most powerful kicks in martial arts.

CHO-GERI – This is called the butterfly kick because all the limbs are spread out during the kick so you look like a butterfly's wings in flight.

PUNCHES (ZUKI)

OI-ZUKI – This lunge punch or jab is the most basic of punches but can definitely come in handy

GYAKI-ZUKI – Even more powerful is the reverse punch or cross punch, which employs most of the body in its motion.

KAGE-ZUKI – You have to be very fast for this hook punch but it's one of Jack's favourites as it's hard to block.

URAKEN-ZUKI – This back fist strike is even quicker and is achieved by forming a fist and striking with the tops of the two largest knuckles.

WHAT'S YOUR FAVOURITE?
Let us know at youngsamurai.com

It all started with a Scarecrow

Puffin is well over sixty years old.
Sounds ancient, doesn't it? But Puffin has never been
so lively. We're always on the lookout for the next big
idea, which is how it began all those years ago.

Penguin Books was a big idea from the mind of
a man called Allen Lane, who in 1935 invented
the quality paperback and changed the world.
**And from great Penguins, great Puffins grew,
changing the face of children's books forever.**

The first four Puffin Picture Books were hatched in 1940 and the
first Puffin story book featured a man with broomstick arms called
Worzel Gummidge. In 1967 Kaye Webb, Puffin Editor, started the
Puffin Club, promising to **'make children into readers'**.
She kept that promise and over 200,000 children became
devoted Puffineers through their quarterly installments of
Puffin Post, which is now back for a new generation.

Many years from now, we hope you'll look back and
remember Puffin with a smile. **No matter what your age
or what you're into, there's a Puffin for everyone.**
The possibilities are endless, but one thing is for sure:
whether it's a picture book or a paperback, a sticker book
or a hardback, **if it's got that little Puffin
on it – it's bound to be good.**